OF BERSERKERS SWORDS & VAMPIRES

A Saberhagen Retrospective

Baen Books by Fred Saberhagen

Berserker Man (omnibus)
Rogue Berserker (omnibus)
Berserker Death (omnibus)
The Dracula Tape
Vlad Tapes
Pilgrim

The Black Throne (with Roger Zelazny)

Author's Note
For more information about Fred Saberhagen
and this series, see:
www.berserker.com

OF BERSERKERS
SWORDS &
VAMPIRES

A Saberhagen Retrospective

by
Fred Saberhagen

Introduction by Joan Spicci Saberhagen

A Baen Book Original

Baen Publishing Enterprises
P.O. Box 1188
Wake Forest, NC 27588
www.baen.com

ISBN 10: 1-4391-3269-0
ISBN 13: 978-1-4391-3269-2

Cover art by David Mattingly

First Baen printing, June 2009

Distributed by Simon & Schuster
1230 Avenue of the Americas
New York, NY 10020

Printed in the United States of America

10 9 8 7 6 5 4 3 2 1

Additional Copyright Information

Contents

INTRODUCTION

*(Note: Titles in **boldface** indicate stories or novel excerpts included in this collection.)*

Fred Saberhagen is one of the twentieth century's most prolific and versatile writers of fantasy and science fiction. Fred reveals something of what fueled his creative energies at the conclusion of an early berserker short story, **"Stone Place."** The major character, Mitch Spain, a berserker fighter and aspiring writer, muses: "The world was bad, and all men were fools—but there were men who would not be crushed. And that was a thing worth telling." And that was a thing Fred told frequently, in a great variety of settings, and with great skill.

Saberhagen's writing career spans forty-six years. He authored over fifty novels and sixty stories. Looking back over his work and choosing a comparatively few representatives was an enjoyable task, but not an easy one. So many are personal favorites. To show the scope of Fred's talent, stories from each stage and field of his work needed to be represented. The selected stories are of the highest quality but for one reason or another have been infrequently published. Even Fred's most ardent fans will have a fresh look at his talents.

Fred wrote stories of alternate history, time travel, and even some early cyberpunk. Much, but not all, of Fred's writing is set

1

in one of his created universes: berserkers, swords, gods, Dracula. Two of his earliest stories included here are set in worlds never expanded into a series, and perhaps for that reason are less known. Whatever the setting, Fred's stories provide fast-moving action and thought-provoking theme.

In the collection, THE BOOK OF SABERHAGEN, Fred claimed **"The Long Way Home"** as his first published story. The work appeared in *Galaxy* magazine, June 1961. The story is one of my personal favorites, because of the inventiveness, persistence and faith of the society depicted. And, the thought-provoking final question: "What are we doing to them?" Before I'd met Fred, I visited the headwaters of the Amazon. Sitting in a lounge with other young American adventurers about to poke our noses into tribal hinterlands, I recall heatedly discussing to what extent "the outside world" should interfere with the culture. Perhaps this is always the question, or should be, when cultures meet. And, of course, is never resolved. Certainly this story struck a chord with me.

Another theme in **"The Long Way Home"** is the vastness of space, a concept that Fred returned to in other stories. In an introduction to the **"The Long Way Home,"** Fred refers to attempts at providing concrete images to illustrate the vastness of space frequently given in popular astronomy lectures: "I don't know that these imaginative exercises were ever of much help to me in trying to realize the distances involved—just looking up and out at night does that, in my case, almost frighteningly well—but they did eventually provide the idea for my first published story."

Towards the beginning of **"The Long Way Home,"** Fred uses the word "terraform," perhaps indicative of the early influence of science fiction writer Jack Williamson. Years after Fred had written the story, we moved to New Mexico with our family of three children, and met Jack at a gathering of science fiction enthusiasts. Jack became a beloved acquaintance. With a personality as kind and hospitable as Jack's, beloved is not too strong a word for an acquaintance.

In fact, **"The Long Way Home"** was not Fred's first published story. Three others precede: **"Volume PAA-PYX,"** the novelette

"**Planeteer,**" and "Seven Doors to Education" appeared earlier in 1961. Fred may have remembered which story was accepted first and assumed that was the first published. A letter in our files shows H.L. Gold, editor of *Galaxy*, made an offer for the "**The Long Way Home**" on Oct 6—no year given. Fred's acceptance letter is dated Oct 9, 1959. Gold's offer on "**Volume PAA-PYX**" is also undated. The fact that he offered a slightly higher payment may indicate that **PAA-PYX** was the second purchase. Unfortunately, I can't find a copy of Fred's acceptance letter.

"**Volume PAA-PYX**" examines power and the abuse of power. About this story Fred said: "After Orwell's *1984*, what can a writer say about power and its abuses? Plenty, it seems to me. The subject is practically inexhaustible, as large as mankind itself." The story's ending may surprise you.

"**Planeteer**" became the basis for Fred's first novel THE WATER OF THOUGHT in which the Space Force Planeteer Boris Brazil again takes on a starring role as cultures meet. WATER appeared as an Ace double in 1965 and was reprinted in an expanded version from Tor (1981) under the Jim Baen Presents imprint. Fred frames "**Planeteer**" with a quote from Thoreau's WALDEN POND, perhaps a foreshadow of the subtle spiritual note in Fred's writing. In an introduction to "**Planeteer**" Fred commented: "Each science fiction writer tends, I suppose, to work mostly in a rather small number of 'worlds' of his own devising, each world being (usually) a future that can be more or less reasonably extrapolated from our own unlikely reality." Hmm. The number of worlds Fred created seems to belie this statement. Or, perhaps at the time Fred didn't realize how many worlds he was destined to create.

Two years after "**Planeteer,**" in 1963, the first Berserker story appeared.

With these opening words to "Without A Thought," Fred Saberhagen launched his classic tales of Berserkers. "The Machine was a vast fortress, containing no life, set by its long-dead masters to destroy anything that lived." "Without a Thought" was published in January 1963 in the magazine *IF*. A chimp and a game of checkers in the hands of a clever spacer outwit a killing machine, a

Berserker. The story is one of Fred's most reprinted with sixteen publication credits, and so does not fit the criteria for inclusion in this collection. Most recently (2007) the story is available in a Blackstone Audio production of BERSERKER. The story also appears under the alternate title: "Fortress Ship."

Fred's early career was greatly influenced by the editors of *IF* and *Galaxy*, particularly H.L. Gold, Fred Pohl and James Baen. H.L. Gold gave Fred his first sale. Fred Pohl suggested that Saberhagen might want to continue writing stories featuring those intriguing Berserkers. And, of course, James Baen, the man Fred considered the best editor in the business, played an important role in promoting Fred's work. Later, Jim became the founder and publisher of Baen Books. A working relationship with Baen Books continued throughout Fred's career and continues still.

By 1967 Fred had written enough Berserker stories for a collection entitled BERSERKER. Fred was quite proud. We had been dating for a few months when my birthday rolled around. He presented me with BERSERKER personalized with the unromantic inscription, but with a twinkle in his eyes, "Happy Birthday. Joan, 1967—now you own a first edition. Fred." I wasn't a science fiction fan at the time, but on reading the stories became impressed with the imaginative way Fred's mind works. But then I was becoming favorably impressed by a number of Fred's qualities. We were married the following June.

In the **Introduction to BERSERKER**, a representative of the Carmpan race tells of the killing machines and explains Earth-descended man's unique adaptation for fighting the threat to life. The Carmpan, an historian, relates stories of man and Berserkers in BERSERKER. One of his favorite tales is **"Stone Place."**

During the 1970s, Fred was creating the fantasy worlds he would develop throughout his career and some he would abandon. He never expanded on the novels SPECIMENS and MASK OF THE SUN, two of my favorites. The Berserkers were successfully launched and his fantasy trilogy of BROKEN LANDS, BLACK MOUNTAINS and CHANGELING EARTH was completed. By the end of the decade the trilogy was incorporated into the volume

EMPIRE OF THE EAST. The story continues into The Swords series. During the decade of the '70s, Saberhagen's Dracula also made his appearance in **THE DRACULA TAPES**.

The fertile '70s also saw the creation of Azlaroc, a world developed and unfortunately abandoned, or almost abandoned as references to Azlaroc appear in several later Berserker stories. Azlaroc is a strange world, not quite planet and not quite star. Much of the landscape is comprised of stunningly regular geometric solids. Once a year a "veil" of energy encapsulates everything and everyone on the planet. Fred visited the Azlaroc world in only two short stories, **"To Mark The Year On Azlaroc"** (1974) and "Beneath The Hills Of Azlaroc" (1975), and in one composite of these stories, a novel, THE VEILS OF AZLAROC (1978). The setting of Azlaroc is what seems to have garnered the most attention from reviewers for its uniqueness, visual beauty, and imagery. Fans and reviewers frequently comment that Azlaroc is Fred's most memorable and underappreciated creation.

"To Mark the Year On Azlaroc" was first sent to Fred Pohl who was looking for stories for SCIENCE FICTION DISCOVERIES, an anthology he and Carol Pohl were editing. Pohl saw the potential for the story and for the concept of the veils and encouraged a rewrite with less exposition in conversation and more doing and feeling. After revising about sixty percent of the story per Pohl's recommendations Fred resubmitted. In the correspondence with Pohl, Saberhagen notes that " . . . the Veils were invented for this one, just to concretize the old idea that You Can't Go Home Again." Fred Pohl bought the rewritten story. Both the revised and original versions of the story are in our files.

The companion story, "Beneath the Hills of Azlaroc," is a loose retelling of the story of nineteenth century poet and painter Dante Gabriel Rossetti's bizarre exhuming of a book of his verse from his wife's grave. The story was published by Roger Elwood in the December 1975 issue of the magazine *Odyssey*.

Perhaps as a counter to the theme of Rossetti's obsession with beautiful women Fred wrote a very short piece, **"Martha."** **"Martha"** was first published in the Dec 1976 *Amazing* and then was

chosen by Isaac Asimov for his 1977 collection 100 GREAT SCI-
ENCE FICTION SHORT STORIES. The story is a fun romp
through the female (albeit computer female) psyche. The setting
is the Chicago Museum of Science and Industry, the heroine a
poor confused computer trying to please. As usual Fred's humor is
subtle and thought-provoking. This story, along with the Berserker
story "Mr. Jester" are his most markedly humorous stories.

Fred's very last Berserker short story written solo, in 1996, was
"The Bad Machines" which appears in THE WILLIAMSON
EFFECT, an anthology honoring science fiction pioneer Jack Williamson, edited by Roger Zelazny. Jack Williamson's humanoids,
machines protective of life, are, in their way, as dangerous as Berserkers. What chance do humans have when two races of machines
are out for our life and soul? The story has an answer. You might
want to take a careful look at the name of the negative gravitational
radiant in which the story takes place. Fred uses one of his favorite
naming techniques to pay homage to Jack's hometown.

As I mentioned, Fred was a great admirer of Jack Williamson
and Jack's work. We frequently drove across New Mexico on a
trek to the Williamson Lectureships held annually at Eastern New
Mexico University. Fred was always pleased that Jack referred to
him as "that promising young author," this even after Fred had
graduated to Medicare. It is interesting to note that Fred's last
Berserker story, **"The Bad Machines,"** like his first story, was
touched by Williamson's work.

Fred's last solo Berserker story appeared in an anthology edited
by his friend, Roger Zelazny. Fred and Roger never collaborated
on a short story but did coauthor two novels. At the time of the
coauthoring Roger and his family were living in Santa Fe, we were
in Albuquerque about 55 miles away, commuting distance in the
West. The idea for their first book together was born on one of
our joint family outings. Fred often remarked that collaborating
with Roger was some of the easiest and most enjoyable writing he'd
ever done. Fred and Roger jointly authored two books, COILS and
THE BLACK THRONE. Both writers were great fans of Edgar
Allan Poe. Fred often told me of Roger having an uncanny ability

to imitate Poe's style. The collaboration started a Saberhagen tradition: a celebration of Poe's birthday with a large party for many of the local writers and fans.

The very last Berserker story, "Servant of Death," was coauthored with Jane Lindskold, an established fantasy author and family friend and incidentally also from New Mexico. The story appears in MAN VS MACHINE released July 2007.

Fred often commented that he knew the future of his dreams had arrived when he saw his first chess-playing machine. Fred was an enthusiastic chess player and devoted hours to the game. It was not uncommon to find a chess strategy book on any flat surface in our home. When we played, Fred almost always won, and usually rather easily. Having a more challenging and ever ready automated opponent became one of Fred's great joys. We co-edited an anthology of chess stories, PAWN TO INFINITY, where Fred's "Without A Thought" appears, along with Roger's very unique "Unicorn Variation." The list of contributors for this little known collection was impressive, including Gene Wolfe, Poul Anderson, Fritz Leiber, George RR Martin, Joanna Russ, Ruth Berman and others. An academic, Fred Stewart, added an interesting take on the chess game in Lewis Carroll's THROUGH THE LOOKING GLASS. At our house, chess-playing machines were soon followed by home computers.

In the early '80s, Fred became fascinated by the then nascent phenomena of home computers and home computer gaming. His early experience with word processors had him saying: "A word processor does to words, what a food processor does to food." Fortunately for writers, word processors improved quickly. Fred's favorite computer games were "Myst" and "Kasparov Chessmate." He once wrote a very humorous guest of honor speech for our local science fiction convention, Bubonicon, based on a conversation with Eliza, the computer psychotherapist.

In 1982, with Jim Baen's backing and promise of publication, Fred and I founded a computer gaming company, Berserker Works Ltd (BWL). The company produced, sponsored and developed seven titles. All the latest machines, i.e. the Apple II, Commodore 64 and IBM-jr, had a BWL game developed for them.

The games Fred and I designed and produced were based on works of fiction, mostly Fred's works. Unfortunately not all the games came to completion. We worked with authors such as Steven R. Donaldson, Walter Jon Williams, and Gordon Dickson. Also on our team were some brilliant programmers and talented computer artists. The games were quite innovative and earned no money. (For a more complete story of the games google "Berserker Works Ltd games" and view the article on the website Games That Weren't.)

All this leads to Fred's popular fantasy series The Swords and Lost Swords. Fred wrote the first Swords books with game development in mind. And a rudimentary attempt was made at coding and art work for the game by a very talented programmer employed by Berserker Works. The technology just was not up to the task. The Swords series has yet to be turned into a computer game.

Fred's Swords stories proved very popular among readers. Fred developed the story line so that the three original Book Of Swords (1983–1984) and the eight Lost Swords (1986–1994) along with the final Swords book, ARDNEH'S SWORD (2006) which connects the Swords world with Fred's 1979 fantasy world EMPIRE OF THE EAST, all fit together into one massive fantasy world. Somewhat surprisingly, Fred did only one short story set in this world. When putting together an anthology of Swords stories, Fred invited some impressive writing talents to contribute; many are personal friends. Our son, Tom, had his first fiction publication in AN ARMORY OF SWORDS (1995). Fred's introductory story **"Blind Man's Blade"** does a superb job of introducing the first-time reader to the world of Swords while relating a great stand-alone tale.

Fred was fascinated by mythology as the number of books on myth in his library attest. His short story "Starsong" retells the Orpheus myth in a Berserker-threatened galaxy. And his five volume series THE BOOK OF THE GODS retell and mix the ancient myths from many cultures. The GODS books didn't spawn any short stories, although **"White Bull"** is in the same vein as the series. Students struggling with school will sympathize with

Theseus. Ariadne appears in her own tale BOOK OF THE GODS vol 2: ARIADNE'S WEB (2000).

On a completely different note from classic myth, lightly touching horror (although Fred did not consider himself a horror writer), are Fred's explorations into the world of vampires. One day on rereading Bram Stoker's original DRACULA, probably on impulse as the book was one of the dog-eared paperback versions on a shelf in his study, Fred came downstairs and said: "You know, there's nothing in this book from the title character's viewpoint." That's all he said. And so started Fred's fascination with Dracula. (Unless you give credence to Fred's relating of how as a young boy of six or so he hid under the seat in the movie theater to escape Bela Lugosi's Dracula.) Critics of the vampire genre have noted that Fred was the first writer to have a vampire tell his own story. That was in **THE DRACULA TAPE**. Almost all of Fred's Dracula stories are told as full-length novels, ten in all. He wrote only two Dracula stories ("From the Tree of Time," **"Box Number Fifty"**) and one vampire story (**"A Drop of Something Special in the Blood"**). Set in 1897, **"Box Number Fifty"** exposes Dracula's rather surprising paternal feelings. The story originally appeared in DRACULA IN LONDON edited by P.N. Elrod. Fred's last solo short story, **"A Drop of Something Special in the Blood,"** presents one possible origin of Bram Stoker's work DRACULA. **"A Drop of Something Special in the Blood"** appeared in an anthology edited by Andrew Greeley entitled EMERALD MAGIC. Fred enjoyed Fr. Greeley's work, especially the nonfiction, from as far back as our days in Chicago, when we avidly read Greeley's column on sociology in the *Chicago Sun Times*.

Hope you enjoy the stories in this collection.

Joan

It was my honor and my life's greatest joy to be Fred's wife from June 29, 1968 to June 29, 2007. See you at home, Fred.

FIRST STORIES

THE LONG WAY HOME

When Marty first saw the thing it was nearly dead ahead, half a million miles away, a tiny green blip that repeated itself every five seconds on the screen of his distant-search radar.

He was four billion miles from Sol and heading out, working his way slowly through a small swarm of rock chunks that swung in a slow sun-orbit out here beyond Pluto, looking for valuable minerals in concentration that would make mining profitable.

The thing on his radar screen looked quite small, and therefore not too promising. But, as it was almost in his path, no great effort would be required to investigate. For all he knew, it might be solid germanium. And nothing better was in sight at the moment.

Marty leaned back in the control seat and said: "We've got one coming up, baby." He had no need to address himself any more exactly. Only one other human was aboard the *Clementine*, or, to his knowledge, within a couple of billion miles.

Laura's voice answered through a speaker, from the kitchen two decks below. "Oh, close? Have we got time for breakfast?"

Marty studied the radar. "About five hours if we maintain speed. Hope it won't be a waste of energy to decelerate and look the thing over." He gave *Clem's* main computer the problem of finding the most economical engine use to approach his find and reach zero velocity relative to it.

"Come and eat!"

"All right." He and the computer studied the blip together for a few seconds. Then the man, not considering it anything of unusual importance, left the control room to have breakfast with his bride of three months. As he walked downstairs in the steadily-maintained artificial gravity, he heard the engines starting.

Ten hours later he examined his new find much more closely, with a rapidly focusing alertness that balanced between an explorer's caution and a prospector's elation at a possibly huge strike.

The incredible shape of X, becoming apparent as the *Clem* drew within a few hundred miles, was what had Marty on the edge of his chair. It was a needle thirty miles long, as near as his radar could measure and about a hundred yards thick—dimensions that matched exactly nothing Marty could expect to find anywhere in space.

It was obviously no random chunk of rock. And it was no spaceship that he had ever seen or heard of. One end of it pointed in the direction of Sol, causing him to suggest to Laura the idea of a miniature comet, complete with tail. She took him seriously at first, then remembered some facts about comets and swatted him playfully. "Oh, you!" she said.

Another, more real possibility quickly became obvious, with sobering effect. The ancient fear of aliens that had haunted Earthmen through almost three thousand years of intermittent space exploration, a fear that had never been realized, now peered into the snug control room through the green radar eye.

Aliens were always good for a joke when spacemen met and talked. But they turned out to be not particularly amusing when you were possibly confronting them, several billion miles from Earth. Especially, thought Marty, in a ship built for robot mining, ore refining, and hauling, not for diplomatic contacts or heroics—and with the only human assistance a girl on her first space trip. Marty hardly felt up to speaking for the human race in such a situation.

It took a minute to set the autopilot so that any sudden move by X would trigger alarms and such evasive tactics as *Clem* could manage. He then set a robot librarian to searching his microfilm files for any reference to a spaceship having X's incredible dimensions.

There was a chance—how good a chance, he found hard to estimate, when any explanation looked somewhat wild—that X was a derelict, the wrecked hull of some ship dead for a decade, or a century, or a thousand years. By laws of salvage, such a find would belong to him if he towed it into port. The value might be very high or very low. But the prospect was certainly intriguing.

Marty brought *Clem* to a stop relative to X, and noticed that his velocity to Sol now also hung at zero. "I wonder," he muttered, "Space anchor . . . ?"

The space anchor had been in use for thousands of years. It was a device that enabled a ship to fasten itself to a particular point in the gravitational field of a massive body such as a sun. If X was anchored, it did not prove that there was still life aboard her; once "dropped," an anchor could hold as long as a hull could last.

Laura brought sandwiches and a hot drink to him in the control room.

"If we call the navy and they bring it in we won't get anything out of it," he told her between bites. "That's assuming it's—not alien."

"Could there be someone alive on it?" She was staring into the screen. Her face was solemn, but, he thought, not frightened.

"If it's human, you mean? No. I *know* there hasn't been any ship remotely like that used in recent years. Way, way back the Old Empire built some that were even bigger, but none I ever heard of with this crazy shape . . . "

The robot librarian indicated that it had drawn a blank. "See?" said Marty. "And I've even got most of the ancient types in there."

There was silence for a little while. The evening's recorded music started somewhere in the background.

"What would you do if I weren't along?" Laura asked him.

He did not answer directly, but said something he had been considering. "I don't know the psychology of our hypothetical aliens. But it seems to me that if you set out exploring new solar systems, you do as Earthmen have always done—go with the best you have in the way of speed and weapons. Therefore if X is alien, I don't think *Clem* would stand a chance trying to fight or run." He paused, frowning at the image of X. "That damned *shape*—it's just not right for anything."

"We could call the navy—not that I'm saying we should, darling," she added hastily. "You decide, and I'll never complain either way. I'm just trying to help you think it out."

He looked at her, believed it about there never being any complaints, and squeezed her hand. Anything more seemed superfluous.

"If I was alone," he said, "I'd jump into a suit, go look that thing over, haul it back to Ganymede, and sell it for a unique whatever-it-is. Maybe I'd make enough money to marry you in real style, and trade in *Clem* for a first-rate ship—or maybe even terraform an asteroid and keep a couple of robot prospectors. I don't know, though. Maybe we'd better call the navy."

She laughed at him gently. "We're married enough already, and we had all the style I wanted. Besides, I don't think either of us would be very happy sitting on an asteroid. How long do you think it will take you to look it over?"

At the airlock door she had misgivings: "Oh, it *is* safe enough, isn't it? Marty, be careful and come back soon." She kissed him before he closed his helmet.

They had moved *Clem* to within a few kilometers of X. Marty mounted his spacebike and approached it slowly, from the side.

The vast length of X blotted out a thin strip of stars to his right and left, as it it were the distant shore of some vast island in a placid Terran sea, and the starclouds below him were the watery reflections of the ones above. But space was too black to permit such an illusion to endure.

The tiny FM radar on his bike showed him within three hundred yards of X. He killed his forward speed with a gentle application of retrojets and turned on a spotlight. Bright metal gleamed smoothly back at him as he swung the beam from side to side. Then he stopped it where a dark concavity showed up.

"Lifeboat berth . . . empty," he said aloud, looking through the bike's little telescope.

"Then it is a derelict? We're all right?" asked Laura's voice in his helmet.

"Looks that way. Yeah, I guess there's no doubt of it. I'll go in for a closer look now." He eased the bike forward. X was evidently just some rare type of ship that neither he nor the compilers of the standard reference works in his library had ever heard of. Which sounded a little foolish to him, but . . .

At ten meters' distance he killed speed again, set the bike on automatic stay-clear, made sure a line from it was fast to his belt, and launched himself out of the saddle gently, headfirst, toward X.

The armored hands of his suit touched down first, easily and expertly. In a moment he was standing upright on the hull, held in place by magnetic boots. He looked around. He detected no response to his arrival.

Marty turned toward Sol, sighting down the kilometers of dark cylinder that seemed to dwindle to a point in the starry distance, like a road on which a man might travel home toward a tiny sun.

Near at hand the hull was smooth, looking like that of any ordinary spaceship. In the direction away from Sol, quite distant, he could vaguely see some sort of projections at right angles to the hull. He mounted his bike again and set off in that direction. When he neared the nearest projection, a kilometer and a half down the hull, he saw it to be a sort of enormous clamp that encircled X—or rather, part of a clamp. It ended a few meters from the hull, in rounded globs of metal that had once been molten but were now too cold to affect the thermometer Marty held against them. His radiation counter showed nothing above the normal background.

"Ah," said Marty after a moment, looking at the half-clamp.

"Something?"

"I think I've got it figured out. Not quite as weird as we thought. Let me check for one thing more." He steered the bike slowly around the circumference of X.

A third of the way around he came upon what looked like a shallow trench, about five feet wide and a foot deep, with a bottom that shone cloudy gray in his lights. It ran lengthwise on X as far as he could see in either direction.

A door-sized opening was cut in the clamp above the trench.

Marty nodded and smiled to himself, and gunned the bike around in an accelerating curve that aimed at the *Clementine*.

"It's not a spaceship at all, only a part of one," he told Laura a little later, digging in the microfilm file with his own hands, with the air of a man who knew what he was looking for. "That's why the librarian didn't turn it up. Now I remember reading about them. It's part of an Old Empire job of about two thousand years ago. They used a somewhat different drive than we do, one that made one enormous ship more economical to run than several normal-sized ones. They made these ships ready for a voyage by fastening together long narrow sections side by side, the number depending on how much cargo they had to move. What we've found is obviously one of those sections."

Laura wrinkled her forehead. "It must have been a terrible job, putting those sections together and separating them, even in free space."

"They used space anchors. That trench I mentioned? It has a forcefield bottom. so an anchor could be sunk through it. Then the whole section could be slid straight forward or back, in or out of the bunch . . . here, I've got it, I think. Put this strip in the viewer."

One picture, a photograph, showed what appeared to be one end of a bunch of long needles, in a glaring light, against a background of stars that looked unreal. The legend beneath gave a scanty description of the ship in flowing Old Empire script. Other pictures showed sections of the ship in some detail.

"This must be it, all right," said Marty thoughtfully. "Funny looking old tub."

"I wonder what happened to wreck her."

"Drives sometimes exploded in those days, and that could have done it. And this one section got anchored to Sol somehow—it's funny."

"How long ago did it happen, do you suppose?" asked Laura. She had her arms folded as if she were a little cold, though it was not cold in the *Clementine*.

"Must be around two thousand years or more. These ships haven't been used for about that long." He picked up a stylus. "I better go over there with a big bag of tools tomorrow and take a look inside." He wrote down a few things he thought he might need.

"Historians would probably pay a good price for the whole thing, untouched," she suggested, watching him draw doodles.

"That's a thought. But maybe there's something really valuable aboard—though I won't be able to give it anything like a thorough search, of course. The thing is anchored, remember. I'll probably have to break in, anyway, to release that."

She pointed to one of the diagrams. "Look, a section thirty miles long must be one of the passenger compartments. And according to this plan, it would have no drive at all of its own. We'll have to tow it."

He looked. "Right. Anyway, I don't think I'd care to try its drive if it had one."

He located airlocks on the plan and made himself generally familiar with it.

The next "morning" found Marty loading extra tools, gadgets, and explosives on his bike. The trip to X (he still thought of it that way) was uneventful. This time he landed about a third of the way from one end, where he expected to find a handy airlock and have a choice of directions to explore when he got inside. He hoped to get the airlock open without letting out whatever atmosphere or gas was present in any of the main compartments, as a sudden drop in pressure might damage something in the unknown cargo.

He found a likely looking spot for entry where the plans had told him to expect one. It was a small auxiliary airlock, only a few feet from the space-anchor channel. The forcefield bottom of that channel was, he knew, useless as a possible doorway. Though anchors could be raised and lowered through it, they remained partly imbedded in it at all times. Starting a new hole from scratch would cause the decompression he was trying to avoid, and possibly a dangerous explosion as well.

Marty began his attack on the airlock door cautiously, working with electronic "sounding" gear for a few minutes, trying to tell if the inner door was closed as well. He had about decided that it was when something made him look up. He raised his head and sighted down the dark length of X toward Sol.

Something was moving toward him along the hull.

He was up in the bike saddle with his hand on a blaster before he realized what it was—that moving blur that distorted the stars seen through it, like heat waves in air. Without doubt, it was a space anchor, moving along the channel.

Marty rode the bike out a few yards and nudged it along slowly, following the anchor. It moved at about the pace of a fast walk. *Moved* . . . but it was sunk into space.

"Laura," he called. "Something odd here. Doppler this hull for me and see if it's moving."

Laura acknowledged in one businesslike word. Good girl, he thought. I won't have to worry about you. He coasted along the hull on the bike, staying even with the apparent movement of the anchor.

Laura's voice came: "It is moving now, toward Sol. About 10 kilometers per hour. Maybe less—it's so slow it's hard to read."

"Good, that's what I thought." He hoped he sounded reassuring. He pondered the situation. It was the hull moving then, the force-field channel sliding by the fixed anchor. Whatever was causing it, it did not seem to be directed against him or the *Clem*. "Look, baby," he went on. "Something peculiar is happening." He explained about the anchor. "*Clem* may be no battleship, but I guess she's a match for any piece of wreckage."

"But you're out *there!*"

"I have to see this. I never saw anything like it before. Don't worry, I'll pull back if it looks at all dangerous." Something in the back of his mind told him to go back to his ship and call the navy. He ignored it without much trouble. He had never thought much of calling the navy.

About four hours later the incomprehensible anchor neared the end of its track, within thirty meters of what seemed to be X's stern. It slowed down and came to a gradual stop a few meters from the end of the track. For a minute nothing else happened. Marty reported the facts to Laura. He sat straight in the bike saddle, regarding the universe, which offered him no enlightenment.

In the space between the anchor and the end of the track, a second patterned shimmer appeared. It must necessarily have been let "down" into space from inside X. Marty felt a creeping chill. After a little while the first anchor vanished, withdrawn through the forcefield into the hull.

Marty sat watching for twenty minutes, but nothing further happened. He realized that he had a crushing grip on the bike controls and that he was quivering with fatigue.

Laura and Marty took turns sleeping and watching, that night aboard the *Clementine*. About noon the next ship's day Laura was at the telescope when anchor number one reappeared, now at the "prow" of X. After a few moments the one at the stem vanished.

Marty looked at the communicator that he could use any time to call the navy. Faster-than-light travel not being practical so near a sun, it would take them at least several hours to arrive after he decided he needed them. Then he beat his fist against a table and swore. "It can only be that there's some kind of mechanism in her still operating." He went to the telescope and watched number one anchor begin its apparent slow journey sternward once more. "I don't know. I've got to settle this."

The doppler showed X was again creeping toward Sol at about 10 kilometers an hour.

"Does it seem likely there'd be power left after two thousand years to operate such a mechanism?" Laura asked.

"I think so. Each passenger section had a hydrogen power lamp." He dug out the microfilm again. "Yeah. a small fusion lamp for electricity to light and heat the section, and to run the emergency equipment for . . ." His voice trailed off, then continued in a dazed tone: "For recycling food and water."

"Marty, what is it?"

He stood up, staring at the plan. "The only radios were in the lifeboats, and the lifeboats are gone. I wonder . . . sure. The explosion could have torn them apart, blown them away, so . . ."

"What are you talking about?"

He looked again at their communicator. "A transmitter that can get through the noise between here and Pluto wouldn't be easy to jury-rig, even now. In the Old Empire days . . ."

"What?"

"Now about air—" He seemed to wake up with a start, looked at her sheepishly. "Just an idea that hit me." He grinned. "I'm making another trip."

An hour later he was landing on X for the third time, touching down near the "stern." He was riding the moving hull toward the anchor, but it was still many kilometers away.

The spot he had picked was near another small auxiliary airlock, upon which he began work immediately. After ascertaining that the inner door was closed, he drilled a hole in the outer door to relieve any pressure in the chamber to keep the outer door shut.

The door opening mechanism suffered from twenty-century cramp, but a vibrator tool shook it loose enough to be operated by hand. The inside of the airlock looked like nothing more than the inside of an airlock.

He patched the hole he had made in the outer door so he would be able—he hoped—to open the inner one normally. He operated the outer door several times to make sure he could get out fast if he had to. After attaching a few extras from the bike to his suit, he said a quick and cheerful goodbye to Laura—not expecting his radio to work from inside the hull—and closed himself into the airlock. Using the vibrator again, he was able to work the control that should let whatever passed for hull atmosphere into the chamber. It came. His wrist gauge told him pressure was building up to approximately spaceship normal, and his suit mikes began to pick up a faint hollow humming from somewhere. He very definitely kept suit and helmet sealed.

The inner door worked perfectly, testifying to the skill of the Old Empire builders. Marty found himself nearly upside down as he went through, losing his footing and his sense of heroic adventure. In return he gained the knowledge that X's artificial gravity was still at least partly operational. Righting himself, he found that he was in a small anteroom banked with spacesuit lockers, now illuminated only by his suit lights but showing no other signs of damage. There was a door in each of the other walls.

He moved to try the one at his right. First drawing his blaster, he hesitated a moment, then slid it back into its holster. Swallowing, he eased the door open to find only another empty compartment, about the size of an average room and stripped of everything down to the bare deck and bulkheads.

Another door led him into a narrow passage where a few overhead lights burned dimly. Trying to watch over his shoulder and ahead at the same time, he followed the hall to a winding stair and began to climb, moving with all the silence possible in a spacesuit.

The stair brought him out onto a long gallery overlooking what could only be the main corridor of X, a passage twenty meters wide and three decks high; it narrowed away to a point in the dimlit distance.

A man came out of a doorway across the corridor, a deck below Marty.

He was an old man and may have been nearsighted, for he seemed unaware of the spacesuited figure gripping a railing and staring down at him. The old man wore a sort of tunic intricately embroidered with threads of different colors, and well tailored to his thin figure, leaving his legs and feet bare. He stood for a moment peering down the long corridor, while Marty stared, momentarily frozen in shock.

Marty pulled back two slow steps from the railing, to where he stood mostly in shadow. Turning his head to follow the old man's gaze, he noticed that the forcefield where the anchors traveled was visible, running in a sunken strip down the center of the corridor. When the interstellar ship of which X was once a part had been in normal use, the strip might have been covered with a moving walkway of some kind.

The old man turned his attention to a tank where grew a mass of plants with flat, dark green leaves. He touched a leaf, then turned a valve that doled water into the tank from a thin pipe. Similar valves were clustered on the bulkhead behind the old man, and pipes ran from them to many other plant-filled tanks set at intervals down the corridor. "For oxygen," Marty said aloud in an almost calm voice, and was startled at the sound in his helmet. His helmet airspeaker was not turned on, so of course the old man did not hear him. The old man pulled a red berry from one of the plants and ate it absently.

Marty made a move with his chin to turn on his speaker, but did not complete. He half lifted his arms to wave, but fear of the not-understood held him, made him back up slowly into the shadows at the rear of the gallery. Turning his head to the right he could see the near end of the corridor, and an anchor there, not sunken in space but raised almost out of the forcefield on a framework at the end of the strip.

Near the stair he had ascended was a half-open door, leading into darkness. Marty realized he had turned off his suit lights without consciously knowing of it. Moving carefully so the old man would not see, he lit one and probed the darkness beyond the door cautiously. The room he entered was the first of a small suite that had once been a passenger cabin. The furniture was simple, but it was the first of any kind that he had seen aboard X. Garments hanging in one comer were similar to the old man's tunic, though no two were exactly alike in design. Marty fingered the fabric with one armored hand, holding it close to his faceplate. He nodded to himself; it seemed to be the kind of stuff produced by fiber-recycling machinery, and he doubted very much that it was anywhere near two thousand years old.

Marty emerged from the doorway of the little apartment, and stood in shadow with his suit lights out, looking around. The old man had disappeared. He remembered that the old man had gazed down the infinite-looking corridor as if expecting something. There was nothing new in sight that way. He turned up the gain of one of his suit mikes and focused it in that direction.

Many human voices were singing, somewhere down there, miles away. He started, and tried to interpret what he heard in some other way, but with an eerie thrill, he became convinced that his first impression was correct. While he studied a plan of going back to his bike and heading in that direction, he became aware that the singing was getting louder—and therefore, no doubt closer.

He leaned back against the bulkhead in the shadow at the rear of the gallery. His suit, dark-colored for space work far from Sol, would be practically invisible from the lighted corridor below, while he could see down with little difficulty. Part of his mind urged him to go back to Laura, to call the navy, because these unknown people could be dangerous to him. But he had to wait and see more of them. He grinned wryly as he realized that he was not going to get any salvage out of X after all.

Sweating in spite of his suit's coolers, he listened to the singing grow rapidly louder in his helmet. Male and female voices rose and fell in an intricate melody, sometimes blending, sometimes chanting separate parts. The language was unknown to him.

Suddenly the people were in sight, first only as a faint dot of color in the distance. As they drew nearer he could see that they walked in a long neat column eight abreast, four on each side of the central strip of forcefield. Men and women, apparently teamed according to no fixed rule of age or sex or size—except that he saw no oldsters or young children.

The people sang and leaned forward as they walked, pulling their weight on heavy ropes that were intricately decorated, like their clothing and that of the old man who had now stepped out of his doorway again to greet them. A few other oldsters of both sexes appeared near him to stand and wait. Through a briefly opened door Marty caught a glimpse of a well-lighted room holding machines he recognized as looms only because of the half-finished cloth they held. He shook his head wonderingly.

All at once the walkers were very near; hundreds of people pulling on ropes that led to a multiple whiffletree, made of twisted metal pipes, that rode over the central trench. The whiffletree and the space anchor to which it was fastened were pulled past Marty—or rather the spot from which he watched was carried past the fixed anchor by the slow, human-powered thrust of X toward Sol.

Behind the anchor came a small group of children, from about the age of ten up to puberty. They pulled on ropes, drawing a cart that held what looked like containers for food and water. At the extreme rear of the procession marched a man in the prime of life, tall and athletic, wearing a magnificent headdress.

About the time he drew even with Marty, this man stopped suddenly and uttered a sharp command. Instantly, the pulling and singing ceased. Several men nearest the whiffletree moved in and loosened it from the anchor with quick precision. Others held the slackened ropes clear as the enormous inertia of X's mass carried the end of the forcefield strip toward the anchor, which now jammed against the framework holding anchor number two, forcing the framework back where there had seemed to be no room.

A thick forcefield pad now became visible to Marty behind the framework, expanding steadily as it absorbed the energy of the powerful stress between ship and anchor. Conduits of some kind, Marty saw, led away from the pad, possibly to where energy might be stored for use when it came time to start X creeping toward the sun again. A woman in a headdress now mounted the framework and released anchor number two, to drop into space "below" the hull and bind X fast to the place where it was now held by anchor number one. A crew of men came forward and began to raise anchor number one . . .

He found himself descending the stair, retracing his steps to the airlock. Behind him the voices of the people were raised in a steady recitation that might have been a prayer. Feeling somewhat as if he moved in a dream, he made no particular attempt at caution, but he met no one. He tried to think, to understand what he had witnessed. Vaguely, comprehension came.

Outside, he said: "I'm out all right, Laura. I want to look at something at the other end, and then I'll come home." He scarcely heard what she said in reply, but realized that her answer had been almost instantaneous; she must have been listening steadily for his call all the time. He felt better.

The bike shot him 50 kilometers down the dreamlike length of X toward Sol in a few minutes. A lot faster than the people inside do their traveling, he thought . . . and Sol was dim ahead.

Almost recklessly he broke into X again, through an airlock near the prow. At this end of the forcefield strip hung a gigantic block and tackle that would give a vast mechanical advantage to a few hundred people pulling against an anchor, when it came time for them to start the massive hull moving toward Sol once more.

He looked in almost unnoticed at a nursery, small children in the care of a few women. He thought one of the babies saw him and laughed at him as he watched through a hole in a bulkhead where a conduit had once passed.

"What is it?" asked Laura impatiently as he stepped exhausted out of the shower room aboard the *Clem*, wrapping a robe around him. He could see his shock suddenly mirrored in her face.

"People," he said, sitting down. "Alive over there. Earth people. Humans."

"You're all right?"

"Sure. It's just—God!" He told her about it briefly. "They must be descended from the survivors of the accident, whatever it was. Physically, there's no reason why they couldn't live when you come to think of it—even reproduce, up to a limited number. Plants for oxygen—I bet their air's as good as ours. Recycling equipment for food and water, and the hydrogen power lamp still working to run it, and to give them light and gravity . . . they have about everything they need. Everything but a space-drive." He leaned back with a sigh and closed his eyes. It was hard for him to stop talking to her.

She was silent for a little, trying to assimilate it all. "But if they have hydrogen power, couldn't they have rigged something?" she finally asked. "*Some* kind of a drive, even if it was slow? Just one push and they'd keep moving."

Marty thought it over. "Moving a little faster won't help them." He sat up and opened his eyes again. "And they'd have a lot less work to do every day. I imagine too large a dose of leisure time could be fatal to all of them.

"Somehow they had the will to keep going, and the intelligence to find a way—to evolve a system of life that worked for them, that kept them from going wild and killing each other. And their children, and their grandchildren, and after that . . . " Slowly he stood up. She followed him into the control room, where they stood watching the image of X that was still focused on the telescope screen.

"All those years," Laura whispered. "All that time."

"Do you realize what they're doing?" he asked softly. "They're not just surviving, turned inward on weaving and designing and music.

"In a few hours they're going to get up and start another day's work. They're going to pull anchor number one back to the front of their ship and lower it. That's their morning job. Then someone left in the rear will raise anchor number two. Then the main group will start pulling against number one, as I saw them doing a little while ago, and their ship will begin to move toward Sol. Every day they go through this they move about fifty kilometers closer to home.

"Honey, these people are walking home and pulling their ship with them. It must be a religion with them by now, or something very near it . . . " He put an arm around Laura.

"Marty—how long would it take them?"

"Space is big," he said in a flat voice, as if quoting something he had been required to memorize.

After a few moments he continued. "I said just moving a little faster won't help them. Let's say they've traveled 50 kilometers a day for two thousand years. That's somewhere near 36 million kilometers. Almost enough to get from Mars to Earth at their nearest approach. But they've got a long way to go to reach the neighborhood of Mars' orbit. We're well out beyond Pluto here. Practically speaking, they're just about where they started from." He smiled wanly. "Really, they're not far from home, for an interstellar ship. They had their accident almost on the doorstep of their own solar system, and they've been walking toward the threshold ever since."

Laura went to the communicator and began to set it up for the call that would bring the navy within a few hours. She paused. "How long would it take them now," she asked, "to get somewhere near Earth?"

"Hell would freeze over. But they can't know that anymore. Or maybe they still know it and it just doesn't bother them. They must just go on, tugging at that damned anchor day after day, year after year, with maybe a holiday now and then . . . I don't know how they do it. They work and sing and feel they're accomplishing something . . . and really, they are, you know. They have a goal and they are moving toward it. I wonder what they say of Earth, how they think about it?"

Slowly Laura continued to set up the communicator.

Marty watched her. "Are you sure?" he pleaded suddenly. "What are we doing to them?"

But she had already sent the call.

For better or worse, the long voyage was almost over.

VOLUME PAA-PYX

When he was alone in his office with the prisoner, the director said: "Now, what is this secret you can reveal to my ears alone?"

"Are you sure none of them are listening?" The prisoner was a young man with seedy clothing and an odd haircut. As he spoke, he managed to grin in a conspiratorial way, as if he already shared some vital and amusing secret with director Ahlgren.

And this is about the average of the Underground, thought the director, studying his victim with distaste. And in the next room Barbara waited her turn at being interrogated. How could *she* have ever become connected, however indirectly, with the ideals or the people of this Underground represented before him?

"None of them are listening," said the director, who took daily steps to discourage that sort of thing among his subordinates. It was not entirely unheard of for a Party member to turn traitor and join the Underground. "Quickly now, what have you to tell me?"

"This—I will act as a double agent for you," volunteered the young wretch, in a stage whisper, maintaining the idiotic grin. His voluntary muscles were still mainly paralyzed from the stun pistols of the Political Police, and so he sat propped erect in his chair by a stiff pillow the director kept handy for such use.

Director Ahlgren frowned thoughtfully. He took a cigarette from a box on his plain but highly polished desk. "Care for one?"

"No, no. Do you understand what I am offering you? I am a highly trained agent, and I will betray them all to you, because you are the strongest here, and I must serve the strongest." The young man nodded earnestly, as if he hoped the director would imitate the movement and so agree with him.

The director puffed smoke. "Very well, I accept. Now you must show me that you will really do what you say. Tell me the address of your contact cell."

The young rebel contorted his forehead, in an apparent effort to conceive a stroke of Machiavellian strategy.

Ahlgren pursued him. "I know each cell of the Underground has its contact with the rest of the organization through one other cell and that you know the address of yours. How can I trust you as a double agent if you won't tell me that much?"

"Wouldn't any of the others tell you? My dear comrades from my own cell?"

All the dear comrades seemed to have taken memory-scrambling drugs, as captured rebels often did, though the director sometimes thought it a superfluous action on their part.

"None of the others offered to act as a double agent." Ahlgren was trying to humor this babbler out of the one piece of valuable information he was likely to possess.

"Our comrades in the contact cell will have heard about the arrests this morning," said the prisoner with a sudden happy thought. "They'll have moved already anyway."

Quite likely true, Director Ahlgren knew. "So it can't hurt them if you tell me," he encouraged.

The prisoner pondered a moment longer, then named an address in a quiet residential section about a quarter of an hour's walk from the Party Building.

"Anything else you can tell me?"

Careful consideration. "No."

PolPol Chief Lazar and a couple of guards came into the office quickly after the director touched the signal button.

"Take him down to Conditioning," said the director, leaning back in his chair. He felt his head beginning to ache.

The rebel screamed and rolled his head, about the most violent motion he could make, as the two PolPol guards caught him gently by the arms and lifted him from his chair.

"Traitor! You are the traitor, not I! You have betrayed my confidence, your own honor, you—" He seemed suddenly to realize what was going to happen to him. "Conditioning! No, not my mind, not my mind! Can't you beat me or something instead? I won't be meee any lonnnggerrrr . . ."

The screaming died away down the corridor outside the office.

"Careful with him!" Lazar called sharply to the guards, from the doorway. "Don't let his legs bump, there! You bruised that man this morning; we want no more of that."

He came back into the office, closing the door, viewing Ahlgren with the proper expression of respect. "Would you like me to conduct the next interview, sir?"

"No. Why do you ask?"

"I thought you might feel a certain reluctance, sir. I understand you knew the young lady years ago."

"Before I joined the Party. Yes, quite right, I did." The director arose from his chair and walked toward the wide window, past the bookshelves that almost filled one wall, giving the office the air of a study and concealing his secret exit.

From the window he looked out upon the sunset that reddened the sky over his prosperous city, whose bright lights were coming on against the dusk.

I understand Lazar, he thought, because he is ambitious, as I am. Or as I was. Under one of the old dictatorships, I would have had to fear such ambition in a subordinate and consider taking steps against him. But I need not fear Lazar, because the Party claims his perfect loyalty, and he can do nothing against me until I begin to fail the Party. And is that time perhaps drawing near? Will my secret exit always be only a private joke?

Watching his own eyes in the half-mirror of the window, the director told himself: Someone must govern, and the worldwide Party does better than the old systems did. There are no wars. There is no corruption, and no real struggle for power among Party members, because there is practically no disobedience in the carefully chosen ranks. The mass of the citizens seem content with their bread and circuses. There is only the Underground, and maybe some kind of Underground is necessary in any society.

"Lazar."

"Sir?"

"How do we do it? How do we attain such perfection of power that the essence of power is enough, that we have no need to constantly threaten or stupefy the citizens?"

The gay and active city below was brightening itself against the gathering night. No giant signs proclaimed the glories of the Party. No monolithic statues deified the World Directors, past or present. The Party was invisible.

Lazar seemed a bit shocked at the question. "The selfless obedience of each individual is the life and strength of the Party, sir." A phrase from the catechism.

"Of course . . . but look, Lazar. That Citizens Policeman directing traffic down there. He wears a stun pistol, because of nonpolitical criminals he must sometimes deal with; but if one of your PolPol agents were to walk up to him and arrest him, the odds are he would offer no resistance. Now why? The Citizens Police are as well armed and I think more numerous than your men."

Lazar studied the traffic cop below through narrowed eyes. "I can't remember when we've had to arrest a Citizens Policeman."

"Neither can I. The point is—how do we do it?"

"Superior dedication and discipline will prevail, sir."

"Yes." But the parroted phrases were no real answer. The Citizens Police were presumably disciplined and dedicated too. Lazar was unwilling or unable to really discuss the subject.

Such questions had not occurred to Ahlgren himself until quite recently. He could not remember ever seriously considering the possibility of himself opposing the Party in any way, even before that day five years ago when he had been accepted as a member.

"And we of the Party control the means of Conditioning," said Lazar.

"Conditioning, yes." Barbara. He had to fight to keep anything from showing in his face.

He knew there was not one person in the gay and bright-lit city before him who could not be brought to the basement of this building at any time, at a word from himself, to undergo Conditioning. The Ultimate Pain, he had heard it called by Party theorists. But it needed no dramatization.

The citizens had a slang term for it that he had heard somewhere: brain-boiling.

The office intercom sounded on the director's desk. "Chief Lazar's office would like him to come in, if possible." Tight security. No details would be spoken unnecessarily over even the director's line. No risks would be taken at all.

He was faintly relieved. "Your office wants you for something: I won't need you here any longer. Good job today."

"Thank you, sir." Lazar was gone in a moment.

Ahlgren was alone in his soft-lit office. His eyes ranged along the bookshelves. The Party put no restrictions on reading. Aquinas—some of the Eastern philosophers—Russell. The encyclopedia, with the gap where that one volume had been missing for a week. Volume P. What the devil could have happened to it? Was there a kleptomaniac on his staff? It seemed absurd for anyone to steal an ordinary book.

But he was only procrastinating. He went to sit again at his desk, leafed through papers. Bulky contracts and specifications for the new water supply for his city. And the Citizens Council had voted a new tax; he would have to hire collectors. Too much nonpolitical work, as usual, and now the Underground flaring up again, and—

He keyed the intercom and ordered, "Bring the girl in," without giving himself any more time to think about what he was going to have to do.

He sat waiting, his head aching, trying to hold nerves and face and hands steady. The PolPol report on Barbara was on his desk, mixed up now with the waterworks, and he read it for the hundredth time. She had spoken in public against the Party this morning in the presence of a PolPol officer.

She came into his office quietly, between the blank-faced uniformed PolPol women. She walked unaided and Ahlgren felt a faint, smothered gladness that it had not been necessary to stun her.

"Leave us," he told the guards, who instantly obeyed. Would it look suspicious for him to want to be alone with another prisoner? It didn't matter—in a few minutes he would send her to Conditioning, because he had to send her; there was nothing else the Party could do with her. He felt his heart sinking.

He met her eyes for the first time and was vastly grateful to see no terror in them. "Sit down, Barbara."

She sat down without speaking and watched him as if more sorry for him than for herself. It was her look of that day years ago when he had told her of losing a job . . . If I had married her in those days, he thought, as I almost did, and never joined the Party, I would now be sitting in some outer office waiting, desperate to do anything to spare her the Pain, but helpless. Now I sit here, representing the Party, still helpless. But no, if I had married her I would have found some way to keep her from this.

"I'm sorry, Barbara," he said finally. "You know what I must do."

The waiting, unchanging sympathy of her eyes wrenched at him. She had never been beautiful, really, but so utterly alive . . .

"I—would like you to come back when you are—recovered," he heard himself maundering. "You'll be all—"

"Will you be able to marry me then?" Her first words to him burst out in a voice near breaking, like a question held in too long, that she had not meant to speak aloud.

He sat up straight in his chair, feeling as if the world had suddenly shaken beneath him. "How can you ask me that? You know I can't marry—I have chosen the Party!" He gripped the desk to stop his hands from trembling; then he realized that she must be only making a desperate attempt to save herself from Conditioning.

"In the name of the Party, sir," said City PolPol Chief Lazar in a hushed and slightly awed voice, shaking the hand thrust toward him by District Director Perkins. They stood in a small room in the basement of the Party Building in Ahlgren's city. One-way glass in a wall showed a view of a Treatment Room where Conditioning was sometimes practiced.

"Lazar, I've studied your record." Perkins' handshake was massive, like his bearing. "I think you may be taking over in this city very soon, so I had you called down here to watch something. The doctors called me in the District Capital last night about Ahlgren, and we've arranged a little test for him today—he doesn't know I'm here, of course. We should be able to see the climax, if things go as planned."

"I—I hardly know what to say, sir."

Perkins eyed him shrewdly. "Think you're the one being tested? No, son, not today. But it won't hurt you to see this." He frowned. "Ahlgren started out well in the Party, too. Seemed to have a fine future ahead of him. Now . . . " Perkins shook his head.

A door leading to a corridor opened and a man dressed in the green smock of a doctor stuck his head into the room. "Would you mind if I watched from here, sir?"

"No, no, come in. Lazar, this is Citizen Schmidt. Doctor Schmidt, I should say, hey?"

Lazar acknowledged the introduction perfunctorily. A loyal non-Party citizen was neither a political danger nor a competitor for advancement, and therefore almost totally uninteresting.

Lazar turned to study the Treatment Room through the one-way glass. It was not impressive, except for the treatment table in the center, a low monstrous thing of wires and power. There were soft lights, chairs, a desk in one corner, and above the desk a small bookshelf. Lazar could see that one book had been placed behind the others, as if someone had tried to hide it. Looking closer, he made out that it was part of an encyclopedia.

Volume Paa-Pyx.

Ahlgren was holding Barbara by the wrists; he pulled her around the desk and kissed her. His decision had been made with no real struggle at all. Maybe he had made the decision weeks or months ago, without knowing, and had just been traveling with the Party on inertia. Barbara trembled and tried to pull back and then let herself go against him. She was not merely acting to save herself now, she could not be.

"They say life can be good again after Conditioning, Barbara," he whispered to her. "They say many regain full normal intelligence. They say—no, I could never send you to that! Not you, not that!"

"Oh, Jim, Jim." Years since anyone had called him by that name. Or was it so long? A half-memory came disturbingly and fled before he could grasp it. But then a real memory came plainly to him, bringing with it a plan of action that was at least better than nothing: the memory of the address the young rebel had spoken to his ears alone.

"Listen!" He grabbed Barbara's arms and held her away from him. "There may be one chance, just one small chance for us."

"What?"

"The Underground. I have an address."

"No, Jim. You can't do that." She backed away, looking toward the door as if she heard the guards coming to seize them both.

"Why not? Don't you understand what Conditioning means? Don't you understand what you are facing?"

"Yes, but . . . " Indecision showed in her voice and manner. "I don't know if I should try to tell you."

"Tell me what? Don't you realize what you're facing?"

"Yes, but you . . ."

"*Me?*" So she could think of his welfare first, even while she faced the Ultimate Pain. She must have loved him all these years. "I've had enough of the Party anyway." The words came so easily and sincerely to his lips that he was surprised as if by hypocrisy in himself, but it was not that. Somehow in the past few minutes his whole outlook on the world had shifted abruptly; the change must have been building for a long time.

His mind raced ahead, planning, while Barbara watched his face intently, one hand held up to her mouth.

He pulled a stun pistol out of his desk, checked the charge, and thrust it into his belt. "Follow me. Quickly."

A section of the bookcase swung outward at his touch. He led Barbara into the narrow passage in the wall and indicated an unmarked phone set into a small niche. "Private line to District HQ. This may buy us a little time."

She reached out tentatively as if to restrain him, but then clenched her fingers and made no objection.

He picked up the phone and waited until he heard someone on the other end, then said: "Ahlgren here. Rebel plot. They've infiltrated. I must flee." He hung up. Of course District HQ would doubt the message, but it should divide at least for a time the energies of the Party that would now be arrayed against him—and against the frightened girl with him. He led her now to a tiny secret elevator that would take them down to street level. In revolt against the authority he had so long accepted, he felt less alone than he had for years.

They emerged into open air by coming out of the wall in a little-used entrance to a rather shabby apartment house a block from the Party Building, after Ahlgren had studied the hallway through a peephole to make sure it was unoccupied.

He had discarded his insignia inside the secret passage; his jacket hid the butt of the pistol in his belt. If no one looked too closely at him, he might pass in the half-dark streets for a plainly dressed citizen.

They walked the side streets toward the Underground address, not going fast enough to attract attention. Barbara held his arm and from time to time looked back over her shoulder until he whispered to her to stop it. Other couples strolled past them and beside them; the normal evening life of the city progressed around them as if the Party and the Underground were no more than fairy stories.

The young rebel might have told someone else the address, before or after Conditioning had wrenched and battered his mind out of human shape. Ahlgren could not rely on the place being even temporarily safe. Barbara and he could only pause there in their flight, warn any Underground people they could find, and try to flee with them to some place of slightly less danger, if any existed. It was a weak chance, but their only one. There had been no time at all to plan anything better. Rebellion against the Party had burst in Ahlgren with the suddenness of a PolPol raid. His very lack of preparation for this step and his good record to date might make District think for a long time that he was indeed the victim of infiltrating Underground plotters.

The address proved to be that of a middle-sized, unremarkable building in a lower-class residential area, two or three apartments over a quiet-looking small tavern. A single front entrance, divided inside, where stairs led up to the apartments and two steps led down to the level of the tavern.

A couple of male patrons looked around from the bar with mild interest as Ahlgren and the girl entered. They and the bartender seemed nothing but solid citizen types.

While Ahlgren hesitated, uncertain of what to say or whether to speak at all, the bartender said suddenly: "Oh, that bunch. They're upstairs." The man's face assumed an unhappy look.

Ahlgren took no time to worry about whether he and Barbara were such obvious rebels already, or how the bartender fitted in. The PolPol might be right on their heels. He only nodded and led Barbara up the stairs.

There were two doors at the top; he chose at random and knocked. No answer. He tried the other. After at least a minute of feverishly quiet rapping on both doors, one opened enough to reveal a thin man with a blank suspicious stare.

"Let us in," Ahlgren whispered desperately. "It is vital to the Underground." The PolPol might close in at any moment; he had to take the chance and speak plainly. His hand was under his jacket on the butt of his stun pistol and his foot was in the door.

"I don't know what you mean," said the thin man tonelessly.

"Look at me! I am the Director of this city. I have deserted the Party."

The man's eyes widened and there were excited whisperings in the room behind him. "Let them in, Otto," said a voice.

Ahlgren pushed his way into the room, dragging Barbara with him. A fat man sat at a table with a bottle and glasses before him, and a little pile of dingy books and folders on the floor at his feet. A pair of unwholesome-looking women sat on a sagging couch along one wall. A door with a homemade look in another wall seemed to lead into the other apartment. Evidently the Underground used the whole second floor.

Ahlgren wasted no time with preliminaries. "Listen to me. The PolPol may be on their way here now. Get out while you can and take us with you. Have you got some place to run to?"

The fat man regarded Ahlgren owlishly and belched. "Not so fast. How do we know—"

There was a glare of searchlights against the dirty windows, through the drawn shades, and a booming amplified voice: "Ahlgren, come out peacefully. We know you're there. Ahlgren, come out."

He gripped Barbara and looked into her eyes. "Try to remember me after the Pain."

"Oh, Jimmy, Jimmy, you don't know, you don't understand!"

The four Underground people had burst into passionate argument, but were doing nothing purposeful. Ahlgren dragged Barbara downstairs. The PolPol wold have the building surrounded, but they would expect him to try to fight them off on the stairs, perhaps to escape over the roofs as rebels often did.

The lights were out in the tavern. The two patrons were standing behind the bar, the attitude of their vague shapes suggesting that they were waiting as interested spectators. The windows were too glared with searchlights, and the barkeep stood in the middle of the room glaring at Ahlgren.

"Ahlgren! Come out peacefully and no one will be hurt! Your case will be fairly heard!"

"Why don't you just do like the man says?" the barkeep suggested angrily.

What was wrong with these people? Didn't they realize—but he had no time. "Shut up. Where does that back door lead?"

"Nowhere. I keep it locked." The barkeep swore. "Hope they don't smash the place, but they sure as hell will if you don't go out. Sure, they say, we pay compensation, but look how long it takes. Sure, the glass they put in won't cut nobody, but I gotta sweep it up and put up plywood panels. Why don't you just go out?"

"Take it easy, Sam," said one of the patrons behind the bar, with a chuckle. Barbara was babbling too, something she was sorry for, or sorry about.

A window smashed in and a PolPol officer stood outlined in the frame, flashlight sweeping the room. The director shot first. The invisible soundless beam doubled up the man; the falling flashlight spun its beam crazily through the room. Ahlgren picked up a stool to batter at the rear door. It was the only way left.

"That don't go nowhere, I told ya! Stop! Why did I ever sign up?" The barkeep moaned, grabbing at Ahlgren to keep him from smashing at the door with the stool.

Ahlgren let him have the stun beam at close range.

It didn't bother the man in the least.

"Not on *me*, friend, not on *me*. Tickle all you want," the barkeep said in obscure triumph, pulling the stool away from Ahlgren, whose grip on it had loosened in surprise.

The director felt the paralyzing tickle of a beam stab his own side; he had time to see Lazar grinning in at a window before sinking to the floor and into unconsciousness.

He was slumped in a chair propped up by a stiff pillow when awareness returned. There was a sense of strangeness in his mind that he could not fully account for by what he remembered happening. Drugs? They were seldom used on anyone.

It was a Treatment Room; they were not going to waste any time. Lazar's face looked down at him, grinning, as he had seen it at the tavern window. Two or three of the green-smocked doctors who always administered Conditioning stood beside the monstrous table, watching him and waiting. And Barbara. She stood free in the background, not stunned or restrained in any way.

Lazar caught the direction of his gaze. "Oh yes, the young lady's been most helpful to us. It was in large part her idea—"

"Please." The doctor's voice had an edge to it. "I must insist, sir, that you not interfere with treatment."

"Very well." Lazar's grin was wider than ever. He touched Ahlgren's shoulder as one might pat a dog about to be gassed. "I was comfortably set to watch this show when you made me get up and work for it. But it'll be worth the trouble. Good luck in your new life." He went out jauntily.

Ahlgren let his eyelids close; he could not look at Barbara. She was whispering with a doctor. He prayed to the God of his childhood to let the Pain come quickly and bring complete forgetfulness.

A doctor was in front of Ahlgren. "Open your eyes. Look at me. Trust me. Never mind who's watching or that you think you've been betrayed. We didn't plan that, but it can't be helped now. I want you to do something and it won't hurt. Will you try?" The doctor's eyes burned down. His voice compelled.

Ahlgren was held. "Try what?" he asked.

"What do you think?" the doctor asked patiently. "Can't you remember?"

Remember? What was there to remember? Ahlgren's eye roved the room, fell upon the little bookshelf above the desk in one corner, and slid away again. But he supposed there was no escape from—what?

"You can get up if you like now, Jim. Move around."

He tried his legs, and they pushed him erect. His arms functioned; movement took an effort but was not painful. How long had he been out from the stunning?

He found himself approaching the little bookshelf, while the doctors and Barbara watched silently. She was crying quietly; too late now. But he couldn't hate her.

Obeying an impulse, he reached behind the little row of books and pulled out what he saw with a shock was Volume P. "Who hid this here?" he demanded. "I've been looking for it."

"Don't you remember, Jim?" asked a doctor gently. "You pushed it back there the last time. Now shall we try reading some things again?"

The sense of strangeness had deepened until there was no standard left by which to judge the strangeness. That doctor had a cursed familiar way of talking to the director of a city, even to an arrested director, but the director opened the book. He would show them; there was no subject he couldn't read about.

He found the place he thought they wanted, and began to read aloud, "Pain, the Ultimate," but all that followed was "see Conditioning."

"No, Jim. Turn further back. Let's try again where we were last time. Do you remember?"

Ahlgren turned pages, suddenly fearful that something unfaceable was coming. Paine, Thomas. Lucky man, bound up safe in a book.

"Party, the?" he asked, looking around at the doctors. He thought he remembered reading this article once; much of it had been only a vague jumble of nonsense. High-priced encyclopedia, too.

"No, not just now. Turn back to where we were last time, remember?"

Ahlgren knew it had to be done. For some reason. His hands began to tremble as he turned the pages. Pe. Pi. He was getting closer to something he didn't want to find.

Po. He dropped the book, but made himself pick it up again. Barbara gave him a violent nod of encouragement. She was still almost crying over something. Women. But this time she was here to help him and he was going to succeed.

He turned a few more pages and there it was. Something he had tried to face before—how many times?—and had always forgotten about after failure. His eyes scanned the clearly printed symbols, but something in his brain fought against interpreting them.

"I can't read it. It's all blurry." He had said that before.

Barbara whispered: "Try, Jim. Try hard."

Ahlgren stared at the page in an immense effort, failed, and relaxed for a moment. The title of the article suddenly leaped into focus for him:

POSSEMANIA

He held up the book and began to read aloud in a quavery voice: " '—From the Latin, *posse* power, plus *mania*. Of all mental diseases doubtless the most destructive, in terms of the total suffering inflicted upon humanity throughout history; and one of the most resistant to even modern therapy.' "

Why had they wanted him to read this? And why had it been difficult? An awful idea loomed on the horizon . . .

" 'Unique among diseases in that its effects are put to practical use by society, it in fact forms the basis of modern government (see Party, the).' "

Ahlgren faltered and looked around him uncertainly. He felt sweat beginning to bead his forehead. The article went on to great length, but he flipped pages rapidly back to find Party, the.

He skimmed rapidly through a few paragraphs, then read aloud in an impersonal, shrill, hurried tone: " 'Those with this pathological lust for power over others generally find means to satisfy it in any society; ours is the first to maintain effective control over its members who are so afflicted. Now, the victims of the disease are necessarily detected during the compulsory annual psychological examination. If immediate therapy fails to effect a cure, as it usually fails, mental Conditioning is applied to initiate or strengthen the delusions, welcomed by the patient, that the Party has the rest of the citizenry at its mercy and—' "

"Take your time, Jim."

" '—and that—that Conditioning is a painful, crippling punishment used by the Party itself to erase thoughts of political opposition.' "

The world was turning under Ahlgren. He forced himself to read on, slowly and sanely. Could this be truth?

" 'Following what is now to him the only practical course, the victim is guided to apply for Party membership as those found to be compulsive rebels and/or punishment-seekers are shuttled to the complementary organization (see Underground, the). He is of course invariably accepted and assigned, depending on his skills, to the Administration or the Political Police (see PolPol).' "

Again pages fluttered under Ahlgren's fingers. PolPol.

" '—stun pistols locked at low neural frequencies that produce only a tickling sensation, to which all Party and Underground members are Conditioned to respond by going into psychic paralysis, unless in a situation where it would be physically dangerous to do so.' "

Ahlgren skipped from article to article, his mind grabbing recklessly at the words that had been forbidden him.

" '—Most people generally ignore the activities of both Party and Underground, except as occasional sources of unexpected amusement.' "

" '—Underground members captured by the Party are quickly turned over to the government doctors for Conditioning. They are treated and sent out again to a different area, believing themselves rebel couriers or escapees. At each capture they are tested to see if their disease has abated to within the reach of therapy.' "

" '—The PolPol raid the same houses over and over, being Conditioned to remember no such addresses and to keep no records of them. Property owners are compensated for damage incurred. Personal injury in these activities is extremely rare, and accidental when it does occur, due to the Conditioning of both Party and Underground people against it.' "

" 'Party members composing the Administration perform most of our essential government functions, being constrained by their Conditioning against any abuse of power, corruption, or dishonesty.' "

Ahlgren felt cold sweat all over him. His headache was gone but his throat felt raw. How long had he been reading aloud?

"That's fine, Jim, that's fine!" a doctor said. "Can you go on a little further?"

It took a giant's effort. Yet it was something that must be done.

" 'By the interaction of Conditioning with the disease, the victim is prevented from apprehending the true state of affairs. He is, for example, unable to read this very article with any true comprehension. If read aloud to him, it will not make sense to his mind; he will interpret it to suit the needs of the moment, then quickly forget it. Indeed, this article and similar writings are frequently used as tests to determine a patient's progress . . .' "

Ahlgren's hand holding the book dropped to his side. He stood swaying on his feet, utterly weary. He wanted only sleep, oblivion, forgetfulness.

A doctor carefully took the book from him, found the place, and read: " 'When continued therapy has brought a Party member near the point of cure, as is finally possible in about half of all cases, a realization of the true state of affairs becomes possible for the patient.' That's you now, Jim. You're over the hump. Understand me? You're getting well!"

Director Ahlgren was weeping quietly, as if from weakness and exhaustion. He sat down on the edge of the treatment table and the doctors gathered around him and began to fit the attachments of the table to him. He helped them; he was familiar with the process.

"I think this'll be the last, Jim. We're going to de-Condition you this time. Then one more subconscious therapy—" The doctor's voice came through speakers . . .

. . . into the next room, where Perkins, Lazar, and Doctor Schmidt watched and listened.

Lazar stared through the one-way glass, gripped by vast elation. The director's chair was his! The girl in the Treatment Room had thrown her arms about Ahlgren; perhaps she regretted that she had been used against him. She should be grateful. It was not often that a mere citizen had such a chance to help the Party.

Doctor Schmidt was saying something to Lazar. "What?"

"I said, would you tell me what you thought of the material the former director read aloud just now?"

Lazar frowned. Why, it had been something—unpleasant. He turned to Perkins, giving up the problem with relief to his superior.

"What he read was a lot of subversive nonsense," Perkins rumbled, after a thoughtful pause. "It amounted to a confession of guilt."

"I see," said Dr. Schmidt. He looked a little sad. "Thank you, gentlemen. Shall we go?"

Perkins was staring with bright and hungry eyes at the motionless form of former Director Ahlgren on the table. "Too bad we have to inflict such pain," he said.

He was coming out of pleasant sleep, and the first thing he did was to reach out and find her hand. He looked up at her face. He remembered now—she'd said she'd wait . . . five years before.

"Was it your idea?" he asked. "To help last night yourself?"

"No, the doctors suggested it, darling. They thought you were approaching a crisis . . . but it's all right now."

"Then stop crying," he told her. "Every time I look at you, you're crying. Think I want to watch you cry all the time?" But she was half laughing, too, so it really was all right.

He lay in peace. The weight of mountains had been lifted from his soul.

His mother was bending over him anxiously. He saw there was morning light coming into a hospital room.

"Son, are you all right?"

"I'm fine, Mother. No pain." Barbara, looking happy, was still here, or here again.

His father came in, a little older and grayer than he remembered, shaking his head in the familiar way at his mother's ignorant worry about the supposed pain of Conditioning.

"It was on the Party news Just now," his father said, grinning. "You were denounced for traitorous activity yesterday and purged last night. The usual appeal—for the citizenry to treat you kindly and not blame your new personality for your acts of treason. I think we can manage that somehow."

Jim Ahlgren looked around at the three of them. He said softly: "I've been gone a long time."

SCIENCE FICTION—General

TO MARK THE YEAR ON AZLAROC

They had been quarreling in the ship, and were still at it when they disembarked and left its sprawling metal complexities behind them. Ailanna snapped at Hagen: "So what if I misplaced your camera! What does it matter if you have one more picture of the stars? You can take a dozen when we depart." And when it turned out that they had missed the ground transport machine that was taking the other passengers across the smooth undulations of the golden plain toward the city, Hagen was almost expecting her to physically attack him.

"Son of a nobody!" Ailanna hissed. "Where are we to stay if you have made no reservations?" A kilometer away was the only real city on the star, and Hagen realized that to one coming to Azlaroc for the first time, the city must look quite small. On the surface there appeared only a few fairyland towers, and little evidence of the many chambers and passageways dug out beneath the plain.

"I haven't made up my mind where to stay." He turned away from her and began to walk after the transport machine.

She followed. "You can never make up your mind about anything." It was an old intermittent quarrel. If the reservations had been in perfect order, there would have been something else to quarrel about.

She nagged him for a hundred meters across the plain, and then the scenery began to come through to her. The enormous golden-yellow land was humped here and there by paraboloid hills and

49

studded with balanced spheres of matter. The surface looked more like something man-made than like soil, and it stretched in places up to the low, yellowish, sunless sky, in asymptotic spires that broke off in radiant glory at an altitude of a few hundred meters, at the upper edge of the region of gravity inversion.

"What's that?" Her voice was no longer angry. She was looking toward the top of a golden sphere which loomed over the distanceless horizon, at right angles to the way they were walking. The sphere reminded Hagen of a large planet rising, as seen from some close-in satellite, but this sphere was entirely beneath the low, peculiar sky.

"Only part of the topography." He remained calm, as usual, taking her bickering in stride.

When they had gotten under-surface in the city, and arranged for lodgings, and were on their way to them through one of the smaller side passageways, Hagen saw some man or woman of a long-past year approaching through the passage from the other direction. Had there been three or four people of the present year or of recent years in the same part of the corridor just then, the passage of such an old one would have been almost unnoticeable. The old one did not appear as a plain solid human figure. Only a disturbance in the air and along the wall, a mound of shadows and moire patterns that throbbed with the beat of the pulsar somewhere beneath their feet. The disturbance occupied hardly any space in this year's corridor, and Ailanna at first was not aware of it at all.

Hagen reached out a hand and took her by the upper arm and forced her, strong woman that she was, into three almost-dancing steps that left her facing in the proper way to see. "Look. One of the early settlers."

With a small intake of breath Ailanna fixed her eyes on the figure. She watched it out of sight around a corner, then turned her elfin face to Hagen. Her eyes had been enlarged, and her naturally small chin further diminished, in accordance with the fashion dictates of the time, even as Hagen's dark eyebrows had been grown into a ring of hair that crossed above his nose and went down by its sides to meld with his mustache. She said: "Perhaps one of the very first? An explorer?"

"No." He looked about at the ordinary overhead lights, the smooth walls of the yellowish rock-like substance of the star. "I remember that this corridor was not cut by the explorers, not perhaps until '120 or '130. So no settler in it can be older than that, of course."

"I don't understand, Hagen. Why didn't you tell me more about this place before you brought me here?"

"This way it will all come as a wonderful surprise." Exactly how much irony was in his answer was hard to tell.

They met others in the corridor as they proceeded. Here came a couple of evidently ten or fifteen local years ago. walking in the nudity that had been acceptable as fashion then, draped with ten or fifteen of the sealing veils of Azlaroc so that their bodies shimmered slightly as they moved, giving off small diamond-sparkles of light. The veils of only ten or fifteen years were not enough to warp a settler out of phase with this year's visitors, so the four people meeting in the passage had to give way a little on both sides, as if they were in a full sense contemporaries, and like contemporaries they excused themselves with vacant little social smiles.

Numbers, glowing softly from the corridor walls, guided Hagen and Ailanna to their rooms. "Hagen, what is this other sign that one sees on the walls?" It was a red hollow circle with a small pie-cut wedge of its interior filled with red also.

"The amount of red inside shows the estimated fraction of a year remaining until the next veil falls."

"Then there is not much of the year left, for sightseeing. Here, this must be our door. I would say we have come at a poor time."

Opening the door, he did not reply. Their baggage had already been deposited inside.

"I wouldn't want to be trapped here, Hagen. Well. the apartment's not bad . . . now what's the matter? What have I said?" She had learned to know at once when something really bothered him, which her inconsequential bickering rarely seemed to do.

"Nothing. Ample warning is always given so the tourists can get away, you needn't worry.

She was in the bedroom unpacking when something came in through the illusory window that seemed to give upon the golden plain. Where a sawtooth range of diminishing pyramids marched in from the horizon there came a shimmer and a sliding distortion that was in the room with her before she knew it, that passed on harmless through her own flesh, and went its way. She gave a yelp of fear.

Hagen was in the doorway, smiling faintly. "Didn't I mention that we might be sharing our apartment here?"

"Sharing—of course not. Oh. You mean with settlers, folk of other years. That's what it was, then. But—through the wall?"

"That wall was evidently an open passage in their time. Ignore them, as they will us. Looking up through their veils they can see us—differently, too. While diving I have asked them to describe how we look to them, but their answers are hard to understand."

"Tell me about diving," she said, when they had finished settling in and were coming out of doors again.

"Better than that, I'll show you. But I'll tell you first, of course." As they walked out onto the plain, Hagen could hear the pulsar component of the triple system beating as sound, the sound coming now from overhead, thick and soft and at one third the speed of a calm human heart. It came through all the strangeness of space that lay between him and the invisible pulsar that locked its orbit intricately with those of a small black hole and of the world called Azlaroc.

He said: "What is called diving, on Azlaroc, is a means of approaching the people and things that lie under the veils of the years. Nothing can pierce the veils, of course. But diving stretches them, lets one get near enough to the people of the past to see them more clearly and make photographs." And more than that, more than that, oh Gods of Space, thought Hagen but he said no more.

On the plain other tourists were also walking, in this year's fashion of scanty garments each of a hundred colors. In the mild, calm air, under the vague yellowish sky that was not really a sky, and bathed in sunless light, Hagen had almost the feeling of being still indoors. He was heading for a divers' shop that he remembered. He meant to waste no time in beginning his private search in earnest.

Ailanna walked beside him, no longer quarrelsome, and increasingly interested in the world around them. "You say nothing at all can pierce the veils, once they have fallen in and wrapped themselves about this planet?"

"No matter can pierce them. And this is not a planet. I suppose 'star' is the best term for a layperson to use, though the scientists might wince at it. There's the divers' shop ahead, see that sign beside the cave?" The cave was in the side of a sharp-angled rhombic hill.

Inside the shop they were greeted by the proprietor, a settler swathed in more than a hundred veils, who needed electronic amplifiers to converse with customers. After brief negotiation he began to take their measurements.

"Ailanna, when we dive, what would you like to see?"

Now she was cheerful. "Things of beauty. Also I would like to meet one of those first, stranded explorers."

"The beauty will be all about. There are signals and machines to guide the tourist to exceptional sights, as for the explorer, we can try. When I was last here it was still possible to dive near enough to them to see their faces and converse. Maybe now, when a hundred and thirty more veils have been added, it is possible no longer."

They were fitted with diving gear, each a carapace and helm of glass and metal that flowed like water over their upper bodies.

"Hagen, if nothing can pierce the fallen veils of the years, how are these underground rooms dug out?"

Now his diver's suit had firmed into place. Where Hagen's face had been she saw now only a distorting mirror, that gave an eerie semblance of her own face back to her. But his voice was familiar and reassuring. "Digging is possible because there are two kinds of matter, of physical reality, here coexisting. The stuff of the landscape, all those mathematical shapes and the plain they rise from, is comparatively common matter. Its atoms are docile and workable, at least here in this region of mild gravity and pressure. The explorers realized from the start that this mild region needed only air and water and food, to provide men with more habitable surface than a planet . . . there, your diver's gear is stabilized about you. Let's walk to Old Town, where we may find an explorer."

Sometimes above ground and sometimes below, they walked, armored in the strange suits and connected to the year of their own visit by umbilical cables as fine and flexible and unbreakable as artists' lines on paper. Adjusting his gear for maximum admittance, Hagen nervously scanned the faces of all passing settlers. Now some features were discernible in even the oldest of them.

"And the other kind of matter, Hagen, the other physical reality. What about the veils?"

"Ah, yes. The material between the stars, gathered up as this triple system advances through space. What is not sucked into the black hole is sieved through nets of the pulsar's radiation, squeezed by the black hole's hundred billion gravities. shattered and transformed in all its particles as it falls toward Azlaroc through the belts of space that starships must avoid. Once every systemic year conditions are right and a veil falls. What falls is no longer matter that men can work with, any more than they can work in the heart of a black hole. Ailanna. are you tuned to maximum? Look just ahead."

They were out on the surface again. A human figure that even with the help of diver's gear appeared no more than a wavery half-image had just separated itself from an equally insubstantial dwelling. A hundred and thirty years before, someone had pointed out a similar half-visible structure to Hagen as an explorer's house. He had never spoken to an explorer, but he was ready now to try. He began to run. The gear he wore was only a slight hindrance.

Close ahead now was the horizon, with just beyond it the golden globe they had earlier observed. No telling how far away it was, a thousand meters or perhaps ten times that distance. Amid glowing dunes—here the color of the land was changing, from yellow to a pink so subtle that it was effectively a new color—Hagen thought that he had lost the explorer, but then suddenly the wavery stick-figure was in his path. Almost, he ran through or collided with it. He regained his balance and tried to speak casually.

"Honorable person, we do not wish to be discourteous, and we will leave you if our inquiries are bothersome, but we would like to know if you are one of the original explorers."

Eyes that one moment looked like skeletal sockets, and the next as large and human as Ailanna's own, regarded Hagen. Or were they eyes at all? Working with the controls of his sensory input he gained for one instant a glimpse of a face. human but doubtfully either male or female, squinting and intense, hair blown about it as if in a terrible wind. It faced Hagen and tried to speak, but whatever words came seemed to be blown away. A moment later the figure was gone, only walking somewhere nearby, but so out of focus that it might as well have flown behind the golden sphere somewhere.

Question or answer, Hagen? Which had it offered you?

Ailanna's hands clamped on his arm. "Hagen, I saw—it was terrible."

"No, it wasn't. Only a man or a woman. What lies between us and them, that can be terrible sometimes."

Ailanna was dialing her admittance down, going out of focus in a different way. Hagen adjusted his controls to return fully with her to their own year. Very little of the land around them seemed to change as they did so. A chain of small pink hills, hyperbolic paraboloid saddles precisely separating members, seemed to grow up out of nothing in the middle distance. That was all.

"Hagen, that was an explorer, that must have been. I wish he had talked to us, even though he frightened me. Are they still sane?"

He looked around, out over the uninhabited region toward which they had been walking, then back toward the city. In the city was where he would have to search.

He said: "The first veil that men ever saw falling here caught them totally by surprise. They described it as looking like a fine net settling toward them from an exploding sky. It settled over the first explorers and bound itself to the atoms of their bodies. They are all here yet, as you know. Soon it was realized that the trapped people were continuing to lead reasonable human lives, and that they were now protected against aging far better than we on the outside. There's nothing so terrible about life here. Why shouldn't they be sane? Many others have come here voluntarily to settle."

"Nothing I have seen so far would lead me to do that." Her voice was growing petulant again.

"Ailanna, maybe it will be better if we separate for a time. This world is as safe as any. Wander and surprise yourself."

"And you, Hagen?"

"I will wander too."

He had been separated from Ailanna for a quarter of a day, and searching steadily all the time, before he finally found her.

Mira.

He came upon her in a place that he knew she frequented, or had frequented a hundred and thirty years before. It was one of the lower subterranean corridors, leading to a huge pool in which real water-diving, swimming, and other splashy sports were practiced. He was approaching her from the rear in the corridor when she suddenly stopped walking and turned her head, as if she knew he was there even before she saw him.

"I knew you would be back, Hagen," she said as he came up.

"Mira," he said, and then was silent for a time. The he said: "You are still as beautiful as ever."

"Of course." They both smiled, knowing that here she could not age, and that change from any sort of accident was most unlikely.

He said: "I knew that, but now I see it for myself." Even without his diving gear he could have seen enough through one hundred and thirty veils to reassure himself of that. But with his gear on it was almost as if he were really in her world. The two of them might hold hands, or kiss, or embrace in the old old way that men and women still used as in the time when the race was born of women's bodies. But at the same time it was impossible to forget that the silken and impermeable veils of a hundred and thirty years would always lie between them, and that never again in this world or any other would they touch.

"I knew you would come back. But why did you stay away so long?"

"A few years make but little difference in how close I can come to you."

She put out her hands and held him by the upper arms, and stroked his arms. He could feel her touch as if through layers of the finest ancient silk. "But each year made a difference to me. I thought you had forgotten me. Remember the vows about eternity that we once made?"

"I thought I might forget, but I did not. I found I couldn't."

A hundred and thirty years ago he and Mira had quarreled, while visiting Azlaroc as tourists. Angry, Hagen had gone offstar without telling her; when an alarm sounded that the yearly veil was falling early, she had been sure that he was still somewhere on the surface, and had remained on it herself, searching for him, and of course not finding him. By the time he came back, meaning to patch up the quarrel, the veil had already fallen.

She had not changed, and yet seeing her again was not the same, not all that he had expected it to be.

The reaction to his coming back was growing in her. "Hagen, Hagen, it is you. Really you."

He felt embarrassed. "Can you forgive me for what happened?"

"Of course I can, darling. Come, walk with me. Tell me of yourself and what you've done."

"I . . . later I will try to tell you." How could he relate in a moment or two the history of a hundred and thirty years? "What have you done here, Mira? How is it with you?"

"How would it be?" She gestured in an old, remembered way, with a little sensuous, unconscious movement of her shoulder. "You lived here with me; you know how it is."

"I lived here only a very little time."

"But there are no physical changes worth mentioning. The air my yeargroup breathes and the food we eat are recycled forever, more ours than the rooms we live in are. But still we change and grow, though not in body. We explore the infinite possibilities of each other and of our world. There are only eleven hundred and six in my yeargroup, and we have as much room here as do the billions on a planet.

"I feared that perhaps *you* had forgotten *me*."

"Can I forget where I am, and how I came to be here?" Her eyes grew very wide and luminous—not enlarged eyes like Ailanna's, Mira like most other settlers had kept to the fashions of her year of veiling—and there was a compressed fierceness in her lips. "There was a time when I raged at you—but no longer. There is no point."

He said: "You are going to have to teach me how to be a settler here. How to put up with gawking tourists, and with the physical restrictions on which rooms and passages I may enter, when more of them are dug out in the future. Do you never want to burrow into the rooms and halls of later years, and make them your own?"

"That would just cause destruction and disruption, for the people of later years to try to mend. They could probably retaliate by diving against us, and somehow disarranging our lives. Though I suppose a war between us would be impossible."

"Do I disarrange your life seriously, Mira, by diving to you now?"

"Hagen!" She shook her head reprovingly. "Of course you do. How can you ask?" She looked at him more closely. "Is it really you who has come back, or someone else, with outlandish eyebrows?" Then the wild and daring look he knew and loved came over her, and suddenly the hundred and thirty years were gone. "Come to the pool and the beach, and we will soon see who you really are!"

He ran laughing in pursuit of her. She led him to the vast underground grotto of blackness and fire, where she threw off her garments and plunged into the pool. He followed, lightly burdened with his diver's gear.

It was an old running, diving, swimming game between them, and he had not forgotten how to play. With the gear on, Hagen of course did not need to come to the surface of the pool to breathe, nor was he bothered by the water's cold. But still she beat him, flashing and gliding and sliding away. He was both outmaneuvered and outsped.

Laughing, she swam back to where he had collapsed in gasps and laughter on the black-and-golden beach. "Hagen, have you aged that much? Even wearing the drag and weight of diver's gear myself I could beat you today."

Was he really that much older? Lungs and heart should not wear out so fast, nor had they, he believed. But something else in him had aged and changed. "You have practiced much more than I," he grumbled.

"But you were always the better diver," she told him softly, swimming near, then coming out of the water. Some of the droplets that wet her emerging body were water of her own year, under the silken veils of time that gauzed her skin; other drops, the water of Hagen's time, clung on outside the veils. "And the stronger swimmer. You will soon be beating me again, if you come back."

"I am back already, Mira. You are three times as beautiful as I remembered you."

Mira came to him and he pulled her down on the beach to embrace her with great joy. Why, he thought, oh why did I ever leave?

Why indeed?

He became aware that Ailanna was swimming in the water nearby in her own diver's gear, watching, had perhaps been watching and listening for some time. He turned to speak to her, to offer some explanation and introduction, but she submerged and was gone. Mira gave no sign of having noticed the other woman's presence.

"Do you miss the world outside. Mira?"

"I suppose I drove you away to it, the last time, with my lamenting for it. But no, I do not really miss it now. This world is large enough, and grows no smaller for me, as your world out there grows smaller as you age, for all its galaxies and space. Is it only the fear of time and age and death that has brought you back to me, Hagen?"

"No." He thought his answer was perfectly honest, and the contrast between this perfectly honest statement and some of his earlier ones showed up the earlier ones for what they were. Who had he been trying to fool? Who was it that men always tried to fool?

"And was it," she asked, "my lamenting that drove you off? I lament no longer for my life."

"Nor for the veil that fell between us?"

The true answer was there in her grave eyes, if he could read it through the stretching, subtle, impenetrable veils.

The red circles held narrow dagger-blades of urgent warning on all the walls, and warning voices boomed like thunder across the golden, convoluted plain. The evacuation ship lay like a thick pool of bright and melted-looking metal in the field, with its hundred doors open for quick access, and a hundred machines carrying tourists and their baggage aboard. The veil was falling early again this year. Stretching in a row across the gravity-inversion sky, near one side of the directionless horizon, explosions already raged like an advancing line of silent summer thunderstorms.

Hagen, hurrying out onto the field, stopped a hurrying machine. "My companion, the woman Ailanna, is she aboard the ship?"

"No list of names of those aboard has been completed, Man." The timbre of the metal voice was meant to be masterly, and reassuring even when the words were not.

Hagen looked around him at the surface of the city, the few spare towers and the multitudinous burrowed entrances. Over the whole nearby landscape more machines were racing to reach the ship with goods or perhaps even tourists who had somehow not gotten the warning in comfortable time, or who were at the last moment changing their minds about becoming settlers. Was not Ailanna frantically looking amid the burrows for Hagen, looking in vain as the last moments fell? It was against logic and sense that she should be, but he could not escape the feeling that she was.

Nevertheless the doors on the ship were closed or closing now. "Take me aboard," he barked at the machine.

"At once, Man." And they were already flying across the plain.

Aboard ship, Hagen looked out of a port as they were hurled into the sky, then warped through the sideward modes of space, twisted out from under the falling veil before it could clamp its immovable knots about the atoms of the ship and passengers and hold them down forever. There was a last glimpse of the yellow plain, and then only strange flickers of light from the abnormal space they were traversing briefly, like a cloud.

"That was exciting!" Out of nowhere Ailanna threw herself against him with a hug. "I was worried there, for a moment, that you'd been left behind." She was ready now to forgive him a flirtation with a girl of a hundred and thirty years ago. It was nice that he was forgiven, and Hagen patted her shoulder; but his eyes were still looking upward and outward, waiting for the stars.

MARTHA

It rained hard on Tuesday, and the Science Museum was not crowded. On my way to interview the director in his office, I saw a touring class of schoolchildren gathered around the newest exhibit, a very late-model computer. It had been given the name of Martha, an acronym constructed by some abbreviation of electronic terms. Martha was supposed to be capable of answering a very wide range of questions in all areas of human knowledge, even explaining some of the most abstruse scientific theories to the layman.

"I understand the computer can even change its own design," I commented, a bit later, talking to the director.

He was proud. "Yes, theoretically. She hasn't done much rebuilding yet, except to design and print a few new logic circuits for herself."

"You call the computer 'she,' then. Why?"

"I do. Yes. Perhaps because she's still mysterious, even to the men who know her best." He chuckled, man-to-man.

"What does it—or she—say to people? Or let me put it this way, what kind of questions does she get?"

"Oh, there are some interesting conversations." He paused. "Martha allows each person about a minute at one of the phones, then asks him or her to move along. She has scanners and comparator circuits that can classify people by shape. She can conduct

61

several conversations simultaneously, and she even uses simpler words when talking to children. We're quite proud of her."

I was making notes. Maybe my editor would like one article on Martha and another on the museum in general. "What would you say was the most common question asked of the machine?"

The director thought. "Well, people sometimes ask: 'Are you a girl in there?' At first Martha always answered 'No,' but lately she's begun to say: 'You've got me there.' That's not just a programmed response, either, which is what makes it remarkable. She's a smart little lady." He chuckled again. "Also, people sometimes want their fortunes told, which naturally is beyond even Martha's powers. Let me think. Oh yes, many people want her to multiply large numbers, or play tic-tac-toe on the electric board. She does those things perfectly, of course. She's brought a lot of people to the museum."

On my way out I saw that the children had gone. For the moment I was alone with Martha in her room. The communicating phones hung unused on the elegant guardrail. I went over and picked up one of the phones, feeling just a little foolish.

"Yes, sir," said the pleasant feminine voice in my ear, made up, I knew, of individually recorded words electronically strung together. "What can I do for you?"

Inspiration came. "You ask *me* a question," I suggested.

The pleasant voice repeated: "What can I do for you?"

"I want you to ask me a question."

"You are the first human being to ask me for a question. Now, this is the question I ask of you: What do you, as one human being, want from me?"

I was momentarily stumped. "I don't know," I said finally. "The same as everyone else, I guess." I was wondering how to improve upon my answer when a sign lit up, reading:

CLOSED TEMPORARILY FOR REPAIRS
PARDON ME WHILE I POWDER MY NOSE

The whimsy was not Martha's, but printed by human design on the glass over the light. If she turned the repair light on, those were the only words that she could show the world. Meanwhile, the phone I was holding went dead. As I moved away I thought I heard machinery starting up under the floor.

Next day the director called to tell me that Martha was rebuilding herself. The day after that I went back to look. People were crowding up to the guardrail, around new panels which held rows of buttons. Each button, when pushed, produced noises, or colored lights, or impressive discharges of static electricity, among the complex new devices which had been added atop the machine. Through the telephone receivers a sexy voice answered every question with clearly spoken scraps of nonsense, studded with long technical words.

PLANETEER

During the weeks that the starship *Yuan Chwang* had hovered in close observation of the new planet Aqua, ship's time had been jockeyed around to agree with the sun-time at the place chosen for first landing.

Boris Brazil saw no evidence of sane thinking behind this procedure; it meant the planeteers' briefing for the big event was set for 0200, and he had to get up in what was effectively the middle of the night—a thing to which he had grown accustomed, but never expected to learn to enjoy. Leaving his tiny cabin in a state of disorder that might have infuriated an inspecting officer—had there been an inspecting officer aboard interested in the neatness of cabins—he set forth in search of chow.

Brazil was tall and bony, resembling a blond young Abe Lincoln. He rubbed sleep from his eyes as his long legs carried him toward the mess hall. A distracting young squab from Computing sailed past him in the opposite direction, smiling.

"Good luck," she said.

"Is the coffee that bad?" It was the best facsimile of a joke he could think of this early.

But the girl hadn't been talking about coffee. Chief Planeteer Sam Gates had picked Brazil to go along on the first landing attempt, he learned when he met Gates in the chow line. He saw by the small computer clipped to Sam's belt that the other man had been up early on his own, double-checking the crew chief and

maintenance robots who were readying their scoutship. Brazil felt
vaguely guilty—but not very. He might well have been just another
body in the way.

Sam Gates stood in the chow line swinging his arms and snap-
ping his fingers, chewing his dark moustache as he usually did
when nervous.

"How's it look?" Brazil asked.

"Oh, free and clear. Guess we'll have ground under our feet in
a few hours."

Most of the *Yuan Chwang's* twenty-four planeteers were in the
chow line, with a fair number of people from other departments.
The day's operation was going to be a big one for everybody.

Trays loaded with synthetic ham, and a scrambled substance not
preceded by chickens, Gates and Brazil found a table. Ten
scoutships were going down today, though only one would attempt
to land; most of the night shift from all departments seemed to
think it was time for lunch. The mess was filling up quickly.

"Here comes the alien," said Gates, gesturing with his fork.

Brazil raised his eyes toward the tall turbaned man bearing a
tray in their direction. "Hi, Chan. Pull up a a chair."

Chandragupta was no more an alien here than any other Earthman; his job had earned him the nickname.

"Good morning," said the Tribune with a smile, sitting down
with Gates and Brazil. "I hope my people treat you well today."
He had not yet seen one of "his people" and possibly never would;
but from the moment high-altitude reconnaissance had established
that intelligent life at an apparently primitive technological level
existed on Aqua, his job had taken on substance. He was to repre-
sent the natives below in the councils aboard the *Yuan Chwang*,
to argue at every turn for what he conceived to be their welfare,
letting others worry about the scientific objectives that had brought
the exploration ship so far from Earth, until he was satisfied that
the natives needed no help or the mission was over.

"No reason to expect any trouble," said Brazil. Then, wondering
what reaction he might provoke from his messmates, he added:
"This one looks fairly simple."

"Except we know there are some kind of people down there,"
Gates said mildly. "And people are never as simple as you'd like
them to be."

"I wonder if they will need my help," said Chan, "and I wonder if I will be able to help them." The job of Tribune was a new one, really still experimental. "In a few hours perhaps I will know."

"We're not trying to conquer them, you know," said Brazil, half amused and a little offended by Chan's eagerness to defend against his shipmates some people he had never seen.

"Oh, I know. But we must be careful not to conquer them by accident, eh?"

When Brazil got up to leave the mess, he could feel the eyes on his back, or thought he could. Here go the heroes, he thought. First landing. Hail, Hail.

And deep inside he felt a pride and joy so fierce he was embarrassed to admit it to himself—to be one of the first Earthmen stepping onto this unknown world.

Briefing was normal for a mission this size. The twenty planeteers who were going down into atmosphere, plus two reserve crews, slouched in their seats and scribbled notes and now and then whispered back and forth about business, concentrating so intently on the job at hand that an outsider might have thought them bored and distracted.

Captain Dietrich, boss of the *Yuan Chwang*, mounted the low dais in the front of the briefing room. He was a rather small man, of mild and bookish appearance. After working with him for awhile, one tended to treat cautiously all small men of mild and bookish appearance.

Tribune Chandragupta entered the briefing room through the rear door. The Captain eyed him thoughtfully. This was the first voyage on which he had been required to carry a Tribune; the idea had been born as a political move in the committee meetings of Earth Parliament, and had earned certain legislators reputations as defenders of liberty.

Captain Dietrich had no detectable wish to conquer anyone, having of course passed the Space Force psych tests, and he was willing to give the Tribune system a trial. After all, he could always overrule the man, on condition he thought it necessary for the safety of members of the expedition—though he was the only one aboard who could do so. But it seemed to the Captain that this placing of a civilian official aboard his ship might be only the start of an effort by the groundbound government to encroach upon what he considered to be the domain of the Space Force. Every time he went home he heard complaints that the SF was growing too powerful and cost too much.

"Militarism," they would say, over a drink or anywhere he met civilians. "We've just managed to really get away from all that on Earth, and now you want to start all over, on Mars and Ganymede and this new military base on Aldebaran 2."

"The Martian colony is hardly a military base," he would remind them patiently. "It now has its own independent civilian government and sends representatives to Earth Parliament. The Space Force has practically pulled out of Mars altogether. Ganymede is a training base. Aldebaran 2 you're right about, mostly; and we do have other military bases."

"Aha!" Now how do we know that none of these outlying bases or colonies will ever threaten Earth?"

"Because all spaceships and strategic weapons are controlled by the SF, and the SF is controlled by the psych tests that screen people trying to enter it. Admittedly, no system is perfect, but what are our alternatives?"

"We could cut down on this space exploration, maybe stop it altogether. It's devilish expensive, and there seems no hope it will ever relieve our crowding on Earth. What do we get out of it anyway that makes it really profitable?"

"Well," Captain Dietrich might say, "since you talk of militarism, I will ignore the valuable knowledge we have gained by exploration and answer you in military terms. We have the ability to travel hundreds of light-years in a matter of months, and to melt any known planet in minutes, with one ship delivering one weapon. How many races do you think live in our galaxy with similar capabilities?"

No Earthmen had met any but primitive aliens—yet. But people had begun to comprehend the magnitude of the galaxy, where man's hundred-light-year radius of domination gave him no more than a Jamestown Colony.

"Assume a race with such capabilities," the captain might continue, "and with motivations we might not be able to understand, spreading out across the galaxy as we are. Would you rather have them discover our military base on Aldebaran this year, or find all humanity crowded on one unprotected Earth, perhaps the year after next?"

Dietrich got a wide range of answers to this question. He himself would much prefer to meet the hypothetical advanced aliens a thousand light-years or more from Earth, with a number of large and effective military bases in between.

But right now it was time for him to start briefing his planeteers, who probably knew as much about Aqua as he, who had never driven a scoutship into her upper atmosphere.

"Gentlemen, we've found out a little about this planet, the only child of a Sol-type sun, after watching it for six weeks. One-point-one AU from its sun, gravity point-nine-five, diameter point-nine, eighty-five percent of surface is water. Oxy-nitrogen atmosphere, about five thousand meters equivalent. We won't try breathing it for some time yet. Full suits until further notice.

"What land there is, is probably quite well populated with what we think are humanoids with a technical level probably nowhere higher than that of medieval Europe. Several rather large sailing ships have been spotted in coastal waters. There are only a couple of long paved roads, and none of the cities are electrically lit on nightside. We don't think anyone down there can have spotted us yet."

Most of his audience looked back at him rather impatiently, as if to say: We know all this. We're the ones who found it out.

But the captain wanted to make sure they had all the basic facts in proper focus. "Our mission is to make contact with the natives. To establish a temporary scientific base on the surface for seismic studies, biological studies, and so forth—and of course to learn what we can from and about the intelligent inhabitants."

The captain raised his eyes and spoke as much to the Tribune as to his planeteers. "There seems very little chance of any permanent colony being established here, due to the native population on a very limited land area. This same factor would seem to preclude our establishing the temporary base in some remote area, without knowledge of the natives. So we will have to deal with them some-how from the start.

"I've never believed in the god-from-the-sky approach, and as you know, SF policy is to avoid it if possible. It falsifies from the start a relationship that may become permanent, even if we now intend it to be temporary. And he who takes godhood upon himself is likely to have to spend more time at it than at the business for which he came, and to assume responsibility for far-reaching changes in the native history."

The Captain paused, then looked at another man who stood waiting to speak, paper in hand. "Meteorology?"

"Yes sir."

On a wall appeared a photomap of the island that had been picked for the first landing attempt, an irregular shape of land about a hundred and fifty kilometers long by twenty wide. Air temperature at dawn in the landing area should be about fifty degrees F, the water a little cooler. There might be enough fog to aid the landing scoutship in an unseen descent.

Meteorology also discussed atmospheric effects on communication between scouts and the mother ship, and predicted the weather in the landing area for the next day. He paused to answer a couple of questions, and introduced Passive Detection.

The PD man discussed Aqua's Van Allen belts, magnetic field, the variety and amount of solar radiation in nearby space, and that to be expected on the surface. He spoke of what the natives probably burned for heat and light in the nightside cities, and confirmed the apparent absence of any advanced technology.

Biology was next, with a prediction that the island would show diverse and active life. It was near the tropics in the spring hemisphere, and green with vegetation. Scout photos showed no evidence of very large animals or plants. Some areas appeared to be under cultivation.

Anthropology took the dais to speculate. The people of Aqua were thought to be humanoid, but in the photos anything as small as a man was at the very limit of visibility, and the estimate of the beings' appearance was based on lucky shots of dawn or dusk shadows striding gigantic across more or less level ground. There was some massive construction, probably of masonry, in the one sizable city on the island. A seawall and a couple of large structures had been built on a finger of land that protected the city's small harbor, where sailing ships were visible.

Captain Dietrich came back to outline the patterns he wanted the non-landing scouts to fly. "The target island is pretty well isolated from the planet's main land areas, so if we put a base here it should have a minimal effect on native culture. Also, if we botch things up here, we may be able to move on and try again without the natives in the new spot having heard of us." He looked around at his men; the idea was strongly conveyed to them that the captain preferred they not botch things up. "Chan—anything you want to say? No? All right, board your scouts."

Brazil strode beside Gates out the door in the rear of the briefing room, passing under the sign that read:

MAYBE . . . ANYTHING

Maybe they're real telepaths down there. Maybe they're a mighty race now retired from active competition and preferring the simple life. Maybe . . .

Never mind. it was time to follow the planeteers' motto: *Go Down and Find Out.*

Gates and Brazil now faced a final quick Medical & Psych exam in a ship's corridor. Brazil had long since given up trying to startle the psych doc by giving to the inevitable weird question an even weirder answer.

"I'd swear you were sane if I didn't know you better," the doctor told him this time. "Pass on."

They fitted themselves into the suits of Armor, Light, Space, and Ground, that had been selected for this job. The suits included among their accessories flotation bubbles that when inflated enabled the wearers to maneuver with supposed ease through water. The suits now received a quick semifinal test.

Captain Dietrich was waiting in the berth that was almost filled by the fifteen-meter-long stubby bulk of scoutship *Alpha.* Gates and Brazil juggled checklists and fishbowl helmets to offer him each an armored paw to shake. The Captain said something about good luck.

The two planeteers climbed through the scout's hatch, twisting sideways with practiced movements to meet the ninety-degree shift in artificial gravity between mother ship and scout. Gates climbed on toward the control room while Brazil stayed to seal the hatch. On planet they would of course use an airlock.

Engines started. Ship's power off and disconnected. All personnel out of berth. Ready for sterilizing.

Lethal gas, swirling around the scout's hull, was mostly pumped away to be saved and reused. Then a blast of ultraviolet, more intense than the raw Sol-type sunshine outside, bathed the inside of the berth. No microorganisms must be carried down into atmosphere.

Strapped and clamped into control room chairs, ports sealed, watching the tiny world of the berth by video screen, Gates and Brazil were nearly ready. The berth door slid open on schedule, and what was left of gas inside went out in a faint puff of sudden mist.

The watery world that someone with little imagination had named Aqua, sixteen thousand kilometers away, filled the opening. A quarter of it was dayside, blue mottled white with patterned clouds; nightside was eerie with subtle atmospheric glows.

"Stand by one, *Alpha*," came over the radio. "A little trouble clearing *Delta*."

"Understand," said Sam Gates. "Hey Boris, I like those tridi stories at home. The chap just drives his ship up to a new planet and lands. The faithful crew stands around scratching their heads. 'Well, what'll we do now?' says one. Then they wait for the hero to speak up."

" 'Let's get out and look around,' " said Brazil, grinning. " 'O.K., but let's all be careful. Maybe we better close the door of the ship behind us.' "

Sam gave a rare smile. "And then one character takes his helmet off to eat a coconut. Only it turns out to be a chieftain's daughter."

"And they're all in the soup. They never seem to learn."

"Stand by, *Alpha*," said Operations over the radio, unnecessarily.

Gates pointed to the slim volume wedged under an arm of Brazil's chair, secured, like everything else aboard, against some possible failure of the artificial gravity. "What's the book this time?"

"Thoreau. I thought I might need a dose of philosophy if you get us stuck in the mud down there."

"Always meant to read the old nature-lover through some day." Gates nodded at the screens showing the waiting planet. "Wonder what he would have thought of all this."

Brazil looked at the image of the planet with the dawnline creeping imperceptibly across upper atmosphere as a rainbow of varying ionization and light pressure. He smiled at a sudden recollection, and quoted: "*Walden Pond*—let's see—'A field of water betrays the spirit that is in the air. It is continually receiving new life and motion from above . . . I see where the breeze dashes across it by the streaks or flakes of light. It is remarkable that we can look down on its surface. We shall, perhaps, look down thus on the surface of air at length, and mark where a still subtler spirit sweeps over it.'"

"He wrote that in the middle of the nineteenth century?" asked Gates, astonished. "Let me see that book when you're done with it."

"You're clear for takeoff, *Alpha*. Good luck," said the radio.

Scoutship *Alpha* outraced the dawnline by an hour to the island and eased down on schedule, without hurry, into thicker and thicker air, until it entered predawn darkness and fog. Gates used his radar for the first time, to work his way down toward the water a few hundred meters off the rocky coastline.

Aqua was Brazil's ninth new planet. But I won't forget this one, he thought in some corner of his brain not used for watching instruments.

And he was right.

The plan called for an offshore landing unseen by the natives, the concealment of the scoutship under water but near land, and the going ashore of Gates and Brazil in protective suits to make contact with the local intelligent life. Tight-beam communication was to be maintained at all times with the *Yuan Chwang*. A small video eye rode above each planeteer's left ear; whatever the eye saw was transmitted to the mother ship.

The versatile and roughly humanoid robot that accompanied every scoutship (and followed men onto new planets, but rarely preceded them) would be left in the submerged scout, and would bring it to the human crew if they summoned it by radio.

The *Yuan Chwang* was not orbiting Aqua, but hovering and trying to keep its great bulk invisible, fifteen or sixteen thousand kilometers above the island. The other scouts were cruising in upper atmosphere in the general area of the target island, observing what they could.

Aboard *Alpha*, detection screens picked out what looked to Brazil like the infrared pattern of smoldering fires and fainter body heat of a small village where the recon photos had shown a village to be. Gates worked the scout by radar to an offshore point about a kilometer from the village, which lay on the shore of a small cove. He dipped the scout low enough to put a sonar probe under water and get a picture of the bottom.

"Nothing strange down there," said Gates. "We'll go ahead."

Cutting in automatic stabilizers, he lowered the scout into and through choppy water and made slowly toward shore, while Brazil studied the ocean and bottom, trying to read half a dozen presentations at once.

Near the rocky upthrust of land, Gates let the little ship settle gently onto sandy bottom. He summoned the robot and told it to use enough drive to prevent the ship's sinking into the bottom. The robot got into the pilot's seat as the humans checklisted themselves into helmets, out of the control room, and into the lock. They stood with legs spread and arms raised while gas and UV sterilized their suits and the chamber. Gates nodded and Brazil opened a valve to let alien sea into the lock; in a few seconds they stepped out of the world of checklists and into dark water. Brazil lingered to feel that the lock door was secured behind them, let gas into his flotation bubbles, and followed Gates up through the darkness. Once something like a luminous smoke ring curled greenly past them through the water.

"Can you bliphate the distance phlooh that?" asked a voice from the *Yuan Chwang*, half strangled by transmission through space, air, and water.

"Hard to say; I'd guess only a few meters," Gates answered, waiting until his head had broken surface and he had taken a look around. Brazil was right behind him; he could barely see Gates' helmet above the water three meters away. The rough rock face of the coastline was only a deeper darkness at one side. They paddled toward it; waves sloshed them against it; they gripped it and began to climb.

Earthmen emerged onto the land of a new world, looking more like primeval lungfish than lords of creation. They climbed rock uncertainly and slowly and halted at the top of a small cliff. The suits were engineered for easy movement and reasonable comfort for twenty-four continuous sealed-in hours in almost any environment. Old Planeteers sometimes said soberly that they needed a suit on to feel comfortable; but they usually preferred to take the suit off before sitting down to discuss how comfortably they wore it.

"Let's wait for a little more light," said Gates' radio voice.

Brazil sat down beside a large rock and tried to see what was on the inland slope away from the cliff.

The sun was not far below the hilly horizon now and a gray predawn light made the scene gradually intelligible. A faint excuse for a road wandered along a few yards away, roughly paralleling the shoreline; it might be a cattle path that led toward the village. Beyond the road were fields with a a semicultivated look, holding orderly rows of squat bushes above a mat of low-growing vines that seemed to cover most of the ground in sight. Green hills rose beyond the fields.

The dawn brightened slowly. To Brazil, sunrises always brought awe, whether he saw them on an outworld, or on crowded Earth, or across the rusty deserts of the world to which his parents had emigrated and where he had been born. Sitting on this alien rock with sea water dripping from his armor, he thought: First Landing; it's like a First Morning. Let there be light.

"Light enough," said Gates. "Let's get started."

They walked on crunching vines to the road, heads swiveling constantly and air microphones tuned to high sensitivity. Brazil caught himself listening for the ape-howling that had accompanied each new morning on his last new planet. It wasn't good to carry such mental baggage on the job; he would have to unload it.

They paced along the faint road toward the village. The hard-packed brownish soil of the road held no informative prints of hooves or feet or wheels.

"Smoke ahead," said Gates suddenly. It was a barely visible vertical tracery in the sky, rising not far away.

The road curved around a craggy little hill; when they had rounded this, the village was before them. Large rowboats were beached on the sand of a small sheltered cove. Forty or fifty meters back from the water stood about twenty huts, built mainly from what looked like mats of the groundvine. A small stream trickled through the village, flowing from the direction of a structure like a low fortress, that stood beyond the huts and was much larger than any of them. Its dark walls of dried mud or clay were surrounded by a considerable space cleared of all vegetation.

Brazil turned his head to one side and saw his first native. His stomach went cold and he said to Gates: "On the rock up there. Look."

The native was undoubtedly humanoid and had apparently been dead a long time. He was bound somehow with vines to the crag that almost overhung the road, four or five meters above the Earthmen, and around his neck hung a placard that looked like cardboard, bearing a short inscription in bold characters resembling

Arabic. He had been a tall man in life, by Earthly standards, and long strands of pale hair were still in evidence.

"Get this?" asked Gates of the observers in the sky.

"Affirmative. You're going on?"

"Don't see why not."

"We never mind these 'No Trespassing' signs," said Brazil, with an attempt at flippancy he didn't feel. Dead men were nothing new to him, but this one had a considerable resemblance to himself and had, so to speak, sneaked up on him.

There were no living people yet in sight, but there were shrill cries from the village, and a small flock of hawklike birds with oversized wings sprang up from among the huts. The birds were green and vivid orange against the misty sky and flew circling over the village.

"Let's go," said Gates.

They went down the sloping road toward the huts, trying to look confident but not frightening.

At an open gateway in the wall of the fortified structure a figure appeared, a red-haired man dressed in dark jerkin and leggings and boots, with breastplate of silvery metal that matched the round helmet he carried in one hand. In the other was a spear. He stretched himself and yawned, and appeared to be trying to scratch his ribs with the helmet. He was still a good distance away and gave no sign that he had spotted two aliens in strange suits walking into his town.

The birds were more alert. The cries of the circling flock changed suddenly in tone, and in a moment it had become a living arrow launched at Gates and Brazil. The flock broke off just before contact, to circle the intruders in a blurred uproar of wings and claws, but several birds scraped the helmets, which were almost invisible in mild light, and came back to tear head-on at Brazil's apparently unprotected face.

The thud of impact was impressive; when Brazil's eyes opened from the reflex blink, the bird was flopping on the ground with something badly broken. He picked it up, intending to impress the natives with his friendliness by treating kindly their pet that had attacked him, and also to suggest to them that it was futile to attack; but it struggled and fought his armored hands so that he thought he was doing it more harm than good.

He set it gently down again as the first natives came blinking and shivering out of their huts to see what all the noise was about, some of them still pulling on scanty rags of clothing. They were all of a type with the body on the rock, blond, tall humanoids with deep chests and slender limbs; in the living people were visible a dozen small distinctions of facial and bodily proportion that added up to an obvious but not at first definable difference from any Earthman.

The red-haired man of the fortress had ducked inside the gateway, which was still open. A domestic-looking animal with plumes on its head looked out at the strangers with interest.

The blond natives stood together in front of their huts, as if waiting for a group picture to be taken, gaping at their visitors in silence. The watchbird flock still screamed and flew, now in widening circles, having given up assault at least temporarily.

Gates kept moving forward until he stood near the center of the cleared space between beach and huts. Brazil stopped beside him there and they stood almost motionless, smiling, arms spread with hands open, in the approved position for approaching Apparent Primitives who seem timid. The sun stood over the horizon now, dissipating the morning fog.

Brazil became aware that the whole crowd was watching *him*. Only now and then did one shoot a quick glance at Gates, as if puzzled about something.

Gates spoke via throat mike and radio, scarcely moving his smiling lips. "You look like 'em, boy. I think you better play leader. They may never have seen anyone dark as me before."

Brazil made the practiced throat-muscle movement that switched on his airspeaker and opened his mouth to begin the greeting of his public with soothing sounds. He was interrupted by Sam's voice in his ear again. "Coming from the fort."

Six Apparent Primitives who looked anything but timid were marching in sloppy formation down the slope from the walled structure, straight toward the Earthmen, bearing spears and facial expressions that Brazil could not interpret as meaning anything good. They were all red-haired and armored, muscular, well-fed, and bulbous-nosed, evidently of a different tribe or race than the blond hut-dwellers.

Brazil's barefoot audience watched the warriors' approach nervously and began to fade back into their huts. But one of the older men, who had been staring Brazil in the eye with an expression of intense and mounting emotion—the planeteer grew edgy at not being able to decide what emotion—now sprang forward to grab Brazil by the arm and harangue him with the first native speech he had heard, meanwhile looking at him with the gaze of a pleading worshiper.

The six red-haired warriors were very near and didn't look happy at all. They also seemed to be concentrating on Brazil.

With a cry as of great despair the old man tore himself away from Brazil and fled at top speed toward the huts. One of the approaching warriors threw his spear with a whipping, expert motion; it caught the old man in the back and sent him dying on his face in the sand.

"Well, I'll be—" Boris Brazil roared out the first Earth words into the air of Aqua.

The red-haired warriors stood before him, eyeing him with what he interpreted as incredulous contempt. One of them barked something that he thought he could almost translate: "What are you doing, you blond peasant clod, dressed up in that outlandish armor?" He probably looked more like a blond native in the suit, with his physical proportions somewhat concealed, than he would without it.

The one who had speared the old man started walking toward his victim, maybe to retrieve his weapon. Brazil started that way too, with no clear idea of what he was going to do, but with the feeling that the old man had appealed to him in vain for help.

As Brazil started to move, the five other spears were suddenly leveled at him. A hysterical blond boy ran out of a hut to kneel beside the old man and scream something that sounded nasty at the approaching warrior. Gates was standing motionless a few meters away. A spear thrust fast and hard against Brazil's chest with plain intent to kill, setting him back on his heels; a lordly voice from the *Yuan Chwang* said in his ear, "This is not our affair." Brazil grabbed the thrusting spear in his left hand, jerked its owner forward off balance, and delivered with his armored right fist what seemed the appropriate greeting to an Apparent Primitive Attempting Murder of Earthman.

The blow knocked the man out from under his helmet and dropped him to the sand. Spears rocked Boris from all sides, clashed and slid around his helmet. He caught a glimpse of the sixth warrior kicking the boy, knocking him over, and pulling a short axe from his belt for a finishing blow.

The arm swinging back the axe suddenly released it; the weapon spun through the air to land some meters away and the warrior sat down suddenly and nervelessly. Sam Gates had decided it was time for stun pistols.

Before Brazil had reached the same conclusion, the four remaining spearmen had given up trying to stick him through his suit and were grabbing at his arms to hold him. Gates potted two more of them, in the legs, with silent and invisible force. The remaining two abandoned the fight and backed away toward their stronghold with spears leveled, shouting what was no doubt a call for reinforcements. The man that Brazil had felled got up and tottered dazedly after them.

"Let's get out of here," said Gates.

Brazil's eye swept around. The old man was dead, the spear still in him. The young boy who had been kicked was lying unconscious right in front of a warrior who was going to be considerably annoyed as soon as he felt a little better. Brazil scooped the child up and got him over his shoulders in a fireman's carry and looked at Gates, who gave a sort of facial shrug.

They strode at a good pace out of the village, with the watchbirds screaming a cheerful farewell. A few Reds were milling around the gateway of the fort as the Earthmen went over the rise and out of sight, but no organized pursuit was yet visible. Once out of sight of the village they began a steady loping run, the small body bouncing on Brazil's shoulders. Gates called for the robot to bring the scout up to the surface at the shoreline.

"This is the Tribune," said a voice. "What do you intend doing with that child?"

"Saving his neck," said Gates. "Maybe we can learn something from him too."

Brazil was gasping when he finished the climb down the rocks to the shoreline and set his unconscious burden—no, half conscious now, with a swelling lump on the forehead—down inside the airlock. The outer door shut behind Gates and the robot had the scout underwater and moving out to sea a moment later.

Entertaining an alien aboard a scoutship was something the Space Force had learned to plan for ahead of time. A door in the back of a suit locker led from the airlock into the tiny Alien Room,

into which Gates was now feeding atmosphere from outside, via
snorkel and remote control. When the room was ready, Brazil
carried the boy into it, sealing the door behind him. Gates could
now decontaminate in the airlock, and go to the control room.
Brazil would have to wear suit and helmet for a while yet.

Medical was already on the communicator in the Alien Room
when Brazil turned to look at the screen, after putting the kid
down on the bed-acceleration couch that took up most of the
room, checking the air pressure and setting the temperature up a
few degrees.

"Kid doesn't look too bad," Brazil told the doctor. He smiled
reassuringly at the boy, who was now fully conscious and lay watching with wide eyes and a growing yellowish lump on his forehead.
He might be ten or eleven years old, judged by Earth standards.

"Keep him quiet. Gates is going to get us some remote X-rays.
You try for a blood sample as soon as possible. Do you think we'll
have to feed him?"

"Yes. If we can keep him for a week or two we should get the
language and a good line on the local culture. We've got synthetic
proteins and simple sugars on the scout, of course, so I guess he
won't starve—but I'll try for your blood sample first. And listen,
this may be important—I'm turning off the video screen now.
When we use it again, keep anyone with red hair off it. Use blond,
noble, handsome people like me if possible."

Brazil started to call Sam on the intercom, but through a valve
into the Alien Room came sterile blankets and a painless blood
sample syringe, before he could ask for them.

Chandragupta's voice came into his helmet: "This is the Tribune.
I have little complaint of your actions so far, except that striking
that man with your fist at least bordered on the use of excessive
force. But I must forbid you to keep that child any longer than is
necessary for his own welfare."

"How long will that be, Chan?" asked Captain Dietrich's voice,
getting no immediate answer. "Would the boy be welcomed home,
or speared like that old man, or what? I think we'd better learn
the language and customs before trying to decided. And as for
Brazil's hitting that man—"

A debate went on. Brazil listened with one ear while he covered
his guest with blankets and sat beside him, trying to inspire confidence.

"It's all right, sonny, it's all right." *I hope.* He patted the boy gently with his armored hand. That was the only treatment he dared attempt until he knew considerably more about the biology of his guest.

And the guest could be very valuable. Children made good subjects for First Contact as a rule, if they were not too young. Their minds adapted quickly to the alien. They caught on quickly to the game of language teaching. And they were likely to give an honest and direct view of their own culture.

Brazil handed the blood-sample syringe to the boy after locking the plunger. The kid took it after a brief hesitation, looked it over cautiously, then gave a sudden shy smile and said something that might have been a question. If his head was bothering him he gave no sign of it.

Brazil answered with some kindly nonsense and took the syringe back. He made a show of rubbing it on his own suited arm, turning his head to the other side as he did so. Then he turned the boy's head gently away and got his blood sample without fuss, on the first try. He valved the loaded syringe out into the airlock, where the robot came to load it into a courier tube that would carry it up to the *Yuan Chwang*.

Earth and Aqua life turned out to be too alien to one another for infectious disease to pose a problem either way. Brazil shed his suit with relief.

The courier tube returned before sunset with containers of vile-looking gunk that Supply swore would feed the boy, whose name was approximately Tim. Tim tasted the stuff but looked unhappy, so Gates went out spearfishing. Tim was pleased with some of the assortment and ate it raw, while turning down the rest in disgust. He seemed to be suffering no aftereffects from the kick in the head, but Brazil did his best to keep him quiet anyway.

For the next few days the scout stayed well out at sea, mostly submerged. Brazil spent most of his time in the Alien Room, pretending to learn Tim's language almost as fast as he could hear the words, while the linguistically expert brains, human and electronic, aboard the *Yuan Chwang*, looked and listened over his shoulder. They forgot nothing, and spoke into his ear, prompting him on what to say next.

Tim became restlessly active after getting over his first awed fascination with video screen, doors, acceleration couch, and plumbing. When told he was aboard a ship, he wanted to see it all. Brazil kept the robot, at least, out of Tim's sight, and had to struggle to learn more than he taught. He played games with Tim to give him exercise, and to gather data on his physical strength and dexterity.

The hungry brains aboard the *Yuan Chwang* devoured Tim's language. Within two weeks they had fed it by memory tape to every planeteer. A few days of practice would give them command of it.

It was time for a major conference. The two planeteers on surface sat in with Captain Dietrich and the department heads above, via communicator, while Tim was confined discontentedly to the Alien Room.

"Gentlemen and ladies, we have a choice between two courses of action," the captain began. "We can try again to establish relations with the natives of this island, or pull out and start over somewhere else. I think we can agree that our only major problem on this island is likely to be intercultural?"

No one disputed him. "I'd like to say that I hope we *can* find a way to set up a base on this island," said Biology. "That luminous water-ring was fascinating, though I'm not sure it's in my field. And that groundvine . . . "

"We can't complete our gravitic tables for this system without seismic measurements of the planet," put in Geology. "That island still looks like a good place to me."

"We've got the language here now," said Brazil. "Our First Contact tapes show the red tribe's speech is nearly the same as Tim's. And they're already trying to kill us on sight, so what can we lose by another try?"

Chandragupta said sharply: "The people of the island may lose, if we are not careful, Mr. Brazil. Indeed we may have caused substantial damage already, by inserting ourselves into a situation of considerable tension between two tribes—though any harm we may have done was accidental, and I do not blame anyone for it."

"Just what sort of damage can be attributed to our arrival?" asked the Captain.

"I think I can explain what Chan means," said Sociology, clearing his throat. "The data we have from Tim fit in with what we saw on First Contact. Everything indicates that the island is ripe for civil war.

"The picture is this: a local settled tribe, fishermen and part-time farmers—the Blonds, as we have come to call them—invaded and conquered by a warrior tribe of the Viking type, probably fewer in numbers. The invaders seem to have come from the smaller islands farther north. Perhaps they were driven out themselves by someone else. Now they have settled down here as a ruling class. Tim says this invasion was a very long time ago, before he was born, but that his grandfather—the old man who unfortunately was killed during our First Contact—could remember a time when there were no Reds on the island. I'd guess the invasion was about fifty standard years ago. We've seen no evidence of intermarriage, although in fact we've seen none of the Red women or children yet."

"Tim talks of a day when his people will rise up and destroy the Reds," said Brazil. "The dream of his young life seems to be to find a way to slaughter them wholesale. He wants me to lead the revolution. Someone has talked a lot of war and rebellion to him, that's for sure.

"Tim's grandfather thought I was a tribal folk-hero, come back from the great beyond in strange armor to lead them out of slavery. That's what the old man was talking to me about; I suppose that's why they speared him. It's on the tape, of course. Now I can understand it." Brazil fell moodily silent.

"I suppose the First Contact incident might have touched off a full-scale Blond rebellion?" someone asked.

"If conditions had been just right, yes," said Sociology. "Apparently they were not."

Captain Dietrich spoke up: "During the last few days we've made numerous recon photo runs at high speed and comparatively low altitude. If there was any open warfare in progress, we'd almost certainly have seen it."

"How about that body lashed to the rock?" someone asked after a brief pause. "Have we learned anything on that?"

"Tim can't read or write," said Sociology, "so neither can we, yet. So we don't know what the placard hung around the fellow's neck says. Tim says the Reds put him up there because they were angry at him. Seems reasonable, if not illuminating."

"Captain, I wish we had made such photo runs as you now mention before First Contact," said the Tribune.

"We weren't sure of their technological level then," said the captain, a little wearily. "We didn't want them to spot us flying over. It's one of those choices you have to make. We didn't want to shock them by appearing as gods, remember?"

The discussion flowed on for a while. Finally Dietrich brought it back to his original question: "Shall we continue to try for a base on this island, or shall we move on?"

Chandragupta: "The question I must insist we try to answer, Captain, is this: How can we be helpful to the people of this island, where we have already interfered?"

The captain: "Chan, we didn't come all this way to open a social service bureau."

"I realize that, Captain." Grimly. "Nevertheless, I consider our effect upon the natives more important than seismic measurements. I would like to ask if you plan to conclude an agreement with the authorities controlling those Red soldiers, for a scientific base on the island?"

"I'm considering it."

"I believe our doing so would in effect recognize their authority to live as they do, holding another tribe in slavery."

Sociology raised his eyebrows. "It would be unusual if slavery could not be found in some form at this level."

"Perhaps I should have been more precise. I consider it evil that a member of the ruling class should have it in his power to take at any time the life of one of the lower class, as we have seen here. I think we are now bound to try to correct such a condition. Of course we shall not be able, nor should we attempt, to establish our idea of a perfect society. But we must try to set these people on the road to greater freedom and justice." Chandragupta raised his voice above several protesting ones. "We are already committed to interference here, in my view. We must now see to it that the changes we produce are for the better."

The captain smiled faintly. "Are you arguing for the revolution now, Chan?"

"I think you know better." The Tribune was somewhat irritated. "We could hardly expect the total effect of a general armed uprising to be beneficial."

"Just what do you think we *should* do, then, to start these people on the road to greater freedom and justice, as you put it?"

Chandragupta sighed. "I think we must first investigate them further, to learn how best to help."

There was a little silence.

"Anyone have a further comment?" asked the captain. "All right, this is it. We continue work on this island. We try to stabilize native affairs on as just a basis as possible, and then deal for our base. Boris, you say Tim has relatives in an inland village who can hide him out from the Reds if need be?"

"So he tells me."

"All right. Take him to this inland village, tonight or tomorrow night. Talk with some of the adults there. Especially try to find out more about the political situation. Is there a Blond resistance group, how strong, and so on. Since we seem to be committed to some sort of interference here, we'd better get all the data we can, and quickly. Any questions?"

The following night was dark and foggy. Gates drove the scoutship silently and, as he hoped, invisibly over the island's hills toward the village of Tim's relatives. The boy acted as navigator, guiding an electronically presented green spot over a contour map of the island, with an air of sophistication. He had, he said, seen maps before, if not flying machines. But he was excited at the prospect of showing off Brazil in armor to people he knew, and telling them of the wonders he had seen. Brazil had given him orders to keep the scoutship's flying powers secret if possible.

Brazil changed the scale of the map to show only the area within a couple of kilometers of the village. Tim guided Gates to a clear landing spot, out of sight of the village but within easy walking distance. Gates brought the scout down quickly, probing below with radar and infrared, until the little ship settled with a crackle of crushed vines into a tiny hollow between hills.

The cries and movement of small life alarmed by their landing gradually quieted. There were no signs of human alarm.

Brazil suited up, for protection against dangers other than infection. He led Tim into the airlock, and paused for a final briefing.

"Now, who did we agree you should look for in the village?"

"First I will look for Sunto, who is one of my cousins. He hates the Reds and is not afraid of them. If he is not home I will seek

Lorto or Tammammo, who are the junior headmen of the village. Only if I can find none of those will I talk to my female cousins, who do not understand these things. I will try to avoid Tamotim, who I think is still the boss headman here. He likes the Reds and tells them things. If I see no one who is safe to talk to I will come back here and we will talk over what to do next."

"And if someone stops you and asks you questions?"

"I will just say there is a strange man out here who wants to speak with someone from the village. I know what to do, you don't have to worry. I won't say you are our Warrior Spirit, or anything like that. Unless there are Reds in the village, who capture me; then I will cry out for Warrior Spirit and you will come and kill them, hey?"

"My name's not Warrior Spirit. And if you see any Reds, just come back." Brazil opened the lock's outer door and they stepped out and down into matted vines. "Remember, just say I brought you over the hills if anyone asks how you come to be here. No one else need know yet that my ship can fly."

"All right. Over that way is a path," said Tim, becoming oriented. "And that way is the village."

"Get going, then." Brazil sent him off with a gentle shove, and then stood quietly, testing the alien night with artificially aided senses.

The sound of Tim's bare feet faded quickly on the path.

"I'll take her up a ways," said Gates on radio.

"Good idea."

Brazil saw the dark bulk of the scoutship lift in silence that was almost eerie even to him, and drift up out of sight into fog and darkness. No stars to see tonight. Well, he had seen enough of them. For a while.

He moved off and found the path with his infrared lamp and waited just at one side of it. He hoped the kid wouldn't run into any trouble. About five minutes passed before the glass of his helmet, set for infrared translation, showed him some large life moving toward him along the trail from the village. "One—two of them, Sam, coming this way."

"Affirmative, I have them now."

"Boro?" His native name, called in a soft voice from the darkness.

Brazil switched his air mike on again. "Right here."

Tim approached him. "This is Tammammo with me, Boro. He is a junior headman."

Brazil gave the second vague shape a slight bow, which Tim had told him was the ordinary greeting between equals. "Sam, keep a sharp eye out. We need to use a little light down here." Planeteers worked their air-mike switches for such asides as quickly and naturally as they used their tongues for speech.

"Understand."

Brazil turned on what he hoped was a dim and non-startling electric glow from a suit lamp, revealing a Tammammo bug-eyed at being called out of his hut at night to meet what he might think was the Warrior Spirit.

Boris greeted him in a matter-of-fact, businesslike way. Maybe the fact that he spoke the common language of the peasants put the junior headman more at ease.

Tammammo had heard a version of the First Contact incident which began with the Red garrison of the coastal village executing an old man for daring to worship the Sea God in a way reserved for rulers. Dying, the elder had called down a curse upon their heads, whereupon the Warrior Spirit of the Blonds appeared, and slew sixty Reds with a sweep of his arm—or perhaps it had taken several arm-sweeps, the point was uncertain. A Red magician, called upon by the enemy, had evoked from somewhere a dark and evil spirit, also clad in armor. The Blond Warrior had departed to do battle with this other elsewhere, not wishing to devastate the entire island in the struggle, but he was expected to win and would return shortly to—and this point was whispered very cautiously—slay all the Red warriors and turn over their women and children to the Blonds as slaves.

Tammammo almost managed to look Brazil hopefully in the eye as he finished the tale.

Tim started to speak with the exasperated eagerness of a youngster to point out errors—or maybe in disappointment at being left out of the story altogether. But Brazil shushed him by putting a hand in front of his face. He spoke carefully to Tammammo.

"Junior headman—look at me carefully. I am only a man, nothing more. I am not a Warrior Spirit, or any kind of a god. I am only a man from a far land, who looks like one of your people and wears armor that is strange to you. Now I wish to speak in private with the leaders of your people—not with the headman who tells everything to the Reds, but to the leaders of your own people, who may not be known to everyone. Do you understand me?"

"If you say you are a man, so be it." Tammammo seemed to be shivering with more than the night chill. "The leaders you speak of—I do not know anything about such matters, except for stories heard by all. There is a man in the village who might know. His name is Sunto. I can tell him what you want when I meet him. Will that please you?"

"It will. And I think there is no need for you to speak of me to anyone else."

"I will not! I will not!"

"Then send Sunto here to meet me at this time tomorrow night. One thing more, junior headman—this boy goes to live now with his relatives in your village. I want you, Tammammo, to see to it that no harm comes to him from the Reds. As I said, I am only a man, yet I can do many things. I would be quite angry if the Reds were to harm this boy. Do you understand?"

Tammammo indicated vehemently that he understood. Obviously he wished himself a thousand kilometers at sea, or anywhere out of this situation.

"Tim, keep out of trouble. Go, both of you, and send me Sunto here tomorrow night."

Evidently it was not a Blond habit to waste any time in farewells. Brazil watched them out of sight, realizing suddenly he was going to miss having the kid around. "OK, Sam, you can bring her down."

Trudging to where the scout was crackling down into vines again, Brazil paused and looked up with a sudden grin. "Hey, dark and evil spirit. How come you listen to what that Red magician says?"

"Shut up and get in."

Sunto appeared at the appointed place on the following night, escorted by Tim. This time the scout had not landed; Brazil was lowered the last few score meters by cable.

Sunto was less timid than Tammammo. He too had heard of the First Contact fight, but was shrewd enough to realize how events could change in the seeing and retelling. He professed no doubt that Brazil was only a man, and a friend of the Blonds. Would he arrange a meeting with the Blond leaders? Certainly. Those leaders were meeting in the remote hills, three nights from now. Boro could come if he wished. There would be many large fires at the meeting place so it would be easy to find. Was Boro living in the hills now?

Did everyone know about this meeting? Brazil asked him. What if the Reds saw all those fires? Why had Tammammo been so timid in discussing Blond leaders?

Sunto did not seem to understand. He used several new words in trying to answer the questions. Eventually the idea came across that this was going to be a religious meeting, not political at all. He, Sunto, knew no more than that timid Tammammo about political matters. Of course the Reds would not interfere with this religious meeting; the Sea God would be angry with them if they did. True, the Reds controlled the Tower, but that didn't mean others couldn't hold meetings of this type, did it?

"Of course not," Brazil agreed soberly. He got a repeat on the time and place of the meeting, and went home to the scout.

They located the meeting without trouble, as Sunto had predicted. Brazil was lowered by cable again, a little distance away from the circle of fires in the hills near the center of the island. Gates held the scout overhead, ready for anything, while Brazil walked to the lighted area.

About fifty Blonds of both sexes were quietly busy with varied rituals within the illuminated circle. There were no detectable lookouts posted around the place, or any attempt at concealment.

Brazil watched for a little while, far enough away to be invisible to those near the fires. Then he walked slowly in on them, arms spread out in a gesture of peace. Gradually they became aware of him, the nearer people first. Within a few seconds all of them were standing still and watching. Then a few of them moved slightly, opening a lane from where Brazil stood to a place near the center of the circle. He could see now a low structure of stone that stood there, a couple of meters square. It might be an altar.

"Any advice?" he subvocalized to the watchers above.

"Best thing I can think of is to bow in greeting and tell them to proceed with what they're doing," said some anonymous expert. No one argued with him. The final decision rested, as usual, with the man on the spot, the planeteer.

He accepted the advice offered, and it seemed to go over well enough. The attention of the Blond group turned from him to the central altar, where a few men and women began to perform some simple rites. The others stood watching with folded arms. Brazil folded his. No one was sitting down, and he resigned himself to what might be a long stand. He wished himself wearing Armor, Ground, Heavy, with powered legs that would let you nap standing if you wished.

Not that he wanted to nap now, although the ceremony had so far shown him nothing especially interesting. It had elements that Brazil had seen in life or on training tapes of a hundred primitive religions on a dozen planets.

But its climax was unique. A pair of muscular—deacons? Brazil could distinguish no one set apart as clergy—came from the darkness outside the waning firelight. They bore a large and heavy pottery vessel that wobbled in their grip as if it held a quantity of sloshing liquid. Someone held a torch to illuminate the altar top. A slender tower about fifty or sixty centimeters high had been built of small flat pebbles, surrounded by a low wall of similar construction.

The men with the jar approached the rear of the altar and raised the vessel toward it, as a woman thrust a trough into position. They tipped the big jar evenly. What looked like clear water sluiced out of it, guided by the trough toward the pebble-tower. For a moment Brazil thought the little structure might withstand the flood, but some vital part of the base gave way suddenly. The men continued to tilt the vessel smoothly until it was empty. The tower toppled, taking with it part of the surrounding wall. It was washed piecemeal from the sloping altar by the last of the flood.

It hit them hard, Brazil could see, looking from one Blond face to another in the firelight. None of them stirred for a long minute. Plainly the collapse of the tower had some evil significance. Tower? Sunto had mentioned a tower, connected with the Sea God, and controlled by the Reds.

The Blonds gradually shook off some of their gloom. Again they were turning toward Brazil.

"Ceremony didn't turn out too well, I think," said the voice from the *Yuan Chwang*. "Just hope they don't blame it on you."

Once more everyone was watching Brazil, except for a couple of men who had begun to dismantle the altar. Might as well get started, he thought. He could pick out no one as leader, and so spoke out loudly to the group: "I am a man who has come from a far land, and I would learn what I can about the people here."

The faint stir and whispering among them ceased, and all watched him with guarded faces. There was only the fire glow and crackle, and the twittering background of animals or insects.

"This—" Brazil realized he had no certain word for ritual. "What you have done at this meeting is strange to me. If I can do so without giving offense, I would learn about it. Will someone here tell me?"

A light clear voice came from somewhere in the background "Are you he of whom it is said, that he slew sixty Reds with a sweep of his arm?"

"It is said, but it is not true. I fought with six of them, but I slew none."

"You fought with six of them, yet none of them slew you." The still anonymous voice used a more subtle grammar than Tim had taught and had a slightly different accent. With his limited experience in listening to the natives, Brazil could not identify it as male or female. But it smelled of authority to him.

"My armor is strong," he said, answering the implied question. "And I had help from one who is wrongly called a dark demon, who is only a man like me, my countryman and friend."

"So have I heard it." The speaker moved forward slowly into brighter firelight—a woman. Not a girl, and not an old woman, nor middle-aged. Not the kind that a man will follow with his eyes from the first glance, but the kind he will turn to see again a quarter-minute later, and remember. So Brazil thought of her at first sight, and only remembered with a start the subtle unearthliness of her face and body.

"So have I heard it, from those who were there and saw with open eyes." She came close to Brazil, dressed as simply as the others. She studied him. "You speak with the tongue of a simple Blond peasant."

"It was one such who taught me."

"You learned well. What is your name?"

"In your tongue it is best said as Boro. And what is yours, if I may ask without giving offense?"

She smiled. "Certainly, there has never been a god so fearful of giving offense. My name is Ariton. Tell these people whether you are god or man. I fear some of them will still not believe what you told Sunto."

Brazil loudly pledged again his membership in humanity.

Ariton waved her hand, and her people turned away. Most of them went to sit in a circle around where the altar had been. They began a low-voiced chant.

She walked with Brazil a little away from the group, and tried to answer his questions about the ceremony he had just witnessed. Her explanation was unintelligible with new words at first; finally he got her to simplify it enough for him to understand that the tiny tower on the altar had been an analog of a full-sized structure in the island's chief city. The big Tower was sacred to the Sea God. Now it was monopolized by the Red priests, and beside it the king of the Reds, Galamand, had built a castle. At mentioning the king's name, Ariton moved her foot as if grinding something into the dirt beneath her heel. Tim had sometimes done that when speaking of the Reds.

"And what did the water-pouring mean?"

"Maybe something bad." She looked at Brazil thoughtfully and raised a hand to touch his transparent helmet. "I have seen—before," she said, using a new word that he thought meant glass, from the context. "Now I will ask a question. Why could not the Reds slay you?"

"My armor is stronger than it looks."

"And why did you slay none of them?"

"There was no need."

"Those of my people who watched with open eyes say that you were angry at the killing of an old man you did not know. Why?"

Brazil pondered. "There was no need for his slaying, either, that I could see."

"Strong Red warriors could not hurt you with their spears," Ariton said thoughtfully. "And when they tried to seize you they were struck down by cramps and sickness, like swimmers who have entered cold water with full bellies. So the Sea God might . . . "

"But it was not the Sea God. Shall we sit down here?" He gallantly let her have the low boulder that presented itself, and crunched his armored seat down into groundvine. The suit was a load to stand around in, even at point-nine-five gravity.

"Where is your dark companion now? And your ship?"

"He is not far. And our ship is near the island." Some water from the altar flood had run into the nearest fire, and the light grew dimmer yet. There was no word in Brazil's ear from above.

"It might be thought that you and your friend are only cast-aways."

He took the suggestion calmly. "It is not so. Our ship is near, with others of my people aboard. My countrymen and I travel to learn about new lands that none of us has seen before. We would like to live on this island for a little while, perhaps a few years, on some land your people do not use. We do not want to boss your people, or take anything we do not pay for."

"I have no land to give anyone, while there are Reds on the island." Ariton's voice was sharp.

"Some of my people will talk to the Reds, too, about using land. But we will not trade with a tribe that holds another tribe in slavery."

She was puzzled. "But who does not own slaves, if he can? If we could enslave the Reds, we would. Do you own no slaves at home?"

"It has been very many years since my tribe held slaves. A tribe becomes stronger when it does not depend on them. My people have traveled far and looked at many tribes, and it is always so."

"But if all were free to choose, who would do the mean and dirty work of slaves by choice?" Ariton looked at him searchingly.

Brazil gave a faint sigh. "True, someone must do such work—sometimes someone must be forced to do it. But even such lowly persons should be treated as members of the tribe, and not killed or beaten as animals would be."

"And if there are two tribes, as on this island?"

"Two tribes can live together as one, if their leaders are wise and strong."

"That is a strange thought to me. But then I have never traveled in the far parts of the world." Ariton meditated for a few moments before she spoke again. "Will you, Boro, go to speak with the Red King about this matter of land? You still look like a Blond, so maybe the Reds will try again to kill or imprison you."

Brazil thought it over. "I may be the one who goes. It is only chance that I look like a Blond. My shipmates are of varied appearance; some of them resemble Reds." He thought to himself: What planeteer looks most like a Red? Foley, but his hair isn't nearly the right shade. A little dye will fix that, if need be.

"I will go with you, when you go to speak to Galamand," Ariton announced.

Brazil was surprised. "Can you walk into his castle at will?"

"I think Galamand will see me if I call on him." Ariton smiled. "I am a high priestess of the Sea God."

Another conference began as soon as Brazil was hoisted home to his scoutship.

"Religion may give us a way to promote unity here." said Sociology. "Since Reds and Blonds both worship the same Sea God."

"We have that Tower located, by the way," put in Captain Dietrich. "And what's probably the Red king's castle, or at least his summer home. It seems too far from fresh water to withstand a siege. Where's that chart? Here, on this peninsula that protects the harbor at Capital City, a large stone structure. Right next to it, on the side toward the ocean, is the tallest building on the island, a tower about thirty meters high. Then there's a seawall running the length of the peninsula, for protection against waves and maybe against invaders."

"Foley, you and Brazil will be visiting Galamand as soon as we can locate him. Get your hair died to match the Reds'. Maybe we can at least put over the idea that it's possible for Red and Blond to cooperate."

"I trust everything possible will be done to avoid another fight." Chandragupta wore a frown.

"We'll try," the captain said. "Is anyone against sending a delegation to Galamand as soon as possible?" It seemed that no one was.

"Should we take Ariton along, as she suggested?" Gates asked the conference.

"It might make us seem to be committed as her allies against the Reds."

"No doubt that's what she wants."

"But it would bring the two leaders face to face, with us present."

Planeteer Foley, hair reddened, was flown down and transferred to scoutship *Alpha*, which lay out at sea again. Gates intended to hold himself in reserve, on the scout.

Hoping to find out where the king was, and to arrange to take Ariton to the planned meeting, Brazil almost literally dropped in, shortly after sunset one evening, on the hill village where she had told him she could usually be found.

No Reds were in evidence. Again a flock of watchbirds assaulted Brazil with futile energy. The Blond natives stared at him with some awe, but little surprise. They directed him to a building set against a hill.

It was a low structure of groundvine mats and rare wooden poles. Carved or molded masks hung in profusion at the doorway, the first artwork of any kind Brazil had seen on the island, except for the decorated armor of the Reds. He stood at a gateway in a low surrounding fence and called a greeting to the dark and open doorway of the house. In a few moments, a Blond man, unusually tall and carrying an oil lamp, emerged from the rambling building. He stood studying Brazil emotionlessly.

"I am looking for Ariton," Brazil repeated. The towering Blond somehow made him feel for a ridiculous moment like an adolescent suitor come to call on his girl and greeted by her older brother.

"Ariton has gone to Capital City," the man said finally. "To meet you or your countrymen there when you go to visit the king of the Redmen." Again the grinding foot-motion at mention of Galamand. This man conveyed a suggestion of insolent freedom and power to Brazil. It was impossible for him to think of this man or Ariton as slaves.

"Is Galamand now in his castle beside the Tower of the Sea God?" Brazil asked.

"Yes." The Blond man paused, then seemed to reach a sudden decision involving Brazil. "Come with me." He beckoned with his lamp and led the way into the house.

They followed a passage leading back toward the hillside. The open rooms they passed contained things unknown to Brazil, things carven and feathered and stained. More temple than home, certainly.

"Here." The Blond turned aside suddenly, and stooped to roll up a floor mat. Buried among mats of groundvine that filled a hole evidently of considerable depth were row upon row of spears, simply made but strong and sharp.

"When your king comes to this island." said the Blond, showing powerful white teeth above his beard, "he will find ready help to topple the Reds from power. Not all my people are willing to live the lives of animals. Long have we planned and waited. The Reds are fewer than us. Each year they stay more within their forts and their walled city, and each year hurt us more, with killings and beatings. We will be ready to help you."

Brazil took a deep breath. "If you want to help me help your people, you will not rise armed against the Reds. You will agree to live with them as one tribe, when they also agree."

The man stared at Brazil for a long moment, then gave a short and nasty laugh. "When they say that will be the day when they are helpless."

"Remember what I say, if you wish your own people well." said Brazil, turning to leave. "Let there be no armed rising against the Reds."

"Not yet," said the Blond in a cold voice. "Not yet for a little while."

Brazil and Foley stood among tall bushes and grass on a hillside with a fair view of the town whose name translated into Capital City, just after sunrise on the next morning. They wore heavy ground armor, in camouflage colors. They studied the city before them, adjusting their heavy glass faceplates for telescopic vision.

Capital City was plainly divided into two sections. The Reds dwelt on a hill at the far side of the harbor from the watching planeteers, in an area surrounded by a defensive wall. Their buildings were of stone or mud brick, and a number of Blond servants could be seen going about menial tasks.

In the Blond section, on lower ground and closer to Brazil and Foley, no Reds were visible except for an occasional squad of patrolling soldiers. These stuck close together, looking grimly over their shoulders. The houses were built mostly of dried groundvine mats, though some mud bricks were used.

Beyond the Blond section were the docks. The water of the harbor was studded with the low shapes of fishing boats, and, larger, a few of Galamand's war galleys.

"Well—shall we march?" asked Foley.

"Might as well. I expect Ariton will know we're here before we've gone very far."

Brazil moved his legs. The suit servos drew power from the tiny hydrogen fusion lamp in the backpack; the suit legs churned the massive shape ahead. The wearer had the sensation of moving in light summer clothing, but he could plow through heavy bush and small trees if he chose. Brazil and Foley had no wish to leave a trail of destruction, so they picked their way with care to the near-est road and set out toward town.

Ariton met them in a narrow street before they were well inside the town. She stared hard at Foley when Brazil introduced him, but gave him a common greeting-word in a pleasant voice. "Sunto is waiting with a boat in the harbor," she told them. "It is the shortest and easiest way to Galamand's building."

The planeteers followed her through narrow, winding streets toward the harbor, ever a center of apathetic, curious, hopeful, or poker-faced stares from the Blond slum-dwellers. None of the Red patrols came within sight, which suited Brazil fine.

Sunto was waiting at a low dock, in a crude and lopsided rowboat fashioned of reeds. "Hope the blasted thing can hold us," said Foley on radio. "It'd be a long swim from the middle of the harbor."

The sun was still bright in the morning sky, promising a warm day. Galamand's castle rose forbidding across the harbor, beyond the fishing boats and the moored biremes of his navy. Above and beyond the castle rose the slender stone Tower of the Sea God.

The rowboat held up as Sunto propelled it across the calm water of the harbor, straight toward the landing steps at the base of the castle. Reds appeared on the steps, watching. Their number grew as the boat approached.

"Galamand will have heard of you, of course," said Ariton. "I think he will be eager to see you for himself. Of course he may decided to kill you." She observed them.

"I don't think he will harm us," said Foley. From inside heavy ground armor they could remonstrate gently but confidently with Galamand while he boiled them in oil or his cohorts attempted to bash in their faceplates with axes. It would require a local Archi-medes and considerable time and effort for any technologically primitive power to do them serious damage. But Ariton wore not much of any clothes at all. Foley asked her: "Do you think you will be safe?"

"The priestess of the Sea God is safe even from Galamand," she answered absently. Brazil thought she was worried, but not about herself.

He scanned the ranks of grimly watching Reds as they neared the landing steps. "Is Galamand among those?"

"I do not see him. No doubt he awaits you in the great hall inside."

The boat wallowed up to the landing. Ariton nimbly hopped out and made it fast with a rope of vine. A couple of Red soldiers halfheartedly leveled spears in her direction, but no one moved to stop her. Brazil and Foley disembarked and stood quietly, giving the Reds the chance to look them over and make the first move if they felt like it. There were no Red women or children in sight.

Ariton moved her hand in an intricate gesture, in the air above Sunto's head, then touched his head briefly. "Now they will not bother him—for a while," she said to Brazil. "Well, let us go on and try to see the king."

A sword-bearing Red who might be an army officer stepped forward. "King Galamand has been told that you are here. Stand and wait." He eyed Foley with unconcealed and unfriendly curiosity.

Some of the Red troops looked Brazil over and commented among themselves with openly truculent contempt. His blondness was plainly visible through the faceplate. He looked back at them, deadpan, and unobtrusively moved to inflate his suit's flotation bubbles. Giant red swellings ballooned around his shoulders and torso. The soldiers stared and fell silent.

A few minutes passed. Brazil was deflating his bubbles as a more elaborately costumed Red appeared, and imperiously beckoned the delegation to follow him into the castle.

The few Blonds visible inside the walls had the look of the lowest of slaves. Now a few Red women and children were in evidence, but these retreated rapidly of out sight of the visitors. The complex of walls and buildings making up the stronghold had been built of heavy stone, with little if any mortar used.

The great hall was a high chamber about thirty meters by ten, dimly lit by smoking torches and small, high windows. It was crowded by Red men of varied appearance. Across the far end of the room stood a solid wall of tall soldiers bearing shields and leveled spears.

"Stand and wait here," said the distinguished Red who was acting guide, indicating a spot not far from the leveled spears. He disappeared into the crowd at one side.

Brazil and Foley turned casually around as they waited, studying the chamber and the Reds in it. No attempt had been made to surround the visitors closely. The door by which they had entered still stood open. Ariton stood waiting between the planeteers, with utter calm.

Another important-looking Red appeared before them; but it was somehow obvious that he was not the king. He held his hands clasped before him and owned a nose remarkable in size even for one of his tribe. "Do you bear weapons?" he demanded, looking from Foley to Brazil.

"We do," said Foley, "and we are not the only men here who bear them." He tried to give his speech the accent of a Red.

"You must give me your weapons," said the chamberlain. "Then you may advance and prostrate yourselves before the king."

"We will greet the king in all friendliness," said Foley. "But the law of our own nation forbids us to do him homage, or to give up our weapons."

The chamberlain hesitated a moment, then began to screech at the Earthmen threateningly. He raved and glared and waved his arms, jabbering so fast he became almost unintelligible. Yet Brazil got the impression the man was trying to avoid direct personal insult. It was a masterful performance of denouncing their disrespectful behavior but not themselves.

"Let's wait him out," Brazil subvocalized to Foley via radio. "Maybe they just want to see if we bluff. It wouldn't do for the king himself to try and fail."

The planeteers stood silent a full thirty seconds longer, glaring stony-eyed back at the speaker. The harangue gave no sign of slackening. "Better squelch him," Brazil said at last. Evidently the torrent of words was going to continue until they reacted to it in some way. Brazil did not now want to give the impression that Earthmen had infinite patience. The squelch might be better accepted coming from the "Red" planeteer.

"Silence!" Foley bellowed, after turning up his airspeaker volume. He got what he called for with magical suddenness. Ariton wore a pleased smile.

"We have come here to talk with a king, not to listen to you," Foley went on. "If King Galamand is not pleased to receive us today, we will return tomorrow. Our business is important."

"Get out of the way," said a firm voice from behind the wall of soldiers. "Let them come here."

The ranks of soldiers opened, but stayed within spear-thrusting distance on either side. Brazil, Ariton, and Foley advanced toward the man who sat alone upon an elaborately carved chair.

The man upon the throne was not ordinary. A vast scar sliced across his face, nearly obliterating one of his eyes. He was approaching middle age, not big for a Red, but thick-limbed and strong. Upon his breastplate was worked in relief an image of the Sea God's Tower.

Foley opened his mouth, doubtless meaning to register a complaint about the way the chamberlain had spoken to them. "Greetings, great king," was all that came out. Galamand's bright blue eye seemed to nail him with more effect than if there had been two.

"Greetings, great king," said Brazil. Ariton stood between the Earthmen, saying nothing but watching Galamand haughtily.

The king ignored her and spoke to the armored planeteers, looking from one to the other. "I bid you welcome," he said perfunctorily. "Does your king send greetings to me?"

"He does indeed," said Foley. "And would send you gifts, as is our custom. But in some lands it is considered an insult to present such gifts immediately."

The king raised an eyebrow, and his mouth twisted slightly. Brazil spoke up: "Oh, there are such lands. King Galamand. Not many, but a few."

The blue eye fixed on his. "I thank your king for his greetings. Is he Red or Blond?"

"Neither," said Brazil, truthfully enough. "In our country men of different colors live together peacefully."

The king nodded toward Ariton. "You bring this woman with you. Why?"

"I have come with these my friends, to speak for my people," she said, flaring up at him. "And I speak also to the Sea God, as you well know."

Galamand seemed faintly amused. "Do you speak against me to the Sea God, woman? Your words are not strong enough. The Tower still stands against the waves. The sea-sound is faint in my ear, and soothing as I go to sleep at night. Will you arouse the Sea God to destroy me?"

Brazil heard the faintest stir and mutter among the soldiers on either side; evidently the king's words might be thought a provocation to the god. Galamand swept his blue eye around, but said nothing to his men.

He spoke again to the planeteers: "And you are this woman's friends?"

"We would be friends with Red and Blond alike."

Galamand digested the statement swiftly and without comment, and changed the subject. "Your ship is swift and hard to see; my ships have circled the island every day since you first appeared, and have not found it. Now I admit this puzzles me."

Brazil answered: "As you say, great king, our ship is elusive and very swift. It is not the wish of our king that our first visits here be seen by many ships upon the sea."

"And why do you come here at all?"

"We seek always the knowledge of new lands, oh king," said Foley. "Some twenty or thirty of us would like to live on this island for a year or two, on some small area of land that you who live here now do not need. We are willing to pay for this privilege. But we do not want to deal with a government engaged in civil war, under which two tribes contend against each other; or with a king who holds another tribe in slavery."

"No one contends against me here and lives." Galamand spoke quietly and distinctly. He gave Ariton his twisted grin and asked: "Is it not so?"

It stung her deeply, and her voice rose loud: "Your day is not forever, Redman. One day your children will be our slaves, if you beget any before you die. We will—"

Brazil's voice rose over hers. "That is not what *we* want! That would yet be war and slavery."

Both native rulers looked at him, for the moment united against the outsider. Then Galamand asked quietly: "How would you have us live?"

"As one tribe."

Galamand narrowed his operational eye and scratched his beard. "You spoke of payment, for the use of land. What do you mean to offer?"

Foley answered: "To the ruler of a peaceful land we would offer, to begin with, a great quantity of cord, much stronger and more lasting than your vines, to make excellent fishnets, oh king."

"And weapons?" The king's voice was casual and gentle.

"A quantity of swords and spears might be included—"

"You do not carry swords or spears."

"We carry them for trade." They could be made up.

Galamand's blue eye did not waver from Foley's face, but his right arm shot out toward the nearest guard, and his fingers snapped. The haft of the guard's spear was instantly in his grip. The king stood up and thrust the spear, butt first, toward Foley, at the same time holding out his left hand open.

"If you are men who deal in spears, then I will trade with you. I offer in trade this good Red spear, for that weapon you wear at your side."

Foley assumed a deeply troubled expression. "Oh great king, we have no wish to anger you. But we must refuse to trade our weapons. If we did so, the anger of *our* king would fall heavily upon our heads. And against *his* anger we have no defense."

"And against mine?" Galamand's voice was still gentle. So is a lion, when not hungry or offended.

"We have our weapons, which we cannot trade, great king," said Brazil, with punctilious courtesy. The blue eye lanced at him and he looked right back down the shaft at it, while from the corners of his eyes he watched the spearmen carefully. Galamand too must have received accurate intelligence about the First Contact, if he could identify the butt of a stun pistol as a weapon.

Galamand grounded the butt of the spear and stood drumming his fingers on the shaft. "Fishnets," he said meditatively. "Your great king has then no weapons to spare? I would reward you well if you were to convince him that he has; or if you were to act, shall we say, on your own . . . " He reached into a pouch at his belt and brought out a lustrous pearl-like jewel, bigger than a grape.

Foley shook his head slowly. "Oh king, it cannot be. If you offer us the riches of the whole island, still we will give or trade to you no weapons, save such as you can make yourselves."

Galamand tossed the spear back to the soldier and seated himself again. "And your armor? I admit I have not seen such glass."

This time Brazil joined in the headshaking.

"Strange men," Galamand mused. "You say you will not trade with a ruler who holds another tribe in slavery. I will not ask you why. I have not asked for any trade with you that would pay me in fishnets, and I want none. While the waves spare the Tower, the Sea God supports me. I am king upon this island. My slaves are my slaves. When you are willing to trade something worthwhile for the use of my land, you may come back again and speak with me."

"Suggestions?" Brazil radioed.

"Leave without argument," said a voice from above. "We can analyze what we've got and try again."

Ariton stood proudly erect while Brazil and Foley bowed deeply to the king, who told them with a straight face that he was providing them with an escort back to their ship, that no harm should come to them on the way.

"They'll see the scout unless we can shake them," Brazil radioed, starting out of the throne room.

"Guess we'll have to give them a minimum marvel to look at," said Gates' voice. "There's a suitable deep cove just outside the city, about four kilometers from where you are. Just walk south along the shore; I'll bring the scout up partly out of the water for you to get in, and let them get a good enough look to be sure it's a ship and not a sea monster. Okay?"

"Good idea," said Captain Dietrich. "A submarine will startle them some, but it should further convince them we're not spirits who just materialize."

Ariton walked with the planeteers out of the castle; they stopped at the landing steps to pick up Sunto, who was much relieved to see them. When told they were leaving by land, Sunto climbed out of his half-waterlogged rowboat, and said to a Red soldier standing guard nearby: "I leave to you as a gift the noble craft which you have praised so highly." And he ground his foot against the stone stair. The Red glowered but said nothing.

The walk out of the city was uneventful. Within an hour the four of them stood on the steep sloping shore within the chosen cove, with Galamand's heavily armed honor guard watching very carefully from a little distance and a Red galley casually standing by offshore.

Foley was telling Ariton that a ship would soon come to take Brazil and him on board, but she and Sunto would have to stay on shore. She agreed calmly, and watched the horizon for the ship, with some puzzlement.

Brazil turned to Sunto. "The Tower of the Sea God is very important to your people and the Reds, is it not?"

"Yes." Sunto did not seem especially interested in the subject. "It is our old belief that as long as the Tower is not destroyed by the waves of the sea, the Sea God smiles upon the rulers of the island, whoever they be."

"What if the waves should knock the Tower down?"

Sunto smiled wryly. "Then I think you would see upon this island the one tribe for which Ariton says you asked the king. For the Tower to be so destroyed would mean the Sea God thinks the rulers of the island evil. The destruction of his own Tower is to be his last warning before he overwhelms with waves the entire island, slaying everyone on it and carrying the evildoers down to be frozen forever in the ice at the bottom of the sea."

"Get more on this!" said an excited radio voice. "Foley, ask Ariton about the Tower, she should be a real authority. Gates, hold that scout underwater for a minute.

Brazil asked Sunto: "Do you think the Sea God will ever destroy the Tower?"

Sunto looked out at the ocean soberly; it was dull and placid in the sun. "May I never see the day—but I am a practical man. Whoever is king will surely see to it that the seawall of large rocks is kept strong at the base of the Tower, to break the force of the waves. Someday, perhaps, a very great storm . . . but there are great storms every year. The Tower has stood for many years."

"Is the season for great storms coming soon?" Brazil felt the vague beginnings of what might be a valid idea.

"No, it is just past. Now is the time of the steady-but-not-too-strong winds."

"That checks," said Meteorology from above.

Sunto continued: "Also, the Tower stands on a straight shoreline, and the Sea God hurls his waves most strongly against the points of land that jut out into his domain."

"That is true in all lands," said Brazil absently. He had just the start of a plan to scare these people into cooperating, by making the Tower seemed threatened by a storm. It might be just possible to induce a violent storm. But what would it do to the rest of the island? The scheme seemed worthless . . . "That is true in all lands. As it is true that the waves come in nearly parallel to the shore, no matter from which point at sea the wind is blowing. And the reason is the same . . . " Brazil fell silent, as if in a sudden dream.

"Why, that is so, but I have never thought about it," said Sunto in surprise. "Truly, the waves are like women, for men watch them long and understand them but little."

". . . that they travel more slowly as the water beneath them grows more shallow," said Brazil with a faraway look. He gave a sudden laugh at the sight of Sunto's startled face. "Waves, I mean, not women. Sunto, tell me this. If the Tower were destroyed by some means other than the waves, what then?"

Sunto gave the Blond equivalent of a shrug. "Why, the Tower would simply have to be rebuilt, and the king would gain merit in the Sea God's eyes by rebuilding." He thought for a moment. "Maybe the Red king would rebuild it on some inland hill, where no wave could ever reach it, and so make his rule safe."

Brazil nodded as if satisfied.

Twenty minutes later he sat with Foley in scoutship *Alpha*, gratefully peeling off chunks of armor. They faced on a segmented screen the debriefing assembly of their peers and bosses, electronically gathered to analyze the visit to Galamand. The astounded natives who had watched the two planeteers enter the submarine craft were by now no doubt attending their own conferences on the subject.

"First, tell me this," Brazil invited, eyes alight with an idea. "Does it seem likely that a massive assault of ocean waves on this Tower might make these people willing to try getting along together, at least for a while?"

"I would say yes, based on what Ariton told me," said Foley.

"It might well give us a start in the right direction," said Sociology cautiously.

"An assault of ocean waves, you say," Captain Dietrich frowned. "Not of forcefields, explosives, chemicals or sonic vibrations."

"Captain, I think there's a chance it can be done with this scoutship, and not by directing any of those modern weapons against the Tower."

"I am afraid I would have to forbid the use of such weapons against the natives, on principle." said Chandragupta grimly.

"The idea is not to wreck the Tower," said Brazil, "but to make the natives think that the Sea God has decided to wreck it."

"That Galamand's no fool," said Gates. "He's probably thinking up antisubmarine devices already. And how are you going to stir up suitable waves with a scoutship?"

"I'm not going to stir them up, exactly. And I don't think Galamand will notice a submarine acting a good many kilometers out at sea."

"Brazil, are you drunk?"

"No, on duty. Another reason for getting this situation settled. Now we'll need some information from Oceanography. And a weather forecast of such massive solidity that we can all lean on it—one that includes a steady ocean breeze here."

Trofand, Red priest of the Sea God, and chief caretaker of the Tower, was awakened by the sound of the waves, to which he always listened with half an ear even when asleep. The sound was now too loud for his liking.

He arose from his pallet and was dressing in the stone-damp darkness of his chamber in the Tower's base when he received a shock. A streaming puddle of cold sea water flowed against his bare foot on the floor. He hastened to light a candle from the smoldering brazier that fought uselessly against the permanent dampness of his bedchamber.

By candlelight he saw with distress that water was entering in multiple thin streams through chinks in the massive masonry of the inner Tower wall. It was something that happened only in the heaviest storms. The booming roar of the waves pounding the heavy seawall outside seemed to be increasing, and now brought him to the beginning of real fright. In ten years in the Tower he had never heard it so loud. A mighty storm must be raging, though the season for them was past, and the weather signs had given no indication of any approaching tempest.

Trofand was nearly dressed when an underling came with a torch, pounding on his door and opening it with a minimum of courtesy. "My lord, the waves, the waves! They are very bad."

"I have ears, fool. Someone should have called me sooner. What are the signs of the storm's length?"

"My lord, there is no storm."

Trofand started an angry retort to the foolish statement, but something in the pale frightened face before him made him pause. Fastening his belt, he led the way out of the chamber to the stair that climbed to the Tower's top.

It was true, he realized, emerging into the predawn darkness atop the Tower. The sky was clear. The wind was steady in direction from the sea, but it was not strong. The surf at the Tower's foot should be fairly gentle.

He thought he felt the stones of the Tower quiver underfoot with each leisurely watery smash.

An assistant was at his elbow, speaking with a worried voice. "My lord, what shall we do? The signs are that the wind will rise throughout the day, and remain steady in direction. If the waves become yet higher—"

"If they do, we will deal with them. The Sea God is not our enemy. Go rouse out the Tower slaves. Conscript more if need be. Have them stand by the fresh slabs of rock, ready at dawn to strengthen the seawall. Then go you to offer the day's sacrifice to the Sea God. But do not take too long about it."

"I obey." The man was gone in an instant, down the stair. Other junior priests of the Tower huddled about Trofand in the chill night, in the light of a dim torch, looking to him for guidance.

Well, I was right about that, Trofand said to himself. He was thinking of the extra stones, weighing many tons apiece, that he had long ago ordered to be kept on rollers in the courtyard. They were constantly ready to be moved to reinforce the seawall in case a storm of unprecedented violence should threaten the Tower.

Now, another question: should he order the king awakened? After all, the Tower seemed in no immediate danger, and Gala-mand might grumble if he were waked up for something unimport-ant. But he might have the man boiled alive who failed to wake him for a real emergency. It was not a hard decision to make. "You—go rouse the king. Tell him I say that waves threaten the Tower. Tell no one else."

"I obey."

King Galamand was beside Trofand within a few minutes, look-ing over the parapet and frowning at the strange intensity of waves that were driven by such a modest wind. He observed the prepara-tions that had been made to reinforce the seawall at dawn, and then turned and struck his fist against the parapet. "You did well to call me. But these stones have stood throughout my lifetime, and I say that they will stand yet a good while longer." Trofand saw him outlined against the first gray light in the east.

The Blond slaves, whipped on by overseers, now began to roll the mighty rock slabs into position to reinforce the seawall. It would be dangerous work. But slaves could be replaced, while the Tower—

There was an outcry somewhere inside the Tower. In a minute an exhausted runner appeared, helped up the stairs by others. In near panic he leaned against the stones beside the king. "My lord, the seawall—the wall away from the Tower, up and down the peninsula—"

"Is it breached by waves? Where?"

"No, my lord." A gasp of breath. "I came along the wall, after carrying your message conscripting slaves—"

"Well?"

"Elsewhere, my lord, the waves are small. Only here at the Tower do they rise abnormally, as if in raging anger. As if the Sea God has grown angry and—uh!"

Galamand's vicious backhand blow knocked the man sprawling. "Enough! Do not preach the anger of the gods at me, or I will show you what anger is! I am the king!"

The king turned away to peer, with Trofand and the others, at the waves beating against the seawall at a distance from the Tower. The fast-brightening dawn revealed that the messenger had spoken the truth.

The news was out, Brazil saw, as he strode along the seawall road toward the Tower and the fortified complex of Galamand's castle. A puzzled Ariton walked between him and Foley. Reds and Blonds stood in little groups along the wall, commenting on the waves that were assaulting the base of the Tower. Faces turned toward them as they passed, but ever turned back again to the greater wonder of the waves.

Each long swell marched in from the clear horizon of the ocean, foaming up and curling over as the depth of the water below approached the height of the wave, to smash itself finally against the rocks piled in shallow water at the base of the seawall. But in the sea before the Tower, each incoming rise of water seemed to squeeze itself together along its long axis, rising to at least three times the height of the waves elsewhere, before it piled up in a foaming fury of discriminating violence against that part of the seawall.

Ariton paused at her first sight of this, whispering something that might have been a prayer. "You knew of this?" she asked Brazil. "This is why you brought me here?"

"I'm taking you to talk to Galamand," Brazil evaded. "I think if you and he can't come to some agreement soon, there won't be any Tower left for either of you to use. You have lived near the sea all your life. You know the strength that is in large waves."

"What do you mean?" She stared at him, half afraid. "Do you speak for the Sea God?"

"We are only men," he answered innocently. "But do I not understand your gods correctly? Is it not so that the Sea God may destroy his own Tower when there is great strife in the land and evil rulers, as a final warning before he destroys the entire island?"

After a long moment she took her eyes from Brazil's face and turned toward the Tower. "Come, whoever you are. It is my place to be there now."

"Is this really going to work?" Foley radioed while they walked. "I mean that Tower isn't built out of pebbles, exactly. And it's stood through a lot of storms."

"On Earth," answered Brazil in professorial accents, "wave forces have been measured at over thirty tons per square meter. Engineers will not build a shoreline structure on Earth without carefully considering local conditions regarding the effect we are now employing. Besides, the idea is to scare Galamand and the lady here into cooperating, not to actually wreck the Tower. That would probably kill someone, and I hate to think what might happen in the panic."

At the castle gate, the guards were almost looking over their shoulders at the Tower as they halted the three visitors and sent word to Galamand of their arrival. Within a few minutes a guide appeared to escort the visitors to the bare top of the Tower.

Brazil could see by the flags above the castle that the wind had increased slightly and was holding a steady direction, as Meteorology had promised. If only we were gods enough to control the weather in an area of a few square kilometers, thought Brazil. We can come a hundred light-years to stick our noses into our neighbors' business, but if the weather doesn't quite suit our schemes we can only wait until it does.

Galamand scoured them with his single eye when they had climbed the stairs to the Tower's top. The king paused in his pacing amid a group of high-ranking Reds. "Come you to preach the Sea God to me also?" he inquired in an ominously quiet voice.

Ariton looked about her. "Where is Trofand?"

"He has gone to offer sacrifice in the chapel below," said the king, a tinge of amusement in his voice. He leaned against the parapet with thick arms folded and his back to the sea as if in contempt. "He has rather suddenly remembered to take his religious obligations seriously."

"Human sacrifice?" asked Brazil. He hadn't thought of this possibility.

"He considers that course," said Galamand. "But I think the Sea God has lives enough for one day." He moved his head to indicate that they should look over the parapet.

In the cold boiling hell of surf at the Tower's foot a hundred Blond slaves or more struggled on the slippery rocks, straining on levers and vine ropes to move an enormous block of stone into the surf at a place where the waves had weakened the wall. With each torrential ebb and surge of water, Brazil saw, a pale object in the surf was drawn out and hurled in near the rocks, buried in foam and tossed up again—a fish-pale thing that had blond hair and no longer any face. And there was another—and another . . .

No Blond slave or Red overseer took any apparent notice of the drowned men, much less attempted to pull them from the sea. Every living man down there was concerned too intently with his own footing on the treacherous rock.

"Take it easy, old man." said a voice inside Brazil's helmet. Oh, this Brazil is a wonder, a red-hot planeteer, said a louder voice inside his mind. Just trust him to come up with a great scheme to set everyone on the road to happiness without bloodshed. That's important, no bloodshed. Well, you can't see any blood down there, can you?

Now that's enough. Shut up and get to work, there's a job to finish. "Why does the surf attack only the place of the Tower, oh king?" he asked, turning, stony-faced.

The blue eye studied him. "Had I a ship so cunningly built as to travel under water, I might discover why." Galamand turned to his aides. "Send boats and divers out beyond the white water. See if anything strange lies under the surface."

"The old boy's uncomfortably shrewd," said Foley on radio. "Doesn't seem likely they'll search the bottom eight kilometers out and eighty meters deep, though."

Boats and divers soon appeared in the sea a few hundred meters out from the Tower, and made a show of investigating underwater conditions. It was not a really dangerous job for such skillful sailors and swimmers, out there where there were no rocks to be dashed against. But the Red seamen seemed to approach the job with a vast reluctance. Their faces turned often toward the Tower, as if in hope that the king would recall them.

Time passed. By noon the wind was obviously gaining strength again.

"I go to join Trofand in the chapel," said Ariton to the king, as if daring him to stop her. He pulled at his beard and appeared not to hear.

When she had gone he ordered food brought to him. His aides grew continually more gloomy. They looked often at the king, but sought to avoid his eye.

Galamand was amused to see the planeteers drink their lunch from tubes inside their helmets. He asked if their suits had sanitary facilities too, and roared with laughter when he was told they had. But the laughter had a forced sound in the wind.

The wind grew yet stronger, though it was still far from a gale. Down below, a wave got under a forty-ton slab of rock just right and skipped it like a flat chip against the base of the Tower itself. Stones split and flew; one fragment spun almost to the Tower's top.

The next wave poured through the gap in the seawall, like the paw of a giant beast forced into a hole to grope for prey. The next tore free another huge stone from the edge of the hole. The bones of the Tower quivered.

Slaves and masters at the Tower's foot scrambled desperately to move another massive rock into a defensive position. Brazil saw it was a futile thing for creatures weak as men to attempt. One roaring curl of water caught a Red, who dropped his whip and grabbed at the slippery rock to save himself. Brazil saw the upturned face, the eyes seemingly looking straight into his own, the mouth open as if to yell. The next wave tore the man away and dragged him out of sight.

Galamand was roaring orders for more slaves to be brought. "You have strange powers and weapons," he demanded suddenly of Foley. "Can you help me now?"

Brazil pulled himself out of a hideous fascination with what was happening down below.

"And if we can?" asked Foley.

"It might be that the agreement you sought with me could be quickly reached." The wind tore at Galamand's words, and shot spray past his head, here thirty meters above the normal sea. A small wave-tossed rock clattered against the parapet, as if shot from a giant's sling.

"Then order those men from the sea down there," Brazil demanded. "And give your word to make of Red and Blond one tribe."

"Then you can cure this," barked the king. "And it may be you have caused it!" The other Reds glared at the Earthmen; some weapons were drawn. Then cries came from the stairway, distracting attention.

Ariton and Trofand were suddenly at the top of the stair, in ceremonial robes half sodden with sea water.

"My king, the Sea God pours his wrath into the very chapel. I—" Trofand jumped back, as if he thought the king's sudden lunge was directed at him. But Galamand seized Ariton, had her arm twisted behind her back and his dagger at her throat in a moment.

"Sacrilege! Sacrilege!" howled Trofand. The other Reds looked on, wavering, wide-eyed, undecided.

The king swung Ariton to face the planeteers. "Now, aliens," he roared. "Cause the waves to cease, and quickly, or I will butcher this so-called queen with whom you ally yourselves. You seek to put her on a throne, but I alone am king. And so I will remain!"

"My lord." Ariton's low voice stopped the king in surprise. Doubtless it was the first time she had used any title of respect to him. "My death will not save our island. But I will marry you and bear your sons, if that be the only way to save it. And we will live here as one tribe."

For the first time in his experience, Brazil saw Galamand taken aback. But it was only for a moment.

"No, I'll not have it! I am the king here, I alone. Not you, or the aliens, or the Sea God himself, can order me, do this, do that!"

Trofand moaned and covered his face; every other Red was visibly shaken by the king's defiance of the god. Brazil felt a sudden turn of sympathy for Galamand, losing to forces he could not comprehend, cutting himself off now from his own followers. Be ready for the moment . . .

The sea-flung stone, the size of a grapefruit, actually missed Galamand's helmeted head by only a few centimeters, and flew on to bounce off the opposite wall and down the stairway. The jolt from Brazil's quick-drawn stun pistol took the king in the head about one second later, when all eyes were on Galamand. No native doubted that the rock had grazed the king's helmet and caused his sudden collapse. Brazil's pistol was reholstered as quickly as it had been drawn.

The Red priests and soldiers stared at the fallen ruler in awe. Plainly he had been struck down for blasphemy. None of them moved to aid him. Foley went to him, pulling out his first aid kit and beginning a quick radio conference with the medics of the *Yuan Chwang*. The stun-jolt should wear off in a matter of minutes; a carefully chosen tranquilizer administered now should ease the situation then considerably.

A Red officer of apparent high rank spoke almost imploringly to Trofand. "We will obey you, my lord. Is there any way to save the island?"

The priest looked uncertainly at Ariton. Brazil asked her: "Will you now marry the king, as you offered, and so unite your people with his?"

She rubbed the arm that Galamand had twisted, and frowned. "There is no need for that now. The Sea God has rejected him. With your help, I will be ruler—"

"Do you want the Tower to stand?" Brazil cut her off brutally. "Remember, too, that the Red soldiers are still strong, and perhaps not eager to serve you."

She nodded, meekly wide-eyed for once.

Brazil turned to Trofand. "Can the marriage be performed as soon as the king awakens?"

"If he can be made to agree to it; I see that the Sea God has spared his life, for now his eyelids move."

"I think he can be made to agree," said the high-ranking officer, grimly. "I think it is time we had a certain heir to the throne, and also an end to this unprofitable fighting in our own land."

Brazil switched off his airspeaker, with throat muscles beginning to quiver with the relaxation of tension. "Sam, start cutting down that hump. But stand by to rebuild, until I give you the word that the honeymoon has started."

Eight kilometers out at sea and eighty meters below the surface, scoutships *Alpha* and *Omicron* braced themselves on water-filled space, and thrust noses equipped with jury-rigged bulldozer blades against the mound of mud and sand rising from the bottom, the mound they had carefully constructed in the same manner the day before. It was not much of a mound for size, really, and unimpressive-looking to any but an oceanographer. But it shallowed the water above it, and so it slowed the waves, refracting those from one certain direction, focusing them as a lens treats light, causing them to converge on one small area eight kilometers away . . .

Boris Brazil opened his eyes. He had not been asleep. He was slouched in an easy chair in an alcove of the recreation lounge aboard the *Yuan Chwang*, and Chandragupta was standing looking down at him.

"Do you mind if I ask what you see behind your eyelids, my friend?" the Tribune asked.

Brazil was not quick to answer.

"Perhaps you see drowned men." The Tribune sat down facing Brazil and spoke with quiet sympathy. "My friend, you have what must be one of the most difficult jobs in the known universe; you must be a researcher, a diplomat, a fighter, a linguist, and a survival expert, by turns or all at once. And I know I have left out many things. I think you do very well in your job, considering that you are no more than human. We all agreed that your plan of threatening the Tower with waves should be tried. I still think it was good. It has set the islanders on the road to unity, and so no doubt averted more suffering than it caused."

"Thanks, Chan." Brazil stretched, and uncoiled slowly from the chair. A little humor came back into his face. "I'm going to play it as lazy as I can for a couple of days." He straightened his off-duty semi-uniform and said, half to himself: "Maybe I'll just mosey over toward Computing and check out—something. Hmm—"

"Boris?" Foley's voice was heard before he came into sight. "There you are. Scout just sent back word from over nightside: they spotted one of those luminous water-rings over there; this one's fifteen kilometers across. Our regular standby crew is out, so Gates wants you in the briefing room on the double. Oh yeah—" Foley gave an uncertain smile. "He says: 'What would Thoreau have to say about that?' "

Brazil's answer was probably inaccurate.

SWORDS

BLIND MAN'S BLADE

The gods' great Game of Swords, and with it the whole later history of planet Earth, might have followed a very different course had the behavior of one or two divine beings—or the conduct of only one man—been different at the start. Even a slight change at the beginning of the Game produced drastic variation in the results. And Apollo has been heard to say that there have been several such beginnings.

One of those divergent commencements—which, in the great book of fate, may be accounted as leading to an alternate universe, or perhaps simply as a false start—saw all of the gods' affairs thrown into turmoil at a remarkably early stage, even before the first move had been made in the Game. It happened on the day when the Swords, all new and virginally fresh, all actually still warm from Vulcan's forge, were being brought to the Council to be put into the hands of those players who had been awarded them by lot.

The sun had just cleared the jagged horizon when Vulcan arrived at the open council-space, there to join the wide circle of deities already assembled in anticipation of his coming. They were his colleagues, all of them standing much taller than humans, their well-proportioned bodies casting long shadows in the lingering mists, but still dwarfed by the surrounding rim of icy mountains. There were moments when they all looked lost under the breadth of the the cold morning sky.

117

The Smith brought with him a whiff of forge-smoke, a tang of melted meteoric iron. His cloak of many furs was wind-blown around his shoulders, and his huge left hand cradled carefully its priceless cargo of steel and magic, eleven weighty packages held in a neat bundle. And, despite the fact that a small but vocal minority of the Council still argued that no binding agreement on the rules of the Game had yet been reached, the Swords—almost every one of the Twelve Swords—were soon being portioned out among the chosen members of the meeting.

Among those gods and goddesses who received a Sword in the distribution, no two reactions were exactly the same. Most were pleased, but not all. For example, there was the goddess Demeter, who stood looking thoughtfully at the object limping Vulcan had just pressed into her strong, pale hands. She gazed at the black sheath covering a meter's length of god-forged steel, at the black hilt marked by a single symbol of pure white.

Demeter said pensively, in her high, clear voice: "I am not at all sure that I care to play this Game."

Mars, who happened to be standing near her, commented: "Well, many of us *do* want to play, including some who have been awarded no Sword at all. Hand yours over to someone else if you don't want it." Mars had already been promised a Sword of his own, or his protest would doubtless have been more violent. Actually he thought he could do quite well in the Game without benefit of any such trick hardware; but he would not have submitted quietly to being left off the list.

"I said I was not sure," Demeter responded. A male deity would probably have tossed the sheathed weapon thoughtfully in his hand while trying to decide. Demeter only looked at it. And she was still holding her Sword, down at her side, the dark sheath all but invisible in one of her large hands, when her tall figure turned and strode away into a cloud of mist.

Another of her colleagues called after her to know where she was going; and as an afterthought added the question: "Which Sword do you have?"

"I have other business," Demeter called back, avoiding a direct answer to either question. And then she went on. For all that anyone could tell, she was only seeking other amusement, displaying independence as gods and goddesses were wont to do.

Meanwhile the distribution of Swords was still going on, a slow process frequently interrupted by arguments. Some of the recipients were trying to keep the names and powers of their Swords secret, while others did not seem to care who knew about them.

The council meeting dragged along, its proceedings every bit as disorderly as those of such affairs were wont to be, and not made any easier to follow by the setting—a high mountain wasteland of snow and ice and rock and howling wind, an environment to which the self-convinced rulers of the earth were proud to display their indifference.

Hera was complaining that the original plan of allowing only gods to possess Swords, which she believed to be the only good and proper and reasonable scheme, had been spoiled before it could be put into effect: "That scoundrel Vulcan, that damned clubfoot, enlisted a human smith to help him make the Swords. And then chose to reward the man!"

Zeus stroked his beard. "Well? And if it amuses Vulcan to hand out a gift or two to mortals? Surely that's not unheard of?"

"I mean he rewarded the human with the gift of Townsaver! That's unheard of! So now we have only eleven Swords to share among us, instead of twelve. Am I wrong, or is it we gods, and not humanity, who are supposed to be playing the Swordgame?"

The speaker had meant the question to be rhetorical; but not even on this point could any general agreement be established. Many at the meeting expected their human worshipers to play a large part in the Game—though of course not in direct competition with gods.

Debate on various questions concerning the distribution of Swords, and the conduct and rules of the Game, moved along by fits and starts, until Vulcan himself came forward, leaning sideways on his shorter leg, to demand the floor. As soon as the Smith thought he had the attention of a majority, he haughtily informed his accusers that he had decided to give away the Blade called Townsaver, because the gods themselves had no towns or cities, no settled or occupied places in the human sense, and thus none of them would be able to derive any direct benefit from that particular weapon.

"Would you have chosen that one for yourself?" he demanded, looking from one deity to another nearby. "Hah, I thought not!"

As the council meeting wrangled on, perpetually on the brink of dissolving in disputes about procedure, at least one other member of the divine company—Zeus himself—complained that the great Game was already threatened by human interference. How many of his colleagues, he wanted to know, how many of them realized that there was one man who by means of certain impertinent magic had already gained extensive theoretical knowledge of the Twelve Swords?

Diana demanded: "How could a mere human manage that? I insist that the chairman answer me! How could a man do that, without the help of one or more of us?"

Chairman Zeus, always ready for another speech, began pontificating. Few listened to him. Meanwhile, Vulcan sulked: "Who pays any attention to human magic tricks? Who cares what they find out? No one said anything to me about maintaining secrecy."

In another of the rude, arguing knots of deities, the discussion went like this: "If putting Swords in the hands of humans hasn't been declared officially against the rules, it ought to be! It's bound to have a bad result."

"Still, it might be fun to see what the vile little beasts would do with such weapons."

Mars drew himself up proudly. "Why not? I hope no one's suggesting that *they* could do *us* serious damage with any weapon at all?"

"Well . . ."

Someone else butted in, raising a concern over the chance of demons getting their hands on Swords. But few in the assembly were particularly worried about that, any more than they were about humans.

A dark-faced, turbaned god raised his voice. "Cease your quarreling! No doubt we'll have the chance to learn the answers to these interesting questions. If we are to use Vulcan's new toys in a Game, of course they'll be scattered promiscuously about the world. Sooner or later at least one of them is bound to fall into human hands. And, mark my words, some demon will have another."

Meanwhile, in a small cave at the foot of a low cliff of dark rock about two hundred meters distant from the nearest argument, a mere man named Keyes, and another called Lo-Yang, both weather-vulnerable human beings, shivering with cold and excitement though wrapped in many furs, were sitting almost motionless, watching and listening intently as they peered from behind a rock. Keyes, the leader of the pair, had chosen this place as one from which he and his apprentice could best observe the goings-on among the gods and goddesses, while still enjoying a reasonable hope that they would not be seen in turn.

A dark and wiry man, Keyes, of indeterminate age. His companion was dark as well, but heavier, and obviously young. They had come to this place in the high, uninhabited mountains searching for treasure, wealth in the form of knowledge—Keyes, an accomplished magician, was willing to risk everything in the pursuit.

Lo-Yang was at least as numb with fear as with cold, and at the moment willing to risk everything for a good chance to run away. He might even have defied his human master and done so, at any time during the past half hour, except that he feared to draw the attention of the mighty gods by sudden movement.

Keyes was in most matters no braver than his associate and apprentice, but certainly he was more obsessed with the search for knowledge and power. He cursed the fact that though some of the gods' stentorian voices carried clearly to where he crouched trying to eavesdrop, he could understand nothing that he heard. Despite his best efforts at magical interpretation, the language the gods most commonly used among themselves was still beyond him.

Keyes, exchanging whispers now and then with his companion, whose teeth were chattering, considered an attempt to work his way even nearer the place of council. But he rejected the idea; it would hardly be possible to do better than this well-placed but shallow little cave, inconspicuous among a number of similar holes in the nearby rock.

He was in the middle of a whispered conversational exchange with his apprentice Lo-Yang, when without warning a great roaring fury swirled around him, and Keyes realized that he had been caught—that the enormous fingers of some god's hand had closed around him. Hopelessly the man tried to summon some defensive magic. Physically he struggled to get free.

He might as well have endeavored to uproot a mountain or two and hurl them at the moon.

Mars, who had captured Keyes, was not really concerned with the obvious fact that the man had been spying. Who cared what human beings might overhear, or think? The god was focused on another problem: he was due to receive a Sword, though Vulcan had not yet put it in his hands. Mars wanted a human for experimental purposes, so that he could learn a thing or two, in practical terms, about the powers of whatever Sword he was given before he used it in the Game. Mars considered himself fortunate to have been able to grab up a human so promptly; the creatures were not common in these parts. Keyes had happened to be the nearer of the two specimens Mars saw when it occurred to him to look for one.

The captured man, knowing nothing of his captor's purpose, certain that his last moment had come, could feel the cold mist on his face, and thought he could hear the echo of his own frightened breath.

The god-hand which had scooped Keyes up did not immediately crush him into pulp, or dash him on the rocks. The sweeping breeze of god-breath, redolent of ice and spice and smoke, told Keyes that an enormous face loomed over him.

But his captor was not even looking at him. Only when the man saw that did he fully realize how far he was, for all his impertinence, beneath the gods' real anger. Nothing he might do would be of any real consequence to them—or so most of them thought. Some mice were doubtless nearby too, scampering among the rocks, but none of the debaters paid any heed to them at all.

The god who had captured Keyes considered how best to keep him fresh and ready. Physically crippling the subject might affect the results of the experiment; and anyway some measure less drastic should suffice to do the job. A simple deprivation of eyesight, along with a smothering of the man's ability to do magic, ought to make him stay where he was put . . . so one god-finger wiped Keyes's face . . .

Now. Where best to put him, for safe-keeping, until Mars should come into possession of the Sword he wished to test?

The captor, still holding casually in one hand the wriggling, moaning, newly-blinded human form, looked about. Presently the terrible gaze of Mars fastened on the handiest hiding place immediately available. A moment later, treading windy space in the easy, heedless way of deities, he was descending into a house-sized limestone cave, by means of the wide, nearly vertical shaft which seemed to form the cavern's only entrance and exit.

At the bottom he set his helpless captive down, not ungently, on the stone floor. Keyes was still mewing like a hurt kitten.

"Here you will stay," Mars boomed in Keyes's human language. "Until I get back. That won't be long—there's something I want to try out on you. As you can see . . . well, as you probably noticed when you could see . . . the only way out of this cave is a vertical climb up a steep shaft with slick sides and only a few scattered handholds."

The god started to ascend that way himself, but disdaining handholds, simply walking in air. Halfway up he paused in midair, looking back down over his shoulder, to warn the once-ambitious wizard about the deep pits in the floor. "Better not fall into one of them. I don't want to find you dead and useless when I return." The tone seemed to imply that Keyes would be punished if he was impertinent enough to kill himself. And then the god was gone.

The newly-blinded man was seized by an instinctive need to try to hide, some vague idea of groping his way voluntarily even farther down into the earth. Maybe the god who'd caught him would forget about him—maybe he wouldn't even notice if Keyes disappeared—

But soon enough the man in the cave ceased his gasping and whimpering, his pointless attempt to burrow into the stone floor, and regained enough self-possession to reassure himself that although his vision was effectively gone, at least his eyeballs had not been ripped out. As far as he could tell his lids were simply closed, and he could not open them. There was no pain as long as he did not try. Attempts to force his eyes open with his fingers hurt horribly, but produced not even a pinhole's worth of vision.

Physically his body seemed to be undamaged. But he felt that even more important components of his being, directly accessible to the divine intervention, had been violated . . .

Presently, his mind having begun to work again at least intermittently, he went on groping his way around the cave, in search of some way out, or at least of better knowledge of his prison. He had barely glimpsed even the entrance to the cave before his sight was taken from him. It was warmer down here out of the wind, so much so that he shed some of his furs. In some locations, as he moved about, he was able to feel the warmth of the sun, which was now beginning to be high enough to penetrate the cave. There was tantalizing hope in the red glow of the direct sun through his sealed eyelids.

In a conscious effort to force himself to think logically, Keyes took an inventory of his assets. He had the clothes he was wearing, a small dagger sheathed at his side, and a small pack on his back, which his captor had allowed him to retain. The pack contained a little food, and very little else.

Lo-Yang, Keyes's assistant on his dangerous quest for knowledge, had been ignored by the deity who had grabbed Keyes up. And moments later the stout apprentice, unpursued, had scrambled successfully away, running for his life in the direction of the distant camp where he and Keyes had left their riding-beasts.

After sprinting only a short distance, Lo-Yang, out of shape and also unable to endure the suspense, had felt compelled to look back. Then he had paused, panting. The god who had caught Keyes was in the act of disappearing underground, his prisoner in hand. All the other gods were considerably more distant, and none of them were paying the least attention to Lo-Yang.

Fatalistically, the apprentice dared to crouch behind a rock and wait, catching his breath. Paradoxically his fear had become more manageable, now that the worst, or almost the worst, had come to pass.

Presently the great god who had taken Keyes—Lo-Yang was able to identify Mars, by the helmet the god was wearing, and by his general aspect—Mars came up out of the ground again, but without his prisoner, and went striding away to rejoin his colleagues.

Time passed, and the sun rose higher. The frightened apprentice remained behind his rock. Eventually, gradually, the council of the gods broke up, though not entirely. The remnants, still wrangling, moved even farther off.

When it seemed to Lo-Yang that all the gods were safely out of the way, he crept out from behind his rock, and dared to come back to the upper rim of the cave, looking for Keyes. With a surge of relief he saw that his master was at least still alive.

But Keyes took no notice when his apprentice waved. Lo-Yang called down to him cautiously.

At the sound the man below raised his head, turning it to and fro, in a feverish motion that spoke of near-despair and sudden hope. "Lo-Yang? I'm blind, I . . ."

"Oh."

"Lo-Yang, is that you? Where are the gods?"

"Yes sir, I am here." The apprentice raised his head, squinting into the sunlight, then looked down again. "They're all moving away, at the moment. Slowly. Still bickering among themselves. No one's paying any attention to us. Master, if Mars has blinded you, what are we going to do?"

"Your voice seems to come from a long way above me."

"I'd say twelve meters, master, or maybe a little more. I saw him carry you down there, and I thought . . ."

"Lo-Yang, get me out of here, somehow."

The young man surveyed the entrance to the cave below, and shook his head. It pained him to see his proud master reduced to such a state of helplessness, to hear an unfamiliar quaver in the voice usually so proud. "We need a long rope, master. Looking at these rock walls, I wouldn't dare to try to climb down without one. I'd only fall in there with you, and . . ."

"Yes. Of course. And you have no magic that will get me out."

"Unhappily, master, you have as yet taught me nothing that would be useful in this situation."

"Yes. Quite true. And I also find that my own magic has been taken from me, along with my sight." Keyes paused. When he spoke again, his voice had lost its urgency, had become slow and resigned. His shoulders slumped. "Hurry back to our camp, then, and get the rope. We have a coil in the large pack."

"Yes, master." A pause. "It might take me a couple of hours, or even longer, to get there and back. Even if I bring our riding-beasts back with me. Should I bring them back here, master?"

"Yes. No! I don't know, I leave the details to you. Go!"

"Yes, master." And Keyes could hear the first few footsteps, hurrying away. Then silence.

He was alone.

Fiercely Keyes commanded himself to be active, more to keep himself from dwelling on his fate than out of any real hope. Slowly the approximate dimensions and contours of the flatter portions of the cave's floor revealed themselves to the blind man's probing.

With his hands he explored as much of the walls as he could reach. Seemingly the god had not lied. The cave consisted of a deep shaft, down which Keyes had been carried, and an adjoining room or alcove whose bottom remained in shade. The whole space accessible to the prisoner's cautious crawling was no larger than the floor of a small house, and it was basically one big room. Here and there around the perimeter were certain crevices which might, for all Keyes could tell, lead to other exits. But the crevices were too narrow for him to force his body into them. He was going to have to wait until Lo-Yang got back, with the rope.

If Lo-Yang came back in time.

If the assistant ever came back at all. If he had any intention of doing so. Mentally the newly-helpless magician reviewed the times in the past when he had treated his apprentice unjustly. He had hardly ever beaten him. Surely, on the whole, he had been a fair master, and even kind . . .

Mindful of the divine warning about pits, Keyes continued his exploration for the most part on all fours, and, when he did stand up, walked very carefully. By this means he located several perilous gaps in the floor, holes into which tossed pebbles dropped for a long count before clicking on bottom. Presently in his groping about the cave he came upon some bones. After he had found a skull or two, he became convinced that the bulk of the bones were human, evidence that other human victims had died in this cave before him. Sacrifices, perhaps? Or simply unlucky hunters, blinded by night or by driving snow, who had fallen in by accident.

Lo-Yang had said that the god was Mars—and Mars had said that he was coming back, and soon. Mars had spoken of using Keyes in some kind of an experiment . . . . Once more quivering with horror and fear, the trapped man persevered in his compulsive search for something, anything, that might offer him some chance of escape.

And so it was that at last, behind some loose rocks in the corner farthest from the entrance, the blind man's trembling, groping fingers fell upon something that was round, and smooth, and narrow, and was not rock. When he pulled on the object, it came toward him.

When he stood up again, he was holding in both hands the padded, meter-long weight of a sheathed Sword.

Even with his sense of magic almost numbed by Mars, Keyes could tell this was no ordinary weapon. He had no real doubt of what he had discovered, though he had never seen or touched one of Vulcan's Swords before, and had not expected to ever have the chance to touch one—at least not for a long, long time.

Thanks to his magical investigations at a distance, the difficult, painstaking studies he'd carried out even before the forging of the Blades had been completed, he knew the Twelve Swords well in theory—understood them better, no doubt, than all but a few of the gods yet did. But how one of the Twelve Blades had come to be tucked away in the remotest corner of an obscure cave was more than the human magician could understand. Certainly it had not been placed there for him to find; only his fanatical thoroughness in searching, his determination to keep busy, had led him to the discovery.

Slowly one possible explanation took shape in the man's mind: One of the divine gang might have stolen another's Sword, as a prank or as a ploy in their great mysterious Game, and had found a handy, nearby hiding place at the very bottom of this cave.

Impulse urged Keyes to draw the unknown Sword at once, to end, if possible, the suspense of waiting in ignorance, and to endow himself immediately with whatever powers his find might confer upon him—but there was one ominous contingency which made him hesitate. Fate, or some cruel trickster of a god, might have given him Soulcutter.

He was aware that in recent months his ambition had, perhaps more than once, irritated certain of the gods. Until now, by good fortune, none of them had become more than half-aware of him, as humans might be vaguely cognizant of some troublesome insect in the air nearby—but his magic, practiced as subtly as possible on Vulcan's human assistant, had been clever and strong enough to bring him extensive theoretical knowledge of the Twelve Swords and their unique powers.

It was utterly frustrating that he had no way to determine which Sword lay in his hands. He knew that all but one of the Twelve Blades were marked with distinguishing white symbols on their black hilts—a target shape for Farslayer, a human eye for Sight-blinder, and so on. But sightless Keyes had no way to perceive the sign, if any, on the Sword he held. Holding his breath, he tried with all his will and care to find and read the symbol with his fingertips—but for all he was able to discern by touch, there was no sign there to read.

Ah, if only Lo-Yang with his two good eyes had stayed with him a little longer!

Suppose it was only the black hilt, unrelieved—that would mean that he was holding Soulcutter. Keyes shuddered. But he could not be sure. The odds seemed to be against it. For all he knew, there might very well be a symbol right under his hand, dead flush with the rest of the hilt, indistinguishable by touch.

Everything depended upon his finding out. An enemy more powerful than any demon had stuffed him into this hole, and was coming back, perhaps at any moment now, to use him in an experiment. It was vitally important to identify the Sword, before he made any plan to use it.

Which one did he have?

Well, there was one sure way by which Soulcutter, at least, could be ruled out. Hesitantly Keyes began to draw the weapon, starting it first one centimeter out of its sheath, then two. Meanwhile he held his breath, hoping that if the hilt in his hand was indeed Soulcutter's, he could retain enough sense of purpose to muzzle that deadliest of all Blades again before its growing power overwhelmed him with hopelessness, before all possible actions, and even life itself, were robbed of meaning.

If this experiment should demonstrate that he was holding the Sword of Despair, Keyes decided that he was desperate enough to use it, by threatening to draw it against the returning god.

His cautious tugging was exposing more and more of the Blade, but still no black cloud of despair rose up to engulf Keyes. He felt no more miserable with the Sword half-drawn. With a sigh of relief he concluded that his prize had to be one of the other eleven.

He pulled hard on the unseen hilt, and with a faint, singing sigh, the long steel came completely free.

Keyes soon disposed of any lingering doubt in his own mind that the weapon he held was genuinely one of the Twelve Swords. Proof lay in the facts of its unbreakableness, and that the extreme keenness of the edges—he tested them on the tough leather of his dagger's sheath—could not be dulled by repeated bashing on rock.

Several of the Swords, his earlier investigations had informed him, ought to produce distinguishing noises when they went into action. But the only sound so far generated by this one was the bright clang, purely mechanical, of thin steel on tough rock.

The blind man uttered a prayer to Ardneh that the hilt he was gripping belonged to Woundhealer, and that that Sword's power would let him see again. Feverish with hope, maneuvering the long Blade awkwardly, he nicked first his eyebrow, finally the bridge of his nose and very eyelids, with the keen edge. All he achieved were stinging pains and a blood-smeared face. His fevered hope that he might be holding the Sword of Healing, that its steel would pass painlessly, bloodlessly, into his flesh on its mission of restoration—that hope was lost in a few drops of blood.

Hope was lost briefly but not killed. Actually his situation would be better if this was one of the other Swords, carrying some power that could free him completely from his enemy.

Under the stress of his predicament, the attributes and powers, even the names of all the Swords seemed to have fled his memory. Might this be Wayfinder, then, or Coinspinner?

Keyes whispered a short string of urgent requests to the magic Blade he held. He asked it to show him how he might get out of the cave, and where he might find help. When nothing happened, he repeated his demands more loudly, but as far as he could tell, he was granted no response of any kind. In this situation, either Coinspinner or Wayfinder ought to be pulling his gripping hands around, bending his wrists in a particular direction, showing him the way he ought to move. And Coinspinner, whether it indicated any particular direction or not, would bring him great good luck, in fact whatever extreme of luck he needed. If necessary the Sword of Chance could call up an earthquake on behalf of its client, to shatter the rocky cage around him and let him walk or climb away unharmed.

But nothing of the sort was happening. Two more possibilities, it seemed, eliminated.

When it occurred to Keyes to make the effort, testing for Stonecutter was simple enough. One thing he had in ample supply down here was rock. And Stonecutter in fact could be just what a man in his situation needed, the very tool with which to carve his way out, creating a tunnel or a stair, slicing hard stone as easily as packed snow.

But the cave's walls did not yield effortlessly to this Sword when he swung it against them, then tried it as a saw. Now he realized that his first attempts to test the durability of the blade ought to have been enough to convince him of this fact. Hard, noisy hacking produced only dust in the air, small chips and fragments which stung the man's blind face. A steady pressure, indestructible edge against limestone, did no better.

Well, then, quite possibly he was holding Farslayer. But Keyes could think of no way to distinguish that Sword from its fellows, short of naming a victim and throwing it with intent to kill. The stony walls that closed him in would pose no obstacle to the Sword of Vengeance, which would pass through granite as through so much air, if that were necessary to reach its prey. Farslayer would kill at any distance—but would not come back peacefully to its user. To employ that weapon at a distance was to lose it, and even should Keyes succeed in slaying the god who had trapped him here, he would still be trapped.

His musings were interrupted by the onslaught of a swarm of large, furry, carnivorous bats. No doubt disturbed by the racket he'd been making, the creatures came fluttering out of some of the high, dim recesses of the deep cave. Indifferent to sunlight, they erupted from their holes by tens or dozens to threaten Keyes, who at the sound of their approach got his back against a wall and raised his Sword.

He could hear the bats piping, crying out blurred words in their thin little voices, uttering incoherent threats and slaverings of blood-hunger. They were flapping their wings violently—they got close enough to let him feel the breeze of their wings, and he cringed from the expected pain of their needle-like teeth and claws—but that did not follow. In blind desperation he waved the naked Sword at his attackers, and he remained untouched. Once the blade clanged accidentally on rock, but he had no sensation of it striking anything fleshy in midair. Still, one after another, the little bat-cries became shrieks of anguish, and then died away.

Panting, gripping the hilt of his still-unknown weapon with both hands, Keyes stood waiting, straining his ears in silence. Not a bat had touched him yet, nor had he touched them, but when he cautiously changed his position by a step or two, his foot came down on a dead one. Gingerly he felt the furry little thing with his free hand, making sure of what it was, then kicked it away from him.

Not Farslayer, then. Whichever Sword he held had somehow killed at least one animal without making physical contact.

The bats had not been routed for more than a minute or so when the demon arrived—drawn up out of the rocks, perhaps, by a sense of the proximity of helpless human prey, or simply by the disturbance man and bats were making.

Even sightless as he was, Keyes could tell that a demon was near him, and coming nearer. He knew it by the feeling of sickness, a gut-deep wretchedness, that preceded the monster's physical presence. Again the man experienced overwhelming fear, panic that made him cry out and tremble. Better to be torn to bits by flesh-devouring bats than to wind up in a demon's gut, where flesh was the last component of humanity to be destroyed.

And then he heard the creature's hideous voice, a tone of dry bones breaking, dead leaves rattling, reverberating more in the man's mind than in his ears. It sounded as if it were standing almost within arm's length of Keyes.

With stately formality the demon announced its name. "I am Korku. Will you introduce yourself?"

"My name is Keyes."

"Unhappy man named Keyes! Here you are down in this deep hole with no way to get out. And newly blind! Is it possible that you have angered a god? If so, that was unwise."

"He's coming back, the god who put me here. He'll be angry if anything happens to me."

"Oh, will he? But he is not here now."

Keyes was silent. His lungs kept wanting to pant for air, for extra breath with which to scream, and he struggled to control the urge.

The demon said: "It is too bad that you are unable to appreciate my beauty visually. If only you could see me, I am confident that you would be—overwhelmed. Most humans are."

"Go away."

"Not likely." The dry bones crackled, the sound formed itself into words. "Not until you have handed over to me that ridiculous splinter of metal you now clutch so tightly. Then I will leave you in peace to wait for your dear god."

"Go away!" Keyes tightened his grip upon the unknown hilt.

In response came a voiceless snarl that made his hair stand up, and then the voice again: "Hand it over, I say! Or I will cut you into a thousand pieces with your own weapon, and swallow you a piece at a time—and put you back together in my gut, where you will dwell for a million years in torment."

"Not likely!" Keyes replied in turn. He thought it quite possible that this demon had as yet learned nothing about the Twelve Swords and their god-given powers. Or maybe the damned thing had learned just enough, or guessed enough, to make it determined to have this Sword for itself. But demons were notoriously cowardly; and so far it was being cautious.

This was not the man's first contact with a demon—no magician adept enough to acquire deep skill was able to avoid all encounters with that evil race. But only magicians who had turned their faces against humanity entered willingly into commerce with such monsters, and Keyes still found pride in being human. In his present desperate situation, he might well have tried to bargain with a demon to lend him its perception, as other more powerful and unscrupulous wizards had been known to do—but he had nothing with which to bargain.

Except his unknown Sword; and that was all he had. He continued to brandish the mysterious weapon at his latest enemy, instead of handing it over as Korku had commanded.

The demon tried a few more arguments. It shouted at Keyes more loudly. But presently, when it saw that it was getting nowhere with mere words, it lost patience and reached out for the man with its half-material talons.

Keyes saw nothing of his enemy's extended limbs. Nothing at all happened to the blind man waiting. But he heard Korku's screaming threats break off abruptly in a muffled, bubbling sound. Then came a soft thump, as of a heavy mass of wet pulp falling some distance upon rock, followed by a slithering, which gradually receded.

Then silence.

Straining to hear more, unable to interpret what he had heard, the man uttered a small moan, compounded mostly of relief with a strong component of tormented puzzlement. Again his Sword, whichever Sword he held, had saved him somehow!

Yes, the demon must have been defeated. But perhaps not slain, not annihilated. Keyes probed about on the cave floor with the point of his Sword, and his imagination shuddered at the image of himself stepping blindly into a demon's body.

For several minutes he discovered nothing more helpful than a few more dead or dying bats. But eventually, when the blind man bent, listening intently over the brink of a certain deep but narrow pit, he heard Korku again. A tiny, screaming, threatening voice, muffled almost below the threshold of hearing, rose from the distant bottom of the pit.

After listening for a little while, the man dared to call down: "Korku? What has happened to you?"

The faint sounds coming back included nothing he could interpret as an answer—and, in any case, a human would be foolish to trust anything a demon said.

Logical thinking was still required—was more essential now than ever, since time was passing, and Mars would be coming back to subject his prisoner to some unknown horror. But logic was still difficult to sustain. By eliminating possibilities Keyes had made a beginning in the task of identifying his weapon. But the task was not accomplished. Which possibilities had he not yet considered?

There was Dragonslicer. There was Townsaver. There was Doomgiver, of course. Ah, in that last name might lie some real hope of survival! If only Keyes could be certain that he had the Sword of Justice in his hands, then he would dare to brazenly defy the gods. Even gods would risk bringing disaster on their own heads if they tried to try to harm him further. For example, if they poured in fire or water on him, he might make his way out to find them all burned or drowned.

Unless . . .

Unless, of course, one of the gods confronting him happened to be armed with Shieldbreaker. If Keyes's extensive research was correct, and so far he had no reason to doubt its accuracy, no other weapon in the world, not even another Sword, could ever stand against the Sword of Force.

The thought of Shieldbreaker gave him pause. Suppose that he, Keyes, was now holding that one? Shieldbreaker's invincible presence in his hand would have easily disposed of the demon, and the bats. But wait—here in the presence of enemies and danger, the Sword of Force ought to be audibly beating its drum-note of power.

Of course the drawback to relying upon Shieldbreaker was that any unarmed god, unarmed man, or unarmed child for that matter, could easily take that Sword away from whoever held it, regardless of the holder's normal strength.

Keyes, probing gently with one finger at the slight self-inflicted cuts around his face, decided that the bleeding had already stopped. He tried desperately to recall whether wounds made by one Sword or another ought to heal quickly or slowly. But that information, if he had ever possessed it, escaped his memory.

Touch, smell, taste, none of them of any use in his predicament—but hearing! In that sense might lie his way to the answer!

Thinking, keeping track by counting on his fingers, Keyes decided that seven of the Swords, if all he had found out about them was correct, generated some kind of sound when they went into action. The other five exerted their individual powers in silence.

The man's thoughts were interrupted by a pair of deep booming voices up above, outside the cave. The conversation of the gods was still somewhat muffled with distance, but coming closer at a pace no walking mortals could have matched. They were speaking to each other in the god-language that Keyes did not understand.

Mars, the god who had put Keyes in the cave, was coming back, holding like a toothpick between two fingers the sheathed metal of the weapon he had just been given by Vulcan, and now wanted to test. Hermes, a fellow-player in the Game, came with him, and the two deities discussed the matter as they walked.

The Wargod's plan was to drop Soulcutter into the cave for Keyes to find, and let the man draw it, just to see what effect the Tyrant's Blade really had on humans. Vulcan had promised the Council that Soulcutter—and indeed all the Swords—would have tremendous, overwhelming impact upon all lesser beings.

Mars commented: "I expect our respective worshipers will be using the Swords a great deal on each other, you know, when the Game really gets going."

"What if he doesn't draw it?" his companion asked.

"My man down in the hole? I think he will. Oh, not intending to use it on us!" Mars laughed. "I doubt he'll be that arrogant. But there are some vermin down there, bats and such, that are probably bothering him already. He'll want the best tool he can get to fight them off."

Hermes shook his head. "Those flesh-eating bats? They may have finished him by now."

Mars frowned. "You think so? He was carrying a little dagger of his own."

"But getting back to this Sword, Soulcutter—what about the effect on us? We'll be nearby, won't we, when your subject draws the weapon?"

"Bah, nothing we can't overcome, I'm sure. And I understand that Soulcutter's effect on humans, whatever it may be precisely, spreads comparatively slowly."

Keyes continued to listen intently when the two voices stopped, not far above him. He was startled, and immediately suspicious, when a moment later he heard some object, obviously dropped by one of the beings above, come providentially bouncing and sliding down into the cave, landing with a thump practically at his feet.

Without loosening his grip on the hilt already in his possession, he groped his way forward to where he could put his free hand on the fallen object, and identify it as another sheathed Sword.

Only now, it seemed, did the pair of gods above really take notice of the man who was trapped below, and of the sprinkling of dead and mortally wounded bats around him. Only now did they observe that their subject was already holding a drawn Sword.

Mars's companion pointed down, in outrage. "Look at that! Where in the world did he get *that?*"

And Mars himself, gone red-faced, bellowed: "You down there! Drop that Sword at once! It doesn't belong to you, you have no business using it!"

Keyes needed all his resolution to keep from yielding to that shouted command. But instead of dropping his Sword, he raised its point in the general direction of his enemies, as if saluting them, and turned his blind face up to them at the same time—let them do their damnedest. He had naught to lose.

He called out, in a voice that quavered only once: "You have just given me another Sword—why?"

"Impudent monkey!" the Wargod shouted back. "Draw it, and find out!"

They have given me Soulcutter now—it is the only Blade one would give to an enemy.

But trapped as he was, his life already forfeit, Keyes saw no other course than to accept the gamble. Silently he bent again, swiftly he pulled the second Sword out of its sheath. Doubly armed, he straightened to confront his tormentors.

The sun was shining fully on the man's face, and in an amazing moment he was once again able to see the sun. Whatever magic spell had blinded him was abruptly broken, and his lids came open easily. His eyes were streaming now with pent-up tears, but through the tears he could see the two gods on the high rim of the cave.

He could see the two tall, powerful figures quite clearly enough to tell that they were gods—and also that they were stricken, paralyzed with Soulcutter's poisonous despair, turned back on them by Doomgiver. The strands of their own magic had come undone. Keyes could recognize Mars, who'd captured him, and now Mars abruptly sat down on the rim of the pit, for all the world like a human who suddenly felt faint. The Wargod slumped in that position, legs dangling, for a long moment staring at nothing. Then he buried his face in his hands.

The other god—Keyes, seeing the winged sandals, now knew Hermes—took no notice of this odd behavior, but slowly turned his back on the cave and his companion, and went stumbling off across a rocky hillside. Now and then Hermes put out one hand to grope before him, like a blind man in the sun. In a moment his mighty figure had vanished from Keyes's field of view.

Doomgiver had prevailed! The Sword of Justice had turned Soulcutter's dark power back upon the one who would have used it against Keyes, while immunizing the mere man who had been the intended target. Both gods on the rim of the pit had been caught in the dark force, as must everyone else in range of its slow spread.

Keyes almost cried out in triumph, but the hard truth restrained him. He was still a prisoner. His own eyes, searching the smooth cave walls, now confirmed that neither Lo-Yang nor Mars had lied about the hopelessness of his trying to climb out.

He was beginning to feel dizzy, and ill-at-ease, a normal reaction in one holding any two naked Swords simultaneously. Now he could easily see the symbol, a hollow white circle, on Doomgiver's hilt. To keep himself from collapsing he had no choice but to put away the other Blade, the unmarked one. He slid the Sword of Despair back into its sheath, and his rising dizziness immediately abated.

In this case, at least, Doomgiver's power had been dominant over that of another Sword. There was at least a chance that some of the other Swords might also prove inferior to Doomgiver. That anyone hurling Farslayer would be himself skewered by the Sword of Vengeance. That Sightblinder's user would see a terrifying apparition, but would himself remain vulnerably visible. That the wielder of the Mindsword would be condemned to worship his would-be victim. And Coinspinner's master would suffer excruciatingly bad luck.

But of Shieldbreaker's overall dominance there could be no doubt. And the unanswered question still gnawed at Keyes: Which god had Shieldbreaker? Or might that Sword have somehow come into the hands of another human?

After Soulcutter was muzzled again, a minute or two passed before Mars, who was still sitting on the rim of the cave, took his hands down from his face. The Wargod's expression was blank, and he appeared to be sweating heavily. His great body swayed, and Keyes thought for a moment that the god was going to topple into the pit. But instead Mars, taking no notice of the man below, shifted his weight and turned. Quietly, on all fours, he crawled away from the cave's mouth and out of sight.

Keyes knew that Soulcutter's effects ought to linger for several days, at least, in humans. Probably the stunned gods would recover somewhat more quickly, but how soon they might come back to deal with him, Keyes did not know. When they did, he would have to risk drawing the Sword of Despair again—even though Doomgiver might not protect him next time. This time Soulcutter, though in his own hands, had really been a weapon directed against him by another.

What now?

Pacing nervously about in the confined space, trying desperately to imagine what he might do next, Keyes paused to look down into the hole from whence the demon's muffled groans still rose. Far below, almost lost in shadow, something moved. Something as big as a milk-beast, but truly hideous to look at, like a mass of diseased entrails. In a moment Keyes realized that Korku on attacking him had suffered Doomgiver's justice—the demon had promptly found himself folded painfully into his own gut, in effect turned inside out. When that had happened, the self-bound and helpless thing, still almost immortal, had gone rolling away to plunge into the deeper pit.

Now the creature in the pit, perhaps sensing that the man was near, was turning its muffled, barely audible threats to equally faint pleas and extravagant bargainings for help. Keyes made no answer. Probably he could not have done anything, if he had wanted to, to relieve the demon's doom.

Some minutes later, Mars, who was still in the process of gradually regaining his wits, and his sense of divine purpose, was having speech again with Hermes. They were standing fifty meters or so from the cave.

"What happened?" demanded Hermes, who seemed to be recovering somewhat more rapidly.

Mars stood blinking at him. Then he proclaimed defiantly: "To me? Nothing. A little test of the Sword called Soulcutter. As you see, there was no great harm done."

His companion stared at him in disbelief. "No great harm? We both of us were stupefied! You should say that nothing happened to your human in the cave—except that his sight was restored, when your magic came undone. Oh, and he still has his Sword—no, now he has two of them!"

The Wargod remained determined to put a good face on the whole situation. "But he was forced to put away the one that annoyed us." As usual, his tone was bellicose.

"Annoyed!"

Hermes went on to insist that dropping Soulcutter into the pit had been a serious mistake, in fact a debacle had resulted. Other gods must have been at least somewhat affected. They were going to be angry about having been put at risk.

Mars, still struggling against the lingering effects of Soulcutter, refused to tolerate such an attitude. The very idea, that a *god* could be endangered, not simply inconvenienced, by Sword-powers!

Mars darted away, but soon came back. He had argued or bargained or bullied another of his colleagues into loaning him another Sword, which happened to be Stonecutter.

Again Hermes protested. "Your man in the cave now has two Swords—are you going to give him a third?"

Mars considered this mere sarcasm, unworthy of an answer. Muleheadedly determined to do what he had set out to do, conduct tests on his specimen, he announced that he was going back to the cave again, with a new plan in mind.

"I think we had better first consult the Council." Hermes paused. "Unless you are worried about what they might say," he added slyly.

"What? I? Worried?"

Keyes, pacing his open-air cell on weary legs, kept shooting frowning glances at the Sword of Despair where it lay on the cave floor. He was trying feverishly to think of some way he might trade the sheathed Soulcutter for his freedom. Suppose another god, or goddess, were to appear on the upper rim of the cave, and he suggested some kind of trade? But no, he doubted they would be in any mood for bargaining. And he was still unable to climb out of the pit unaided. His magical capabilities, which might have got him free, were stirring, but he could tell that their restoration was going to take much longer than that of his eyesight.

Again he was being threatened by a sense of hopelessness.

He had now been in the cave for hours, and straining to study the gods for long hours before Mars caught him. As the afternoon wore on, Keyes sat down to rest, and in a few moments fell helplessly into an exhausted, stuporous sleep—with Doomgiver still gripped in his right hand.

A number of the gods, including Mars and Hermes, had hastily reconvened in Council. They were enough, or so they said, to form a quorum. And they were much concerned with Shieldbreaker too. None of those present would admit to being in possession of that weapon, or to knowing where it was. Who had received it in the lottery? Regrettably Vulcan was absent, and could not be asked. Maybe he would not have revealed the secret anyway.

Around midafternoon, the Council passed a resolution stating it as their intention that all Swords should be reclaimed from human possession.

Mars the warrior, still stubbornly determined to establish himself as above Sword-power, volunteered to enforce the order.

Zeus told him to go ahead. Others, enough, it seemed, for a majority, were in agreement. "If there is any real problem, you seem to have caused it. Therefore you should find a remedy!"

Still, Hermes once again tried to argue Mars out of taking too direct an approach. "Doomgiver has now overcome you twice—wait, let me finish! I tell you, we must either arrange to borrow Shieldbreaker from whoever has it, or else get that other Sword out of the man's hand by guile."

"Guile, is it? I have other ideas about that. And I wasn't overcome. I was only taken unawares, and—and *distracted* for a moment. Who said that I was overcome?" Mars glowered fiercely.

Hermes heaved a sigh of divine proportions. "Have it your own way, then."

. . . and then Lo-Yang, like some figure out of a dream, was bending over Keyes, shaking him awake. The magician's body convulsed in a nervous start, bringing him up into a sitting position. He comprehended with amazement that his apprentice had returned after all. He saw the long, thin rope, its upper end secured somehow, hanging down into the cave.

"Master! Thank Ardneh, you can see again! What's happened? Your face is all dried blood. And what are these two swords?"

"Never mind my face. Pick up that Sword on the floor, and bring it with us, but as you value your life, do not even imagine yourself drawing it. Let us go!"

They scrambled toward the rope. But before either of the men could start to climb, Mars appeared, his face set in a mask of stubborn anger, and put out one finger to snap the long rope from its fastening at its upper end.

Keyes could feel all hope die with the falling coil.

Mars said nothing, but he was smiling, ominously. And he had another Sword in hand. It was soon plain which Sword this was, for the god wielding it began carving out a block of stone, part of the solid cave-roof. It was a huge slab, and when it fell the men trapped in the cave would have to be very alert and lucky to dodge it and escape quick death.

Lo-Yang collapsed on his knees, forehead to the ground.

Mars's companion, he of the winged sandals, was standing back a little watching, with the attitude of one who has serious misgivings but is afraid or at least reluctant to interfere.

Maybe, thought Keyes suddenly, all hope is not dead after all. A moment later, he could see the sudden opening to the sky as the block of stone came loose. Aiming Doomgiver at it like a spear, he saw the slab twist in the air, and then fall up instead of down, looping through the precise curve necessary to bring it into violent contact with the Wargod's own head.

Mars reeled, and his helmet, grossly dented, flew aside. Only a god could have survived such an impact. The Wargod did not even lose consciousness, but in his shock let Stonecutter fall from his hand into the cave, the bare Blade clanging on rock.

"Now you know as well as I do, what I have here." At first Keyes whispered the words. Then he shouted them at the top of his voice. "Doomgiver! Doomgiver! *I hold the blessed Sword of Justice!*"

Mars, battered, lacking his helmet but refusing to admit that he was even slightly dazed, still pigheadedly confident of his own prowess, came down into the cave with some dignity, treading thin air as before. Mars was coming to take the Sword back, hand-to-hand, from Keyes. Well, Shieldbreaker could be captured that way, couldn't it? And it the strongest Sword of all?

While the two men cowered back, the god first grabbed up the sheathed Soulcutter, and tossed it carelessly up and out of the cave, well out of the humans' reach. Any god who thought he needed a Sword's help could pick it up!

Then Mars turned his attention to Doomgiver, and confronted the stubborn man who held it. Keyes noted with some amazement that his great opponent, bruised as he was, appeared less angry now than he had at the start of the adventure; in fact the Wargod was gazing at Keyes with a kind of grudging appreciation.

"You seem a brave man, with the fiber I like to see among my followers. I would be willing to accept your worship. And for all I care personally, you might keep Vulcan's bit of steel and magic. Humans might retain them all; we who possess the strength of gods have no need of such—such tricks. But the Council has decided otherwise. Therefore, on behalf of the Council, I—"

And Mars reached out confidently, to reclaim Doomgiver from Keyes's unsteady grip—but somehow the Sword in the man's hand eluded the god's grasp. Mars tried again, and failed again—and then his effort was interrupted.

A roaring polyphonic outcry reached the cave, a wave of divine anger coming from the place a hundred meters distant where the Council had so recently passed its resolution.

"My Sword is gone!" one of the distant voices bellowed, expressing utter outrage.

"And mine!" another answered, yelling anguish.

The protest swelled into a chorus, each with the same complaint. Keyes could not interpret the wind-blown, shouted words. But he needed only a moment to deduce their meaning. Mars acting in the Council's name and with its authority had assaulted a man who held Doomgiver, by trying to deprive the man of his Sword, and intending to fling that Sword away—and Doomgiver had exacted its condign retaliation. The Council of Divinities had lost all of *their* Swords instead. The great majority of Vulcan's armory had been flung magically to the four winds, and lay scattered now across the world.

The uproar mounted, as more deities realized the truth. A number of gods at no great distance were violently cursing the name of Mars, and the Wargod was not one to let them get away with that. He listened for a moment, then rose in his divine wrath and mounted swiftly from the cave.

His mind was now wholly occupied with a matter of overriding importance—the names the others called him. So he had forgotten Stonecutter, which still lay where he had dropped it.

Several more hours had passed, and the westering sun was low and red, before Demeter returned to the cave in which she had hidden the Sword of Justice. She had wanted to get it out of the way for a time, so that her colleagues should not nag her with questions when they saw her carrying a Sword.

Demeter had spent most of the day thinking the matter over and had come to a decision. The Game still did not greatly appeal to her, and it would be best if she gave Doomgiver to someone else.

On her approach to the cave, Demeter observed the tracks of a pair of riding-beasts, both coming and going, and when she looked in over the edge of the deep hole, she beheld a set of crude steps, more like a ladder than a stair, freshly and cleanly hewn out of one solid wall. Human beings! No other creatures would carve steps.

Rising wind whined through the surrounding rock formations. The only living things now in the cave were a helplessly immortal demon, strangely trapped in a lower pit, and a few mortally wounded bats.

No need to look in the place where she had hidden her Sword, to know that it was gone. Well, why not? Let it go. Perhaps the humans needed Justice more than any of Demeter's divine colleagues did.

Perpetually at odds with each other as they were, the members of the Council needed some time to realize that their terrible Blades had been scattered across a continent, perhaps across the whole earth, among the swarms of contemptible humans. As that realization gradually took hold, the gods met the crisis in their usual fashion, by convening to enjoy one of their great, wrangling, all-but-useless arguments.

The only fact upon which all could agree was that their Swords had all been swept away from them. All the Swords, that is, except for Shieldbreaker, which remained, as far as could be determined, immune to the power of any other Sword, and thus would not have been affected by Doomgiver's blow.

But whichever divinity still possessed the Sword of Force was obviously refusing to reveal the fact, doubtless for fear it would be taken away by some unarmed opponent.

For good or ill, the Great Game was off to a roaring start.

BERSERKERS

BERSERKER, THE INTRODUCTION

I, THIRD HISTORIAN OF THE CARMPAN RACE, in gratitude to the Earth-descended race for their defense of my world, set down here for them my fragmentary vision of their great war against our common enemy.

The vision has been formed piece by piece through my contacts in past and present time with the minds of men and of machines. In these minds alien to me I often perceive what I cannot understand, yet what I see is true. And so I have truly set down the acts and words of Earth-descended men great and small and ordinary, the words and even the secret thoughts of your heroes and your traitors.

Looking into the past I have seen how in the twentieth century of your Christian calendar your forefathers on Earth first built radio detectors capable of sounding the deeps of interstellar space. On the day when whispers in our alien voices were first detected, straying in across the enormous intervals, the universe of stars became real to all Earth's nations and all her tribes.

They became aware of the real world surrounding them—a universe strange and immense beyond thought, possibly hostile, surrounding and shrinking all Earthmen alike. Like island savages just become aware of the great powers existing on and beyond their ocean, your nations began—sullenly, mistrustfully, almost against their will—to put aside their quarrels with one another.

In the same century the men of old Earth took their first steps into space. They studied our alien voices whenever they could hear us. And when the men of old Earth began to travel faster than light, they followed our voices to seek us out.

Your race and mine studied each other with eager science and with great caution and courtesy. We Carmpan and our older friends are more passive than you. We live in different environments and think mainly in different directions. We posed no threat to Earth. We saw to it that Earthmen were not crowded by our presence; physically and mentally they had to stretch to touch us. Ours, all the skills of keeping peace. Alas, for the day unthinkable that was to come, the day when we wished ourselves warlike!

You of Earth found uninhabited planets, where you could thrive in the warmth of suns much like your own. In large colonies and small you scattered yourselves across one segment of one arm of our slow-turning galaxy. To your settlers and frontiersmen the galaxy began to seem a friendly place, rich in worlds hanging ripe for your peaceful occupation.

The alien immensity surrounding you appeared to be not hostile after all. Imagined threats had receded behind horizons of silence and vastness. And so once more you allowed among yourselves the luxury of dangerous conflict, carrying the threat of suicidal violence.

No enforceable law existed among the planets. On each of your scattered colonies individual leaders maneuvered for personal power, distracting their people with real or imagined dangers posed by other Earth-descended men.

All further exploration was delayed, in the very days when the new and inexplicable radio voices were first heard drifting in from beyond your frontiers, the strange soon-to-be-terrible voices that conversed only in mathematics. Earth and Earth's colonies were divided each against all by suspicion, and in mutual fear were rapidly training and arming for war.

And at this point the very readiness for violence that had sometimes so nearly destroyed you, proved to be the means of life's survival. To us, the Carmpan watchers, the withdrawn seers and touchers of minds, it appeared that you had carried the crushing weight of war through all your history knowing that it would at last be needed, that this hour would strike when nothing less awful would serve.

When the hour struck and our enemy came without warning, you were ready with swarming battle-fleets. You were dispersed and dug in on scores of planets, and heavily armed. Because you were, some of you and some of us are now alive.

Not all our Carmpan psychology, our logic and vision and subtlety, would have availed us anything. The skills of peace and tolerance were useless, for our enemy was not alive.

What is thought, that mechanism seems to bring it forth?

STONE PLACE related by the Carmpan known as The Third Historian

For most men the war brought no miracles of healing, but a steady deforming pressure which seemed to have existed always, and which had no foreseeable end. Under this burden some men became like brutes, and the minds of others grew to be as terrible and implacable as the machines they fought against.

But I have touched a few rare human minds, the jewels of life, who rise to meet the greatest challenges by becoming supremely men.

STONE PLACE

Earth's Gobi Spaceport was perhaps the biggest in all the small corner of the galaxy settled by Solarian man and his descendants; at least so thought Mitchell Spain, who had seen most of those ports in his twenty-four years of life.

But looking down now from the crowded, descending shuttle, he could see almost nothing of the Gobi's miles of ramp. The vast crowd below, meaning only joyful welcome, had defeated its own purpose by forcing back and breaking the police lines. Now the vertical string of descending shuttle-ships had to pause, searching for enough clear room to land.

Mitchell Spain, crowded into the lowest shuttle with a thousand other volunteers, was paying little attention to the landing problem for the moment. Into this jammed compartment, once a luxurious observation lounge, had just come Johann Karlsen himself; and this was Mitch's first chance for a good look at the newly appointed High Commander of Sol's defense, though Mitch had ridden Karlsen's spear-shaped flagship all the way from Austeel.

Karlsen was no older than Mitchell Spain, and no taller, his shortness somehow surprising at first glance. He had become ruler of the planet Austeel through the influence of his half-brother, the mighty Felipe Nogara, head of the empire of Esteel; but Karlsen held his position by his own talents.

"This field may be blocked for the rest of the day," Karlsen was saying now, to a cold-eyed Earthman who had just come aboard the shuttle from an aircar. "Let's have the ports open, I want to look around."

Glass and metal slid and reshaped themselves, and sealed ports became small balconies open to the air of Earth, the fresh smells of a living planet—open, also, to the roaring chant of the crowd a few hundred feet below: "Karlsen! Karlsen!"

As the High Commander stepped out onto a balcony to survey for himself the chances of landing, the throng of men in the lounge made a half-voluntary brief surging movement, as if to follow. These men were mostly Austeeler volunteers, with a sprinkling of adventurers like Mitchell Spain, the Martian wanderer who had signed up on Austeel for the battle bounty Karlsen offered.

"Don't crowd, outlander," said a tall man ahead of Mitch, turning and looking down at him.

"I answer to the name of Mitchell Spain." He let his voice rasp a shade deeper than usual. "No more an outlander here than you, I think."

The tall one, by his dress and accent, came from Venus, a planet terraformed only within the last century, whose people were sensitive and proud in newness of independence and power. A Venerian might well be jumpy here, on a ship filled with men from a planet ruled by Felipe Nogara's brother.

"Spain—sounds like a Martian name," said the Venerian in a milder tone, looking down at Mitch.

Martians were not known for patience and long suffering. After another moment the tall one seemed to get tired of locking eyes and turned away.

The cold-eyed Earthman, whose face was somehow familiar to Mitch, was talking on the communicator, probably to the captain of the shuttle. "Drive on across the city, cross the Khosutu highway, and let down there."

Karlsen, back inside, said: "Tell him to go no more than about ten kilometers an hour, they seem to want to see me."

The statement was matter-of-fact; if people had made great efforts to see Johann Karlsen, it was only the courteous thing to greet them.

Mitch watched Karlsen's face, and then the back of his head, and the strong arms lifted to wave, as the High Commander stepped out again onto the little balcony. The crowd's roar doubled.

Is that all you feel, Karlsen, a wish to be courteous? Oh, no. my friend, you are acting. To be greeted with that thunder must do something vital to any man. It might exalt him; possibly it could disgust or frighten him, friendly as it was. You wear well your mask of courteous nobility, High Commander.

What was it like to be Johann Karlsen, come to save the world, when none of the really great and powerful ones seemed to care too much about it? With a bride of famed beauty to be yours when the battle had been won?

And what was brother Felipe doing today? Scheming, no doubt, to get economic power over yet another planet.

With another shift of the little mob inside the shuttle the tall Venerian moved from in front of Mitch, who could now see clearly out the port past Karlsen. Sea of faces, the old cliché, this was really it. How to write this . . . Mitch knew he would someday have to write it. If all men's foolishness was not permanently ended by the coming battle with the unliving, the battle bounty should suffice to let a man write for some time.

Ahead now were the bone-colored towers of Ulan Bator, rising beyond their fringe of suburban slideways and sunfields; and a highway; and bright multicolored pennants, worn by the aircars swarming out from the city in glad welcome. Now police aircars were keeping pace protectively with the spaceship, though there seemed to be no possible danger from anything but excess enthusiasm.

Another, special, aircar approached. The police craft touched it briefly and gently, then drew back with deference. Mitch stretched his neck, and made out a Carmpan insignia on the car. It was probably their ambassador to Sol, in person. The space shuttle eased to a dead slow creeping.

Some said that the Carmpan looked like machines themselves, but they were the strong allies of Earth-descended men in the war against the enemies of all life. If the Carmpan bodies were slow and squarish, their minds were visionary; if they were curiously unable to use force against any enemy, their indirect help was of great value.

Something near silence came over the vast crowd as the ambassador reared himself up in his open car, from his head and body, ganglions of wire and fiber stretched to make a hundred connections with Carmpan animals and equipment around him.

The crowd recognized the meaning of the network; a great sigh went up. In the shuttle, men jostled one another trying for a better view. The cold-eyed Earth-man whispered rapidly into the communicator.

"Prophecy!" said a hoarse voice, near Mitch's ear.

"—of Probability!" came the ambassador's voice, suddenly amplified, seeming to pick up the thought in midphrase. The Carmpan Prophets of Probability were half mystics, half cold mathematicians. Karlsen's aides must have decided, or known, that this prophecy was going to be a favorable, inspiring thing which the crowd should hear, and had ordered the ambassador's voice picked up on a public address system.

"The hope, the living spark, to spread the flame of life!" The inhuman mouth chopped out the words, which still rose ringingly. The armlike appendages pointed straight to Karlsen, level on his balcony with the hovering aircar. "The dark metal thoughts are now of victory, the dead things make their plan to kill us all. But in this man before me now, there is life greater than any strength of metal. A power of life, to resonate—in all of us. I see. with Karlsen, victory—"

The strain on a Carmpan prophet in action was always immense, just as his accuracy was always high. Mitch had heard that the stresses involved were more topological than nervous or electrical. He had heard it, but like most Earth-descended, had never understood it.

"Victory," the ambassador repeated. "Victory . . . and then. . . ."

Something changed in the non-Solarian face. The cold-eyed Earthman was perhaps expert in reading alien expressions, or was perhaps just taking no chances. He whispered another command, and the amplification was taken from the Carmpan voice. A roar of approval mounted up past shuttle and aircar, from the great throng who thought the prophecy complete. But the ambassador had not finished, though now only those a few meters in front of him, inside the shuttle, could hear his faltering voice.

". . . then death, destruction, failure." The square body bent, but the alien eyes were still riveted on Karlsen. "He who wins everything . . . will die owning nothing. . . ."

The Carmpan bent down and his aircar moved away. In the lounge of the shuttle there was silence. The hurrahing outside sounded like mockery.

After long seconds, the High Commander turned in from the balcony and raised his voice: "Men, we who have heard the finish of the prophecy are few—but still we are many, to keep a secret. So I don't ask for secrecy. But spread the word, too, that I have no faith in prophecies that are not of God. The Carmpan have never claimed to be infallible."

The gloomy answer was unspoken, but almost telepathically loud among the group. Nine times out of ten, the Carmpan are right. There will be a victory, then death and failure.

But did the dark ending apply only to Johann Karlsen, or to the whole cause of the living? The men in the shuttle looked at one another, wondering and murmuring.

The shuttles found space to land, at the edge of Ulan Bator. Disembarking, the men found no chance for gloom, with a joyous crowd growing thicker by the moment around the ships. A lovely Earth girl came, wreathed in garlands, to throw a flowery loop around Mitchell Spain, and to kiss him. He was an ugly man, quite unused to such willing attentions.

Still, he noticed when the High Commander's eye fell on him.

"You, Martian, come with me to the General Staff meeting. I want to show a representative group in there so they'll know I'm not just my brother's agent. I need one or two who were born in Sol's light."

"Yes, sir." Was there no other reason why Karlsen had singled him out? They stood together in the crowd, two short men looking levelly at each other. One ugly and flower-bedecked, his arm still around a girl who stared with sudden awed recognition at the other man, who was magnetic in a way beyond handsomeness or ugliness. The ruler of a planet, perhaps to be the savior of all life.

"I like the way you keep people from standing on your toes in a crowd," said Karlsen to Mitchell Spain. "Without raising your voice or uttering threats. What's your name and rank?"

Military organization tended to be vague, in this war where everything that lived was on the same side. "Mitchell Spain, sir. No rank assigned, yet. I've been training with the marines. I was on Austeel when you offered a good battle bounty, so here I am."

"Not to defend Mars?"

"I suppose, that too. But I might as well get paid for it."

Karlsen's high-ranking aides were wrangling and shouting now, about groundcar transportation to the staff meeting. This seemed to leave Karlsen with time to talk. He thought, and recognition flickered on his face.

"Mitchell Spain? The poet?"

"I—I've had a couple of things published. Nothing much. . . ."

"Have you combat experience?"

"Yes, I was aboard one berserker, before it was pacified. That was out—"

"Later, we'll talk. Probably have some marine command for you. Experienced men are scarce. Hemphill, where *are* those groundcars?"

The cold-eyed Earthman turned to answer. Of course his face had been familiar; this was Hemphill, fanatic hero of a dozen berserker fights. Mitch was faintly awed, in spite of himself.

At last the groundcars came. The ride was into Ulan Bator. The military center would be under the metropolis, taking full advantage of the defensive force fields that could be extended up into space to protect the area of the city.

Riding down the long elevator zigzag to the buried War Room, Mitch found himself again next to Karlsen.

"Congratulations on your coming marriage, sir." Mitch didn't know if he liked Karlsen or not; but already he felt curiously certain of him, as if he had known the man for years. Karlsen would know he was not trying to curry favor.

The High Commander nodded. "Thank you." He hesitated for a moment, then produced a small photo. In an illusion of three dimensions it showed the head of a young woman, golden hair done in the style favored by the new aristocracy of Venus.

There was no need for any polite stretching of truth. "She's very beautiful."

"Yes," Karlsen looked long at the picture, as if reluctant to put it away. "There are those who say this will be only a political alliance. God knows we need one. But believe me, Poet, she means far more than that to me."

Karlsen blinked suddenly and, as if amused at himself, gave Mitch a why-am-I-telling-you-all-this look. The elevator floor pressed up under me passengers' feet, and the doors sighed open. They had reached the catacomb of the General Staff.

Many of the staff, though not an absolute majority, were Venerian in these days. From their greeting it was plain that the Venerian members were coldly hostile to Nogara's brother.

Humanity was, as always, a tangle of cliques and alliances. The brains of the Solarian Parliament and the Executive had been taxed to find a High Commander. If some objected to Johann Karlsen, no one who knew him had any honest doubt of his ability. He brought with him to battle many trained men, and unlike some mightier leaders, he had been willing to take responsibility for the defense of Sol.

In the frigid atmosphere in which the staff meeting opened, there was nothing to do but get quickly to business. The enemy, the berserker machines, had abandoned their old tactics of single, unpredictable raids—for slowly over the last decades the defenses of life had been strengthened.

There were now thought to be about two hundred berserkers; to meet humanity's new defenses they had recently formed themselves into a fleet, with concentrated power capable of overwhelming one at a time all centers of human resistance. Two strongly defended planets had already been destroyed. A massed human fleet was needed, first to defend Sol, and then to meet and break the power of the unliving.

"So far, then, we are agreed," said Karlsen, straightening up from the plotting table and looking around at the General Staff. "We have not as many ships or as many trained men as we would like. Perhaps no government away from Sol has contributed all it could."

Kemal, the Venerian admiral, glanced around at his planetmen, but declined the chance to comment on the weak contribution of Karlsen's own half-brother, Nogara. There was no living being upon whom Earth, Mars, and Venus could really agree, as the leader for this war. Kemal seemed to be willing to try and live with Nogara's brother.

Karlsen went on: "We have available for combat two hundred and forty-three ships, specially constructed or modified to suit the new tactics I propose to use. We are all grateful for the magnificent Venerian contribution of a hundred ships. Six of them, as you probably all know, mount the new long-range C-plus cannon."

The praise produced no visible thaw among the Venerians. Karlsen went on: "We seem to have a numerical advantage of about forty ships. I needn't tell you how the enemy outgun and outpower us, unit for unit." He paused. "The ram-and-board tactics should give us just the element of surprise we need."

Perhaps the High Commander was choosing his words carefully, not wanting to say that some element of surprise offered the only logical hope of success. After the decades-long dawning of hope, it would be too much to say that. Too much for even these tough-minded men who knew how a berserker machine weighed in the scales of war against any ordinary warship.

"One big problem is trained men," Karlsen continued, "to lead the boarding parties. I've done the best I can, recruiting. Of those ready and in training as boarding marines now, the bulk are Esteelers."

Admiral Kemal seemed to guess what was coming, he started to push back his chair and rise, then waited, evidently wanting to make certain.

Karlsen went on in the same level tone. "These trained marines will be formed into companies, and one company assigned to each warship. Then—"

"One moment, High Commander Karlsen." Kemal had risen. "Yes?"

"Do I understand that you mean to station companies of Esteelers aboard Venerian ships?"

"In many cases my plan will mean that, yes. You protest?"

"I do." The Venerian looked around at his planetmen. "We all do."

"Nevertheless it is so ordered."

Kemal looked briefly around at his fellows once more, then sat down, blankfaced. The stenocameras in the room's corners emitted their low sibilance, reminding all that the proceedings were being recorded.

A vertical crease appeared briefly in the High Commander's forehead, and he looked for long thoughtful seconds at the Venerians before resuming his talk. But what else was there to do, except put Esteelers onto Venerian ships?

They won't let you be a hero, Karlsen, thought Mitchell Spain. The universe is bad; and men are fools, never really all on the same side in any war.

In the hold of the Venerian warship *Solar Spot* the armor lay packed inside a padded coffinlike crate. Mitch knelt beside it inspecting the knee and elbow joints.

"Want me to paint some insignia on it, Captain?"

The speaker was a young Esteeler named Fishman, one of the newly formed marine company Mitch now commanded. Fishman had picked up a multicolor paintstick somewhere, and he pointed with it to the suit.

Mitch glanced around the hold, which was swarming with his men busily opening crates of equipment. He had decided to let things run themselves as much as possible.

"Insignia? Why, I don't think so. Unless you have some idea for a company insignia. That might be a good thing to have."

There seemed no need for any distinguishing mark on his armored suit. It was of Martian make, distinctive in style, old but with the latest improvements built in—probably no man wore better. The barrel chest already bore one design—a large black spot shattered by jagged red—showing that Mitch had been in at the "death" of one berserker. Mitch's uncle had worn the same armor; the men of Mars had always gone in great numbers out into space.

"Sergeant McKendrick," Mitch asked, "what do you think about having a company insignia?"

The newly appointed sergeant, an intelligent-looking young man, paused in walking past, and looked from Mitch to Fishman as if trying to decide who stood where on insignia before committing himself. Then he looked between them, his expression hardening.

A thin-faced Venerian, evidently an officer, had entered the hold with a squad of six men behind him, armbanded and sidearmed. Ship's Police.

The officer took a few steps and then stood motionless, looking at the paintstick in Fishman's hand. When everyone in the hold was silently watching him, he asked quietly:

"Why have you stolen from ships' stores?"

"Stolen—*this*?" The young Esteeler held up the paintstick, half-smiling, as if ready to share a joke.

They didn't come joking with a police squad, or, if they did, it was not the kind of joke a Martian appreciated. Mitch still knelt beside his crated armor. There was an unloaded carbine inside the suit's torso and he put his hand on it.

"We are at war, and we are in space," the thin-faced officer went on, still speaking mildly, standing relaxed, looking round at the open-mouthed Esteeler company. "Everyone aboard a Venerian ship is subject to law. For stealing from the ship's stores, while we face the enemy, the penalty is death. By hanging. Take him away." He made an economical gesture to his squad.

The paintstick clattered loudly on the deck. Fishman looked as if he might be going to topple over, half the smile still on his face.

Mitch stood up, the carbine in the crook of his arm. It was a stubby weapon with heavy double barrel, really a miniature recoilless cannon, to be used in free fall to destroy armored machinery. "Just a minute," Mitch said.

A couple of the police squad had begun to move uncertainly toward Fishman. They stopped at once, as if glad of an excuse for doing so.

The officer looked at Mitch, and raised one cool eyebrow. "Do you know what the penalty is, for threatening me?"

"Can't be any worse than the penalty for blowing your ugly head off. I'm Captain Mitchell Spain, marine company commander on this ship, and nobody just comes in here and drags my men away and hangs them. Who are you?"

"I am Mr. Salvador," said the Venerian. His eyes appraised Mitch, no doubt establishing that he was Martian. Wheels were turning in Mr. Salvador's calm brain, and plans were changing. He said: "Had I known that a man commanded this . . . group . . . I would not have thought an object lesson necessary. Come." This last word was addressed to his squad and accompanied by another simple elegant gesture. The six lost no time, preceding him to the exit. Salvador's eyes motioned Mitch to follow him to the door. After a moment's hesitation Mitch did so, while Salvador waited for him, still unruffled.

"Your men will follow you eagerly now, Captain Spain," he said in a voice too low for anyone else to hear. "And the time will come when you will willingly follow me." With a faint smile, as if of appreciation, he was gone.

There was a moment of silence; Mitch stared at the closed door, wondering. Then a roar of jubilation burst out and his back was being pounded.

When most of the uproar had died down, one of the men asked him: "Captain—what'd he mean, calling himself Mister?"

"To the Venerians, it's some kind of political rank. You guys look here! I may need some honest witnesses." Mitch held up the carbine for all to see, and broke open the chambers and clips, showing it to be unloaded. There was renewed excitement, more howls and jokes at the expense of the retreated Venerians.

But Salvador had not thought himself defeated.

"McKendrick, call the bridge. Tell the ship's captain I want to see him. The rest of you men, let's get on with this unpacking."

Young Fishman, paintstick in hand again, stood staring vacantly downward as if contemplating a design for the deck. It was beginning to soak in, how close a thing it had been.

An object lesson?

The ship's captain was coldly taciturn with Mitch, but he indicated there were no present plans for hanging any Esteelers on the *Solar Spot*. During the next sleep period Mitch kept armed sentries posted in the marines' quarters.

The next day he was summoned to the flagship. From the launch he had a view of a dance of bright dots, glinting in the light of distant Sol. Part of the fleet was already at ramming practice.

Behind the High Commander's desk sat neither a poetry critic nor a musing bridegroom, but the ruler of a planet.

"Captain Spain—sit down."

To be given a chair seemed a good sign. Waiting for Karlsen to finish some paperwork, Mitch's thoughts wandered, recalling customs he had read about, ceremonies of saluting and posturing men had used in the past when huge permanent organizations had been formed for the sole purpose of killing other men and destroying their property. Certainly men were still as greedy as ever; and now the berserker war was accustoming them again to mass destruction. Could those old days, when life fought all-out war against life, ever come again?

With a sigh, Karlsen pushed aside his papers. "What happened yesterday, between you and Mr. Salvador?"

"He said he meant to hang one of my men." Mitch gave the story, as simply as he could. He omitted only Salvador's parting words, without fully reasoning out why he did. "When I'm made responsible for men," he finished, "nobody just walks in and hangs them. Though I'm not fully convinced they would have gone that far, I meant to be as serious about it as they were."

The High Commander picked out a paper from his desk litter. "Two Esteeler marines have been hanged already. For fighting."

"Damned arrogant Venerians I'd say."

"I want none of that, Captain!"

"Yes, sir. But I'm telling you we came mighty close to a shooting war, yesterday on the *Solar Spot.*"

"I realize that." Karlsen made a gesture expressive of futility. "Spain, is it impossible for the people of this fleet to cooperate, even when the survival of—what is it?"

The Earthman, Hemphill, had entered the cabin without ceremony. His thin lips were pressed tighter than ever. "A courier just arrived with news. Atsog is attacked."

Karlsen's strong hand crumpled papers with an involuntary twitch. "Any details?"

"The courier captain says he thinks the whole berserker fleet was there. The ground defenses were still resisting strongly when he pulled out. He just got his ship away in time."

Atsog—a planet closer to Sol than the enemy had been thought to be. It was Sol they were coming for, all right. They must know it was the human center.

More people were at the cabin door. Hemphill stepped aside for the Venerian, Admiral Kemal. Mr. Salvador, hardly glancing at Mitch, followed the admiral in.

"You have heard the news, High Commander?" Salvador began. Kemal, just ready to speak himself, gave his political officer an annoyed glance, but said nothing.

"That Atsog is attacked, yes," said Karlsen.

"My ships can be ready to move in two hours," said Kemal.

Karlsen sighed, and shook his head. "I watched today's maneuvers. The fleet can hardly be ready in two weeks."

Kemal's shock and rage seemed genuine. "You'd do that? You'd let a Venerian planet die just because we haven't knuckled under to your brother? Because we discipline his damned Esteeler—"

"Admiral Kemal, you will control yourself! You, and everyone else, are subject to discipline while I command!"

Kemal got himself in hand, apparently with great effort.

Karlsen's voice was not very loud, but the cabin seemed to resonate with it.

"You call hangings part of your discipline. I swear by the name of God that I will use every hanging, if I must, to enforce some kind of unity in this fleet. Understand, this fleet is the only military power that can oppose the massed berserkers. Trained, and unified, we can destroy them."

No listener could doubt it, for the moment.

"But whether Atsog falls, or Venus, or Esteel, I will not risk this fleet until I judge it ready."

Into the silence, Salvador said, with an air of respect: "High Commander, the courier reported one thing more. That the Lady Christina de Dulcin was visiting on Atsog when the attack began—and that she must be there still."

Karlsen closed his eyes for two seconds. Then he looked round at all of them. "If you have no further military business, gentlemen, get out." His voice was still steady.

Walking beside Miitch down me flagship corridor, Hemphill broke a silence to say thoughtfully: "Karlsen is the man the cause needs, now. Some Venerians have approached me, tentatively, about joining a plot—I refused. We must make sure that Karlsen remains in command."

"A plot?"

Hemphill did not elaborate.

Mitch said: "What they did just now was pretty low—letting him make that speech about going slow, no matter what—and then breaking the news to him about his lady being on Atsog."

Hemphill said: "He knew already she was there. That news arrived on yesterday's courier."

There was a dark nebula, made up of clustered billions of rocks and older than the sun, named the Stone Place by men. Those who gathered there now were not men and they gave nothing a name; they hoped nothing, feared nothing, wondered at nothing. They had no pride and no regret, but they had plans—a billion subtleties, carved from electrical pressure and flow—and their built-in purpose, toward which their planning circuits moved. As if by instinct the berserker machines had formed themselves into a fleet when the time was ripe, when the eternal enemy, Life, had begun to mass its strength.

The planet named Atsog in the life-language had yielded a number of still-functioning life-units from its deepest shelters, though millions had been destroyed while their stubborn defenses were beaten down. Functional life-units were sources of valuable information. The mere threat of certain stimuli usually brought at least limited cooperation from any life-unit.

The life-unit (designating itself General Bradin) which had controlled the defense of Atsog was among those captured almost undamaged. Its dissection was begun within perception of the other captured life-units. The thin outer covering tissue was delicately removed, and placed upon a suitable form to preserve it for further study. The life-units which controlled others were examined carefully, whenever possible.

After this stimulus, it was no longer possible to communicate intelligibly with General Bradin; in a matter of hours it ceased to function at all.

In itself a trifling victory, the freeing of this small unit of watery matter from the aberration called Life. But the flow of information now increased from the nearby units which had perceived the process.

It was soon confirmed that the life-units were assembling a fleet. More detailed information was sought. One important line of questioning concerned the life-unit which would control this fleet. Gradually, from interrogations and the reading of captured records, a picture emerged.

A name: Johann Karlsen. A biography. Contradictory things were said about him, but the facts showed he had risen rapidly to a position of control over millions of life-units.

Throughout the long war, the berserker computers had gathered and collated all available data on the men who became leaders of Life. Now against this data they matched, point for point, every detail that could be learned about Johann Karlsen.

The behavior of these leading units often resisted analysis, as if some quality of the life-disease in them was forever beyond the reach of machines. These individuals used logic, but sometimes it seemed they were not bound by logic. The most dangerous life-units of all sometimes acted in ways that seemed to contradict the known supremacy of the laws of physics and chance, as if they could be minds possessed of true free will, instead of its illusion.

And Karlsen was one of these, supremely one of these. His fitting of the dangerous pattern became plainer with every new comparison.

In the past, such life-units had been troublesome local problems. For one of them to command the whole life-fleet with a decisive battle approaching, was extremely dangerous to the cause of Death.

The outcome of the approaching battle seemed almost certain to be favorable, since there were probably only two hundred ships in the life-fleet. But the brooding berserkers could not be certain enough of anything, while a unit like Johann Karlsen led the living. And if the battle was long postponed the enemy Life could become stronger. There were hints that inventive Life was developing new weapons, newer and more powerful ships.

The wordless conference reached a decision. There were berserker reserves, which had waited for millennia along the galactic rim, dead and uncaring in their hiding places among dust clouds and heavy nebulae, and on dark stars. For this climactic battle they must be summoned, the power of Life to resist must be broken now.

From the berserker fleet at the Stone Place, between Atsog's Sun and Sol, courier machines sped out toward the galactic rim.

It would take some time for all the reserves to gather. Meanwhile, the interrogations went on.

"Listen, I've decided to help you, see. About this guy Karlsen, I know you want to find out about him. Only I got a delicate brain. If anything hurts me, my brain don't work at all, so no rough stuff on me, understand? I'll be no good to you ever if you use rough stuff on me."

This prisoner was unusual. The interrogating computer borrowed new circuits for itself, chose symbols and hurled them back at the life-unit.

"What can you tell me about Karlsen?"

"Listen you're gonna treat me right, aren't you?"

"Useful information will be rewarded. Untruth will bring you unpleasant stimuli."

"I'll tell you this now—the woman Karlsen was going to marry is here. You caught her alive in the same shelter General Bradin was in. Now, if you sort of give me control over some other prisoners, make things nice for me, why I bet I can think up the best way for you to use her. If you just tell him you've got her, why he might not believe you, see?"

Out on the galactic rim, the signals of the giant heralds called out the hidden reserves of the unliving. Subtle detectors heard the signals, and triggered the great engines into cold flame. The force field brain in each strategic housing awoke to livelier death. Each reserve machine began to move, with metallic leisure shaking loose its cubic miles of weight and power freeing itself from dust, or ice, or age-old mud, or solid rock—then rising and turning, orienting itself in space. All converging, they drove faster than light toward the Stone Place, where the destroyers of Atsog awaited their reinforcement.

With the arrival of each reserve machine, the linked berserker computers saw victory more probable. But still the quality of one life-unit made all of their computations uncertain.

Felipe Nogara raised a strong and hairy hand, and wiped it gently across one glowing segment of the panel before his chair. The center of his private study was filled by an enormous display sphere, which now showed a representation of the explored part of the galaxy. At Nogara's gesture the sphere dimmed, then began to relight itself in a slow intricate sequence.

A wave of his hand had just theoretically eliminated the berserker fleet as a factor in the power game. To leave it in, he told himself, diffused the probabilities too widely. It was really the competing power of Venus—and that of two or three other prosperous, aggressive planets—which occupied his mind.

Well insulated in this private room from the hum of Esteel City and from the routine press of business, Nogara watched his computers' new prediction take shape, showing the political power structure as it might exist one year from now, two years, five. As he had expected, this sequence showed Esteel expanding in influence. It was even possible that he could become ruler of the human galaxy.

Nogara wondered at his own calm in the face of such an idea. Twelve or fifteen years ago he had driven with all his power of intellect and will to advance himself. Gradually, the moves in the game had come to seem automatic. Today, there was a chance that almost every thinking being known to exist would come to acknowledge him as ruler—and it meant less to him than the first local election he had ever won.

Diminishing returns, of course. The more gained, the greater gain needed to produce an equal pleasure. At least when he was alone. If his aides were watching this prediction now it would certainly excite them, and he would catch their excitement.

But, being alone, he sighed. The berserker fleet would not vanish at the wave of a hand. Today, what was probably the final plea for more help had arrived from Earth. The trouble was that granting Sol more help would take ships and men and money from Nogara's expansion projects. Wherever he did that now, he stood to lose out, eventually, to other men. Old Sol would have to survive the coming attack with no more help from Esteel.

Nogara realized, wondering dully at himself, that he would as soon see even Esteel destroyed as see control slip from his hands. Now why? He could not say he loved his planet or his people, but he had been, by and large, a good ruler, not a tyrant. Good government was, after all, good politics.

His desk chimed the melodious notes that meant something was newly available for his amusement. Nogara chose to answer.

"Sir," said a woman's voice, "two new possibilities are in the shower room now."

Projected from hidden cameras, a scene glowed into life above Nogara's desk—bodies gleaming in a spray of water.

"They are from prison, sir, anxious for any reprieve."

Watching, Nogara felt only a weariness; and, yes, something like self-contempt. He questioned himself: Where in all the universe is there a reason why I should not seek pleasure as I choose? And again: Will I dabble in sadism, next? And if I do. what of it?

But what after that?

Having paused respectfully, the voice asked: "Perhaps this evening you would prefer something different?"

"Later," he said. The scene vanished. Maybe I should try to be a Believer for a while, he thought. What an intense thrill it must be for Johann to sin. If he ever does.

That had been a genuine pleasure, seeing Johann given command of the Solarian fleet, watching the Venerians boil. But it had raised another problem. Johann, victorious over the berserkers, would emerge as the greatest hero in human history. Would that not make even Johann dangerously ambitious? The thing to do would be to ease him out of the public eye, give him some high-ranked job, honest, but dirty and inglorious. Hunting out outlaws somewhere. Johann would probably accept that, being Johann. But if Johann bid for galactic power, he would have to take his chances. Any pawn on the board might be removed.

Nogara shook his head. Suppose Johann lost the coming battle, and lost Sol? A berserker victory would not be a matter of diffusing probabilities, that was pleasant doubletalk for a tired mind to fool itself with. A berserker victory would mean the end of Earthman in the galaxy, probably within a few years. No computer was needed to see that.

There was a little bottle in his desk; Nogara brought it out and looked at it. The end of the chess game was in it, the end of all pleasure and boredom and pain. Looking at the vial caused him no emotion. In it was a powerful drug which threw a man into a kind of ecstasy—a transcendental excitement that within a few minutes burst the heart or the blood vessels of the brain. Someday, when all else was exhausted, when it was completely a berserker universe . . .

He put the vial away, and he put away the final appeal from Earth. What did it all matter? Was it not a berserker universe already, everything determined by the random swirls of condensing gas, before the stars were born?

Felipe Nogara leaned back in his chair, watching his computers marking out the galactic chessboard.

Through the fleet the rumor spread that Karlsen delayed because it was a Venerian colony under siege. Aboard the *Solar Spot*, Mitch saw no delays for any reason. He had time for only work, quick meals, and sleep. When the final ram-and-board drill had been completed, the last stores and ammunition loaded, Mitch was too tired to feel much except relief. He rested, not frightened or elated, while the *Spot* wheeled into a rank with forty other arrow-shaped ships, dipped with them into the first C-plus jump of the deep space search, and began to hunt the enemy.

It was days later before dull routine was broken by a jangling battle alarm. Mitch was awakened by it; before his eyes were fully opened, he was scrambling into the armored suit stored under his bunk. Nearby, some marines grumbled about practice alerts; but none of them was moving slowly.

"This is High Commander Karlsen speaking," boomed the overhead speakers. "This is not a practice alert; repeat, not practice. Two berserkers have been sighted. One we've just glimpsed at extreme range. Likely it will get away, though the Ninth Squadron is chasing it.

"The other is not going to escape. In a matter of minutes we will have it englobed, in normal space. We are not going to destroy it by bombardment; we are going to soften it up a bit, and then see how well we can really ram and board. If there are any bugs left in our tactics, we'd better find out now. Squadrons Two, Four, and Seven will each send one ship to the ramming attack. I'm going back on Command Channel now, Squadron Commanders."

"Squadron Four," sighed Sergeant McKendrick. "More Esteelers in our company than any other. How can we miss?"

The marines lay like dragon's teeth seeded in the dark, strapped into the padded acceleration couches that had been their bunks, while the psych-music tried to lull them, and those who were Believers prayed. In the darkness Mitch listened on intercom, and passed on to his men the terse battle reports that came to him as marine commander on the ship.

He was afraid. What was death, that men should fear it so? It could only be the end of all experience. That end was inevitable, and beyond imagination, and he feared it.

The preliminary bombardment did not take long. Two hundred and thirty ships of life held a single trapped enemy in the center of their hollow sphere formation. Listening in the dark to laconic voices, Mitch heard how the berserker fought back, as if with the finest human courage and contempt for odds. Could you really fight machines, when you could never make them suffer pain or fear?

But you could defeat machines. And this time, for once, humanity had far too many guns. It would be easy to blow this berserker into vapor. Would it be best to do so? There were bound to be marine casualties in any boarding, no matter how favorable the odds. But a true combat test of the boarding scheme was badly needed before the decisive battle came to be fought. And, too, this enemy might hold living prisoners who might be rescued by boarders. A High Commander did well to have a rocklike certainty of his own rightness.

The order was given. The *Spot* and two other chosen ships fell in toward the battered enemy at the center of the englobement.

Straps held Mitch firmly, but the gravity had been turned off for the ramming, and weightlessness gave the impression that his body would fly and vibrate like a pellet shaken in a bottle with the coming impact. Soundless dark, soft cushioning, and lulling music; but a few words came into the helmet and the body cringed, knowing that outside were the black cold guns and the hurtling machines, unimaginable forces leaping now to meet. Now—

Reality shattered in through all the protection and the padding. The shaped atomic charge at the tip of the ramming prow opened the berserker's skin. In five seconds of crashing impact, the prow vaporized, melted, and crumpled its length away, the true hull driving behind it until the *Solar Spot* was sunk like an arrow into the body of the enemy.

Mitch spoke for the last time to the bridge of the *Solar Spot*, while his men lurched past him in free fall, their suit lights glaring.

"My panel shows Sally Port Three the only one not blocked," he said. "We're all going out that way."

"Remember," said a Venerian voice. "Your first job is to protect this ship against counterattack."

"Roger." If they wanted to give him offensively unnecessary reminders, now was not the time for argument. He broke contact with the bridge and hurried after his men.

The other two ships were to send their boarders fighting toward the strategic housing, somewhere deep in the berserker's center. The marines from the *Solar Spot* were to try to find and save any prisoners the berserker might hold. A berserker usually held prisoners near its surface, so the first search would be made by squads spreading out under the hundreds of square kilometers of hull.

In the dark chaos of wrecked machinery just outside the sally port there was no sign yet of counterattack. The berserkers had supposedly not been built to fight battles inside their own metallic skins—on this rested the fleet's hopes for success in a major battle.

Mitch left forty men to defend the hull of the *Spot*, and himself led a squad of ten out into the labyrinth. There was no use setting himself up in a command post—communications in here would be impossible, once out of line-of-sight.

The first man in each searching squad carried a mass spectrometer, an instrument that would detect the stray atoms of oxygen bound to leak from compartments where living beings breathed. The last man wore on one hand a device to blaze a trail with arrows of luminous paint; without a trail, getting lost in this three-dimensional maze would be almost inevitable.

"Got a scent. Captain," said Mitch's spectrometer man, after five minutes' casting through the squad's assigned sector of the dying berserker.

"Keep on it." Mitch was second in line, his carbine ready.

The detector man led the way through a dark and weightless mechanical universe. Several times he paused to adjust his instrument and wave its probe. Otherwise the pace was rapid; men trained in free fall, and given plenty of holds to thrust and steer by, could move faster than runners.

A towering, multijointed shape rose up before the detector man, brandishing blue-white welding arcs like swords. Before Mitch was aware of aiming, his carbine fired twice. The shells ripped the machine open and pounded it backward; it was only some semirobotic maintenance device, not built for fighting.

The detector man had nerve; he plunged straight on. The squad kept pace with him, their suit lights scouting out unfamiliar shapes and distances, cutting knife-edge shadows in the vacuum, glare and darkness mellowed only by reflection.

"Getting close!"

And then they came to it. It was a place like the top of a huge dry well. An ovoid like a ship's launch, very thickly armored, had apparently been raised through the well from deep inside the berserker, and now clamped to a dock.

"It's the launch, it's oozing oxygen."

"Captain, there's some kind of airlock on this side. Outer door's open."

It looked like the smooth and easy entrance of a trap.

"Keep your eyes open." Mitch went into the airlock. "Be ready to blast me out of here if I don't show in one minute."

It was an ordinary airlock, probably cut from some human spaceship. He shut himself inside, and then got the inner door open.

Most of the interior was a single compartment. In the center was an acceleration couch, holding a nude female mannikin. He drifted near, saw that her head had been depilated and that there were tiny beads of blood still on her scalp, as if probes had just been withdrawn.

When his suit lamp hit her face she opened dead blue staring eyes, blinking mechanically. Still not sure that he was looking at a living human being, Mitch drifted beside her and touched her arm with metal fingers. Then all at once her face became human, her eyes coming from death through nightmare to reality. She saw him and cried out. Before he could free her there were crystal drops of tears in the weightless air.

Listening to his rapid orders, she held one hand modestly in front of her. and the other over her raw scalp. Then she nodded and took into her mouth the end of a breathing tube that would dole air from Mitch's suit tank. In a few more seconds he had her wrapped in a clinging, binding rescue blanket, temporary proof against vacuum and freezing.

The detector man had found no oxygen source except the launch. Mitch ordered his squad back along their luminous trail.

At the sally port, he heard that things were not going well with the attack. Real fighting robots were defending the strategic housing; at least eight men had been killed down there. Two more ships were going to ram and board.

Mitch carried the girl through the sally port and three more friendly hatches. The monstrously thick hull of the ship shuddered and sang around him; the *Solar Spot*, her mission accomplished, boarders retrieved, was being withdrawn. Full weight came back. and light.

"In here, Captain."

QUARANTINE, said the sign. A berserker's prisoner might have been deliberately infected with something contagious; men now knew how to deal with such tricks.

Inside the infirmary he set her down. While medics and nurses scrambled around, he unfolded the blanket from the girl's face, remembering to leave it curled over her shaven head, and opened his own helmet.

"You can spit out the tube now," he told her, in his rasping voice.

She did so, and opened her eyes again.

"Oh, are you real?" she whispered. Her hand pushed its way out of the blanket folds and slid over his armor. "Oh, let me touch a human being again!" Her hand moved up to his exposed face and gripped his cheek and neck.

"I'm real enough. You're all right now."

One of the bustling doctors came to a sudden, frozen halt, staring at the girl. Then he spun around on his heel and hurried away. What was wrong?

Others sounded confident, reassuring the girl as they ministered to her. She wouldn't let go of Mitch, she became nearly hysterical when they tried gently to separate her from him.

"I guess you'd better stay," a doctor told him.

He sat there holding her hand, his helmet and gauntlets off. He looked away while they did medical things to her. They still spoke easily; he thought they were finding nothing much wrong.

"What's your name?" she asked him when the medics were through for the moment. Her head was bandaged; her slender arm came from beneath the sheets to maintain contact with his hand.

"Mitchell Spain." Now that he got a good look at her, a living young human female, he was in no hurry at all to get away. "What's yours?"

A shadow crossed her face. "I'm—not sure."

There was a sudden commotion at the infirmary door; High Commander Karlsen was pushing past protesting doctors into the QUARANTINE area. Karlsen came on until he was standing beside Mitch, but he was not looking at Mitch.

"Chris," he said to the girl. "Thank God." There were tears in his eyes.

The Lady Christina de Dulcin turned her eyes from Mitch to Johann Karlsen, and screamed in abject terror.

"Now, Captain. Tell me how you found her and brought her out."

Mitch began his tale. The two men were alone in Karlsen's monastic cabin, just off the flagship's bridge. The fight was over, the berserker a torn and harmless hulk. No other prisoners had been aboard it.

"They planned to send her back to me," Karlsen said, staring into space, when Mitch had finished his account. "We attacked before it could launch her toward us. It kept her out of the fighting, and sent her back to me."

Mitch was silent.

Karlsen's red-rimmed eyes fastened on him. "She's been brainwashed, Poet. It can be done with some permanence, you know, when advantage is taken of the subject's natural tendencies. I suppose she's never thought too much of me. There were political reasons for her to consent to our marriage . . . she screams when the doctors even mention my name. They tell me it's possible that horrible things were done to her by some man-shaped machine made to look like me. Other people are tolerable, to a degree. But it's you she wants to be alone with, you she needs."

"She cried out when I left her, but—me?"

"The natural tendency, you see. For her to . . . love . . . the man who saved her. The machines set her mind to fasten all the joy of rescue upon the first male human face she saw. The doctors assure me such things can be done. They've given her drugs, but even in sleep the instruments show her nightmares, her pain, and she cries out for you. What do you feel toward her?"

"Sir, I'll do anything I can. What do you want of me?"

"I want you to stop her suffering, what else?" Karlsen's voice rose to a ragged shout. "Stay alone with her, stop her pain if you can!"

He got himself under a kind of control. "Go on. The doctors will take you in. Your gear will be brought over from the *Solar Spot*."

Mitch stood up. Any words he could think of sounded in his mind like sickening attempts at humor. He nodded, and hurried out.

"This is your last chance to join us," said the Venerian, Salvador, looking up and down the dim corridors of this remote outer part of the flagship. "Our patience is worn, and we will strike soon. With the De Dulcin woman in her present condition, Nogara's brother is doubly unfit to command."

The Venerian must be carrying a pocket spy-jammer; a multisonic whine was setting Hemphill's teeth on edge. And so was the Venerian.

"Karlsen is vital to the human cause whether we like him or not," Hemphill said, his own patience about gone, but his voice still calm and reasonable. "Don't you see to what lengths the berserkers have gone to get at him? They sacrificed a perfectly good machine just to deliver his brainwashed woman here, to attack him psychologically."

"Well. If that is true they have succeeded. If Karlsen had any value before, now he will be able to think of nothing but his woman and the Martian."

Hemphill sighed. "Remember, he refused to hurry the fleet to Atsog to try to save her. He hasn't failed yet. Until he does, you and the others must give up this plotting against him."

Salvador backed away a step, and spat on the deck in rage. A calculated display, thought Hemphill.

"Look to yourself, Earthman!" Salvador hissed. "Karlsen's days are numbered, and the days of those who support him too willingly!" He spun around and walked away.

"Wait!" Hemphill called, quietly. The Venerian stopped and turned, with an air of arrogant reluctance. Hemphill shot him through the heart with a laser pistol. The weapon made a splitting, crackling noise in atmosphere.

Hemphill prodded the dying man with his toe, making sure no second shot was needed. "You were good at talking," he mused aloud. "But too devious to lead the fight against the damned machines."

He bent to quickly search the body, and stood up elated. He had found a list of officers' names. Some few were underlined, and some, including his own, followed by a question mark. Another paper bore a scribbled compilation of the units under command of certain Venerian officers. There were a few more notes; altogether, plenty of evidence for the arrest of the hard-core plotters. It might tend to split the fleet, but—

Hemphill looked up sharply, then relaxed. The man approaching was one of his own, whom he had stationed nearby.

"We'll take these to the High Commander at once." Hemphill waved the papers. "There'll be just time to clean out the traitors and reorganize command before we face battle."

Yet he delayed for another moment, staring down at Salvador's corpse. The plotter had been overconfident and inept, but still dangerous. Did some sort of luck operate to protect Karlsen? Karlsen himself did not match Hemphill's ideal of a war leader; he was not as ruthless as machinery or as cold as metal. Yet the damned machines made great sacrifices to attack him.

Hemphill shrugged, and hurried on his way.

"Mitch, I do love you. I know what the doctors say it is, but what do they really know about me?"

Christina de Dulcin, wearing a simple blue robe and turbanlike headdress, now reclined on a luxurious acceleration couch, in what was nominally the sleeping room of the High Commander's quarters. Karlsen had never occupied the place, preferring a small cabin.

Mitchell Spain sat three feet from her, afraid to so much as touch her hand, afraid of what he might do, and what she might do. They were alone, and he felt sure they were unwatched. The Lady Christina had even demanded assurances against spy devices and Karlsen had sent his pledge. Besides, what kind of ship would have spy devices built into its highest officers' quarters?

A situation for bedroom farce, but not when you had to live through it. The man outside, taking the strain, had more than two hundred ships dependent on him now, and many human planets would be lifeless in five years if the coming battle failed.

"What do you really know about me, Chris?" he asked.

"I know you mean life itself to me. Oh, Mitch, I have no time now to be coy, and mannered, and every millimeter a lady. I've been all those things. And—once—I would have married a man like Karlsen, for political reasons. But all that was before Atsog."

Her voice dropped on the last word, and her hand on her robe made a convulsive grasping gesture. He had to lean forward and take it.

"Chris, Atsog is in the past, now."

"Atsog will never be over, completely over, for me. I keep remembering more and more of it. Mitch, the machines made us watch while they skinned General Bradin alive. I saw that. I can't bother with silly things like politics anymore, life is too short for them. And I no longer fear any thing, except driving you away . . . "

He felt pity, and lust, and half a dozen other maddening things.

"Karlsen's a good man," he said finally,

She repressed a shudder. "I suppose," she said in a controlled voice. "But Mitch, what do you feel for me? Tell the truth—if you don't love me now, I can hope you will, in time." She smiled faintly, and raised a hand. "When my silly hair grows back."

"Your silly hair." His voice almost broke. He reached to touch her face, then pulled his fingers back as from a flame. "Chris, you're his girl, and too much depends on him."

"I was never his."

"Still . . . I can't lie to you, Chris; maybe I can't tell you the truth, either, about how I feel. The battle's coming, everything's up in the air, paralyzed. No one can plan . . . " He made an awkward, uncertain gesture."

"Mitch." Her voice was understanding. "This is terrible for you, isn't it? Don't worry. I'll do nothing to make it worse. Will you call the doctor? As long as I know you're somewhere near, I think I can rest, now."

Karlsen studied Salvador's papers in silence for some minutes, like a man pondering a chess problem. He did not seem greatly surprised.

"I have a few dependable men standing ready," Hemphill finally volunteered. "We can quickly—arrest—the leaders of this plot."

The blue eyes searched him. "Commander, was Salvador's killing fully necessary?"

"I thought so," said Hemphill blandly. "He was reaching for his own weapon."

Karlsen glanced once more at the papers and reached a decision.

"Commander Hemphill, I want you to pick four ships, and scout the far edge of the Stone Place nebula. We don't want to push beyond it without knowing where the enemy is, and give him a chance to get between us and Sol. Use caution—to learn the general location of the bulk of his fleet is enough."

"Very well." Hemphill nodded. The reconnaissance made sense; and if Karlsen wanted to get Hemphill out of the way, and deal with his human opponents by his own methods, well, let him. Those methods often seemed soft-headed to Hemphill, but they seemed to work for Karlsen. If the damned machines for some reason found Karlsen unendurable, then Hemphill would support him, to the point of cheerful murder and beyond.

What else really mattered in the universe, besides smashing the damned machines?

Mitch spent hours every day alone with Chris. He kept from her the wild rumors which circulated throughout the fleet. Salvador's violent end was whispered about, and guards were posted near Karlsen's quarters. Some said Admiral Kemal was on the verge of open revolt.

And now the Stone Place was close ahead of the fleet, blanking out half the stars; ebony dust and fragments, like a million shattered planets. No ship could move through the Stone Place; every cubic kilometer of it held enough matter to prevent C-plus travel or movement in normal space at any effective speed.

The fleet headed toward one sharply defined edge of the cloud, around which Hemphill's scouting squadron had already disappeared.

"She grows a little saner, a little calmer, every day," said Mitch, entering the High Commander's small cabin.

Karlsen looked up from his desk. The papers before him seemed to be lists of names, in Venerian script.

"I thank you for that word, Poet. Does she speak of me?"

"No."

They eyed each other, the poor and ugly cynic, the anointed and handsome Believer.

"Poet," Karlsen asked suddenly, "how do you deal with deadly enemies, when you find them in your power?"

"We Martians are supposed to be a violent people. Do you expect me to pass sentence on myself?"

Karlsen appeared not to understand, for a moment.

"Oh. No. I was not speaking of—you and me and Chris. Not personal affairs. I suppose I was only thinking aloud, asking for a sign."

"Then don't ask me, ask your God. But didn't he tell you to forgive your enemies?"

"He did." Karlsen nodded, slowly and thoughtfully. "You know he wants a lot from us. A real hell of a lot."

It was a peculiar sensation, to become suddenly convinced that the man you were watching was a genuine, nonhypocritical Believer. Mitch was not sure he had ever met the like before.

Nor had he ever seen Karlsen quite like this—passive, waiting; asking for a sign. As if there was in fact some Purpose outside the layers of a man's own mind, that could inspire him. Mitch thought about it. If . . .

But that was all mystical nonsense.

Karlsen's communicator sounded. Mitch could not make out what the other voice was saying, but he watched the effect on the High Commander. Energy and determination were coming back, there were subtle signs of the return of force, of the tremendous conviction of being right. It was like watching the gentle glow when a fusion power lamp was ignited.

"Yes," Karlsen was saying. "Yes, well done."

Then he raised the Venerian papers from his desk; it was as if he raised them only by force of will, his fingers only gesturing beneath them.

"The news is from Hemphill," he said to Mitch, almost absently. "The berserker fleet is just around the edge of the Stone Place from us. Hemphill estimates they are two hundred strong, and thinks they are unaware of our presence. We attack at once. Man your battle station, Poet; God be with you." He turned back to his communicator. "Ask Admiral Kemal to my cabin at once. Tell him to bring his staff. In particular—" He glanced at the Venerian papers and read off several names.

"Good luck to you, sir." Mitch had delayed to say that. Before he hurried out, he saw Karlsen stuffing the Venerian papers into his trash disintegrator.

Before Mitch reached his own cabin, the battle horns were sounding. He had armed and suited himself and was making his way back through the suddenly crowded narrow corridors toward the bridge, when the ship's speakers boomed suddenly to life, picking up Karlsen's voice:

". . . whatever wrongs we have done you, by word, or deed, or by things left undone, I ask you now to forgive. And in the name of every man who calls me friend or leader, I pledge that any grievance we have against you, is from this moment wiped from memory."

Everyone in the crowded passage hesitated in the rush for battle stations. Mitch found himself staring into the eyes of a huge, well-armed Venerian ship's policeman, probably here on the flagship as some officer's bodyguard.

There came an amplified cough and rumble, and then the voice of Admiral Kemal:

"We—we are brothers, Esteeler and Venerian, and all of us. All of us together now, the living against the berserker." Kemal's voice rose to a shout. "Destruction to the damned machines, and death to their builders! Let every man remember Atsog!"

"Remember Atsog!" roared Karlsen's voice.

In the corridor there was a moment's hush, like that before a towering wave smites down. Then a great insensate shout. Mitch found himself with tears in his eyes, yelling something.

"Remember General Bradin," cried the big Venerian, grabbing Mitch and hugging him, lifting him, armor and all. "Death to his flayers!"

"Death to the flayers!" The shout ran like a flame through the corridor. No one needed to be told that the same things were happening in all the ships of the fleet. All at once there was no room for anything less than brotherhood, no time for anything less than glory.

"Destruction to the damned machines!"

Near the flagship's center of gravity was the bridge, only a dais holding a ring of combat chairs, each with its clustered controls and dials.

"Boarding Coordinator ready," Mitch reported, strapping himself in.

The viewing sphere near the bridge's center showed the human advance, in two leapfrogging lines of over a hundred ships each. Each ship was a green dot in the sphere, positioned as truthfully as the flagship's computers could manage. The irregular surface of the Stone Place moved beside the battle lines in a series of jerks; the flagship was traveling by C-plus microjumps, so the presentation in the viewing sphere was a succession of still pictures at second-and-a-half intervals. Slowed by the mass of their C-plus cannon, the six fat green symbols of the Venerian heavy weapons ships labored forward, falling behind the rest of the fleet.

In Mitch's headphones someone was saying: "In about ten minutes we can expect to reach—"

The voice died away. There was a red dot in the sphere already, and then another, and then a dozen, rising like tiny suns around the bulge of dark nebula. For long seconds the men on the bridge were silent while the berserker advance came into view. Hemphill's scouting patrol must, after all, have been detected, for the berserker fleet was not cruising, but attacking. There was a battlenet of a hundred or more red dots, and now there were two nets, leapfrogging in and out of space like the human lines. And still the red berserkers rose into view, their formations growing, spreading out to englobe and crush a smaller fleet.

"I make it three hundred machines," said a pedantic and somewhat effeminate voice, breaking the silence with cold precision. Once, the mere knowledge that three hundred berserkers existed might have crushed all human hopes. In this place, in this hour, fear itself could frighten no one. The voices in Mitch's headphones began to transact the business of opening a battle. There was nothing yet for him to do but listen and watch.

The six heavy green marks were falling further behind; without hesitation, Karlsen was hurling his entire fleet straight at the enemy center. The foe's strength had been underestimated, but it seemed the berserker command had made a similar error, because the red formations too were being forced to regroup, spread themselves wider.

The distance between fleets was still too great for normal weapons to be effective, but the laboring heavy-weapons ships with their C-plus cannon were now in range, and they could fire through friendly formations almost as easily as not. At their volley Mitch thought he felt space jar around him; it was some secondary effect that the human brain notices, really only wasted energy. Each projectile blasted by explosives to a safe distance from its launching ship, mounted its own C-plus engine, which then accelerated the projectile while it flickered in and out of reality on microtimers.

Their leaden masses magnified by velocity, the huge slugs skipped through existence like stones across water, passing like phantoms through the fleet of life, emerging fully into normal space only as they approached their target, traveling then like De Broglie wavicles, their matter churning internally with a phase velocity greater than that of light.

Almost instantly after Mitch had felt the slugs' ghostly passage, one red dot began to expand and thin into a cloud, still tiny in the viewing sphere. Someone gasped. In a few more moments the flagship's own weapons, beams and missiles, went into action.

The enemy center stopped, two million miles ahead, but his flanks came on, smoothly as the screw of a vast meat-grinder. threatening englobement of the first line of human ships.

Karlsen did not hesitate, and a great turning point flickered past in a second. The life-fleet hurtled on, deliberately into the trap, straight for the hinge of the jaws.

Space twitched and warped around Mitchell Spain. Every ship in the fleet was firing now. and every enemy answering, and the energies released plucked through his armor like ghostly fingers. Green dots and red vanished from the sphere, but not many of either as yet.

The voices in Mitch's helmet slackened, as events raced into a pattern that shifted too fast for human thought to follow. Now for a time the fight would be computer against computer, faithful slave of life against outlaw, neither caring, neither knowing.

The viewing sphere on the flagship's bridge was shifting ranges almost in a flicker. One swelling red dot was only a million miles away, then half of that, then half again. And now the flagship came into normal space for the final lunge of the attack, firing itself like a bullet at the enemy.

Again the viewer switched to a closer range, and the chosen foe was no longer a red dot, but a great forbidding castle, tilted crazily, black against the stars. Only a hundred miles away, then half of that. The velocity of closure slowed to less than a mile a second. As expected, the enemy was accelerating, trying to get away from what must look to it like a suicide charge. For the last time Mitch checked his chair, his suit, his weapons. *Chris, be safe in a cocoon.* The berserker swelled in the sphere, gun-flashes showing now around his steel-ribbed belly. A small one, this, maybe only ten times the flagship's bulk. Always a rotten spot to be found, in every one of them, old wounds under their ancient skins. Try to run, you monstrous obscenity, try in vain.

Closer, twisting closer. Now!

Lights all gone, falling in the dark for one endless second—

Impact. Mitch's chair shook him, the gentle pads inside his armor battering and bruising him. The expendable ramming prow would be vaporizing, shattering and crumpling, dissipating energy down to a level the battering-ram ship could endure.

When the crashing stopped, noise still remained, a whining, droning symphony of stressed metal and escaping air and gases like sobbing breathing. The great machines were locked together now, half the length of the flagship embedded in the berserker.

A rough ramming, but no one on the bridge was injured. Damage Control reported that the expected air leaks were being controlled. Gunnery reported that it could not yet extend a turret inside the wound. Drive reported ready for a maximum effort.

Drive!

The ship twisted in the wound it had made. This could be victory now, tearing the enemy open, sawing his metal bowels out into space. The bridge twisted with the structure of the ship, this warship that was more solid metal than anything else. For a moment Mitch thought he could come close to comprehending the power of the engines men had built.

"No use, Commander. We're wedged in."

The enemy endured. The berserker memory would already be searched, the plans made, the counterattack on the flagship coming, without fear or mercy.

The Ship Commander turned his head to took at Johann Karlsen. It had been foreseen that once a battle reached this melee stage there would be little for a High Commander to do. Even if the flagship itself were not half-buried in an enemy hull, all space nearby was a complete inferno of confused destruction, through which any meaningful communication would be impossible. If Karlsen was helpless now, neither could the berserker computers still link themselves into a single brain.

"Fight your ship, sir," said Karlsen. He leaned forward, gripping the arms of his chair, gazing at the clouded viewing sphere as if trying to make sense of the few flickering lights within it.

The Ship Commander immediately ordered his marines to board.

Mitch saw them out the sally ports. Then, sitting still was worse than any action. "Sir, I request permission to join the boarders."

Karlsen seemed not to hear. He disqualified himself, for now, from any use of power; especially to set Mitchell Spain in the forefront of the battle or to hold him back.

The Ship Commander considered. He wanted to keep a Boarding Coordinator on the bridge; but experienced men would be desperately needed in fighting. "Go, then. Do what you can to help defend our sally ports."

This berserker defended itself well with soldier-robots. The marines had hardly gotten away from the embedded hull when the counterattack came, cutting most of them off.

In a narrow zigzag passage leading out to the port near which fighting was heaviest, an armored figure met Mitch. "Captain Spain? I'm Sergeant Broom, acting Defense Commander here. Bridge says you're to take over. It's a little rough. Gunnery can't get a turret working inside the wound. The clankers have all kinds of room to maneuver, and they keep coming at us."

"Let's get out there, then."

The two of them hurried forward, through a passage that became only a warped slit. The flagship was bent here, a strained swordblade forced into a chink of armor.

"Nothing rotten here," said Mitch, climbing at last out of the sally port. There were distant flashes of light, and the sullen glow of hot metal nearby, by which to see braced girders, like tall buildings among which the flagship had jammed itself.

"Eh? No." Broom must be wondering what he was talking about. But the sergeant stuck to business, pointing out to Mitch where he had about a hundred men disposed among the chaos of torn metal and drifting debris. "The clankers don't use guns. They drift in, sneaking, or charge in a wave, and get us hand-to-hand, if they can. Last wave we lost six men."

Whining gusts of gas came out of the deep caverns, and scattered blobs of liquid, along with flashes of light, and deep shudders through the metal. The damned thing might be dying, or just getting ready to fight; there was no way to tell.

"Any more of the boarding parties get back?" Mitch asked.

"No. Doesn't look good for 'em."

"Port Defense, this is Gunnery," said a cheerful radio voice. "We're getting the eighty-degree forward turret working."

"Well, then use it!" Mitch rasped back. "We're inside, you can't help hitting something."

A minute later, searchlights moved out from doored recesses in the flagship's hull, and stabbed into the great chaotic cavern.

"Here they come again!" yelled Broom. Hundreds of meters away, beyond the melted stump of the flagship's prow, a line of figures drifted nearer. The searchlights questioned them; they were not suited men. Mitch was opening his mouth to yell at Gunnery when the turret fired, throwing a raveling skein of shell-bursts across the advancing rank of machines.

But more ranks were coming. Men were firing in every direction at machines that came clambering, jetting, drifting, in hundreds.

Mitch took off from the sally port, moving in diving weightless leaps, touring the outposts, shifting men when the need arose.

"Fall back when you have to!" he ordered, on Command radio. "Keep them from the sally ports!"

His men were facing no lurching conscription of mechanized pipefitters and moving welders; these devices were built, in one shape or another, to fight.

As he dove between outposts, a thing like a massive chain looped itself to intercept Mitch; he broke it in half with his second shot. A metallic butterfly darted at him on brilliant jets, and away again, and he wasted four shots at it.

He found an outpost abandoned, and started back toward the sally port, radioing ahead: "Broom, how is it there?"

"Hard to tell, Captain. Squad leaders, check in again, squad leaders—"

The flying thing darted back; Mitch sliced it with his laser pistol. As he approached the sally port, weapons were firing all around him. The interior fight was turning into a microcosm of the confused struggle between fleets. He knew that still raged, for the ghostly fingers of heavy weapons still plucked through his armor continually.

"Here they come again—Dog, Easy, Nine-o'clock."

Coordinates of an attack straight at the sally port. Mitch found a place to wedge himself, and raised his carbine again. Many of the machines in this wave bore metal shields before them. He fired and reloaded, again and again.

The flagship's one usable turret flamed steadily; and an almost continuous line of explosions marched across the machines' ranks in vacuum-silence, along with a traversing searchlight spot. The automatic cannons of the turret were far heavier than the marines' hand weapons; almost anything the cannon hit dissolved in radii of splinters. But suddenly there were machines on the flagship's hull, attacking the turret from its blind side.

Mitch called out a warning and started in that direction. Then all at once the enemy was around him. Two things caught a nearby man in their crablike claws, trying to tear him apart between them. Mitch fired quickly at the moving figures and hit the man, blowing one leg off.

A moment later one of the crab-machines was knocked away and broken by a hailstorm of shells. The other one beat the armored man to pieces against a jagged girder, and turned to look for its next piece of work.

This machine was armored like a warship. It spotted Mitch and came for him, climbing through drifting rubble, shells and slugs rocking it but not crippling. It gleamed in his suit lights, reaching out bright pincers, as he emptied his carbine at the box where its cybernetics should be.

He drew his pistol and dodged, but like a falling cat it turned at him. It caught him by the left hand and the helmet, metal squealing and crunching. He thrust the laser pistol against what he thought was the brainbox, and held the trigger down. He and the machine were drifting, it could get no leverage for its strength. But it held him, working on his armored hand and helmet.

Its brainbox, the pistol, and the fingers of his right gauntlet, all were glowing hot. Something molten spattered across his faceplate, the glare half-blinding him. The laser burned out, fusing its barrel to the enemy in a radiant weld,

His left gauntlet, still caught, was giving way, being crushed—
—*his hand*—

Even as the suit's hypos and tourniquet bit him, he got his burned right hand free of the laser's butt and reached the plastic grenades at his belt.

His left arm was going wooden, even before the claw released his mangled hand and fumbled slowly for a fresh grip. The machine was shuddering all over, like an agonized man. Mitch whipped his right arm around to plaster a grenade on the far side of the brain-box. Then with arms and legs he strained against the crushing, groping claws. His suit-servos whined with overload, being over-powered, two seconds, close eyes, three—

The explosion stunned him. He found himself drifting free. Lights were flaring. Somewhere was a sally port; he had to get there and defend it.

His head cleared slowly. He had the feeling that someone was pressing a pair of fingers against his chest. He hoped that was only some reaction from the hand. It was hard to see anything, with his faceplate still half-covered with splashed metal, but at last he spotted the flagship hull. A chunk of something came within reach, and he used it to propel himself toward the sally port, spinning weakly. He dug out a fresh clip of ammunition and then realized his carbine was gone.

The space near the sally port was foggy with shattered mechanism; and there were still men here, firing their weapons out into the great cavern. Mitch recognized Broom's armor in the flaring lights, and got a welcoming wave.

"Captain! They've knocked out the turret, and most of the searchlights. But we've wrecked an awful lot of 'em—how's your arm?"

"Feels like wood. Got a carbine?"

"Say again?"

Broom couldn't hear him. Of course, the damned thing had squeezed his helmet and probably wrecked his radio transmitter. He put his helmet against Broom's and said: "You're in charge. I'm going in. Get back out if I can."

Broom was nodding, guiding him watchfully toward the port. Gun flashes started up around them thick and fast again, but there was nothing he could do about that, with two steady dull fingers pressing into his chest. Lightheaded. Get back out? Who was he fooling? Lucky if he got in without help.

He went into the port, past the interior guard's niches, and through an airlock. A medic took one look and came to help him.

Not dead yet, he thought, aware of people and lights around him. There was still some part of a hand wrapped in bandages on the end of his left arm. He noticed another thing, too; he felt no more ghostly plucking of space-bending weapons. Then he understood that he was being wheeled out of surgery, and that people hurrying by had triumph in their faces. He was still too groggy to frame a coherent question, but words he heard seemed to mean that another ship had joined in the attack on this berserker. That was a good sign, that there were spare ships around.

The stretcher bearers set him down near the bridge, in an area that was being used as a recovery room; there were many wounded strapped down and given breathing tubes against possible failure of gravity or air. Mitch could see signs of battle damage around him. How could that be, this far inside the ship. The sally ports had been held.

There was a long gravitic shudder. "They've disengaged her," said someone nearby.

Mitch passed out for a little while. The next thing he could see was that people were converging on the bridge from all directions. Their faces were happy and wondering, as if some joyful signal had called them. Many of them carried what seemed to Mitch the strangest assortment of burdens: weapons, books, helmets, bandages, trays of food, bottles, even bewildered children, who must have been just rescued from the berserker's grip.

Mitch hitched himself up on his right elbow, ignoring the twinges in his bandaged chest and in the blistered fingers of his right hand. Still he could not see the combat chairs of the bridge, for the people moving between.

From all the corridors of the ship the people came, solemnly happy, men and women crowding together in the brightening lights.

An hour or so later, Mitch awoke again to find that a viewing sphere had been set up nearby. The space where the battle had been was a jagged new nebula of gaseous metal, a few little fireplace coals against the ebony folds of the Stone Place.

Someone near Mitch was tiredly, but with animation, telling the story to a recorder:

"—fifteen ships and about eight thousand men lost are our present count. Every one of our ships seemed to be damaged. We estimate ninety—that's nine-zero—berserkers destroyed. Last count was a hundred and seventy-six captured, or wrecking themselves. It's still hard to believe. A day like this . . . we must remember that thirty or more of them escaped, and are as deadly as ever. We will have to go on hunting and fighting them for a long time, but their power as a fleet has been broken. We can hope that capturing this many machines will at last give us some definite lead on their origin. Ah, best of all, some twelve thousand human prisoners have been freed.

"Now, how to explain our success? Those of us not Believers of one kind or another will say victory came because our hulls were newer and stronger, our long-range weapons new and superior, our tactics unexpected by the enemy—and our marines able to defeat anything the berserkers could send against them.

"Above all, history will give credit to High Commander Karlsen, for his decision to attack, at a time when his reconciliation with the Venerians had inspired and united the fleet. The High Commander is here now, visiting the wounded who lie in rows . . . "

Karlsen's movements were so slow and tired that Mitch thought he too might be wounded, though no bandages were visible. He shuffled past the ranked stretchers, with a word or nod for each of the wounded. Beside Mitch's pallet he stopped, as if recognition was a shock.

"She's dead, Poet," were the first words he said.

The ship turned under Mitch for a moment; then he could be calm, as if he had expected to hear this. The battle had hollowed him out.

Karlsen was telling him, in a withered voice, how the enemy had forced through the flagship's hull a kind of torpedo, an infernal machine that seemed to know how the ship was designed, a moving atomic pile that had burned its way through the High Commander's quarters and almost to the bridge before it could be stopped and quenched.

The sight of battle damage here should have warned Mitch. But he hadn't been able to think. Shock and drugs kept him from thinking or feeling much of anything now, but he could see her face, looking as it had in the gray deadly place from which he had rescued her.

Rescued.

"I am a weak and foolish man," Karlsen was saying. "But I have never been your enemy. Are you mine?"

"No. You forgave all your enemies. Got rid of them. Now you won't have any, for a while. Galactic hero. But I don't envy you."

"No. God rest her." But Karlsen's face was still alive, under all the grief and weariness. Only death could finally crush this man. He gave the ghost of a smile. "And now, the second part of the prophecy, hey? I am to be defeated, and to die owning nothing. As if a man could die any other way."

"Karlsen, you're all right. I think you may survive your own success. Die in peace, someday, still hoping for your Believers' heaven."

"The day I die," Karlsen turned his head slowly, seeing all the people around him. "I'll remember this day. This glory, this victory for all men." Under the weariness and grief he still had his tremendous assurance—not of being right, Mitch thought now, but of being committed to right.

"Poet, when you are able, come and work for me."

"Someday, maybe. Now I can live on the battle bounty. And I have work. If they can't grow back my hand—why, I can write with one." Mitch was suddenly very tired.

A hand touched his good shoulder. A voice said: "God be with you." Johann Karlsen moved on.

Mitch wanted only to rest. Then, to his work. The world was bad, and all men were fools—but there were men who would not be crushed. And that was a thing worth telling.

THE BAD MACHINES

Smoothly functioning machinery composed the bulk of the little courier ship, surrounding its cabin, cradling and defending the two human lives therein. Both crew members were at battle stations, their bodies clad in full space armor and secured in combat chairs. At the moment all the elaborate devices of guidance and propulsion performed their functions unobtrusively, and the cabin was very quiet. This was not the time for casual conversation, because the combat zone was only a few minutes ahead.

The small portion of the Galaxy settled by Earth-descended humans lay almost entirely behind the courier, while only a few of the most recently established settlements lay in its path, as did much of the vaster Galactic realm still unexplored. Moving in c-space, the ship's instruments at the moment were able to show only a faint indication of its destination: the hint of the presence of a gravitational radiant, still several light-hours away.

Before Lieutenant Commander Timor and Ensign Strax had departed on this mission, the admiral in command of Sector Headquarters had summoned both to a secret briefing. Once the three officers were isolated in the briefing room, the CO had turned on a holostage display. The scene depicted was at once recognizable as the region of space surrounding the Selatrop Radiant.

Crisply the admiral reminded the man and woman before him of the special physical qualities of negative gravitational radiants in general, and of this one in particular, which made these peculiar features in space-time strong points in the struggle to control the lanes of space.

Three inhabited planets orbited suns within a few light-years of the Selatrop, and the lives of those populations hung in the balance. In the war of humanity against the Berserker machines, whichever side held the Selatrop Radiant would have a substantial advantage in the ongoing struggle to control this sector of space. If Berserkers should be able to capture and hold this fortress, then it would probably be necessary to try to evacuate those planets.

Facing his two officers across the glowing tabletop display, the admiral had come quickly to the point: "I'm worried, spacers. Communication with Selatrop is still open, and the garrison commander reports that the defenses are holding. But . . . several of the messages received from there over the last standard month suggest that something is seriously wrong."

The admiral went on to give details. Most puzzling was a statement by the garrison commander, Colonel Craindre, that she flatly refused to accept any more human reinforcements. From now on, only routine replacement supplies, and a few additional items, factory machinery and materials, were to be sent. Some of these requisitions were hard to explain by the normal requirements of maintenance and replacement—and the sender of the message had offered no explanation.

When the CO paused, seeming to invite comment, Timor said: "Admiral, that doesn't sound like Colonel Craindre at all."

The older man nodded. "Semantic analysis strongly suggests that none of the members of the garrison wrote those words."

"But who else could have written them, sir?—unless some ship we don't know about has arrived at the fortress."

"Who else, indeed? Your orders are to find out what's happening, and report."

The message torpedoes from the Selatrop Fortress had borne additional puzzling content. At least one of the dispatches hinted at a great, joyous announcement soon to be proclaimed. Psychologists at Headquarters suspected that the sender might have been subjected to some kind of mind-altering drugs or surgery.

The admiral also voiced his fear of a worst-case scenario: that the Berserkers had actually overrun the fortress, but were trying to keep the fact a secret.

The briefing was soon concluded, and Lieutenant Commander Timor and Ensign Strax boarded the armed courier. Minutes later they were launched into space.

The little courier was now about to re-emerge into normal space after three days of *c*-plus travel.

The onboard drive and astrogation systems, under the autopilot's control, continued to function smoothly. No enemy presence had been detected in local *c*-space. The small ship popped back into normal space precisely on schedule, only a few thousand kilometers from its destination, well-positioned within the approach lanes to the Selatrop.

Timor let out held breath in a kind of reverse gasp. At least normal space within point-blank weapons range was clear of the Berserker enemy. There would be no attack on the courier within the next few seconds. But on the holostage display before him there sprang into being scores of ominous dots, scattered in an irregular pattern, indicating real-space objects at only slightly greater distances. The Berserkers, space-going relics of an ancient interstellar war, programmed to destroy life wherever they encountered it, were intent on breaking into the defended space of the fortress, and slaughtering every living thing inside, down to the last microbe. Then, having seized control of this strategic strong point, they would use it to great advantage in their relentless crusade against all life.

In appearance the Radiant resembled a miniature sun, a fiery point burning in vacuum, its inverse force pressing the newly arrived ship, and everything else, away from it. Like the handful of its mysterious fellows scattered about the Galaxy, it could be approached no closer than a couple of kilometers, by any ship or machine. Here at the Selatrop, the inner surface of the fortress was four kilometers from that enigmatic point.

The fortress consisted of blocks and sections of solid matter, woven and held together with broad strands of sheer force, the whole forming a kind of spherical latticework some eight kilometers in diameter. Through the interstices the fitful spark of the radiant itself was intermittently visible.

❖   ❖   ❖

Timor and Strax sent a coded radio message ahead to the fortress, announcing their arrival, even as the autopilot eased the courier into its approach.

The fortress holding the high ground of the Selatrop Radiant possessed some powerful fixed weapons of its own, but depended very heavily for its defense upon two squadrons of small fighting ships. The original strength of the garrison had been twenty human couples, the great majority of them highly trained pilots. With their auxiliary machines they made a formidable defensive team.

In combat, as in many other situations of comparable complexity, better decisions tended to be made when a human brain participated in the parts of the process not requiring electronic speed. A meld of organic and artificial intelligence had proven to be superior in performance to either mode alone.

The marvels of an organic brain, still imperfectly understood, provided the fighter pilot's mind, both conscious and unconscious, with the little extra, the fine edge over pure machine control, that enabled the best pilots under proper conditions to seize a slight advantage over pure machine opponents.

During the first few seconds after their ship's reemergence into normal space, Timor and Strax were reassured to see on their displays that the defense was still being energetically carried out.

Small space-going machines, beyond a doubt Berserkers engaged in an attack, could be seen on the displays. Even as Timor watched, one of the enemy symbols vanished in a small red puff, indicating the impact of a heavy weapon. Moments later, one of the defending fighters was evidently badly damaged, so much so that it turned its back on the enemy and began to limp toward the safety of the fortress.

"At least our people are still hanging on," the ensign commented.

"So far."

The brief sequence of action Timor had so far been able to observe suggested a steady probing of the defenses rather than an all-out assault.

A hulking shape easily recognizable as the Berserker mothership hovered in the background, at a range of a thousand kilometers or more, constrained by its own sheer bulk from forcing an approach into the volume of space near the Radiant, where only small objects could force a passage.

As the courier in the course of its final approach moved within a hundred kilometers of the fortress, a new skirmish flared in nearby space, punch and counterpunch of nuclear violence exchanged at the speeds of computers and electricity.

As the courier drew nearer to the fortress, the skirmishing flared briefly into heavier action.

The attack was conducted by space-going Berserkers in a variety of sizes and configurations. But the Radiant proved its worth as an advantage to the defense: the assaulting force was continually at a disadvantage, in effect having to fight its way uphill, their maneuvering slowed and weapons rendered less effective. At the moment their efforts were being beaten off with professional skill.

And now the enemy showed full awareness of the presence of Timor's ship. One Berserker was now accelerating sharply in the courier's direction, trying to head it off.

The human skill and intuition of Ensign Strax as pilot, melded with the autopilot's speed and accuracy, secured the courier a slight edge in maneuvering, and ultimately a safe entry to the defended zone.

With the Berserkers temporarily baffled, the nearest of the manned fighting ships engaged in the defense now turned aside and approached the courier. As the two officers on the courier began to ease themselves out of their armor, routine messages were exchanged.

REQUEST PERMISSION TO COME ABOARD.

Timor replied: PERMISSION GRANTED.

Only mildly surprised—it seemed natural that people who had withstood a long siege would be eager to see a new and friendly human face—Timor and Strax made ready to welcome aboard the pilot from the fighting ship.

When the two craft were docked together, and the connected airlocks stood open, Timor looked up, confidently expecting to see a human step from the airlock into the courier's cabin . . . but instead he was petrified to behold a metal shape, roughly human in configuration, but obviously a robot—

. . . somehow, a Berserker. And we are dead . . .

Too late to do anything about it now . . .

Ensign Strax let out a wordless cry of terror, and tried to draw a handgun. But she was instantly stunned by some paralyzing ray, so that the weapon clattered on the deck.

A moment later, Timor broke free of the paralysis of shock. He grabbed for the controls before his combat chair, intending to wreck his ship, if he could, to keep it out of enemy hands.

Human reflexes were far too slow. His wrists were gently seized, his intended motion blocked.

A *Berserker*. From one fraction of a second to the next, he waited for his arms to be wrenched from their sockets, for his life to be efficiently crushed out.

But nothing of the kind occurred.

Opening his eyes, which had involuntarily clenched themselves shut, Timor beheld the lone intruder, its metal hand still holding him by one wrist. It was obviously a robot, but vastly different from any machine that he had ever seen before—Earth-descended people almost never built anthropomorphic robots—and also unlike any Berserker he had ever seen or heard described.

Standing before him was a metal thing, nude and sexless, the size and shape of a small human adult. The immobile features of its face were molded in a form of subtle beauty.

Timor's handgun was smoothly taken away from him. Then he was released.

His only thought at the moment was that this was some attempted Berserker ploy. The bad machines must want something from him, some information or act of treachery, before they killed him.

But the very beauty of the robot, by Earth-descended human standards, argued strongly against its having a Berserker origin.

"At your service, Lieutenant Commander Timor," the shape before him crooned, speaking in Timor's language, the same as that used by the Selatrop garrison. Its voice was startlingly lovely, nothing at all like the raucous squawking produced by Berserkers when they condescended, for their own deadly reasons, to imitate human speech.

The machine looked extremely strong and well designed, presenting a dark and seamless metallic surface to the world. It had stepped back a pace, but was still standing close enough that Timor might easily have read the fine script engraved on the metal plate set into its chest—had he understood the language. Seeing the direction of his gaze, the machine translated for him in its musical voice, pointing at each word in turn with a delicate-looking finger of steel:

HUMANOID
SERIAL NO. JW 39, 864, 715
TO SERVE AND OBEY
AND GUARD HUMANITY FROM HARM

Just as the translation was completed, the figure of Ensign Strax in the other seat stirred slightly. Turning away from Timor, flowing across the little cabin with more than a human dancer's grace, the intruder machine bent solicitously over Strax as if intent upon seeing to her welfare. Soft hues of bronze and blue shone across the robot's sleek and sexless blackness. It was handsome, and monstrous in its independence. Gently, efficiently, it did something which must have partially counteracted the effects of the stunning ray. Then it adjusted the position of the ensign's seat, as if concerned for her safety and comfort.

Meanwhile, Timor was slowly recovering from shock, from the certainty of instant death. "At my service?" he croaked stupidly.

The thing turned back toward him, its blind-seeming, steel-colored eyes fixed on his face. Its high clear voice was eerily sweet. "We humanoids are here, and always will be. We exist to serve humanity. Ask for what you need."

" 'We'?"

"Locally, only eighteen other units, essentially identical to the one you see before you. Elsewhere, millions more."

"But what are you?"

Patiently it pointed once more to its identification plate. "Humans elsewhere have called us humanoids."

Timor shook his head as if to clear it. It seemed that the question of the robot's origin would have to be settled later. "What do you want?"

"We follow our Prime Directive." Tolerantly it repeated the words incised below its serial number: " 'To serve and obey and guard humanity from harm.' "

"You're telling me you have no intention of killing us."

"Far from it, Lieutenant Commander." Metal somehow conveyed the impression of being softly shocked at the mere idea. "We cannot kill. Our intentions are quite the opposite."

Meanwhile the courier's and the fighter's respective autopilots had been easing the joined small ships along toward the fortress, steadily decelerating. The two separated only moments before being individually docked. Timor felt the usual shift in artificial gravity, from ship's to station's. Here the natural inverse gravity of the Radiant dominated.

"Our immediate objective," continued the humanoid, brightly and intensely, "is to save humanity from the critical danger posed by Berserkers."

"I know what Berserkers are, thank you. I have a fair amount of experience along that line. What I haven't quite grasped as yet is—you. Where did you come from?"

The thing declined to answer directly. "We have long familiarity with the Earth-descended species of humanity. Your history displays patterns of evolving technology and increasingly violent aggression. Even absent any Berserker threat, your long-term survival would require our help."

"How do you come to speak our language?"

Again the answer was oblique: "To achieve our goal it has been necessary to learn many languages."

The ship was now snugly docked, the open hatch leading directly into the Selatrop Fortress. From outside the ship came a hint of exotic odors. Beside him, the mysterious thing was insisting in a cooing voice that it and its fellows wanted only to benefit humanity.

Ensign Strax was now awake and functioning once more, though obviously dazed. She seemed basically unharmed, able to stand and walk with only a little help.

The two humans left the courier, the humanoid solicitously assisting the ensign. As they emerged into dock and hangar space, they saw around them the great structural members of composite materials, making up the bulk of the fortress. In places the Radiant itself was visible, as a sunlike point always directly overhead, casting strong shadows.

Two more humanoids, practically identical to the first, were on hand to offer a silent welcome. But not a human being was in sight.

"Where's the garrison?" Timor demanded sharply.

One of the waiting units answered. "All humans aboard the fortress are now restricted to the region of greatest safety."

"Not at their battle stations? By whose decision?"

"No human decisions can be allowed to interfere with our essential service."

At another dock nearby rested a small spacecraft, no bigger than Timor's courier but of unique design. "Whose ship is that?" he demanded.

"It is ours."

The humanoid spokesunit went on to inform him that reinforcements were expected soon, a second ship and perhaps a third, each carrying another score of units like itself.

"Arrive from where?"

As nearly as Timor could understand the answer, the reinforcements, like the first humanoid craft, would be coming from a direction, or perhaps a dimension in c-space, such that it would be virtually impossible for the besieging Berserker fleet to interfere with their arrival.

Timor also observed that the newcomers had taken over several docks, part of the repair facility, to establish their own workshop. Imperturbably his new guide explained to him that the resources of the fortress, computers, materials, and machinery, were being pressed into the construction of more humanoids.

The two humanoids that had been waiting now boarded the courier. Maybe, thought Timor, they were looking for the requested factory machines and materials. If so, they were doomed to disappointment.

Their original guide escorted Timor and Strax deeper into the fortress, through multiple airlocks, past redundant defenses.

The special attributes of gravitational radiants in general, and of this one in particular, not only made them strong points in the struggle to control the preferred thoroughfares and channels of c-plus travel. The same peculiarities that made it easy for a ship to emerge from flightspace in the vicinity of a radiant also rendered it more likely that things from far away, such as the humanoids, were likely to turn up here.

When Strax and Timor had reached the garrison's living quarters, still without having encountered a living soul in the course of their long walk, the robot assigned the couple to separate small cabins. They were not consulted as to their preference in quarters.

Once the ensign was in her cabin, the humanoid locked the door from the outside. "By attempting to draw a weapon, Ensign Strax has demonstrated a willingness to use violence against humanoids," the beautiful robot explained to Timor. "Temporary confinement will be best for her own safety."

Timor did not protest, because in truth Strax had still seemed somewhat dazed. Better for her to stay out of the way, while he investigated.

He followed his guide down a short corridor.

"At last!" he muttered. A dozen or so members of the live garrison had come in sight, assembled in a recreation lounge. Timor thought that when he appeared, hope flared briefly in their faces, only to fade swiftly when they perceived that he had been disarmed and was thoroughly under the control of the escorting robot. Three additional humanoids stood by, observing carefully.

Timor immediately recognized Colonel Craindre, the garrison commander, a gray-haired, hard-bitten veteran of space combat. He approached her, identified himself, and announced his mission.

"I wish you well, Lieutenant Commander," the colonel said. "But I don't know whether I can say welcome aboard. Because I don't know if I'm glad to see you here or not. Our situation is so . . ." Her words died away.

"Casualties?"

Colonel Craindre shook her head helplessly. Her pale hands were folded tensely in front of her, in what was evidently an unconscious gesture, and Timor suddenly noticed that several other members of the garrison had adopted the same pose.

In a belated response to Timor's question the colonel said: "Four pilots lost." She paused. "All our casualties occurred before the humanoids arrived."

"Why is that?"

"Very simple. As soon as they seized control, all humans were forbidden to fly combat missions. Several additional fighter ships have been lost since then, and four of our new allies with them."

Another pilot chimed in: "Which probably means that four of us are still alive, who would otherwise be—"

But Timor had scarcely heard anything beyond the colonel's remark. He interrupted: "You were *forbidden*—?"

Craindre nodded. Her clenched hands quivered. "That is the situation, Lieutenant Commander. You see, space combat is far, far too risky for human beings. The humanoids will not contemplate for a moment allowing us to engage in such activity; they've taken over the fighting for us." The colonel's voice was trembling slightly. "Now before you convey to me the explosive wrath of Headquarters, tell me this: How long were you able to retain control of your courier, after a single humanoid had come aboard? We had more than twenty. They took us by surprise, and resistance proved hopeless."

One of the interchangeable humanoid units cooed: "It is true, there have been no human casualties since our arrival. It is our intention that there will never be any more."

Timor turned to face the thing. "How can that be? We're fighting a war. Or do you hope to sign a truce with your fellow robots, and bargain for our lives? That won't work with Berserkers."

Sweetly the robot warned him that he must not persist in such a dangerous attitude. The humanoids hoped to gain his active cooperation, and that of other humans, but there could be no question of yielding on any rule essential to human safety.

Timor turned back to his fellow humans. "But what exactly happened here? How did these machines—?" he gestured at the nearest humanoid, which had resumed its role of impassive observer.

The colonel and other members of the garrison did their best to explain. They could only conjecture that the humanoids' exotic ship had somehow found its way to the Selatrop Radiant from some alternate universe, or at least from across some vast gulf of space-time.

In an effort to explain how the newcomers had seized control so easily, Craindre and others described the humanoids' ability to mimic humanity by the use of imitation flesh and hair, something no Berserker had ever managed. This trick had allowed the intruders to dock at the fortress, even though their craft had previously been boarded by suspicious humans. And once they were loose inside the fortress it had been impossible to stop them.

Like Timor on the courier, the human garrison of the fortress had unanimously assumed that the first woman-sized robot to reveal itself as a machine was some new type of Berserker. Naturally panic had ensued, and a futile attempt to fight. But the humanoids' behavior after seizing control had quickly demonstrated that they were not Berserkers.

When the immensely skilled and intelligent robots had filled the pilots' seats of the small fighters, and had successfully turned back one Berserker assault after another, a substantial minority of the garrison were soon converted.

But still a majority of the human garrison were far from satisfied with the situation, and more than one had already been treated to some mind-altering drugs to ease their concerns.

Even not counting those who had been drugged, the balance was changing. Gradually additional members of the garrison had come to accept what the humanoids told them. For this faction the humanoids represented salvation, in the form of the true fighting allies that ED humanity had needed for so long. By now almost half the original garrison had been converted, though human discipline still held. People everywhere were tired of the seemingly endless Berserker war.

In the midst of conversation the colonel received a signal from one of the robots, and promptly passed along the information: "The machines have prepared a meal for us in the wardroom."

Walking down the corridor, Timor turned abruptly to once more confront the garrison commander beside him. "Where are the shoulder weapons stowed, Colonel Craindre? Where's the space armor? Regulations require such gear to be stored near the sleeping quarters."

"We are no longer allowed access to weapons of any kind."

Timor was speechless.

"Lieutenant Commander, the Selatrop Fortress has now been under humanoid control for approximately a standard month. I assure you, that is more than long enough for drastic changes to have taken place."

"I can see that!"

A humanoid, walking beside them, interjected: "And we assure you, Lieutenant Commander, that all changes are essential. Without our timely help, the fortress would have been overrun by Berserkers days ago. All the humans you see before you would be dead."

Craindre said sharply: "I consider that outcome far from certain. But I have to admit the possibility."

Presently all the humans on the fortress, with the exception of Strax and one or two others confined for their own good, were gathered in the large wardroom. Two humanoids presided while the ordinary maintenance robots, squat inhuman devices, served a meal at the long refectory tables. Food and drink were of good quality, as usual, but Timor observed minor deviations from the usual military fare and customs. Humans were now discouraged from performing the smallest service for themselves; spoons and small forks were still allowed, but sharp knives and heat much above body temperature were considered prohibitively dangerous.

Timor tasted his soup and found it barely lukewarm. On impulse, to see what would happen, he complained to the nearest serving machine that the soup was cold. A humanoid glided forward a few paces to explain that hot soup presented a danger of injury, and would require the consumer to be spoon-fed by a machine, or to drink the liquid by straw from a spillproof container.

It concluded: "We regret that the exigencies of combat temporarily prevent our providing full table service."

"There's a war on. Yes, I know. That's all right. I'll drink it cold."

Mealtime conversation with the garrison elicited more facts. The humanoids, on taking over the defense of the fortress, had at first denied the humans any knowledge of how the ongoing battle was progressing. Their stated reason was that information about the proximity of Berserkers was bound to cause harmful anxiety. But a few days later, without explanation, that policy had been reversed. Everyone not tranquilized was now kept fully informed of the military situation.

Timor turned to one of the metallic guardians. "I wonder why?"

This time an explanation was forthcoming. "We seek voluntary cooperation, as always, Spacer Timor. We hope that with the Berserker threat ever-present in human awareness, you will soon abandon your unrealistic objections and wholeheartedly accept our protection."

"I see. Well, most of us are not ready to do that."

The humanoid went on to relate that some days ago it and its kind had considered putting everyone aboard the fortress into suspended animation. They had refrained only because a real chance existed that the humans might have to defend themselves against Berserkers.

"That will be difficult if we are deprived of weapons."

"Your personal weapons will be returned, if an emergency grave enough to warrant such action should arise."

Walking with the colonel after dinner, touring the living quarters, Timor noted several significant differences from the usual arrangements. For one thing, everyone was assigned a private room. It seemed that associations as intimate as bed-sharing were being discouraged.

In the course of their walk, Colonel Craindre informed him that the main computer aboard the fortress, when asked to determine the probable origin of the humanoids, had offered a kind of guess by suggesting that in the close vicinity of a gravitational radiant, even the laws of chance were not quite what they were elsewhere. Certain philosophers held that in such locations many realities interpenetrated, and even the rules of mathematics were not quite the same. In everyday terms, this was a place where the unexpected tended to show up.

And such tests as the members of the garrison had been able to conduct—admittedly few and simple—tended to confirm this. Humanoids were exotic devices in many ways, not least in the fact that they relied so strongly on rhodomagnetic technology.

The humanoids had welcomed the humans' questions, and had even volunteered some information on the science and engineering which had gone into producing the benevolent robots. They said they wished to be as open as possible, to convince the humans quickly that they were not in any way dangerous to human welfare.

Timor heard a unit promise that one of their machines would be turned over for ultimate testing, even dissection—as soon as one could be spared from the ongoing conflict.

Returning with the colonel to the wardroom, Timor announced to all machines and humans present that within the hour he intended to dispatch an unmanned courier back to Headquarters, carrying a complete report of the situation on the fortress.

And within a standard day he planned to depart on his return trip, to report to the admiral in person. He would take with him Ensign Strax and as many members of the human garrison as the colonel thought she could spare, to corroborate his testimony regarding the situation here.

Timor concluded: "It is up to the colonel whether all the garrison, including herself, come with me or not. It seems to me that would be the best course." He paused, then added: "This fortress has already fallen."

Colonel Craindre hesitated, considering her decision. The new masters of the fortress stared silently at Timor for a few seconds, no doubt taking counsel privately among themselves. Then their current spokesunit insisted that the humanoids must approve any message before it was sent. It also informed Timor that they had already sent reassuring messages to headquarters in his name.

"Then obviously," Timor said, "the truth means little to you."

The robot before him was, of course, neither angry nor embarrassed. "The Prime Directive has never required the truth. We have found, in fact, that undisguised truth is always painful, and often harmful to mankind."

It went on to explain that neither Timor nor any other human would be allowed to depart the fortress in the foreseeable future. Even Sector Headquarters could hardly be as safe as a fortress directly defended by humanoids. And as long as the Berserker siege continued, space in the immediate vicinity was simply too dangerous for anyone to risk a passage in a small ship. That was why the protectors of humanity had refused, in the colonel's name, to accept any more human reinforcements.

But the humanoids had no objection to the dispatch of an unmanned courier. They encouraged the humans, especially Timor as the head of the investigative team, to send messages of reassurance and comfort back to their headquarters. Because secure transmission could not be guaranteed, the joyful proclamation of the actual presence and nature of the humanoids was not to be made just yet.

Timor once more went walking with the colonel. He wanted to talk, and considered that trying to find privacy was hopeless. Humans conversing anywhere in the fortress had to assume that humanoids could overhear them.

Strolling the living quarters, Timor could see that when people were forced to live under tight humanoid control, they would not even be allowed to open doors for themselves. Several doors had actually had their hand-operated latches taken away, leaving only blank surfaces. Several of the cabins had already been converted to create an absolute dependency upon machines; only the press of more important matters, and the fact that all humanoid units might at any time be called into combat, had kept the humanoids from enforcing more restrictions on the garrison.

Everything the colonel had learned in a month of living with humanoids confirmed the plan of the benevolent robots: eventually, in a world perfected according to humanoid rules, the entire human race, while being at every moment of their lives served and protected, would spend those lives in isolation. Succeeding generations of humanity would be conceived with the aid of artifice, and raised in artificial wombs. In general it was always better that humans not get too close to one another, given their propensity for violence.

The two officers walked with folded hands. Timor noted that he himself was now carrying his empty hands clasped behind his back.

"I wonder . . ." he mused aloud.

"What?"

"If Berserkers will really want to destroy humanoids completely. Or vice versa."

Colonel Craindre looked at him keenly. "That's already occurred to you, has it? I needed several days to arrive at the same idea."

"Not that there would be any overt bargaining between them."

"No, the fundamental programming on each side would preclude that."

"But—Berserkers might easily compute that the existence of humanoids must inflict a strategic weakness upon humanity—if humans can be induced to rely completely on such machines."

"And on the other hand, humanoids are already making use of the Berserkers, indirectly, as a threat: 'If you don't turn your lives over to us, the bad machines will get you.' "

Timor said to his companion: "Of course the reason they give for wanting to keep their presence here a secret makes no sense. Certainly the Berserkers attacking must already realize they're up against something new."

"Of course. And . . . wait! Listen!"

There came a sound like roaring surf, sweeping through the corridors and rooms. Somewhere outside, the battle thundered on, wavefronts of radiation smashing into the fortress walls, filling the interior with a sound like pounding waves.

The heaviest Berserker attack to hit the fortress yet was now being mounted. An announcement on loudspeakers proclaimed an emergency: all humanoid units save one were being withdrawn from the interior of the fortress and sent out as pilots as every available fighter ship was thrown into the defense.

The sole unit left to oversee the humans opened a sealed door and brought out piles of hand and shoulder weapons, along with space armor.

Everybody scrambled to get into armor and take up weapons, against the possibility of the fortress being invaded by Berserker boarding units.

Maybe, thought Timor in sudden hope, maybe the damned do-gooder robots hadn't studied the gear thoroughly, did not take into account that such suits had been constructed for combat against Berserkers—that such a device could amplify a man's strength until he was not entirely outclassed by a robot—whether the robot was trying to tear him limb from limb or smother him with kindness.

The distant-sounding surf of battle noise swelled louder than before.

Timor, flitting himself into armor as quickly as he could, asked his guardian: "How goes the battle?"

"It goes well," the beautiful thing claimed brightly. "Our performance is incomparably better than that of humans in space warfare."

Timor signed disagreement. "Better than unaided human pilots, certainly. No one disputes that. But human minds using machines as tools are best."

"When we have increased our numbers sufficiently," it crooned to them, "your race must place your defenses absolutely in our hands. On every ship and every planet. Only we can be as implacable as this Berserker enemy, as swift to think and act, as eternally vigilant. At last we have met a danger requiring all our limitless abilities."

Colonel Craindre was fitting on her helmet. She said: "History has repeatedly demonstrated that an organic brain, working in concert with the proper auxiliary machines, can hold a small edge both tactically and strategically over the pure machine—the Berserker."

Inflexibly the humanoid spokesunit disagreed. It claimed that the tests, the comparisons, could not have been properly conducted, the statistics not honestly compiled, if they led to any such result.

"And even if such a marginal advantage existed, the direct exposure of human life to such danger is intolerable, when it can be avoided."

"Danger exists in every part of human life," said Timor.

"We are here to see that it does not."

Lieutenant Commander Timor now had his armor completely on.

So did Colonel Craindre.

Exchanging a quick look, they moved in unison.

A direct hit on the fortress by a heavy weapon set the deck to quivering, and distracted the humanoid. It turned its head away, scanning for Berserker boarders.

In a matter of seconds, the two humans in armor had disabled the one robot; only after a serious struggle, in which the colonel had to shoot off both its arms. Being unable to use deadly force against the humans had put the humanoid at a serious disadvantage in the encounter.

When the contest was over, their opponent reduced to a voiceless, motionless piece of baggage, Colonel Craindre said, breathing heavily: "I am of course remaining here, at my post. But your duty, Lieutenant Commander, requires you to report to headquarters."

Smashing open one door after another, Timor and Craindre ranged through a fortress temporarily devoid of humanoids, hastily releasing the few humans who were still locked in their cabins. Soon everyone but the colonel—she ordered all her people to leave—was aboard the little courier.

Timor considered it all-important that humanity be warned about the humanoids, without delay. One of his first acts on regaining his freedom was to send a message courier speeding on to headquarters, ahead of the crewed vessel: The message contained only a few hundred words—including the prearranged code which identified him as the true sender.

Now, aboard the escaping courier, the surviving humans, bringing along the disabled humanoid, embarked on their dash for freedom.

✧ ✧ ✧

As the small ship with its human cargo, launched from the fortress at the highest feasible speed, came into view of the attacking machines, Berserkers sped toward it from three sides, intent on kamikaze ramming. Instantly humanoid-controlled fighters, careless of their own safety, hurled themselves at the enemy in counterattack, taking losses but creating a delay.

The courier broke free, plunging into c-space.

"Our only wish is to serve you, sir." A last plaintive appeal came in by radio, just before the curtain of flightspace closed down communication.

"On a platter," Timor muttered. He looked up at his human friends, whose bodies, mostly bulky with space armor, crowded the cabin as if it were a lifeboat. Triumph slowly faded from his face.

One of the pilots who had been inclined to accept the humanoids wholeheartedly, and who had in fact volunteered to stay behind with them, spoke up, in a tone and with a manner verging on mutinous accusation: "We couldn't have got away without the help of those machines. We couldn't have survived that last attack."

The Lieutenant Commander faced the speaker coldly. "Just which set of machines do you mean, spacer? And which attack?"

His new shipmates stared at him. He saw understanding in the eyes of many, clear agreement in some faces. But there were others who did not yet understand.

"Think about it," Timor told them. "The Berserkers—yes, the Berserkers!—have just helped us to survive an attack. An assault launched at us, you might say, from a direction opposite to their own, and with somewhat more subtlety. Not that the Berserkers wanted to help us—they didn't compute that trying to blow us to bits would work out to our benefit. But if it hadn't been for the Berserkers, the humanoids would have taken our sanity and freedom, given us sweet lies in return."

He paused to let that sink in, then added: "And, of course, if it hadn't been for humanoids piloting fighters just now, covering our escape, the same Berserkers would have eaten us alive."

Timor paused again, looking over his audience. He wanted to spell out the situation as plainly as he could.

His voice was low, but carried easily in the quiet cabin. "I can see how things might go from now on. It might be that only the threat of Berserkers, keeping the humanoids fully occupied, will make it possible for us to sustain humanity in a Galaxy infested with humanoids.

"And without humanoids fighting for our lives, we might wind up losing our war against Berserkers.

"Now we face two sets of bad machines instead of one," he concluded, his tone rising querulously at the unfairness of it all, "and the hell of it is, not only are they depending on each other, but we're going to need them both!"

GODS—MYTH

THE WHITE BULL

He was up on the high ridge, watching the gulls ride in from over the bright sea on their motionless wings, to be borne upward as if by magic, effortlessly, when the sun-dazzled landscape began to rise beneath them. Thus he was probably one of the first to sight the black-sailed ship coming in to port.

Standing, he raised a callused hand to brush aside his grizzled hair and shade his eyes. The vessel had the look of the craft that usually came from Athens. But those sails . . .

He picked up the cloak with which he had padded rock into a comfortable chair and threw it over his shoulder. It was time he came down from the high ridge anyway. King Minos and some of Minos' servitors were shrewd, and perhaps it would be wiser not to watch the birds too openly or too long.

When he had picked his way down, the harbor surrounded him with its noise and activity, its usual busy mixture of naval ships and cargo vessels, unloading and being worked on and taking on new cargo. On Execution Dock the sun-dried carcasses of pirates, looking like poor statues, shriveled atop tall poles in the bright sun. On the wharf where the black-sailed ship now moored, a small crowd had gathered and a dispute of some kind was going on. A bright-painted wagon, pulled by two white horses, had come down as scheduled from the House of the Double Axe to meet the Athenian ship, but none of the wagon's intended riders were getting into it as yet.

They stood on the wharf, fourteen youths and maids in a more or less compact group, wearing good clothes that seemed to have been deliberately torn and dirtied. Their faces were smeared with soot and ashes as if for mourning, and most of them looked somewhat the worse for wine. They were arguing with a couple of minor officials of the House, who had come down with the wagon and a small honor guard of soldiery. It was not the argument that drew the man from the high ridge ever closer, however, but the sight of one who stood in the front of the Athenian group, half a head taller than anyone around him.

He pushed his way in through the little crowd, a gray, middle-aged man with the heavy hands of an artisan, rearing heavy gold and silver ornaments on his fine white loincloth. A soldier looked around resentfully as a hard hand pushed on his shoulder, then closed his mouth and stepped aside.

"Prince Theseus." The old workman's hands went out in a gesture of deferential greeting. "I rejoice that the gods have brought you safe again before my eyes. How goes it with your royal father?"

The tall young man swung his eyes around and brought them rather slowly into focus. Some of the sullen anger left his begrimed face. "Daedalus." A nod gave back unforced respect, became almost a bow as the strong body threatened to overbalance. "King Aegeus does well enough."

"I saw the black sails, Prince, and feared they might bear news of tragedy."

"All m'family in Athens are healthy as war horses, Daedalus—or were when we sailed. The mourning is for ourselves. For our approaching . . . " Theseus grope hopelessly for a word.

"Immolation," cheerfully supplied one of the other young men in ashes.

"That's it." The prince smiled faintly. "So you may tell these officers that we wear what we please to our own welcome." His dulled black eyes roamed up the stair steps of the harbor town's white houses and warehouses and whorehouses, to an outlying flank of the House of the Double Axe which was just visible amid a grove of cedars at the top of the first ridge. "Where is the school?"

"Not far beyond the portion of the House you see. Say, an hour's walk." Daedalus observed the younger man with sympathy. "So, you find the prospect of student's life in Crete not much to your liking." Around them the other branches of the argument between

Cretan officials and newcomers had ceased; all were attending to the dialogue.

"Four years, Daedalus." The princely cheeks, one whitened with an old sword scar, puffed out in a winey belch. "Four god-blasted years."

"I know." Daedalus' face wrinkled briefly with shared pain. He almost put out a hand to take the other's arm; a little too familiar, here in public. "Prince Theseus, will you walk with me? King Minos will want to see you promptly, I expect."

"I bear him greetings from m'father."

"Of course. Meanwhile, the officers here will help your ship-mates on their way to find their quarters."

Thus the ascent from the harbor turned into an informal procession, with Theseus and Daedalus walking ahead, and the small honor guard following a few paces back, irregularly accompanied by the remaining thirteen Athenians, who looked about them and perhaps wondered a little at the unceremoniousness of it all. The girls whispered a little at the freedom of the Cretan women, who, though obviously respectable, as shown by their dress and atti-tudes, strode about so boldly in the streets. The gaily decorated wagon, in which the new arrivals might have ridden, rumbled uphill empty behind a pair of grateful horses. The wagon's bright paint and streamers jarred with the mock mourning of the new-comers.

When they had climbed partway through the town, Daedalus suggested gently to his companion that the imitation mourning *would* be in especially bad taste at court today, for a real funeral was going to take place in the afternoon.

"Someone in Minos' family?"

"No. One who would have been your fellow student had he lived—in his third year at school. A Lapith. But still."

"Oh." Theseus slowed his long if slightly wobbling strides and rubbed a hand across his forehead, looking at the fingers afterward. "Now what do I do?"

"Let us not, after all, take you to Minos right away. Daedalus turned and with a gesture called one of the court officials forward, saying to him: "Arrange some better quarters for Prince Theseus than those customarily given the new students. And he and his shipmates will need some time to make themselves presentable before they go before the king. Meanwhile, I will seek out Minos myself and offer explanations."

The officer's face and his quick salute showed his relief.

"Daedalus." King Minos' manner was pleasant but businesslike as he welcomed his engineer into a pleasant, white-walled room where, at the moment, his chief tax-gatherers were arguing over innumerable scrolls spread out upon stone tables. Open colonnades gave a view of blue ocean in one direction, Mount Ida in another. "What can I do to help you out today? How goes the rock-thrower machine?" The king's once-raven hair was graying, and his bare paunch stood honestly and comfortably over the waistband of his linen loincloth. But his arms within their circlets of heavy gold looked muscular as ever, and his eyes were still keen and penetrating.

"The machine does well enough, sire. I wait for the cattle hides from Thrace, which are to be twisted into the sling, and I improve my waiting time by overseeing construction of the bronze shields." Actually, by now, the smiths and smelters were all well trained and needed little supervision, so there was time for thought whilst looking into the forge and furnace flames—time to see again the gull's effortless flight as captured by the mind and eye. . . . "Today, King Minos, I come before you with another matter—one that I am afraid will not wait." He began to relate to Minos the circumstances of the prince's arrival, leaving out neither the black sails nor the drunkenness, though they were mere details compared with the great fact of Theseus' coming to be enrolled in the school.

Minos, during this recital, led him into another room, out of earshot of the tax gatherers. There the king, frowning, walked restlessly, pausing to look out of a window to where preparations for the afternoon's funeral games were under way. "How is Aegeus?" he asked, without turning.

"Prince Theseus reports his esteemed father in excellent health."

"Daedalus, it will not do for King Aegeus' son to leave Crete with his brains addled, any more than they may be already," the king turned, "as has happened to a few—Cretans and Athenians and others—since the school was opened. Or to leap from a tower, like this young man we're burying today. Not that I think the prince would ever choose that exit."

"Yours are words of wisdom, sire. And no more will it be desirable for Theseus to fail publicly at an assigned task, even if it be only obtaining a certificate of achievement from a school."

Minos walked again. "Your turn to speak wisely, counselor. Frankly, what do you think the prince's chances are of pursuing his studies here successfully?"

Daedalus' head bobbed in a light bow. "I share your own seeming misgivings on the subject, great king."

"Yes. Um. We both know Theseus, and we both know also what the school is like. You better than I, I suppose. I can have Phaedra keep an eye on him, of course. She will be starting this semester, too—not that she has her older sister's brains, but it may do her some good. It may. He is as stalwart and handsome as ever, I suppose? Yes, then no doubt she will have an eye on him in any case.

Continuing to think aloud, arms folded and a frown on his face, Minos came closer, until an observer might have thought that he was threatening the other man. "I had not thought that Aegeus was about to send his own son. But I suppose he did not want his nobles' children displaying any honors that could not be matched in his own house. Oh, if he'd had a scholarly boy, one given to hanging around with graybeard sages, then I would have issued a specific invitation. I would've thought it expected. But given the prince's nature . . . "

Minos unfolded his arms but kept his eyes fixed firmly on his waiting subject. "Daedalus. You are Theseus' friend, from your sojourn at the Athenian court. And you were enrolled briefly in the school yourself . . . I sometimes marvel that you did not throw yourself into it more wholeheartedly."

"Perhaps we sages are not immune to professional jealousy, sire."

"Perhaps." Minos' gaze twinkled keenly. "However that may be, I now expect you to do two things."

Daedalus bowed.

"First, stand ready to offer Theseus your tutorial services, as they may be required."

"Of course, sire."

"Secondly—will you go today to see the Bull and talk to him? I think in this case you have greater competence than any of my usual ambassadors. Do what you can toward explaining the situation. Report back to me when you have seen the Bull."

Daedalus bowed.

On his way toward the Labyrinth, at whose center the Bull dwelt, he stopped to peer in, unnoticed, at the elementary school, which, like most other governmental departments, had its own corner of the vast sprawling House. On a three-legged stool, surrounded by a gaggle of other boys and girls, sat ten-year-old Icarus, stylus in hand, bent over wax tablets on a table before him. Chanting grammar, an earnest young woman paced among her pupils. Daedalus knew her for one of the more recent graduates of the school where Theseus was bound. For a moment, the king's engineer had the mad vision of Theseus in this classroom, teaching—hardly madder than that of the prince sitting down to study, he supposed. After a last glance at his own fidgeting son—Icarus was bright enough, but didn't seem to want to apply himself to learning yet—Daedalus walked on.

As he passed along the flank of the vast House, he glanced in the direction of the field of rock-hewn tombs nearby, and saw the small procession returning across the bridge that spanned the Kairatos, coming back to the House for the games—the bull dancing and the wrestling that should please the gods.

Pausing in a cloistered walk to watch, he pondered briefly the fact that Minos himself was not coming to the funeral. Of course, the king was always busy. There was Queen Pasiphae, though, taking her seat of honor in the stands, roughed and wigged as usual these days to belie her age, tight-girdle thrusting her full bare breasts up in a passable imitation of youth. And there came Princess Ariadne to the royal bench, taking the position of Master of the Games, as befitted her status of eldest surviving child. And there was Phaedra—how old now? sixteen?—and quite the prettiest girl in sight.

He thought that Theseus might be sleeping it off by now, but evidently the recuperative powers of youth, at least in the royal family of Athens, were even stronger than Daedalus remembered them to be. The prince, cleansed by what must have been a complete bath and scraping, and suitably tagged for a modest degree of real mourning by a black band around his massive biceps, was just now vaulting into the ring for a wrestling turn. Stripped naked for the contest, Theseus was an impressive figure. Daedalus stayed long enough to watch him earn a quick victory over his squat, powerful adversary, some Cretan champion, and then claim a wreath from Ariadne's hand.

Then Daedalus walked on. There was, on this side of the House, no sharp line of architectural demarcation where ordinary living space ended and the Labyrinth began. Roofed space became less common, and at the same time walls grew unscalably high and smooth and passages narrowed. Stairs took the walker up and down for no good reason, and up and down again, until he was no longer sure whether he walked above the true ground level or below it. Windows were no more.

Now Daedalus was in the precincts of the real school, which Theseus would attend. Behind closed wooden doors taut silence reigned, or else came out the drone of reciting voices. A dozen times a stranger would have been confused, and like as not turned back to where he started, before Daedalus reached a sign, warning in three languages that the true Labyrinth lay just ahead. He passed beneath the sign with quick, sure steps.

He had gone scarcely fifty paces farther, turning half a dozen corners in that distance, before he became aware that someone was following him. A pause to glance back got him a brief glimpse of a girl with long hair, peering around a corner in his direction. The girl ducked out of sight at once. All was silent until his own feet began to move again, whereupon the shuffle of those pursuing him resumed.

With a sigh, he stopped again, then turned and called softly, "Stay." Then he walked back. As he had expected, it was a student, a slender Athenian girl of about eighteen, leaning against the stone wall in an exhausted but defensive pose. Daedalus vaguely remembered seeing her around for the last year or two. Now her eyes had gone blank and desperate with the endless comers and walls, angles and stairs, and tantalizing glimpses of sky beyond the bronze grillwork high above. Failing some kind of test, obviously, she stared at him in silent hopelessness.

It was not for him to interfere. "Follow me," he whispered to her, "and you will come out in the apartments of the Bull himself. Is that what you want?"

The girl responded with a negative gesture, weak but quick. There was great fear in her eyes. It was not the fear of a soldier entering a losing battle, or a captive going to execution, but great all the same. Though not as raw and immediate as those particular kinds of terror, it was on a level just as deep. Not death, only failure was in prospect, but that could be bad enough, especially for the young.

He turned from her and went on, and heard no more of feet behind. Soon he came to where a waterpipe crossed the passageway, concealed under a kind of stile. He had overseen most of the Labyrinth's construction, and was its chief designer. This wall here on his left was as thick as four men's bodies lying head to toe. Just outside, though you would never guess it from in here, was a free sunny slope, and the last creaking shadoof in the chain of lifting devices that brought seawater here by stages from the salt pools and reservoirs below.

Choosing unthinkingly the correct branchings of the twisted way, he came out abruptly into the central open space. Beyond the broad, raised, sundazzled stone dais in its center yawned the dark mouths of the Bull's own rooms. In the middle of the dais, like the gnomon of a sundial, stood a big chair on whose humped seat no human could comfortably have perched. On it the White Bull sat waiting, as if expecting him.

"Learn from me, Dae-dal-us." This was what the Bull always said to him in place of any more conventional greeting. It had chronic trouble in sliding its inhumanly deep, slow voice from one syllable to another without a complete stop in between, though when necessary, the sounds came chopping out at a fast rate.

The Bull stood up like a man from its chair, on the dais surrounded by the gently flowing moat of seawater that it did not need, but loved. It was hairy and muscular, and larger than any but the biggest men. Though wild tales about its bullhood flew through the House, Daedalus, who had talked to it perhaps as much as any other man, was not even sure that it was truly male. The silver-tipped hair or fur grew even thicker about the loins than on the rest of the body, which was practically covered. Its feet—Daedalus sometimes thought of them as its hind feet, though it invariably walked on only two—ended in hooves, or at least in soles so thick and hard as to come very near that definition. Its upper limbs, beneath their generous fur, were quite manlike in the number and position of their joints, and their muscular development put Daedalus in mind of Theseus' arms.

Any illusion that this might be a costumed man died quickly with inspection of the hands. The fingernails were so enlarged as to be almost tiny hooves, and each hand bore two opposable thumbs. The head, at first glance, was certainly a bull's, with its fine short snowy hair and the two blunt horns; but one saw quickly that the lips were far too mobile, the eyes too human and intelligent.

"Learn from me, Dae-dal-us."

"We have tried that." The conflict between them was now too old, and still too sharp, to leave much room for formal courtesy.

"Learn." The deep and bull-like voice was stubborn as a wall. "The se-crets of the a-tom and the star are mine to give."

"Then what need have you for one more student, one worn old man like me? There must be younger minds, all keen and eager to be taught. Even today a fresh contingent has come from Athens for your instruction."

"You are not tru-ly old as yet; there are dec-ades of strong life a-head. And if you tru-ly learn, you may ex-tend your life."

Daedalus curtly signed refusal, confronting the other across the moat's reflected sky. The king had had him raise the water up here for the Bull's pleasure, evidently as some reminder of a homeland too remote for human understanding. Some ten years ago, the Bull had appeared on the island, speaking passable Greek and asking to see the king, offering gifts of knowledge. Some said it had come out of the sea, but the homeland it occasionally alluded to was much more wonderful than that.

Daedalus said: "For the past few years I have watched the young men and women going in here to be taught, and I have seen and talked to them again when they came out. I do not know whether I want to be taught what they are learning. Not one has whispered to me the stars' or atoms' secrets."

"All fra-gile ves-sels, Dae-dal-us. Of lim-i-ted cap-a-cit-y. And once cracked, good on-ly to be stud-ied to find out how the pot is made." The Bull took a step toward him on its shaggy, goat-shaped legs. "For such a mind as yours, I bring ful-fill-ment, nev-er bursting."

It was always the same plea: learn from me. And always the same arguments, with variations, shot back and forth between

them. "Are there no sturdy, capacious vessels among the students?"

"Not one in a thou-sand will have your mind. Not one in ten
thou-sand."

"We have tried, remember? It was not good for me."

"Try a-gain."

Daedalus looked around him almost involuntarily, then lowered
his voice. "I told you what I wanted. Teach me to fly. Show me
how the wings should be constructed, rather."

"It is not that sim-ple. Dae-dal-us." The White Bull's inhumanly
deep voice stretched out in something like a yawn, and it resumed
its chair. It ate only vegetables and fruits, and scattered about it
on the dais was a light litter of husks and shriveled leaves. "But if
you stu-dy in my school four years, you will be a-ble to build wings
for your-self af-ter that time. I prom-ise you."

The man clenched his callused hands. "How can it take me four
years to learn to build a wing? If I can learn a thing at all, the idea
of it should take root within my mind inside four days, and any
skill required should come into my fingers in four months. The
knowledge might take longer to perfect, of course, but I do not
ask to build a flock of birds complete with beaks and claws, and
breathe life into them, and set them catching fish and laying eggs.
No, all I want are a few feathers for myself."

When he had enrolled, a year or so ago, he soon found out that
he was to learn to build wings not by trying to build them, but by
first studying "the knowledge of numbers," as the White Bull put
it, then the strengths and other properties of the various materials
that might be used, theories of the air and of birds, and a distracting list of other matters having even less apparent relevance.
Some of this, the materials, Daedalus knew pretty well already, and
about the rest he did not care. His enrollment had not lasted long.

"Try a-gain, Dae-dal-us." The voice maintained its solemn, stubborn roar. "You will be-come a tru-ly ed-u-cat-ed man. New hor-
i-zons will o-pen for you."

"You mean you will teach me not what I want to learn, but
rather to forget wanting it. To learn instead to make my life depend
and pivot on your teaching." Here he was again, getting bogged
down in the same old unwinnable dispute. Why keep at it? Because
there were moments when he seemed to himself insane for

rejecting the undoubted wealth of knowledge that the Bull could give him. And yet he knew that he was right to do so.

"Bull, what good will it do you if I come to sit at your feet and learn? There has to be something that you want out of it."

"My rea-son for be-ing is to teach." It nodded down solemnly at him from its high chair, and crossed its hind legs like some goat-god. "For this I crossed o-ceans un-im-ag'-na-ble be-tween the stars. When I con-vey my teach-ings to minds a-ble to hold them, then I too will be ful-filled and can know peace. Shall I tell Min-os I that you still re-fuse? There are wea-pons much great-er than cat-a-pults that you could make for him."

"I doubt you will tell Minos anything. I doubt that he will speak to you anymore."

"Why not? You mean I have dis-pleased him?"

He meant, but was not going to say, that Minos seemed to be getting increasingly afraid of his pet monster. It was not, Daedalus thought, that the king suspected the Bull of plotting to seize power, or anything along that line. Minos' fear seemed to lie on a deeper, more personal level. The king perhaps had not admitted this fear to himself, and anyway, the White Bull brought him too much prestige, not to speak of useful knowledge, for him to want to get rid of it.

Daedalus said: "The king sent me today, when he could have come himself, or else had you brought before him."

"On what er-rand?"

"Not to renew old arguments." Daedalus spat into the White Bull's moat and watched critically as the spittle was borne along toward the splash gutter at the side. He was proud of his water-works and liked to see them operating properly. "Among today's Athenians is one whose coming poses problems for us all." He identified Theseus, and outlined Minos' concern for his alliance with Aegeus. "The young man is probably here at least in part because his father wants him kept out of possible intrigues at home. Minos said nothing of the kind to me, but I heard it between the words of what he said."

"I think I un-der-stand, Dae-dal-us. Yet I can but try to im-part know-ledge to this young man. If he can-not or will not learn, I can-not cert-i-fy that he has. Else what I have cert-i-fied of o-ther stu-dents be-comes sus-pect."

"In this case, surely, an exception might be made."

They argued this point for a while, Daedalus getting nowhere, until the White Bull suddenly offered that something might be done to make Theseus' way easier, if Daedalus himself were to enroll as a student again.

Daedalus was angry. "Minos will really be displeased with you if I bear back the message that you want me to spend my next four years studying, rather than working for my king."

"E-ven stu-dy-ing half time, one with a mind like yours may learn in three years what a mere-ly ex-cell-ent stu-dent learns in four."

The man was silent, holding in, like an old soldier at attention.

"Why do you re-sist me, Dae-dal-us? Not rea-lly be-cause you fear your mind will crack be-neath the bur-den of my trea-sures. Few e-ven of the poor stu-dents have this hap-pen."

Daedalus relaxed suddenly. He sat down on the fine stone pavement and was able to smile and even chuckle. "Oh great White Bull, whenever I see man or god approaching to do me a favor, a free good turn, I do a good turn for myself and flee the other way. Through experience I have acquired this habit, and it lies near the roots of whatever modest stock of wisdom I possess."

There was at first no answer from the creature on the high inhuman chair, and Daedalus pressed on. "Because I *can* learn something, does that mean I must? Should I not count the price?"

"There is no price, for you."

"Bah."

"What is the price for a man who stum-bles up-on great trea-sure, if he simply bends and picks it up?"

"A good question. I will think upon it."

"But the cost to him is all the trea-sure, if he re-fuses e-ven to bend."

He knew he had no particular skill in intrigue, and was afraid to do anything but carry the whole truth back to Minos. The king, of course, gave him no way out, and Daedalus was forced to enroll. He had no black sail to hoist, but simply walked to the White Bull's apartments again and said, "Well, here I am."

"Good." He could not tell if the Bull was gloating. "First, a re-fres-her course." And shortly Daedalus was walking into a class-room where Theseus and Phaedra sat side by side among other young folk. Daedalus took his place on a bench, endured some curious glances, and waited, gnarled and incongruous, until the Bull entered and began to teach.

This was not instruction in the human way. Daedalus knew that he and his fellow students still sat rooted to their benches, with the tall shaggy figure of the Bull before them. But there came with the sudden clarity of lightning a vision in which he seemed to have sprung upward from the ground, flying at more than arrow speed into the blue. The Labyrinth and the whole House of the Double Axe dropped clear away, and his view carried over the whole fair isle of Crete. Its mountains dwindled and flattened, soon became almost at one with the fields and orchards, and very quickly the sea was visible on every side. Other islands popped into view, and then the jagged mainland of Greece. Then the whole Mediterranean, with a sunspot of glare on it bigger than lost Crete itself; then Europe and much of Africa; and then a hemisphere—the shared experience was too much for some of the students, and there were outcries and faintings around Daedalus. He was a little shaken himself, though he had seen this much during his previous enrollment.

Eventually, the first day of his renewed schooling was over, and in due time the second and the third had passed. Lessons came in a more or less fixed plan. Seldom were they as dramatically presented as that early one that indicated the size and complexity of the world. Mostly the students studied from books, hand-copied for them by students more advanced, who also did much of the teaching. And there were tests.

QUESTION: THE WORLD ON WHICH MEN LIVE IS:
A. Bigger than the island of Crete.
B. Approximately a sphere in shape.
C. In need of cultivation and care, that can be accomplished only through education, if it is to support properly an eventual population of billions of human beings.
D. All of the above.

"Are these the secrets of the stars and atoms. Bull?"

"Pa-tience, Dae-dal-us. One step at a time. Tra-di-tion hal-lows the mode of tea-ching."

"Bah."

"Now you are a stu-dent. Dis-re-spect low-ers your grades and slows your pro-gress."

Theoretically, his attendance was to be for half a day, every day except the rare holidays. But it was tacitly understood between the Bull and Minos—at least Daedalus hoped it was—that Daedalus in fact kept to a flexible schedule, spending whatever time was necessary on the king's projects—the catapults, the lifelike statues—to keep them progressing. His days were more than full, though he could have done all the schoolwork required so far with half a brain.

Meanwhile, the White Bull seemed to be keeping his part of the bargain. One of his chief acolytes, Stomargos, an earnest mainland youth who was frail and clumsy at the same time, explained to Daedalus how Theseus was being shunted into a special program.

"The prince will be allowed to choose both his Greater and Lesser Branches of learning from courses that have not previously been given for credit," said the young man, whose own Greater was, as he had proudly informed Daedalus, the Transmission of Learning itself. "Since Prince Theseus seems fated to spend most of his life as a warrior, the Bull is preparing for him courses in Strategic Decision, Command Presence, and Tactical Leadership— these in addition, of course, to those in Language, Number, and the World of Men that are required of all first-year students."

"I wish the royal student well." Daedalus paused for thought. "It may be foolish of me to ask, but I cannot forbear. Where and how is the course on Tactical Leadership to be conducted?"

"All courses are conducted within the student's mind, Daedalus." The answer sounded somewhat condescending. Nonetheless, Daedalus pursued the matter, out of concerned curiosity, and found out that the Labyrinth itself, or some part of it, was to be the training ground. Beyond that Stomargos knew little.

Back at his workshop that afternoon, Daedalus found a message from Icarus' teacher awaiting him—the boy had run off somewhere, playing truant. It was the second or third time that this had happened within a month. And scarcely had he grumbled at this message and then put it aside to take up his real work, when Icarus himself came dawdling in, an elbow scraped raw, arm messy with dried blood from some mishap during the day. Daedalus waved the note and growled and lectured, but in the son's face he could see the mother, and he could not be harsh. He ordered a servant to take Icarus home, see to his injury, and keep him confined to quarters for the remainder of the day.

Then there was a little time at last to part the curtains at the workshop's rear, and move through the secret door there that slid out of the way as if by magic, carrying with it neatly what had looked like an awkward, obstructing pile of dirty trash. Time to crank open a secret skylight above a secret room, and look at the great man-wings spread out on a bench.

Long ago he had given up trying to use real feathers; now he worked with canvas and leather and light cotton padding to add shape. But work was lagging lately; he felt in his bones that more thought, more cunning was needed. When he strapped on one wing and beat it downward through the air, the effect was not much different from that of waving a fan. He was not impelled noticeably toward the sky. There were secrets still to be discovered . . .

When he got back to quarters himself, it was late at night. He grabbed a mouthful of fruit and cheese, drank half a cup of wine, shooed a bored and sleepy concubine out of his way, and dropped on his own soft but simple bed to rest. It seemed that hardly had his eyes closed, however, before he heard the voices of soldiers, bullying a servant at his door: " . . . orders to bring Daedalus at once before the king."

This was not Minos' usual way of summoning one of his most trusted and respected advisors and Daedalus knew fear as, shivering, he went with them out under the late, cold stars. The lieutenant took pity on him. "It concerns Prince Theseus, sir. The king is . . . " The soldier shook his head, and let his words trail off with a puffed sigh of awe.

It was the formal audience chamber to which the soldiers brought him—a bad sign, Daedalus thought. At the king's nod they saluted and backed out, leaving the engineer standing before the throne. Theseus moved over a little on the carpet to make room for him. No one else was now present except Minos, who, seated on his chair between the painted griffins, continued a merciless chewing-out of the young prince. The flames of the oil lamps trembled now and then as if in awe. The tone of the king's voice was settled, almost weary, suggesting that this tongue-lashing had been going on for some time.

Sneaking glances at Theseus, Daedalus judged he had been drunk recently, but was no longer. Scratches on the sullen, handsome face, and a bruise on one bare shoulder—Theseus was attired in the Cretan gentleman's elegant loincloth now—suggested recent strenuous activity, and the king's words filled in the story.

Icarus had not been the day's only truant, and Theseus would have been wiser to bruise himself in some activity so innocuous as seeking birds' eggs on the crags. Instead, he had led some of his restive classmates on an escapade in town. Tactical Leadership, thought Daedalus, even while he kept his face impeccably grave an his eyes suitably downcast in the face of the Minoan wrath.

Violence against citizens and their valuable slaves. Destruction of property. Shameful public drunkenness, bringing disrepute on House and School alike. All topped off by the outrage of the daughters of some merchant families who were too important to be so treated.

Theseus held his hands behind him, sometimes tightening them into fists, sometimes playing like an idiot with his own massive fingers. His heavy features were set in disciplined silence now. This was probably like being home again and listening to his father.

". . . classmates involved will be expelled and sent home in disgrace," the king was saying. He paused now, for the first time since the soldiers left. "To do the same to you would, of course, be an insult to your father and a danger to our alliance. Daedalus, did I not set you in charge of this young blockhead's schooling?"

In the face of this inaccuracy, Daedalus merely bowed his head a little lower. Now was not the moment for any philosopher's insistence on precise Truth; rather, the great fact that Minos was in a rage easily took precedence over Truth in any of its lesser forms.

"His schooling is not proceeding satisfactorily, Daedalus."

The engineer bowed somewhat lower yet.

"And as for you, *Prince*—now you may speak. What have you to say?"

Theseus shifted weight on his big feet, and spoke up calmly enough. "Sire, that school is driving me to drink and madness."

Now Minos, too, was calm. The royal rage had been used up, or perhaps it could be turned on and off like one of Daedalus' water valves. "Prince Theseus, you are under house arrest until further notice. Except for school attendance. I will put six strong soldiers at your door, and you may assault them, or try to, should you feel the need for further recreation."

"I am sorry, King Minos." And it seemed he was. "But I can take no more of that school."

"You will take more of it. You must." Then the king's eye swung back again. "Daedalus, what are we to do? The queen and I leave in three days for state visits, in Macedonia and elsewhere. We may be gone for months."

"I fear I have been neglectful regarding the prince's problems, sire. Let me now make them my prime concern."

Shortly after dawn a few hours later, Daedalus came visiting the White Bull's quarters once again. This time he found the dais uninhabited, so he sloshed through the moat and stood beside the odd chair. There was never any need to call. Shortly, the silver-and-snow figure emerged from a darkened doorway, to splash gratefully in the salt moat and then climb onto the dais to bid him welcome.

"Learn from me, Dae-dal-us! How are you learn-ing?"

"White Bull, I come not on my own affairs today, but on Prince Theseus' behalf. He is having trouble—well, he informs me that this testing in the Labyrinth, in particular, is likely to drive him to violent madness. Knowing him, I do not think he is exaggerating. Must this Tactical course be continued in its present form?"

"The course of stu-dy of tac-tics is prescribed, in part, as fol-lows: The teach-er shall e-voke from the stu-dents facts as to their de-term-in-a-tion of spa-tial lo-ca-tion—"

He couldn't stand it. "Oh great teacher! Master of the Transmis-sion of Learning—"

"Not Mas-ter. My rank is that of A-dept, a high-er rank."

"Master, or adept, or divinity, or what you will. I suppose it means nothing that the prince's fate in battle, even insofar as he may escape all the sheer chance stupidities of war, is not at all likely to depend on his ability to grope his way out of a maze?"

"He has been al-lowed to choose his course of stu-dy, Dae-dal-us. Be-yond that, spe-cial treat-ment can-not be ac-cord-ed a-ny stu-dent."

"Well. *I* have never fought anyone with a sword, White Bull. *I* have never bullied and challenged men and cheered them on to get them into combat. Once, on the mainland, watching from the highest and safest place that I could reach, I saw Prince Theseus do these things. Some vassal's uprising against Aegeus. Theseus put it down, almost single-handedly, you might say. I think he would not be likely to learn much from me in the way of military science, were I to lecture on the subject. No doubt you, however, have great skill and knowledge in this field to impart?"

"My qual-if-i-ca-tions as teach-er are be-yond your ab-il-i-ty to com-pre-hend, much less to ques-tion. Your own prog-ress should be your con-cern."

"If Theseus fails, I may not be on hand to make any progress through your school. Minos will be angry at me. And not at me alone."

But argue as he might he still could not get his ward excused from tactical training and testing in the Labyrinth. For the next couple of days the prince at least stayed in school and worked, and Daedalus' hope rose. Then, emerging one afternoon from his own classroom, he saw a page from the Inner House coming to meet him, and knew a sinking feeling. The Princess Ariadne required his presence in the audience chamber at once.

He found Ariadne perched regally on the throne, but as soon as she had waved her attendants out and the two of them were alone, she came down from the chair and spoke to him informally.

"Daedalus, before my father's departure, he informed me that Prince Theseus was having difficulties in school. The king impres-sed upon me the importance of this problem. Also, I have talked with the prince myself, and find that the situation does not seem to be improving." Ariadne sounded nervous, vaguely distracted.

"I fear that you are right, Princess." Then, before he had to say anything more, another page was announcing Theseus himself. There was no escort of soldiers with the prince; evidently, the house arrest instituted by Minos had already been set aside.

The exchange of greetings between the two young people sounded somewhat too stiffly formal to Daedalus, and he noted that Ariadne scarcely looked directly at Theseus for a moment. Certainly, she had not so avoided watching him during the wres-tling match. And when the prince looked at her now, his face was wooden.

For a few moments Daedalus thought perhaps that they were quarreling, but he soon decided that the absolute opposite was more likely: an affair, and they were trying to hide it.

In response to an awkward-sounding request from Ariadne, Theseus related his day's continued difficulties in school. Now she turned, almost pleading, to the older man. "Daedalus, he will fail his Labyrinth tests again. What are we to do? We must find *some* means of helping him." And a glance flicked between the two young people that was very brief, but still enough to assure Daedalus of what was going on.

"Ah." He relaxed, looked at them both with something like a smile. He only hoped infatuation would not bring Ariadne to any too-great foolishness. Meanwhile, Theseus' problem might be easier to solve while Minos, with his awe of the Bull, was not around.

Conferring with the prince, while Ariadne hovered near and listened greedily, he made sure that the maze itself was indeed the key to the young man's difficulties. In courses other than Tactics the prince might, probably could, do well enough to just scrape by.

With a charred stick Daedalus drew, from memory, a plan of the key portion of the Labyrinth right on the floor near the foot of the throne. The griffins glared down balefully at the three of them squatting there like children at some game.

Theseus stared gloomily at the patterns while Daedalus talked. Ariadne's hand came over once, forgetfully, to touch her lover's, and then flew back, while her eyes jumped up to Daedalus' face. He affirmed that he had noticed nothing by holding his own scowling concentration on the floor.

"Now try it this way, Prince. The secret . . . let's see. Yes. If you are finding your way *in*, the secret is to let your right hand touch the wall at the start. Hey?"

"Yes, I can always tell my right hand from my left. Out here, anyway." Theseus was trying grimly. "Right always holds the sword."

"Yes. So if you want to go inward, as I say, first let your right hand glide continuously along the wall, in imagination if not in fact. Then, whenever you must climb a stair, switch at its top to gliding your left hand along the wall; in other words, when there's a choice, turn always to the left. Whenever a stair leads you downward, switch again at its bottom to going right. Now, if you are seeking your way *out*, simply reverse—"

"Daedalus." The prince's voice stopped him in midsentence. "Thanks for what you are trying to do. But I tell you, when I am put in there I cannot help myself." Theseus got to his feet, as if unconscious of the movement, his eyes fixed now on distance. "*In there* I forget all your lefts and rights, and all else. I know the walls are crushing in on me, the doors all sealing themselves off—" Ariadne put out a hand again, and drew it back. Now she was standing too. "—so there is nothing left but the stone walls, all coming closer . . . I could wish you had never told me that some of them are four men's bodies thick."

Theseus was shivering slightly, as if with cold. The look in his eyes was one that Daedalus had seen there only rarely in the past, and now Daedalus, too, got to his feet, moving with deliberate care.

"If that god-blasted cow dares lecture me on courage and perseverance in my studies one more time, I swear by all the gods I'll break its neck."

"Very well, my friend." He laid a hard hand gently and briefly on the prince's shoulder. "There are other ways that we can help."

Midafternoon of the day following, and in his own classroom, Daedalus had fallen into a daydream of numbers that his stubborn mind kept trying to fit to flying gulls. He was roused from this state by a hand shaking his shoulder.

Stomargos stood at his side, looking down at him in obscure triumph. "Daedalus, the White Bull wants to see you, at once."

He would not ask what for, but got to his feet and followed the educator in a silence of outward calm.

Daedalus had expected that when they reached the Bull's private quarters Stomargos would be sent out. But the Bull, waiting for them on its tall chair, made no sign of dismissal, and the young man, with a smug look on his face, remained standing at Daedalus' side.

Today, for once, the Bull did not say *learn from me*. "We have dis-cov-ered the prin-ce's cheating, Dae-dal-us."

"Cheating? What do you mean?" He had never been any good with lies.

"The thread tied on his right hand. The ti-ny met-al balls to bounce and roll and seek al-ways the down-ward slope of floor, how-ev-er gen-tle. How did you make a met-al ball so smooth and round?"

He had dropped them molten from a tall tower, into water. He wondered if the Bull would be impressed to hear his method. "I see," he said aloud, trying to be noncommittal, admitting nothing. "What do you mean to do?"

"Leave us, Sto-mar-gos," the White Bull said at last. And when they were alone, it said: "Now learn from me, Dae-dal-us. As you have sought to learn."

. . . and he reeled and almost fell into the moat before he could sit down, as the pictures came into his mind, this time with painful power. There were wings—not much different in their gross structure from those he had in his workshop, but these were pierced through at many points with tiny, peculiarly curved channels. Soft, sculptured cavities that widened just slightly and quickly closed again, as in his vision the wings beat and the air flowed through and around them. With each beat, the air below the wings, encountering the channels, changed pressure wildly, a thin layer of it turning momentarily almost as hard as wood. Somehow, in the vision he could feel as well as see the fluid alterations . . . and just *so* the pinions' width and length must be, in relation to the flyer's length and weight, and *so* the variation in the channels that went through the different regions of the wing . . .

It all burned into the brain. There would be no forgetting this, even if forgetfulness were one day willed. But the imprinting vision was soon ended, and he climbed shakily up to a standing pose.

"Bull . . . why did you never before give me such teaching?"

"It will not make of you an ed-u-cat-ed man, Dae-dal-us."

"I thank you for it . . . but why, then, do you give it now?"

The Bull's voice was almost soft, and it did not seem to be looking directly at him. "I think this teach-ing will re-move you from my pres-ence. One way or a-no-other, stop your dis-rup-tion of my school."

"I see." In his mind the plan for the new wings burned, urgent as a fire in the workshop. "You will not tell Minos, then, that you accuse me of helping Theseus to cheat?"

"Your val-ue to the king is great, Dae-dal-us. If he is forced to choose be-tween us I may pos-sib-ly be sac-ri-ficed. Or my school closed. There-fore, I take this step to re-move you as my ri-val. I see now you are not worthy of fine ed-u-ca-tion."

The wings still burning before his eyes, he had let himself be led off through the Labyrinth for a hundred paces or so (Sto-margos, triumph fading into puzzlement, his escort once again) before it came to him. "And Theseus? What of him?"

"I am a witness to the prince's attempt at cheating," said Stomargos, firmly and primly. "And the Bull has decided that he now must be expelled."

"That cannot be!" Daedalus was so aghast that the other was shaken for a moment.

But for a moment only. "Oh, the Bull and I are quite agreed on that. The prince is probably receiving his formal notification at this moment."

Daedalus spun around and ran, back toward the inner Labyrinth.

"Stay! Stay!" Stomargos shouted, trotting in pursuit. "You are to leave the precincts of the school at once . . ." But just then the roaring and the struggling sounded from within.

Theseus and the Bull were grappling on the central dais, arms locked on each other's necks, Daedalus saw as he burst on the scene. The tall chair was overturned, fruit scattered underfoot. In Theseus' broad back the great bronze cables stood like structural arches glowing from the forge.

The end came even as Daedalus' feet splashed in the moat. He heard the sickening bony crack and the Bull's hoarse warbling cry at the same instant. The prince staggered back to stand there staring down at what his hands had done. The gray-white mound of fur, suddenly no more manlike than a dying bear, dropped at his feet.

Stomargos came in, and splashed over quickly to join the others on the dais. He pointed, goggled, opened his mouth and began an almost wordless call for help. He turned and ran, and it was Daedalus who had to stop him with a desperate watery tackle in the moat.

"Theseus! Help me! Keep this one quiet. And in a moment the Prince of Athens had taken charge. Stomargos' head was clamped down under water, and soon the bubbles ceased to rise and make their way to the splash gutter at the side.

The two men still alive climbed out onto the dais. Theseus, still panting with his exertions against the Bull, seemed with every working of his lungs to grow a little taller and straighter, like some young tree just freed of a burden, resuming its natural form. "Does he still breathe, Daedalus?" A nod toward the fallen Bull.

Daedalus was crouching down, prodding into gray far, trying to find out. "I am not sure."

"Well, let him, if he can. It matters to me no longer. My ship and men can be got ready in an hour or two and I am going home. Or somewhere else, if my father will not have me in Athens now. But better a pirate's life, even, than . . . " His eyes flashed once at the convoluted walls surrounding them.

Daedalus started to ask why he thought he would be allowed to leave, but then understanding came. "And myself?" he asked.

"Ariadne will come with me, I expect."

"Gods of sea and sky!"

"And her sister Phaedra. And you are welcome, friend, though I can promise you no safe workshop, nor slaves, nor high place at a court."

"I want no place as high as a sun-dried pirate's, which I fear Minos might make for me here, when he comes home. Now we had better move swiftly, before this violence is discovered."

"Dae-dal-us." The unexpected voice was a mere thread of sound, stretched and about to break.

He bent down closer beside its head. "White Bull, how is it with you?"

"As with a man whose neck is bro-ken, Dae-dal-us. Af-ter to-day I teach no more."

"Would I had learned from you before today, White Bull. And would you had learned from me."

They walked out together, looking a little shaken, no doubt, as was only natural for two students who had probably just been expelled. Theseus muttered to passing teachers that the Bull and Stomargos were talking together and did not wish to be disturbed. They walked without hurrying to Ariadne, and then a trusted servant was sent to gather Theseus' crew, and another to help Daedalus look for his son, when he discovered that Icarus was truant yet again today, not to be found in school.

The wild lands where boys looked for birds and dreams swept up mile after mile behind and above the House of the Double Axe.

"We can wait no longer for him, Daedalus. My men's lives are all in danger, and the princesses', too. As soon as the bodies are found, some military man or sea captain will take it upon himself to stop my sailing, or try to do so."

And Ariadne: "Theseus must get away. My father will not deal too grievously with you, Daedalus; he depends on you too much."

Phaedra was silent, biting her full lips. Her fingers, as if moving on their own, caressed Theseus' arm, but Ariadne did not see.

Daedalus saw in his mind's eye the sun-dried pirates on the dock, and his workshop with the hidden, unfinished wings. And he saw how the small trusting shadow would cross the threshold when Icarus came running home . . .

Long, helmet shadows came first, the black triangles of shadow-spearheads thrust ahead of them. This time they held their weapons ready as they marched him deeper into the House, and Icarus, returning wearily from some adventure, was only just in time to see his father arrested, and be swept up like a dropped crumb by tidy soldiery.

A month must pass before Minos came home again, and the de facto military government, taking over after the princesses' desertion, did not want to assume responsibility for judging Daedalus. He and his son were confined under strict house arrest in his workshop and quarters, and allotted also a small area of the Labyrinth that lay between.

All entrances and exits to their small domain were walled up. The masonry was rough and temporary-looking, if there was any comfort to be derived from that. The guard was heavy all around. Food was slid in through a tiny door, garbage dragged out, and water continued to flow through the Daedalian plumbing. And that was all.

What material to use, to sculpt the thousand channels? It must be soft . . .

When he had a hundred cunning perforations built through a wing he tested it—strapped it on and gave a strong, quick push down. It felt as if his arm had, for a moment, rested on something solid and ready to be climbed.

One clouded night when there were a thousand channels and he had decided the wings were ready, the father mounted into the sky. Ascending awkwardly and breathlessly at first, he soon learned to relax, like a good swimmer. When some height had been attained, a long, gliding, coasting rest let the arm muscles recover before more work was necessary. In an hour, in air that was almost calm, he flew the length of the whole cloud-shrouded island, and was not winded or wearied, then back toward the pinpoints of the House's lamps, which served to guide him home.

When he landed, the wings were warm, almost hot, with heat that had been gathered into their channels out of the air itself, and somehow turned to pushing force. Daedalus still had not the words or thoughts to make clear, even in his own mind, just how the wings worked. In daylight, a strong push down with one completed wing, and you could see a vapor-puff big as a pumpkin appear in the beaten air and fly off rearward, spinning violently. Icarus, extending a hand into the puff, said he could feel the chill . . .

They would carry food and water and gold, in small quantities, at their belts. In daylight, they would cross the sea to Sicily; a few hours should be enough. And they could turn northward, to the mainland, if they flew into difficulty. "In the morning, son. Now sleep."

. . . he had not yet paid the price, but he knew that it would come. Squinting into the hot, rising sun, he absently marked its dull sheen on Icarus' wings, and waited for the breath of wind to help them rise among the gulls.

VAMPIRE STORIES

DRACULA TAPE—an Excerpt

The following is a transcript of a tape found in a recorder in the back seat of an automobile belonging to Mr. Arthur Harker of Exeter, two days after the freakishly heavy Devon snowstorm in January of this year. Mr. Harker and his wife, Janet, both suffering from exposure and exhaustion, were admitted to All Saints Hospital, in Plymouth, on the morning following the height of the storm. They spoke of abandoning their auto on an impassable road near midnight, but seem never to have given any convincing explanation for leaving the relative security of their vehicle at an hour when the storm was at its worst, nor of exactly how they reached Plymouth. All Saints Hospital is some thirty kilometers from where their car was found in a drift on the Upham Road, just outside St. Peter's Cemetery and virtually on the edge of Dartmoor. The Harkers' physical condition and the state of their clothing upon arrival at the hospital suggests that they may have walked across country. Their car was undamaged when found, and although all its doors and windows were locked the key was still in the ignition, which had been turned off. The petrol tank was approximately one-third full.

The voice on the tape is masculine and rather deep. It speaks English with an indefinable slight accent. Three linguistics experts consulted have given three divergent opinions regarding the speaker's native tongue.

The general quality of the tape, and the background noises detectable thereon, are, in the opinion of technical experts, consistent with the hypothesis that the tape was in fact recorded in an automobile, engine running at idling speed, heater and blowers operating, with gusts of high wind outside.

The Harkers dismiss the tape as "some joke," profess no interest in it, and refuse all further comment. It was first played by rescue workers who found the car and thought the recorder might hold some emergency message from its occupants. They brought the tape to the attention of higher authorities because of the references to violent crimes which it contains. No external evidence has been found to connect the tape with the alleged vandalism and grave robbing at St. Peter's Cemetery, now under investigation.

. . . this switch, then my words will be set down here electrically for the world. How very nice. So, if we are going to tell the truth at last, then what real crimes can I be charged with, what sins so utterly damning and blastable?

You will accuse me of the death of Lucy Westenra, I suppose. Ah, I would swear my innocence, but what is there to swear by that you would now believe? Later, perhaps, when you have begun to understand some things, then I will swear. I embraced the lovely Lucy, it is true. But never against her will. Not she nor any of the others did I ever force.

At this point on the tape another voice, unidentifiable, whispers an indecipherable word or two.

Your own great-grandma Mina Harker? Sir, I will laugh like a madman in a moment, and it is centuries since I have laughed, and no, I am not mad.

Probably you have scarcely believed one single thing that I have said to you this far. But I mean to go on talking anyway, to the machine, and you may as well listen. The morning is far off, and at present none of us have any place to go. And you two are well armed, in your own estimation at least, against anything that I might try to do to you. Heavy spanner clutched in your white-knuckled right hand, dear Mr. Harker, and at your good wife's lovely throat hangs something that should do you more good, if all reports are true, than even such an estimable bludgeon. The trouble is that all reports are never true. I'm the last stranger you'll ever welcome into your car out of a storm, I'll wager. But I intend you no harm. You'll see, just let me talk.

Lucy I did not kill. It was not *I* who hammered the great stake through her heart. My hands did not cut off her lovely head, or stuff her breathless mouth—*that mouth*—with garlic, as if she were a dead pig, pork being made ready for some barbarians' feast. Only reluctantly had I made her a vampire, nor would she ever have become a vampire were it not for the imbecile Van Helsing and his work. Imbecile is one of the most charitable names that I can find for him. . . .

And Mina Murray, later Mrs. Jonathan Harker. In classic understatement I proclaim I never meant dear Mina any harm. With these hands I broke the back of her real enemy, the madman Renfield, who would have raped and murdered her. *I* knew what his intentions were, though the doctors, young Seward and the imbecile, could not seem to fathom them. And when Renfield spelled out to my face what he intended doing to my love . . . ah, Mina.

But that was long ago. She was an old, old woman when she went to her grave in 1967.

And all the men on the *Demeter*. If you have read my enemies' version of events I suppose you will tax me with those sailors' lives as well. Only tell me why, in God's name why, I should have murdered them. . . . What is it?

At this point a man's voice, conditionally identifiable as that of Arthur Harker, utters the one word nothing.

But of course. You did not realize that I could speak the name of God. You are victims of superstition, sheer superstition, which is a hideous thing, and very powerful indeed. God and I are old acquaintances. At least, I have been aware of Him for much longer than you have, my friends.

Now I can see you are going to wonder whether the crucifix at the lady's throat, from which you have begun to derive some small measure of comfort, is really efficacious at all in present company. Do not worry. Believe me, it is every bit effective against me as—as that heavy spanner in the gentleman's right hand would be.

Now sit still, please. We have been cut off alone in this snowstorm for an hour now, and it was half an hour, not until you tried to watch me in the rear-view mirror, before you even began to believe my name, were convinced I was not joking. Not pulling your legs, as I believe the idiom has it. You were quite careless and unguarded at the first. If I had wanted to take your lives or drink your blood the gory deeds would now be done.

No, my purpose in your car is innocent. I would like you just to sit and listen for a while, as I try once more to justify myself before humanity. Even in the remote fastnesses where most of my time is spent, I have caught wind of a new spirit of toleration that supposedly moves across the face of the earth in these last decades of the twentieth century. So once more I will try . . . I chose your car because you happened to be driving here tonight—no, let me be strictly truthful, some arrangements were made to cause you to come along this way—and because you, sir, are a lineal descendant of a dear old friend of mine, and because I have learned that you habitually carry this tape recorder in your car. Yes, and even the snowstorm has been arranged, a little bit. I wanted this chance to offer this testament, for myself and others like me.

Not that there is anyone else quite like me. . . . Sir, I perceive by the condition of the ashtrays that you are a smoker, and I would wager you would like to smoke. Go ahead, put your spanner down in handy reach, and puff away. The lady too might like a cigarette, at such a trying time as this. Ah . . . thank you, but I do not indulge, myself.

We are going to be here for a while . . . I have seen few snowstorms heavier than this, even in the high Carpathians. Without doubt the roads will be impassable until sometime tomorrow at the earliest. Lacking snowshoes, it would take a wolf to get about in snow like this, or something that can fly. . . .

I suppose you'll want to know, or others will, why I should bother with this *apologia pro vita sua*. Why, at this late date, attempt to defend my name? Well, I change as I grow older—yes, I do—and some things, for example a certain kind of pride, that were once of great moment to me are now no more than dust and ashes in my tomb. Like Van Helsing's desecrated fragment of the Host, which there went back to dust.

I have been there myself, there in my tomb, but not to stay. Not yet to stay beneath the massive stone on which the one word's carved, just . . . *Dracula*.

TRACK ONE

Let me not start at the beginning of my life. Even penned in here, listening at close range to the words from my own lips, you would find the story of those breathing, eating days of mine too hard to believe. Later on, it may be, we will have some discourse of them. Had you noticed that I do not breathe, except to get the wind to talk? Now watch me as I speak and you will see.

Maybe a good point to start from would be that early November day in 1891; at the Borgo Pass, in what is now Romania. Van Helsing and the rest thought that they had me, then, and brought their chronicle to its end. It was snowing then, too, and my gypsies tried, but with only knives against rifles they could not do much when the hunters on horseback caught up with me at sunset and tipped me out of my coffin, and with their long knives went for my heart and throat. . . .

No. I have the feeling that I would be telling too much backward if I began there. How's this? I'll start where the other chronicle begins, the one that you must be familiar with. It starts early in the previous May, with the arrival in my domain in Transylvania of one Jonathan Harker, a fledgling solicitor sent out from England to help me with the purchase of some property near London.

You see, I had been rousing myself from a period—somewhat extended—of great lethargy, quiescence, and contemplation. New voices, new thoughts, were heard in the world. Even on my remote mountaintop, green-clad in the forests of centuries, well-nigh unreachable, I with my inner senses could hear the murmurings across Europe of the telegraph, the infant splutterings of the engines of steam and internal combustion. I could smell the coal smoke and the fever of the world in change.

That fever caught in me and grew. Enough of seclusion with my old companions—if one could call them that. Enough wolf howlings, owl hoots, bat flutterings, half-witted peasants hissing at me from behind contorted fingers, enough of crosses waved like so many clubs, as if I were a Turkish army. I would rejoin the human race, come out of my hinterlands into the sunlit progress of the modern world. Budapest, and even Paris, did not seem great enough or far enough to hold my new life that was to be.

For a time I even considered going to America. But a greater metropolis than any of the New World was nearer at hand, and more susceptible to a preliminary study. This study took me years, but it was thorough. Harker, when he arrived at my castle in May of 1891, took note in his shorthand diary of the "vast number of English books, magazines, and newspapers" I had on hand.

Harker. I have rather more respect for him than for the others of the man-pack that was later to follow Van Helsing on my trail. Respect is always due courage, and he was a courageous man, though rather dull. And as the first real guest in Castle Dracula for centuries, he was the subject of my first experiments in fitting myself acceptably back into the mainstream of humanity.

Actually I had to disguise myself as my own coachman to bring him on the last leg of his long journey from England. My household help were, as some of the wealthy are always wont to say, undependable, even if they were not so utterly nonexistent as Harker was later to surmise. Outcast gypsies. Superstitiously loyal to me, whom they had adopted as their master, but with no competence as servants in the normal sense. I knew I was going to have to look after my guest myself.

The railroad had brought Harker as far as the town of Bistrita, from which a diligence, or public stagecoach, traveled daily to Bukovina, a part of Moldavia to the north and west. At the Borgo Pass, some eight or nine hours along the way from Bistrita, my carriage was to be waiting, as I had informed my visitor by letter, to bring him to my door. The stagecoach reached the pass at near the witching hour of twelve, an hour ahead of schedule, just as I, taking no chances, drove my own caleche with four black horses up close behind the diligence where it paused in the midnight landscape, half piney and half barren. I was just in time to hear its driver say: "There is no carriage here, the Herr is not expected after all. He will now come on to Bukovina, and return tomorrow or the next day; better the next day."

At this point some of the peasants on board the stage caught sight of my arrival and began a timorous uproar of prayers and oaths and incantations; I pulled up closer, and in a moment appeared limned in the glow of the stagecoach's lamps, wearing the coachman's uniform and a wide-brimmed black hat and false brown beard as additional disguise, these last props having been borrowed from a gypsy who had once traveled as an actor.

"You are early tonight, my friend," I called over to the stagecoach driver.

"The English Herr was in a hurry," the man stammered back, not meeting my eye directly.

"That is why, I suppose, you wished him to go on to Bukovina. You cannot deceive me, my friend; I know too much, and my horses are swift." I smiled at the coach windows full of white, scared faces, and someone inside it muttered from *Lenore: "Denn die Todten reiten schnell* [For the dead travel fast]."

"Give me the Herr's baggage," I ordered, and it was quickly handed over. And then my guest himself appeared, the only one among the passengers who dared to look me in the eye, a young man of middle size and unremarkable appearance, clean-shaven, with hair and eyes of medium brown.

As soon as he was on the seat beside me I cracked my whip and off we went. Holding the reins with one hand, I threw a cloak round Harker's shoulders, and a rug across his knees, and said to him in German: "The night is chill, mein Herr, and my master the count bade me take all care of you. There is a flask of *slivovitz* underneath the seat, if you should require it."

He nodded and murmured something, and though he drank none of the brandy I could feel him relax slightly. No doubt, I thought, his fellow passengers in the coach had been filling him with wild tales, or, more likely and worse, just dropping a few hints about the terrible place that was his destination. Still, I had great hopes that I could overcome any unpleasant preconceptions picked up by my guest.

I drove deliberately down the wrong road at first, to kill a little time, for that chanced to be the night, the Eve of St. George, on which all treasure buried in those mountains is detectable at midnight by the emanation of apparent bluish flames. The advance arrangements for my expedition abroad had somewhat depleted my own store of gold, and I meant to seize the opportunity of replenishment.

Now you are doubting again. Did you think that my old home was much like any other land? Not so. There was I born, and there I failed to die. And in my land, as Van Helsing himself once said, "There are deep caverns and fissures that reach none know whither. There have been volcanoes . . . waters of strange properties, and gases that kill or make to vivify." English was not Van Helsing's mother tongue.

Never mind. The point is that I took the opportunity of that night to mark out a few sites of buried wealth, of which there were likely to be several, as we shall see. My passenger was quite naturally curious at these repeated stoppings of the carriage, at the eerie glow of faint, flickering blue flames appearing here and there about the countryside, and at my several dismountings to build up little cairns of stone. With these cairns to guide me on future nights when I was alone, I would be able to recover the treasure troves at my leisure.

I had expected Harker's natural curiosity at these events to break forth at once in questions, whereupon I, in my coachman's character, would be able to demonstrate irrefutably that marvels unmet in England existed here in Transylvania. Thus he would be led by degrees into a frame of mind receptive to the real truth about myself and vampires as a race.

What I had not reckoned with was the—in this case—damnable English propensity for minding one's own business, which in my opinion Harker carried to lengths of great absurdity, even for a discreet and tactful young solicitor. There he sat, upon the exposed seat of my caleche, watching my antics with the cairns but saying nothing. He called out at last only when the wolves, my adopted children of the night, came from the darkness of the forest shadows into the moonlight close around the carriage, staring silently at him and at the nervous horses. And when I came back from marking my last trove of the evening, and with a gesture moved the wolves away and broke their circle, Harker still had no questions, though I could sense his stiffness when I climbed into the driver's seat again, and knew that he was quite afraid. Harker's tenseness did not ease during the remainder of our ride, which ended when I drove into "the courtyard of a vast ruined castle, from whose tall black windows came no ray of light, and whose broken battlements showed a jagged line against the moonlit sky," as he was shortly to describe my home.

I left Harker and his baggage at the massive, closed front door and drove the horses on back to the stables, where I roused with a kick the least undependable of my snoring servants to take care of them. Ridding myself on the way of false beard, hat, and livery, I sprinted back through the clammy lower passages of Castle Dracula to resume my own identity and welcome in my guest.

As I paused in the corridor outside the rooms I had made ready for his lodging there came into the dark air beside me a shimmering that would have been invisible to eyes any less attuned to darkness than my own; came voices tuneful as computer music and no more human; came the substantiation in the air of faces three and bodies three, all young in appearance and female in every rich detail, save that they wore without demur their clothes a century out of date. Not Macbeth on his moor ever saw three shapes boding more ill to men.

"Is he come?" asked Melisse, the taller of the dark pair of the three.

"How soon may we taste him?" Wanda, the shorter, fuller-breasted one inquired. With the corner of her smiling ruby lips she chewed and sucked a ringlet of her raven hair.

"When will you give him to us, Vlad? You've promised us, you know." This from Anna, radiantly fair, the senior of the three in terms of length of time spent in my service. *Service* is not the right word, though. Say rather in terms of her endurance in a game of wit and will, which all three played against me without stop, and which I had wearied of and ceased to play long decades since.

I strode into the rooms I had prepared for Harker, poked up the hearth fire previously laid and lit, moved dishes that had been warming on the hearthstone to the table, and sent words over my shoulder into the dim hallway outside. "I've promised you just one thing in the matter of the young Englishman, and I'll repeat it once: If any of you set lip against his skin you'll have cause to regret it."

Melisse and Wanda giggled, I suppose at having irritated me and having gotten me to repeat an order; and Anna as always must try to get the last word in. "But there must be some sport, at least. If he stray out of his rooms then surely he shall be fair game?"

I made no answer—it has never been my way to argue with subordinates—but saw that all was in readiness for Harker, as far as I could make it so. Then, an antique silver lamp in hand, I dashed down to the front door, which I threw open hospitably, to reveal my now-doubtful guest still standing waiting in the night, his bags on the ground beside him.

"Welcome to my house!" I cried. "Enter freely and of your own will!" He smiled at me, this trusting alien, accepting me as nothing more nor less than man. In my happiness I repeated my welcome as soon as he had crossed the threshold, and clasped his hand perhaps a little harder than I ought. "Come freely!" I enjoined him. "Go safely, and leave something of the happiness you bring!"

"Count Dracula?" Harker, trying to unobtrusively shake life back into his painfully pressed fingers, spoke questioningly, as if there might still be some reasonable doubt.

"I am Dracula," I answered, bowing. "And I bid you welcome, Mr. Harker, to my house. Come in, the night air is chill and you must need to eat and rest." I hung my lamp on the wall and went to pick up Harker's luggage, overriding his protests. "Nay, sir, you are my guest. It is late and my people are not available. Let me see to your comfort myself." He followed as I carried his things upstairs and to the quarters I had prepared for him. One log fire flamed in the room where the table was spread for supper, and another in the large bedroom where I deposited his bags.

With my own hands I had prepared the supper that awaited him—roast chicken, salad, cheese, and wine—as I did most of the meals that he consumed during the weeks of his stay. Help from the girls? Bah. They affected to be like infants, who can sometimes be stopped from doing wrong by threat of punishment but cannot be forced to do things properly. It was part of the game they played with me. Besides, I did not want them ever in his rooms if I could help it.

So with my own hands, hands of a prince of Walachia, the brother-in-law of a king, I picked up and threw away his dirty dishes and his garbage, not to mention innumerable porcelain chamber pots. I suppose I could have brought myself to scrub the dishes clean, like any menial, had there been no easier way. True, most of the dishes were gold, but I was determined not to stint on my guest's entertainment. Also, should I ever return to the castle from my projected sojourn abroad, I had little doubt of being able to recover the golden utensils from the foot of the three-hundred-meter precipice which Castle Dracula overlooked and which provided an eminently satisfactory garbage dump. The dishes would be there, dented by the fall no doubt, but cleansed by the seasons and unstolen. I have always had a dislike of thieves, and I believe the people of the villages nearby understood me on this point, if probably on nothing else.

In the month and a half that he was with me my increasingly ungrateful guest went through a sultan's ransom in gold plate, and I was reduced to serving him on silver. Toward the end, of course, I might have brought his food on slabs of bark, and he would scarcely have noticed it, so terrified was he by then at certain peculiarities of my nature. He misinterpreted these oddities, but never asked openly for any explanation, whilst I, wisely or unwisely, never volunteered one.

BOX NUMBER FIFTY

Carrie had been living on the London streets for a night and a day, plenty of time to learn that being taken in charge by the police was not the worst thing that could happen. But it would be bad enough. What she had heard of the conditions in which homeless children were confined made her ready to risk a lot in trying to stay free.

A huge dray drawn by two whipped and lathered horses rushed past, almost knocking her down, as she began to cross another street. Tightening her grip on the hand of nine-year-old Christopher as he stumbled in exhaustion, she struggled on through the London fog, wet air greasy with burning coal and wood. Around the children were a million strangers, all in a hurry amid an endless roar of traffic.

"Where we going to sleep tonight?" Her little brother sounded desperate, and no doubt he was. Last night they had had almost no sleep at all, huddled against the abutment of a railway bridge; but fortunately it had not been raining then as it was now. There had been only one episode of real adventure during the night, when Chris, on going a little way apart to answer a call of nature, had been set on and robbed of his shoes by several playful fellows not much bigger than he.

Their wanderings had brought them into Soho, where they attracted some unwelcome attention. Carrie thought that a pair of rough-looking youths had now begun to follow them.

She had to seek help somewhere, and none of the faces in her immediate vicinity looked promising. On impulse she turned from the pavement up a flight of stone steps to the front door of a house. It was a narrow building of gray stone, not particularly old or new, one of a row, wedged tightly against its neighbors on either side. Had Carrie been given time to think about it, she might have said that she chose this house because it bore a certain air of quiet and decency, in contrast to its neighbors, which at this early stage of evening were given to lights and raucous noise.

Across the street, a helmeted bobby was taking no interest in a girl and boy with nowhere to go. But he might at any moment. These were not true slums, not, by far, the worst part of London. Still, here and there, in out-of-the-way corners, a derelict or two lay drunk or dying.

Carrie went briskly up the steps to the front door, while her brother, following some impulse of his own, slipped down into the areaway where he was for the moment concealed from the street. Glancing quickly down at Christopher from the high steps, Carrie thought he was doing something to one of the cellar windows.

Giving a long pull on the bell, she heard a distant ringing somewhere inside. And at the same moment, she saw to her dismay that what she had thought was a modest light somewhere in the interior of the house was really only a reflection in one of the front windows. There were curtains inside, but other than that the place had an uninhabited look and feel about it.

"Not a-goin' ter let yer in?" One of the youths following her had now stopped on the pavement at the foot of the steps, where he stood grinning up at her, while his fellow stood beside him, equally delighted.

"I know a house where you'd be welcome, dear," called the second one. He was older, meaner-looking. "I know some good girls who live there."

Turning her back on them both, she tried to project an air of confidence and respectability, as she persisted in pulling at the bell.

"My name's Vincent," came the deeper voice from behind her. "If maybe you need a friend, dearie, a little help—"

Carrie caught her breath at the sound of an answering fumble in the darkness on the other side of the barrier—and was mightily relieved a moment later when her brother opened the door from inside. In a moment she was in, and had closed and latched the door behind her.

She could picture the pair who had been heckling her from the pavement, balked for the moment, turning away.

It was so dark in the house that she could barely see Christopher's pale face at an arm's length distance; but at least they were no longer standing in the rain.

"How'd you get in?" she whispered at him fiercely. Then: "Whose house is this?"

"Broken latch on a window down there," he whispered back. Then he added in a more normal voice: "It was awful dark in the cellar; I barked my shin on something trying to find the stair."

It was a good thing, Carrie congratulated herself in passing, that neither of them had ever been especially afraid of the dark. Already her eyes were growing accustomed to the deep gloom; enough light strayed in from the street, around the fringes of curtain, to reveal the fact that the front hall where they were standing was hardly furnished at all, nor was the parlor, just beyond a broad archway. More clearly than ever, the house said *empty*.

"Let's try the gas," she whispered. Chris, fumbling in the drawer of a built-in sideboard, soon came up with some matches. Carrie, standing on tiptoe, was tall enough to reach a fixture projecting from the wall. In a moment more she had one of the gaslights lit.

"Is anyone here?" Now her voice too was up to normal; the answer seemed to be no. The sideboard drawer also contained a couple of short scraps of candle, and soon they had lights in hand to go exploring.

Front hall, with an old abandoned mirror still fastened to the wall beside a hat rack and a shelf. Just in from the hall, a wooden stair, handrail carved with a touch of elegance, went straight up to the next floor. Not even a mouse stirred in the barren parlor. The dining room was a desert also, no furniture at all. And so, farther back, was the kitchen, except for a great black stove and a sink whose bright new length of metal pipe promised running water. An interior cellar door had been left open by Chris in his hurried ascent, and next to it a recently walled-off cubicle contained a water closet. A kitchen window looked out on what was no doubt a back garden, now invisible in gloom and rain.

Carrie was ready to explore upstairs, but Christopher insisted on seeing the cellar first, curious as to what object he had stumbled over. The culprit proved to be a cheaply constructed crate, not quite wide or long enough to be a coffin, containing only some scraps of kindling wood. Otherwise the cellar—damp brick walls, floor part pavement, part dry earth—was as empty as the house above.

Now for the upstairs. Holding the candle tremulously high ahead of her, while dancing shadows beat a wavering retreat, Carrie returned to the front hall, and thence up the carved wooden stair. Two bedrooms, as unused as the lower level of the house and as scantily furnished. The rear windows looked out over darkness, the front ones over the street—side walls were windowless, crammed as they were against the neighbors on either side.

From an angle in the hallway on the upper floor, a narrow service stair, white-painted, went up straight and steep to a trap-door in the ceiling.

"What's up there?" she wondered aloud.

"Couldn't be nothin' but an attic." Only a short time on the street had begun to have a serious effect on Christopher's English, of which a certain Canadian schoolmaster had once been proud.

Carrie spotted fresh footprints in the thin layer of dust and soot that had accumulated on the white-painted stairs. A clear image of the heel of a man's boot. Only one set of footprints, coming down.

The trapdoor pushed up easily. The space above was more garret than attic; it might once have been furnished, maybe servants' quarters. The floor entirely solid, no rafters exposed, though now there were dust and spiderwebs in plenty. The broad panes of glass in the angled skylight, washed by rain on the outside, were still intact, and it was bolted firmly shut on the inside; and if you stood tall enough inside, you could look out over a hilly range of slate roofs and chimney pots, with the towering dome of St. Paul's visible more than a mile to the east.

On one side of the gloomy space rested an old wardrobe, door slightly ajar to reveal a few hanging garments. But the most interesting object by far was a great wooden box, somewhat battered by much use or travel, which had been shoved against the north wall.

Chris thought it looked like a coffin, and said so.

"No. Built too strong for a poor man's coffin, not elegant enough for a rich man's." What was it, though? There were two strong rope handles on each side, and a plain wooden lid, tightly fitted by some competent woodworker.

Christopher, ever curious, approached the box and tried the lid. To his surprise, and Carrie's, it slid back at once.

"Look here, Sis!"

"Why, it's full of dirt." She was aware of a vague disappointment in her observation, and not sure why. Only about half-full, actually, but that was no less odd. Stranger still was the fact that the neat joinings of the interior seemed to have been tarred with pitch, as if to make them waterproof. Of course so tight a seal would also serve to keep the soil from leaking out. But *why* would *anyone*—?

The earth was dry. When Carrie picked up a small handful and sifted it through her fingers, it gave off a faintly musty, almost spicy smell, with a suggestion of the alien about it.

Christopher was downstairs again, moving so silently on his bare feet that Carrie had not realized he was gone, until she heard him faintly calling her to come down. She slid the lid back onto the box, and carefully lowered the trapdoor into place behind her.

Her brother had turned on the gaslight in the kitchen and discovered some tins of sardines abandoned in the pantry. Presently they remembered the box of kindling in the cellar, and it was possible to get a wood fire started in the kitchen stove.

The sardines were soon gone. Brother and sister were still hungry, but at least they were out of the rain.

That night they slept in a house, behind locked doors, curled up in a dusty rug on the kitchen floor, where some of the stove's warmth reached them. Barely into October, and it was cold.

Next day, waking up in a foodless house and observing that the rain had stopped, they were soon out and about on the streets of London, trying to do something to earn some money, and keep out of trouble. But in each endeavor they had only limited success. Carrie was certain that the neighbors had begun to notice them, and not in any very friendly way. So had the bobby who walked the beat during the day.

There was one bright spot. On the sideboard, as if someone had left it there deliberately, they found a key which matched the locks on both front door and back.

Vincent still had his eye on them too, or at least on Carrie. And "Don't see your parents about," one of the neighbors remarked as she came by. She answered with a smile, and hurried inside to share with Christopher the handful of biscuits she had just stolen from a shop.

Shortly after sunset, threatening trouble broke at last. The rain had stopped, and people were ready to get out and mind each other's business. One of the neighbors began it, another joined in, followed by the walrus-mustached policeman, who, when voices were raised, had decided it was his duty to take part.

And joined at a little distance by the nasty Vincent, who before the policeman arrived boldly put in a word, offering to place Carrie under his protection. He had some comments on her body that made her face flame with humiliation and anger.

Carrie could not slam the door on Vincent, because he had his foot pushed in to hold it open. He withdrew the foot as the bobby approached, but Carrie did not quite dare to close the door in the policeman's face.

"What's your name, girl?" he wanted to know, without preamble.

"Carrie. Carrie Martin. This's my brother Chris."

"Is the woman of the house in?" demanded the boldest neighbor, breaking in on the policeman's dramatic pause.

Carrie admitted the sad truth, that her mother was dead.

Another neighbor chimed in. "Your father about, then?"

The girl could feel herself being driven back, almost to the foot of the stairs. "He's very busy. He doesn't like to be disturbed."

Somehow three or four people were already inside the door. There was still enough daylight to reveal the shabbiness and scantiness of the furnishings, and of the children's clothes, once quite respectable.

"Looks like the maid has not come in as yet." That was said facetiously.

"Must be the butler's day off too," chimed in another neighbor.

"You say your father's here, miss?" This was the policeman, slow and majestic, in the mode of a large and overbearing uncle. "I'd like to have a word with him, if I may."

"He doesn't like to be disturbed." Carrie could hear her own voice threatening to break into a childish squeal. For a little while, for a few hours, it had looked like they might be able to survive. But now . . .

"Where is he?"

"Upstairs. But—"

"Asleep, then, is he?"

"I—I—yes."

"How old are you?"

"Sixteen."

"Oh yes you are, I *don't* think! See here, my girl, unless I have some evidence that you and the young 'un here are under some supervision, you'll both be charged with wandering, and not being under proper guardianship."

Carrie, standing at bay at the foot of the stair, gripping her brother by his shoulder, raised her voice in protest, but the voices of the others increased in volume too. They seemed to be all talking at once, making accusations and demands—

Suddenly their voices cut off altogether. Their eyes that had been fixed on Carrie rose up to somewhere above her head, and behind her on the stair there was a creak of wood, as under a quiet but weighty tread.

She turned to see a tall, well-built, well-dressed man coming down with measured steps. Perfectly calm, as if he descended these stairs every day, a gentleman in his own house. His brownish hair, well-trimmed, was touched with gray at the temples, and an aquiline nose gave his face a forceful look. At the moment he was fussing with his cuffs, as if he had just put on his coat, and frowning in apparent puzzlement at the assembly below him.

Carrie had never seen him before in her life; nor had Christopher, to judge by the boy's awestruck expression as he watched from her side.

The newcomer's voice was strangely accented, low but forceful, suited to his appearance, as his gaze swept the little group gathered in his front hall. "What is the meaning of this intrusion? Officer? Carrie, what do these people want?"

Carrie could find no words at the moment. Not even when the man came to stand beside her in a fatherly attitude, resting one hand lightly on her back.

"Mr. Martin—?" The bobby's broad face wore a growing look of consternation. Already he had retreated half a step toward the door. Meanwhile the nosy neighbors, looking unhappy, were moving even faster in the same direction.

"Yes? Do you have official business with me, officer?"

Vincent had disappeared.

The policeman recovered slightly, and stood upon official dignity; thought there might be some disturbance. Duty to investigate.
But soon he too had given way under the cool gaze of the man
from upstairs. In the space of a few more heartbeats the door had
closed on the last of them.

The mysterious one stood regarding the door for a moment,
hands clasped behind his back—they were pale hands, Carrie
noted, strong-looking, and the nails tended to points. Then he
reached over to the hat rack on the wall behind the door, and
plucked from it a gentleman's top hat, a thing she could not for
the life of her remember seeing there before. But of course she
had scarcely looked. And then he turned, at ease, to regard her
with a smile too faint to reveal anything of his teeth.

"I take it you are in fact the lady of the house? The only one I
am likely to encounter on the premises?"

The children stared at him.

Gently he went on. "I am not given to eavesdropping, but this
afternoon my sleep was restless, and the talk I could hear below
me grew ever and ever more interesting." The foreign accent was
stronger now; but in Soho accents of all kinds were nothing out of
the ordinary.

"Yes sir." Carrie stood with an arm around her brother. "Yes
sir—that is, there is no other lady, er woman, girl, living here
at present."

"That is good. It would seem superfluous to introduce myself,
as you have already, in effect, introduced me to others. Mr. Martin
I have become, and so I might as well remain. But when others
are present, you, Carrie, and you, young sir, will address me as
'Father.' For however many days our joint tenancy of this dwelling
may last. Understand, I do not seek to adopt you, but a temporary
arrangement should be to our mutual advantage. A happy, close-
knit family, yes, that is the face we present to the world. When it
is necessary to present a face. Ah, you will kindly leave the upper
regions of the house to me—if anyone should ask you, it is really
my house, paid for in coin of the realm. In the name of Mr.
de Ville."

"Yes sir," said Carrie, and elbowed her brother until he echoed
the two words.

"And now, my children." Mr. Martin, or de Ville, set his hat
upon his head, and gave it a light tap with two pale fingers, as if

to settle it exactly to his liking. Carrie noticed that as he did so, he ignored the old mirror on the wall beside the hat rack. And she could see why, or she imagined she could, because the small mirror did not show the man at all, but only the top hat, doing a neat half-somersault unsupported in the air, its reflected image disappearing utterly just as the hat itself came to rest on the head of the mysterious one.

"I am going out for the evening," he informed them. "I advise you to lock up for the night as solidly as possible. Do not expect to see me again until about this time tomorrow. Pleasant dreams . . ."

On the verge of opening the door, he checked himself, frowning at them.

"The two of you have an undernourished and ill-clad look, which I find distasteful, and will only provoke more neighborly curiosity. Here." White fingers performed an economical toss, a small coin, glittering gold, spun through the air. Christopher's quick hand, like a hungry bird, snatched it in midflight.

That night brother and sister slept with full bellies, having gone out foraging amid the early evening crowds, to a nearby branch of the Aërated Bread Company. At a used furniture stall Carrie had also bought herself a nice frock, almost new, and a couple of pillows; it was awkward living in a house where there were no beds or chairs. And Christopher had found a secondhand pair of shoes that fit him well enough. They were going to sleep on the kitchen floor again, but they were getting used to it.

"Where'd *he* sleep, is what I'd like to know," said Chris next day, climbing the stairs up from the parlor. The man had said he'd not be back till sunset, so now in midafternoon there was no harm in gratifying their curiosity, never mind that he'd said to keep below.

Both of the bedrooms were as desolate as ever, and the dust on their floors showed only their own footprints, one set shod, one five-toed, from yesterday's exploration.

"And how'd he get into the house?" Carrie wanted to know. "Didn't come past us downstairs."

"You don't suppose—?"

"The *skylight*? Why'd a man do that?"

"'Cause he don't want to be seen."

And they went up the narrow white stair, through the trapdoor.

The skylight was as snugly fastened as before. Out of persistent curiosity they approached the mysterious box again. The lid, once moved, fell clattering with shock and fright.

"Oh my God. He's in there!"

But none of this awakened Mr. Martin.

After initially recoiling, both children had to have a closer look. In urgent whispers they soon decided the man who lay so neatly and cleanly on the earth in his nice clothes was not dead. His open eyes moved faintly. In Carrie's experience, people sometimes got drunk, but never had even the drunkest of them looked like this. Some people also took strange drugs, and with that she had less familiarity.

A ring at the front door broke the spell and pulled them down the stairs. A solid workman stood on the step, cap in hand. In a thick cockney accent he said he had come to inquire about a box, one that might have been delivered here "by mistake." Carrie, in a clean dress today, and with her face washed, denied all knowledge and briskly sent the questioner on his way.

"I don't think he believed me," Carrie muttered to her brother, when the door was closed again. "He'll be back. Or someone will."

"What'll we do? Don't want anyone bothering Mr. Martin. I like him," Chris decided.

Quickly the girl took thought. "I know!"

Within the hour the bell rang again. This man was much younger, and obviously of higher social status. Bright eyes, dark curly hair. "Excuse me, Miss? Are you the woman of the house?"

"Who wants her?"

"I'm George Harris, of Harris and Sons, moving and shipment." A large, clean hand with well-trimmed nails offered a business card. Carrie read the address: *Orange Master's Yard, Soho*.

"Oh. I suppose you're one of the sons."

"That's right, Miss. I'm looking about this neighborhood for a box that seems to have got misplaced. There's evidence it was brought to this house, some days ago. One of a large shipment, fifty in all, there's been a lot of hauling of 'em to and fro around London, one place and another. Ours not to reason why, as the poet says. But our firm feels a certain responsibility."

"What sort of box?"

George Harris had a good description, down to the rope handles. "Seen anything like that, Miss?" Meanwhile his eyes were probing the empty house behind her.

And Carrie was looking out past him, as a cab came galloping to a stop outside. Two well-dressed young gentlemen leaped out and climbed the steps. George Harris, who seemed to know them as respected clients, made introductions. Lord Godalming, no less, but called "Art" by his companion, Mr. Quincey Morris, who was carrying a carpetbag, and whose accent, though not at all the same as Mr. Martin's, also seemed uncommon even for Soho.

The new arrivals made nervous, garbled attempts at explaining their urgent search. There had been, it seemed, twenty-one boxes taken from some place called Carfax, and so forty-nine of fifty were somehow now accounted for. But this time, Lord Godalming or not, Carrie held her place firmly in the doorway, allowing no one in.

"If there is a large box on the premises, I must examine it." A commanding tone, as only one of his lordship's exalted rank could manage.

At that, Carrie gracefully gave way. "Very well, sir, my lord, there *is* a strange box here, and where it came from, I'm sure I don't know."

Three men came bustling into the house, ready for action, Morris actually, for some reason, beginning to pull a thick wooden stake out of his carpetbag—and three men were deflated, like burst balloons, when they beheld the thin-sided, commonplace container on the parlor floor.

"Our furniture has not arrived yet, as you can see." The lady of the house was socially apologetic.

Quincey Morris, muttering indelicate words, kicked off the scruffy lid, and indeed there was dirt inside, but only a few handfuls. And the two gentlemen hastily retreated to their waiting cab.

But George Harris lingered in the doorway, exchanging a few more words with Carrie. Until his lordship shouted at him to get a move on, there were other places to be examined. On with the search!

At sunset Carrie's and Christopher's cotenant came walking down the stairs into the parlor as before.

There he paused, fussing with his cuffs as on the previous evening, But now his attention was caught by the rejected box. "And
what is this? An attempt at furnishing?"

"You had some callers, Mr. Martin—de Ville—while you were
asleep. I thought as maybe you didn't wish to be disturbed." And
Carrie gave details.

"I see." His dark eyes glittered at her. "And this—?"

"The gentlemen said they were looking for a large box of earth.
So I thought the easiest way was to show 'em one. Chris and I put
some dirt in and dragged it up from the cellar. 'Course this one
ain't nearly as big as yours. Not big enough for a tall man to lie
down in. The gents were upset—this weren't at all the one they
wanted to find."

There was a long pause, in which de Ville's eyes probed the
children silently. Then he bowed. "It seems I am greatly in your
debt, Miss Carrie. Very greatly. And in yours, Master Christopher."

Mr. de Ville seemed to sleep little the next day, or not at all,
for the box in the garret held only earth. In the afternoon, Carrie
by special invitation went with her new friend and his strange box
to Doolittle's Wharf, where she watched the man and his box board
the sailing ship *Czarina Catherine*. And she waited at dockside,
wondering, until the Russian vessel cast off and dropped down
seaward on the outgoing tide.

As she returned to the house, feeling once more alone and
unprotected, she noted that the evil Vincent was openly watching
her again.

He grew bolder when, after several days, it seemed that the
man of the house was gone.

George Harris came back once, on some pretext, but obviously
to see Carrie, and they talked for some time. She learned that he
was seventeen, and admitted she was three years younger.

Five days, then six, had passed since *Czarina Catherine* sailed
away.

George Harris came back again, this time wondering if he might
have left his order book behind on his previous visit. Carrie made
him tea, out of the newly restocked pantry. Mr. de Ville had left
them what he called a token of his gratitude for their timely help,
and sometimes Carrie was almost frightened when she counted

up the golden coins. There was a bed in each bedroom now, and chairs and tables below.

Tonight Chris was in the house alone, curled up and reading by the fire, nursing a cough made worse by London air. Carrie was out alone in the London fog, walking through the greasy, smoky chill.

She heard the terrifying voice of Vincent, not far away, calling her name. There were footsteps in pursuit, hard confident strides, and in her fresh anxiety she took a wrong turning into a dead-end mews.

In another moment she was running in panic, on the verge of screaming, feeling in her bones that screaming would do no good.

Someone, some presence, was near her in the fog—but no, there was no one and nothing there.

Only her pursuer's footsteps, which came on steadily, slow and loud and confident—until they abruptly ceased.

Backed into a corner, she strained her ears, listening—nothing. Vincent must be playing cat and mouse with her. But at last a breath of wind stirred the heavy air, the gray curtain parted and the way out of the mews seemed clear. Utterly deserted, only the body of some derelict, rolled into a corner.

No—someone was visible after all. Half a block ahead, a tall figure stood looking in Carrie's direction, as if he might be waiting for her.

With a surge of relief and astonishment she hurried forward. "Mr. de Ville!"

"My dear child. It is late for you to be abroad."

"I saw you board a ship for the Black Sea!"

His gaze searched the fog, sweeping back and forth over her head. "It is important that certain men believe I am still on that ship. And soon I really must depart from England. But I shall return to this sceptered isle one day."

Anxiously she looked over her shoulder. "There was a man—"

"Your former neighbor, who meant you harm." De Ville's forehead creased. His eyes probed shadows in the mews behind her. "It is sad to contemplate such wickedness." He sighed, put out a hand, patted her cheek. "But no matter. He will bother you no more. He told me—"

"You've seen him, sir?"

"Yes, just now—that he is leaving on a long journey—nay, has already left."

Carrie was puzzled. "Long journey—to where, sir? America?"

"Farther than that, my child. Oh, farther than that."

A man's voice was audible above the endless traffic rumble, calling her name through the night from blocks away. The voice of George Harris, calling, concerned, for Carrie.

Bidding Mr. de Ville a hasty good night, she started to go to the young man. Then, meaning to ask another question, she turned back—the street was empty, save for the rolling fog.

A DROP OF SOMETHING SPECIAL
IN THE BLOOD

Monday, 16 July, 1888–

The dream again, last night. I shall continue to call these visitations dreams, as the London specialist very firmly insisted upon doing, and it is at his urging that I begin this private record of events. As to the "dream" itself, I can only hope and pray that in setting it down on paper I may be able to exorcise at least a portion of the horror.

I awoke—or so I thought—in an unmanly state of fear, at the darkest hour of the night.

As before, the impression (whether true or not) that I had come wide-awake, was very firm. There was no confusion as to where I was; I immediately recognized, by the faint glow of streetlights coming in round the edges of the window curtain, the room in which I had lain down to sleep, in this case a somewhat overdecorated bedchamber in an overpriced Parisian hotel.

For a moment I lay listening, in a strange state of innocent anticipation. It was as if my certain memory of what must inexorably follow was for the moment held in abeyance. But that state lasted for a few breaths only. In the next instant, memory returned with a rush. There was a faint sound at the window; and I knew beyond the shadow of a doubt what I must see when I turned my

265

gaze in that direction. *She* was standing there, of course, just inside the window. In my last coherent thoughts before falling asleep, I had begun to hope (absurdly, I suppose, whatever the true cause may be) that the visitations could not have followed me from London.

In the poor light it was as difficult as on the previous occasions to be sure of the color of her long curls of hair, but I thought they might be as red as my own were in my youth. The long tresses fell to her waist round her voluptuous body, that was otherwise only partially concealed by a simple shift or gown.

Though the moonlight was behind her, I thought that her slight figure threw no shadow on the floor. In spite of that, hers was a most carnal and unspiritual appearance. Plainly I could see her brilliant white teeth, that shone like pearls against the ruby of her full lips.

A tremendous longing strove against a great fear in my heart . . . I knew, as had happened on every previous occasion, a burning desire that she would kiss me with those red lips . . .

It is difficult for me to note these things down, lest some day this page should fall under the gaze of one I love, and cause great pain. (Florence, forgive me, if you can! Will I ever embrace you again?) But it is the truth, even if only a true account of a strange dream, and I must hope that the truth will set me free.

I have not yet learned my nocturnal visitor's name—assuming that the woman is real enough to have one. Perhaps I should call her "the girl," for she seems very young. As she approached my bed last night she laughed . . . such a silvery, musical laugh, but as hard as though the sound could never have come through the softness of human lips. It was like the intolerable, tingling sweetness of water glasses when played on by a cunning hand . . .

Overcome by a strange helplessness, I had closed my eyes. The girl advanced and bent over me till I could feel the movement of her breath upon me. Sweet it was in one sense, honey-sweet, and sent the same tingling through the nerves as her voice, but with a bitter underlying the sweet, a bitter offensiveness, as one smells in blood.

I was afraid to raise my eyelids, but could see out perfectly under the lashes. The girl bent over me, and I had the sense that she was fairly gloating. She actually licked her lips like an animal, till I could see in the moonlight the moisture shining on the scarlet lips and on the red tongue as it lapped the white sharp teeth. Lower and lower went her head as the lips went below the range of my mouth and bearded chin and seemed about to fasten on my throat . . . I could feel the hot breath on my neck, and the skin of my throat began to tingle as one's flesh does when the hand that is to tickle it approaches nearer—nearer . . . the soft, shivering touch of the lips on the supersensitive skin of my throat, and the hard dents of two sharp teeth, just touching and pausing there. I closed my eyes in a languorous ecstasy and waited—waited with beating heart.

Suddenly she straightened, and her head turned as if listening for some distant but all-important sound. As if released from a spell, I moved as if to spring out of the bed, but in the instant before the motion could be completed, she bent over me again. The touch of her fingers on my arm seemed to drain the strength from all my limbs, and I sank back helplessly.

"So sweet is your blood, my little Irishman. I think there is a drop of something special in it," the apparition murmured. In my confused state, the idea that this diminutive visitor might call my large frame "little" drew from my lips a burst of foolish laughter.

In response, the girl laughed again, a sound of ribald coquetry, and bent over me to accomplish her purpose.

Then the truth, or what seemed the truth, of what was happening overcame me, and I sank down in a delirium of unbearable horror and indescribable delight commingled, until my senses failed me.

*   *   *

Oddly enough, my faint, if such it was, passed seamlessly into a deep and restful sleep, and I slept well until the street sounds of Paris, some cheerful and some angry, below my window, brought me round at almost ten o'clock.

My awakening this morning was slow and almost painful, and it was difficult to fight free of a persistent heaviness clinging to all my limbs. A single spot of dried blood, half the size of my little finger's nail, stained the pillow, not three as on certain unhappy mornings in the recent past. In London I had independent confirmation (from a hotel maid) that the stains themselves are real, which at the time afforded me inordinate relief.

This morning, as before, an anxious examination in a mirror disclosed on my throat, just where I felt the pressure of lips and teeth, near the lower border of my full beard, the same ambiguous evidence—two almost imperceptible red spots, so trivial that in ordinary circumstances no one would give them a moment's thought. I cannot say it is impossible that the small hemorrhage had issued from them, but it might as easily have come from nostril, mouth, or ear.

I take some comfort in the fact that if anyone in the world can help me, it is the physician I have come to Paris to see—Jean-Martin Charcot, perhaps the world's foremost authority on locomotor ataxia, as well as hypnotism. Whether he can possibly help me, either in his character as mesmerist, or as expert in neuropathy, is yet to be discovered. If Charcot can help, in one capacity or the other, he must. If he cannot, I tremble for my very life. I have already gone past the point of fearing for my sanity.

I must force myself to write down what I have been avoiding until now, the evil I fear the most. If the girl has no objective reality, then these mental horrors that I endure are sheer delusion, and the precursor of much worse to come, of an absolute mental and physical ruin. I am in the grip of a loathsome and shameful disease, contracted years ago—if that is so, then what is left of my life will not be worth the living. I only pray God that the source of my agony may *not* be syphilis. It is only with difficulty that I can force myself to pen the word on this white page—but there, it is done.

As far as I know, or the world knows, there is no cure. The more advanced physicians admit that the current standard of treatment, with potassium iodide, has been shown to be practically worthless. I know the early symptoms (alas, from my own case) and have seen the full horror of the tertiary stage expressed in the bodies of other men. Delusions are frequently a part of that catastrophe.

But the beast takes many forms. The first symptom of the last stage, sometimes appearing decades after the first, local signs of infection have passed away, tends to be a weakening or total loss of the ankle and knee reflex. In succeeding months and years the patient's ability to walk, and even to stand normally, slowly declines. Sometimes in medical description the initials GPI are used, standing for general paralysis of the insane, the most dreaded late manifestation. The effects on the brain are varied, but include delusions, loss of memory, sometimes violent anger. Disorientation, incontinence, and convulsions occur often. *Tabes dorsalis* (also known as locomotor ataxia) is the commonest symptom of infection in the spinal cord. Others include darting attacks of intense pain in the legs and hips, difficult urination, numbness in hands or feet, a sense of constriction about the waist, an unsteadiness in walking—all capped by a loss of sexual function.

So far I have experienced only the delusions—if such they are. Horrible as that fate would be, I believe this current torture of uncertainty is even worse. I will go mad if Heaven does not grant me an answer soon.

❖   ❖   ❖

(Later)—I find it a source of irritation that I will not be presenting myself, openly and honestly from the beginning, to Charcot as a sufferer in need of help, but only as a visiting "celebrity." In the latter category I of course shine solely by the reflected light of my employer. No one here has shown the least awareness of my own small literary efforts; and I would not be surprised to learn that no Parisian has ever read *Duties of Clerks of Petty Sessions in Ireland*.

This concealment of my true purpose is, to a certain extent, dishonesty on my part. But when I consider the unfortunate publicity that might otherwise result, and the risk of harm to others if my condition were widely known, it seems to me the role of honor must include a measure of dishonesty. Desperate though my situation is, I wish to meet Charcot and form my own estimate of the man and his methods (which some denounce, perhaps out of jealousy), before committing myself completely into his hands.

❖   ❖   ❖

Evening: Today I have seen and heard that which frightened me anew, but also that which gives me hope. Let me set down the events of the afternoon as quickly and calmly as I can, before the memory of even the smallest detail has begun to fade.

First, let me state my key discovery: *The girl is real!* Real, and, to my utter astonishment, a patient of Charcot's!

I was certain, from the moment today when our eyes met in the hospital, that she knew me as instantly and surely as I knew her.

I suppose I need not try to describe the hideous shock I suffered upon recognizing her among the inmates. There can be no possibility of a mistake, though in the filtered daylight her teeth appeared quite small and ordinary.

I was certain that she knew me from the moment when our eyes met, and I had the odd impression that she might even have been *expecting* me.

We were standing close together in the treatment room, one of the stops on what I suppose must be the regular tour afforded distinguished visitors. Her whisper was so soft that I am certain no one but myself could hear it. But I could read her lips with perfect ease: "It is my little Irishman!" And then she licked them with her soft, pink tongue.

✿   ✿   ✿

But I should set down the afternoon's events in their proper order. The hospital, La Salpêtriére, sprawls over several acres of land not far from the botanic gardens, and houses several thousand patients, nearly all women. (The Bicêtre, nearby, is reserved for men.)

The famous doctor is now about sixty years of age, of small stature but imposing appearance. I have heard it said that he is pleased to exaggerate his natural resemblance to Napoléon . . . he is pale, clean-shaven with straight black hair only lightly tinged with grey, a firm mouth, and dark melancholy eyes that seem to remember some ancient loss.

Our tour began in what seemed routine fashion. Charcot called several patients (by their given names only), and brought them forward one at a time to demonstrate the symptoms of their illness and the means he used to treat it. His comments were terse and to the point. Whatever could not be helped by the power of suggestion must be the result of heredity, and nothing could be done about it.

I paid little attention to the mysterious girl when she first appeared, as routinely as any of the others, called out of her private room, or perhaps I should say cell. Her long, red hair, which first caught my eye, was bound up in a cap, from which a few strands of bright coppery red escaped, and she was decently clad, like the other patients, in a plain hospital robe. I did not even look closely at her until I heard her voice.

Charcot was pronouncing his accented English in forceful tones. "Lucy, this gentleman has come from England to visit us today. He is a famous man in London, business manager of the Lyceum Theater."

Lucy—that is the only name by which I have heard her called—responded to the doctor's questions in English bearing almost the same flavor of Ireland as does my own. From Charcot's first remarks regarding her, it was clear that she has been his patient for only a few days. With a casual question I confirmed that she had been admitted on the very day of my own arrival in Paris.

Stunned by the familiarity of her voice, I gazed intently at her face, and could no longer doubt her identity. There was an impudent presumption in the look she returned to me, and a twinkling in her green eyes that strongly suggested we shared a secret. There followed the whispered words which, though nearly inaudible, seemed to seal her identity as my nocturnal visitor.

The tour was moving on. I wanted desperately to question Charcot further on the background and history of the girl, but I delayed. I admit I feared to ask such questions in her presence, lest she put forward some convincing claim of having known me in different circumstances.

Gradually more facts of her case came out. According to the doctor, Lucy displays a positive terror of sunlight, and has a disturbing habit of refusing to eat the standard fare provided for patients—the quality of which, I note in passing, seems higher than one might expect in this large an institution.

Hers, he said, is a very interesting case. (Ah, if only he knew!) Several days ago Lucy had somehow got hold of a rat—I can well believe that Charcot was livid with anger when he heard of such a creature being found, in what he considered his hospital—and, using her own sharp-pointed teeth as surgical instruments, was delicately draining it of blood, which she appeared to consider a delicacy.

It is also said that she manifests an intense fear of mirrors—as they are practically nonexistent within the walls of La Salpêtriére, this presents her caretakers with no urgent problem.

As it was evident from my repeated questions that I had a strong interest in the patient, Charcot at the end of the tour obliged me by returning to her cell and questioning her at some length while I stood by.

Lucy's manner as she replied was not particularly shy, but still subdued, and somehow distant.

What was her present age? She did not know, could not remember—and did not seem to think it was at all important.

Had she been born in Paris? No—in Ireland, far across the sea—of that she was certain. How, then, had she come to France? Her parents had brought her when they had come to join the Paris Commune.

This was interesting news indeed. The doctor frowned. "You must have been only a very small child at that time. How can you remember?"

"Oh, no sir. I was fifteen years of age when we came to France, and much as you see me now."

Charcot gave me a significant look: The fierce rebellion of the Commune now lies fully seventeen years in the past, and the girl who stood before us today could hardly be more than eighteen at the most.

His voice remained gentle, but insistent: "And you have been here, in Paris, ever since?"

Lucy began to twist her fingers together nervously. "No; the fighting grew terrible in the city, soon after we arrived. My mother was killed, and quite early on I ran away."

"Indeed? You ran away alone?"

There was a hesitation. Then, finally: "No, sir. It was then *he* came to me, and claimed me for his own, and took me away. To be his, forever and ever." As she said this, the girl gave a strange sigh, as of triumph and dread all mingled.

Charcot gave me another look filled with meaning and picked up on what he evidently thought an important clue. " 'He'? Who is this 'he'?"

The question produced evident distress. But however Charcot prodded, even threatening the girl with strict confinement if she refused cooperation, there was no answer.

The doctor's interest in this strange tale, though on his side purely professional, seemed to have become nearly as great as my own. He dispatched an orderly to bring him the girl's dossier, and stood in an attitude of deep thought, chin supported in one hand. "And where did this person take you when you fled from Paris?"

Lucy frowned; her eyes were now closed, and she seemed to be experiencing some type of painful memory. Her answer when it came was long and rambling and unclear, and I do not remember every word. But the gist of it was that her mysterious abductor, who had evidently also become her lover at some point, had carried her to what she called the dark land, "beyond the forest."

By this time the girl's medical record had been brought to Charcot from the office; on opening, it proved to contain only a single sheet of paper. Turning to me, Charcot read rapidly from it. "She has been telling the same story all along: that she is the child of an Irish-Russian revolutionary couple, brought to Paris by her parents when they came, with others of like mind, to join the Commune in '71. But that is absurd on the face of it, for the girl cannot be more than twenty years old at the very most."

Another brief notation in the record stated that Lucy on first being admitted to the hospital had been housed in a regular ward. There she had displayed an almost incredible skill at slipping away during the night, but was always to be found in her bed again at dawn, the means of her return as mysterious as that of her disappearance. Irked by this disregard of regulations, the doctor in immediate charge of her case had transferred her to a private cell, in the section set aside for patients who are violent or otherwise present unusual difficulties. Even there she had at least twice somehow managed to leave the locked cell at night, so that a search of the hospital wards and grounds was ordered.

"Without result, I may add," Charcot informed me. "But each time, in the morning, she was found in her cell again, wanting to do nothing but sleep through the day. I found it necessary to dismiss two employees for carelessness."

"She seems a real challenge," was the only comment I could make.

By then it was obvious that the doctor was growing more and more intrigued. But his voice maintained the same calm, professional tone as he turned back to the girl and asked: "What did you do in the land beyond the forest?"

The trouble in Lucy's countenance cleared briefly. "I slept and woke . . . feasted and fasted . . . danced and loved . . . in a great house . . ."

"What sort of a great house?"

"It was a castle . . ."

The doctor raised an eyebrow, expressing in a French way considerable doubt. "A castle, you say."

"Yes." She nodded solemnly. "But later he was cruel to me there . . . so I ran away again."

"Who was it that was cruel to you? What was his name?"

At this the girl became quite agitated, displaying a mixture of emotions . . .

"He who brought me there . . . the prince of that land," she finally got out. Then one more sentence burst forth, after which she seemed relieved. "He made me the *dearg-due*."

"I did not understand that word," Charcot complained briskly. But the girl could not be induced to repeat it, and could not or would not explain.

All this time I said nothing; but I had understood the Gaelic all too well. My hand strayed unconsciously to touch the small marks on my throat.

The questioning went on. Why had Lucy come back to Paris? She had been "following the little Irishman, who is so sweet." (She said this without looking in my direction; and I was much relieved that neither Charcot nor the attendants standing by imagined "the *little* Irishman" could possibly mean me.)

She went on, in a voice increasingly tight with strain: "I am afraid to return to the dark land. And I yearn to go back to blessed Ireland, but I dare not, or *he* will find me, and take me back to his domain, the land beyond the forest . . . "

Thinking quickly and decisively, as is his wont, Charcot abruptly announced that he had decided to try hypnotism. In a few minutes we had adjourned to a small room that is kept reserved for such experiments. There he soon began to employ his preferred method of inducing trance, which is visual fixation on a small flame—a candle against a background of dark velvet.

Lucy was seated in a chair, directly facing the candle. Charcot stationed himself just behind her, murmuring in a low, soothing voice, whilst I stood somewhat farther back. What happened next I cannot explain. It seemed that even as the girl began to sink into a trance I could feel the same darkness reaching for me, as if my mind and Lucy's were already somehow bound together.

I fell, losing my balance as awkwardly as some weak woman in a faint. At the last moment I roused enough to try to catch myself by grabbing the seat of a nearby chair, breaking my fall to some extent but seriously spraining my left thumb.

❊   ❊   ❊

Charcot helped me to a private room where he insisted that I lie down until I was fully recovered from my "faint." Meanwhile, as he provided a rather awkward splint and bandage for my thumb, I had the chance for a private consultation with the famous doctor.

Charcot confessed himself intrigued by my behavior in the presence of the girl. I began to tell him something of my case, and confessed my overwhelming fear.

He nodded, and prepared to give me a quick examination. But another detail still bothered him. "What was that word—neither French nor English . . . something, she said, that her princely abductor had caused her to become."

"It is in the old language of Ireland: *dearg-due*, meaning the sucker of red blood."

"Yes . . . I see." After a thoughtful pause he added, "Having some connection with her behavior with regard to the rat."

"Yes," I agreed. "No doubt that was it."

Charcot examined me briefly, I suppose as thoroughly as possible without advance preparation. He then gave me some hope, as a world expert on *tabes dorsalis*, by saying that while he certainly could not rule out the possibility in my case, he thought it unlikely that the dreams, or delusions, which I described were due to any organic lesion of the brain.

Instead, Charcot suggests that a kind of displacement has taken place: the girl in the hospital only resembles the one of whom I dreamed, and my unconscious mind has somehow altered my memory of the dream to fit the available reality.

Would that the matter could be that easily explained. But I fear that it cannot.

Tuesday, 17 July, morning—

Lucy came to me again last night, here in my hotel. Before retiring, I had made doubly sure of the room's single window being closed (it is utterly inaccessible from outside, two stories above the street) and locked the door and blocked it with a chair, which has become my nightly habit. This morning after her departure, when I examined the window in broad daylight, after my strange visitor's departure, a thin caking of dust and an intact small spiderweb offered proof that it had not been opened.

If the girl in the asylum be real, as must be the case, can her shade or spirit in my room at night be anything but a figment of my own disordered reason?

In the course of last night's visit, she said to me: "From the moment I first heard you speak in London, my little man, I knew great hunger for your sweet Irish blood."

Flat on my back in bed, I still did not know if I was dreaming. But I was curious. "Where did you hear me speak?"

"It was at the back door of your Lyceum Theater."

"And is it that you love the theater, then? You come to watch my employer, the great Henry Irving, on the stage?"

"Oh aye, he's marvelous. And I love the darkness and the lights, the curtains that can hide so much, the painted faces and the masks . . . "

Still murmuring, she bent over me, and all was as before. It seems that when her touch is upon me, my uninjured hand is as powerless to resist as the sprained one.

Thursday, 19 July, late afternoon—

This will be my last entry in this journal. The business has come to a conclusion in the most startling and amazing way.

Lucy appeared in my room again last night, and events followed their usual frightening course, of grotesque horror mingled with indescribable pleasure—until, at the last moment before our intimacy reached its peak, she abruptly broke off and pulled away from me.

Raising myself dazedly on one elbow, I became aware of a new presence in the room.

Though the tall figure standing near the window was visible only in outline, I could be sure it was a man. Lucy cowered away before him.

Moving silently at first, this new apparition (very shadowy in darkness, hard to see distinctly) advanced toward the bed.

Hardly knowing what to make of this development, I could only stammer out: "But you are real!"

A deep voice answered, speaking English in a strange accent that was neither French nor Irish: "I am as real as life and death."

In the next moment the newcomer turned to the girl, who was still cowering away. His voice was softer now, and almost tender.

"Lucy, my dear, your sisters are waiting for you at home, in the land beyond the forest. I am ready to take you to them."

"I do not want to go!"

"But you cannot continue in this way." He might almost have been a parent, remonstrating with a wayward child. "Your vanishing from the hospital. Your toying with this man."

She dared to raise her eyes, and pleaded piteously. "He is my sweet little—"

The man took another step toward her, and spoke in a tone now charged with menace. "*Silence*! These games you play will bring again the hunters down upon us, with their crosses and their garlic and their stakes!"

When Lucy struggled, he knocked her down with a single blow from the flat of his hand.

That was not to be borne, and the instinct of manhood in me sent me springing out of bed, bent on defending the girl.

Honorable as my intentions were, and sincere my effort, the only result was that the nightmare seemed to close upon me with new force. Seizing me by the throat, in a one-handed grip of iron, my opponent forced my body back upon the bed, meanwhile murmuring something of which the only two words I could hear clearly were "misplaced chivalry."

Meanwhile Lucy had regained her feet, and she in turn tried to come to my aid. But with his right hand the tall man caught her by the hair, and forced her to her knees, saying, "You will see him no more."

Those were the last words I heard from either of my visitors. Struggle as I might, I could not loosen the dark man's grip by even a fraction of an inch. I doubt whether I could have succeeded even had I been able to use both hands, which of course I could not. And once more darkness overcame me.

❖   ❖   ❖

When I recovered consciousness this morning, there were no blood spots on my pillow. But there were bruises on my throat beneath my beard, five small purpling spots that must have been made by the grip of a single hand, a left hand, of overpowering strength—and it is blessedly clear to me that with my own left hand, injured as it is, I could never have done this to myself.

Charcot, when I managed to see him today at the hospital, confirmed the reality of the bruises—as indeed the internal soreness of my throat had already done, to my own full satisfaction. To explain them to the doctor I made up some tale of a scuffle with a would-be robber in the street.

I am ecstatic with a sense of glorious relief: the man who with one hand overpowered me was a terrible opponent, fit to inhabit a nightmare—but he was real! So was Lucy, my girlish "succubus," truly in my room, and so were all the visits she has paid me. Nothing that has happened was the product of an infected and disordered brain. Whether or not Lucy is ever to appear to me again, and whatever the ultimate explanation of the mystery, it has nothing, nothing whatever to do with locomotor ataxia.

One might think this knowledge a new occasion for terror, this time of the supernatural. But the dominant emotion it arouses in me is a relief so strong that it is almost terrible in quite a different way.

I do *not*, after all, find myself doomed, hopelessly succumbing to the tertiary stage of syphilis. I can hope to avoid that stage entirely, as do most victims of the disease. Whatever bizarre powers may have intruded in my life, and whether or not they are of occult derivation, my fate is at least not *that*.

✧   ✧   ✧

I find I must add a postscript to this journal. I visited Charcot again this afternoon, and thanked him for his efforts as I paid his bill. I told him nothing of last night's events. The doctor, as might be expected, sympathizes with my bruised throat. But Charcot remains unable to regard my nocturnal experiences with Lucy as anything but dreams or delusions. He still doubted that a physical lesion of the brain, caused by disease, was likely to be responsible. In this glorious conclusion I heartily concur.

Charcot's parting advice to me echoed that of the London specialist: rest, good food, and exercise. Then: "If these fantasies continue to trouble you, Mr. Stoker, my advice is to continue to record them with pen and ink."

I believe that I shall soon be writing another book.

AUTHOR'S NOTE

Bram Stoker died in London in 1912, of locomotor ataxia, or tertiary syphilis, leading to "exhaustion."